S0-AIY-465

STORK MOUNTAIN

ALSO BY MIROSLAV PENKOV

East of the West

STORK MOUNTAIN

MIROSLAV PENKOV

S

SCEPTRE

ROCKDALE CITY
LIBRARY

The Book House

24.5.16

2250

First published in USA in 2016 by Farrar, Straus and Giroux

First published in Great Britain in 2016 by Sceptre
An imprint of Hodder & Stoughton
An Hachette UK company

1

Copyright © Miroslav Penkov 2016

The right of Miroslav Penkov to be identified as the Author of the
Work has been asserted by him in accordance with the Copyright,
. Designs and Patents Act 1988.

All rights reserved. No part of this publication may be reproduced, stored in a
retrieval system, or transmitted, in any form or by any means without the prior
written permission of the publisher, nor be otherwise circulated in any form of
binding or cover other than that in which it is published and without a similar
condition being imposed on the subsequent purchaser.

All characters in this publication are fictitious and any resemblance to real
persons, living or dead is purely coincidental.

A CIP catalogue record for this title is available from the British Library

Hardback ISBN 978 1 473 62218 0
Trade Paperdback ISBN 978 1 473 63291 2
Ebook ISBN 978 1 473 62219 7

Printed and bound by McPhersons Printing Group

Hodder & Stoughton policy is to use papers that are natural, renewable
and recyclable products and made from wood grown in sustainable forests.
The logging and manufacturing processes are expected to conform to the
environmental regulations of the country of origin.

Hodder & Stoughton Ltd
Carmelite House
50 Victoria Embankment
London EC4Y 0DZ

www.sceptrebooks.com

FOR KYOKO

Visita Interiora Terrae Rectificando
Invenies Occultum Lapidem

—ALCHEMICAL MOTTO

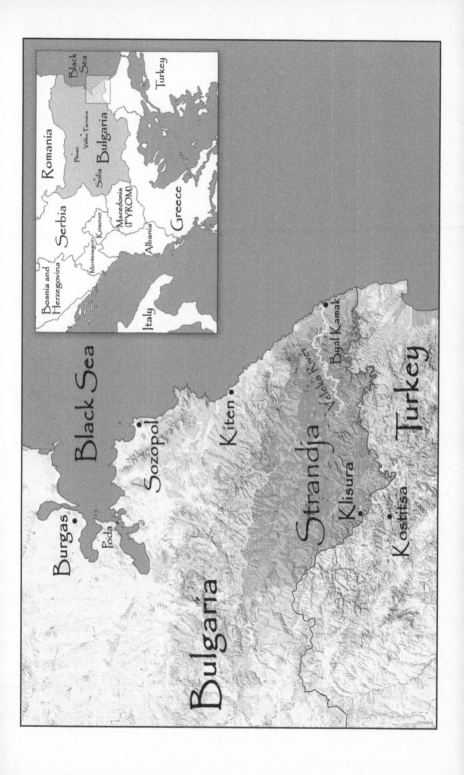

PART
ONE

· ONE ·

SOMEONE WAS BEATING THE DOOR of the station and I heard a man cry out, "Let us in, you donkeys. The storm's on my tail and inching closer." But I hadn't slept in thirty hours and maybe I was dreaming of voices. Or maybe I didn't want to get up, snug as I was on the floor in the corner. The handful of peasants around me began to stir, uneasy. The stench of wet wool, of sweat and tobacco, rose like mist from their ancient bodies and the waiting room fogged up. I knew they expected *me*, the young boy, to wrestle the door open, to let into safety whoever was out there. So I pretended that I was sleeping.

I had arrived on a bus from Sofia early that morning, a four-hour wobble east to the middle of nowhere. "You wait here," the driver had told me, "for the bus to Klisura. It comes around noon. A blue bus. With a big sign. *To Klisura*. Will you be able to read it?" He'd spoken to me the way people speak to foreigners, drunks, or the dim-witted. I'd smiled and nodded and wondered which of the three he'd thought I was.

Outside, the fist kept pounding. A growing wind whipped the windows and their glass creaked on the verge of breaking. Through the veil of my eyelashes, I spied an old woman make for the door, limping. An old man got up to help her. Next thing I knew, wind was roaring around us, much too scorching for the middle of April.

When they shut the door again I heard the man who'd been banging, now on the inside. "*Ashkolsun*, Grandma." Then I saw him, slapping sand off his tracksuit trousers, off his brown leather jacket. He kissed the old woman's forehead and, without as much as a glance at the people around him, marched to one end of the station, where old benches had been piled up, all the way to the ceiling.

"You come here and help me," he called, still not turning.

By the door there now stood a young woman. A girl really, in blue shalwars and a silk dress; it seemed like she'd sprung out from the nothing. She was untying her headscarf, white with roses imprinted on it, but when the man called, she rushed to aid him. They lugged the bench together, a good five, six meters.

"And my demijohn?" he said. "Did you forget it?" Once more the girl sprinted back to the exit, her face as red as the roses, her bare feet kicking up the sand she'd tracked in.

At once I felt lighter. The eyes of the peasants, which had crushed me for hours, had now latched on to the couple. I didn't blame them. I too wanted to know what the girl was doing, but I was afraid her man would catch me staring. So I moved to the window to watch her reflection in secret.

And at the window, I saw the storm approaching. There was a road outside the station, fissured by heat, frost, and hail, and a vast, barren field beyond it. Two rows of wind turbines stretched on the horizon, and scattered across the field I counted a dozen small mounds. Thracian tombs; I knew that much. In the distance, beyond the mounds and the turbines, a wall of red sand was pouring from the sky, violent, muddy, and racing in our direction.

"Simooms," said a voice beside me. "Scoop up sand from the Saharan desert. Bring it here, across two thousand kilometers."

A plume of smoke hit the glass on the inside and bounced back to choke me. When the smoke settled, I saw an old man reflected, ghostly transparent, except for his thick mustache the color of rusted metal.

"My missus makes me dye it," he said, smoothing the hairs and nodding at a withered woman on one of the benches. Dressed in a black skirt, black apron, black headscarf, she resembled a shadow. The old man turned his gaze to the girl in the corner. "I reckon if I wasn't married, I'd steal her." And he coughed a long time in place of laughter.

I had the urge to tell him there were no simooms in Bulgaria, never had been. But who was I to correct him? Maybe even the climate had changed in my absence. Were we in danger? Should I step away from the window? But asking him required I speak the language I hadn't used in so many years, and this scared me far more than a sandstorm.

I crawled back to my corner. On her bench, the girl was eating an apple. Her man was asleep, his arms wrapped around a wicker demijohn, the cigarette in his mouth still burning. I allowed myself to stare more boldly until at last the girl caught me. She bit hard into the apple, smiled, and began chewing, her lips aglow with sweet juice. Something slammed the side of the station, a deafening shatter.

"There, there," I heard Red Mustache saying. He'd returned to his wife, who now rocked back and forth in her seat, in fear.

"Vah, vah," she answered. Like a soft song, "Vah, vah."

And out of nowhere, she gave out a shrill cry.

"Welcome, welcome, Saint Kosta." Her rocking sped up and she crossed herself time and again with zeal. One by one the few women beside her stood up and hurried to the other side of the station. One by one they crouched on the floor and covered their faces with their motley headscarves. The girl in the corner perked up, threw away the apple, and wiped her palms in her shalwars.

"Don't be afraid, my dears," the woman in black told them. "It's just Saint Kosta arriving. And his good mother coming behind him." Her husband kept speaking, but again she wouldn't listen. In vain she tried to reach her rubber galoshes, in vain to unhook them. Her undone scarf flapped like the wings of a black bird. Her cheeks had turned to red apples, and when she looked at me, though just for a moment, she appeared as youthful as the girl in the corner.

"Don't be afraid," she told me kindly. She wiped her tears with the scarf and tied it.

Red Mustache lowered himself on the ground before her, unhooked her galoshes, and began to massage her feet, swollen and pinkish.

"There, there," he told her.

"Vah, vah," she whispered, and the tears rolled on.

It grew dark around us. The storm had swallowed the station. Fists of wind slammed it and tiles flew off the roof with a terrible clatter. Endless grains hammered the windows, and I thought any minute the glass would shatter. And through all this, I could see the sun blazing, red in the red mist—simoom, from the Saharan desert.

"That's right, my sweet dove," croaked the old woman. "Fear nothing. It's only Saint Kosta." But it wasn't to me she was speaking.

The girl had gone to the window. Fearless, reckless, she'd glued her palms to the glass as if she meant to pass through it. Her body shivered and I could see her face reflected, her wet lips twisting in a thin smile. The storm that had made me crouch on the ground in fear beckoned her to come closer.

An underground thump shook the station. The glass rippled like water and then burst into pieces.

I managed to shut my eyes before the sand lashed me. My lungs filled up with fire and I felt as if I were drowning. Wind thrashed; the women were crying and more glass was breaking around us. Next, somebody's hand was pulling me deeper into the station.

"Grab a bench," someone shouted. "Turn it over." We were pulling benches from the tall pile, me and the peasants, building a shelter and crouching behind it.

"I told you, my dears," the old woman kept croaking. "No need to fear."

I'm not sure how long we sat this way, our bodies pressed one against the other, like soldiers in a trench before battle. Sand whirlpooled around us and I had to keep my eyes shut tightly, but after a while I could breathe better and the wind no longer howled with the same force.

When someone splashed my face I jumped, startled. Red wine, warm and stinging.

"Wash the sand off," said the man with the leather jacket. He carried his demijohn along the line and poured wine on people's faces. His girl was sitting beside me, her hair spilling free over her shoulders, her face black with the streaming wine and the sand, which had turned muddy. Mud and wine trickled on the floor and the sour smell of grapes mixed with the dust of the sandstorm.

I wanted to ask the girl how she was feeling. Had the glass cut her? But once more I was ashamed of speaking. Besides, she kept her eyes closed, as before, smiling. I too closed mine and tried to steady my breathing. The wine was hot on my tongue and salty; the sand scraped my throat each time I swallowed.

"Wake up, boy. Take this." Someone shoved in my hand a piece of bread, a chunk of white cheese. Red Mustache had opened his wife's basket and was passing food to the peasants. She didn't seem to mind it, herself sucking a morsel. I wasn't that hungry, but it felt good to be eating, each bite pushing away the darkness. And so we ate, hidden behind the benches, fearful and relieved and excited. An eerie silence had filled the station, and when someone hiccupped, a woman burst out laughing. In no time we were all gasping, not in the least sure what was so funny. Only the girl by my side kept quiet. Her eyes swam under their closed lids, her face now entirely drained of color.

I turned to see her better and it was then that I touched the blood pooling between us. The wine had obscured it— black blood, thick and sticky, oozing through the sleeve of her silk dress.

"Are you touching my wife?" her husband barked, and jumped up, ready to fight me.

"She's cut," I mumbled. "Look, she's bleeding." My tongue felt limp, unresponsive, but I kept babbling until the man understood me. He pulled back the sleeve and we saw the girl's wrist, slashed open.

"Sweet mother," the man said, "I feel dizzy." He stumbled back and collapsed against the wall of the station. The peasants flocked around the girl like vultures. One slapped her face; another told her to wake up. Her eyes flicked open—as black and shiny as the blood flowing—and she gave us a sweet smile.

"I feel like a feather."

"We need to stop the bleeding," I heard myself saying. I pulled off the headscarf and wrapped it around the girl's wrist, then showed an old man where to press it, not to let go. In a daze I sprinted to retrieve my backpack, sand still lashing through the broken windows, though no longer as harshly.

"Are you a doctor?" someone asked, so I said no, I wasn't. But I carried a first aid kit, knew how to dress wounds. I kept babbling, drunk on the sound of my language or on the adrenaline maybe.

Once I'd tied the makeshift bandage the girl's eyes opened.

"I could do with some water."

I brought my bottle to her lips and she drank a few small sips.

"Stay away from my wife, you hear me?" Her husband had sprung up to his feet once more, but when he saw the blood pool his face twisted and he sat back down.

"Mouse heart," a woman's voice whispered, and the peasants burst out laughing. Even the girl giggled.

"What kind of a man fears blood?" someone mumbled.

"How does he slay *kurban*, then?"

The man rose again with great effort. He pushed through

the crowd, scooped his wife up, and, leaving a trail of bloody steps in the sand, carried her to the other side of the station. He laid her down on the floor and in his spite began to remove her bandage.

"Another man touching my wife," he said, fuming. "And you fools are laughing." In the end he threw away the bandage and wrapped the scarf around his wife's wrist.

"Mouse heart, am I?"

I looked about. But the others only shrugged and crept back to the benches. Even Red Mustache didn't seem too bothered.

For some time I watched the blood-soaked bandage on the floor, where it gathered black sand. I watched the man pressing his wife's wound, his eyes fixed on the stripped beams of the ceiling. Then I picked up my backpack and hurried to the most distant corner.

Outside, sand hung in midair like a dry mist, but the worst of the storm had passed us. I leaned my head against the wall, closed my eyes, and listened. The sand whooshing, whispering, drumming against the roof and the empty panes of the windows. What in the world was I doing back in this country, chasing after a man I hadn't seen in fifteen years? A man I hadn't spoken to in the last three. My flesh and blood. My childhood hero. A man who'd vanished without a word even.

I pulled out the tourist map I'd bought in Sofia that morning and spread it before me. There, in the southeast corner of Bulgaria, spilled the Strandja Mountains. There was the delta of the Veleka River, the coast of the Black Sea. There loomed Turkey and the border, like the bottom of a maiden's skirt, a capricious maiden who teases her suitors, lifts the hem to show one of them her ankle, then hides it and shows it to another—Greece, Bulgaria, then Turkey, like this for thirteen hundred years. And there on the hem, in the hills of the Strandja, written on the map in a font different from that of all other villages around it, was nestled Klisura. It was to Klisura I was now headed. It was in Klisura that my grandfather was hiding.

I folded up the map and returned it to my backpack. Behind the barricade the woman in black was calm now. Her husband had treated a few other men to his tobacco, and thin strings of smoke rose to the ceiling. The man in the leather jacket kept pressing his wife's wrist, his face paler than hers, which was now flushed and sweaty. She spoke to him sweetly, her voice small, distant, her head lolled on his shoulder. And twenty miles to the south, in Klisura, at this very moment, my grandfather ate lunch or pulled a bucket from the well, read a book or readied himself for his afternoon nap. Not suspecting that his grandson was coming near. To call him to account for his hurtful disappearance? I only wished my reasons for returning were this noble and this pure.

· TWO ·

OUR MOTHERS COULD DO IT ALL—each one was certified to be a tailor, a cook, a doctor, a mechanic. Our fathers were trained to wage war, to build schools and bridges, herd sheep, plow fields. Each one could go to the Olympics at only the shortest notice—lift weights, run a marathon, all in the same day. My grandfather earned two medals—gold and silver, both from the same competition. And he was sixty. Yes, triple jump. I'd show you the medals but Grandpa thought them worthless trinkets. He'd tossed them in the trash.

Our scientists had established a lunar colony, a base on Mars. Our schools operated their own cosmodromes and each child was taught to pilot his own space rocket. To graduate from first grade, a student was expected to orbit Earth. What was it like? Fantastic. The first few times.

Your Legos built you castles and ours built us guns. Each morning in school, before we drank our milk, we lined up in neat rows, pulled out the AKs from our bags, took them apart and put them back together in under forty seconds' time. Our land was most fertile—strawberries the size of apples and apples the size of melons. The melons as big as cars. Our cars were tanks. They heated up with sunlight in the day and shone at night, like thousands of heroic suns. The sun would never set on our Homeland.

Until it did. Yes, I remember. I was old enough. The earth trembled, the skies grew dark, and nothing was the same again. The winter stretched for years. The lines for bread and cheese—for days. Release the dogs! Throw out the cats! Who could afford to keep a pet? Small children, old men and women would vanish from the lines—snatched by the vicious packs and torn apart. Then it was our turn to flood the streets. Where once there had been mothers, fathers, sisters, and brothers now spilled a faceless mob.

We were living with my grandpa at the time. Yes, the Olympic medalist. He was also a history teacher, so he managed to stay employed. But Father lost his job and wanted out. He said, we either leave or perish. They woke me up one night and made me pack a suitcase. No, no, they said, no AKs, no grenades—just clothes and shoes. I could hear the mob chanting outside our apartment complex, ravenous, hateful, and the dogs howling, so we used a secret passageway, underground, to reach the cosmodrome at school.

Grandpa picked me up, kissed me on my forehead, and fastened my seat belt in the rocket seat. One day, I'll come for you, I told him. My mother counted: ten, nine, eight . . . My father pressed the button and the engines roared. The rocket shook, took off. From high above, I saw a thousand other rockets fleeing, their engines like blooming peonies in the dark.

You don't know what a peony is. Well, what flowers do you weave into your wreaths and garlands? For celebrating May 24, of course. The day of the Cyrillic alphabet? The Cyrillic . . . *А, б, в* . . .

Yes, it seems to me now that I learned my English through telling lies. Then again, lies have always been more charming than the truth.

· THREE ·

THE BUS ARRIVED with great Bulgarian punctuality—an hour and twenty minutes late. I must have dozed off, because when its horn echoed through the station I started and didn't know right away where I was. The young husband and his injured girl still sat in their corner, her head resting against his shoulder, her eyes closed. Red Mustache and his wife still hid behind the barricade. But most other peasants had left—on an earlier bus, which I'd missed somehow.

I picked up my backpack and sprinted for the door.

"Hey, funny talker," Red Mustache called. "Give us a hand, will you?"

Outside, the bus sounded its horn again. I could read its sign well, scribbled on a checkered sheet in blue pen.

"To Klisura, is it?" the young husband asked, while I struggled to pick up the old couple's sacks and baskets.

"Yes, sir," I mumbled. "I think so."

On his shoulder his girl let out a giggle.

"You go to sleep," he told her, "that's not our bus," and covered her face with his thick palm. She laughed again and I could see her eyes, watching me, between the gaps of his fingers.

And then we were outside—me and the old couple. The bus's headlights cast thick yellow ropes through the sand that hung in the air; its wipers fought to keep the grains away, but for some reason, its doors remained closed for us.

Sand pricked my face and filled my mouth with every breath. I hesitated, then kicked the door. And then again, until it opened. I let the old ones climb in first, then followed.

"A vandal, eh!" the driver said, and clicked his tongue. "A door-kicker." I paid my fare and dropped off the bags with their owners. "You take care of yourself," I told Red Mustache, and he showed me his swollen gums, on which glistened grains of sand.

"You *are* a funny talker."

There were very few other people in the bus, but even so I walked all the way to the backseat.

"Next stop," the driver announced, and I could see that he was looking at me in the rearview mirror, "Klisura."

I tousled my hair, dusted off the collar of my jacket. Sand flew around me and fell in dunes at my feet. Then, as if something made me, I turned around and looked out the back window. And this is how I saw him.

A black figure in the red. A giant with flapping wings.

The bus began to move. The giant waved, his wings flapped, he fell behind and vanished in the fog.

"Stop," I shouted. I ran all the way to the front. "Open the doors."

The driver stopped the bus. "Are you," he said slowly,

"speaking in English?" I realized what I'd done in my excitement. "A man," I said in Bulgarian. "Behind the bus."

At that moment a fist slammed on the doors. A black figure filled the small window, a Bedouin who'd wrapped a shirt, the color of red wine, around his face. He grumbled and I recognized a few words only, *mother*, *yours*, enough to catch the gist.

"Another vandal, by the looks of it," the driver said, and apathetically pressed the necessary button. The doors flew open and a sheet of sand hurled itself upon us.

"Klisura?" the Bedouin asked from the threshold. The black wings flapped madly on his chest and I realized that he was holding a hen, or maybe a chicken, whose head had been covered over with a tarpaulin pouch.

"Buy a ticket and I'll tell you," the driver said, but waved him in.

With the doors closed, the man stood motionless, catching his breath. Sand seeped from his elbows as he held the hen to his chest, from the hen's wings when they flapped.

"You're usually two hours late," he said to the driver.

"Consider it a miracle," the driver said, and rubbed his thumb against his index finger.

The man turned to face me. "My boy, hold this," he said, and shoved the hen in my direction. I jumped back, startled. Someone laughed behind me. Not wanting to appear a coward, I seized the chicken, which screamed and slapped me with its wings.

"It's fine if you're scared," the man said, not letting go, and something mocking rang in his voice. I yanked the bird out of his grip. A victorious pleasure—now I'll show him— washed over me and then, when the chicken dug its talons into my forearm, a blinding pain.

"He didn't get you with his claws now, did he?" the man said, and his eyes sparkled.

"Can't feel a thing," I lied.

"That sleeve's turning red," the driver noticed. He snatched the money the man had offered him and counted it twice. I was ready to pass out a little, when finally the man took back his hen.

The floor, seats, windows, and ceiling buzzed and we started rattling down the road. From the backseat I watched the man up front, no longer a glorious Bedouin, unwrap the shirt around his face with one hand and hold the chicken with the other. Layer after layer fell, like a mummy unbandaged, to finally reveal his wrinkled skin, his bony, hollowed cheeks, his sharp and pointy chin.

A heaviness settled in my stomach as though I'd drunk too much cold water too quickly. I had been certain of it all along and all along, it seemed, I had been wrong. This man was not my grandfather.

· FOUR ·

I WAS EIGHT WHEN COMMUNISM FELL in Bulgaria. 1989. My parents and I lived in Grandpa's apartment, crammed like broilers, because we had no money to rent, let alone buy, our own place. Father and Grandpa fought constantly. Mother wept and threatened divorce. At first they tried to spare me, but then, it's difficult to yell discreetly in a coop.

At least we weren't hungry. My grandfather was too well connected for hunger to keep us in its fist. The butcher, the baker, the fruit-and-vegetable seller—they had all been his students once.

"Wake up," Grandpa would whisper at my bedside, already bundled up in his thinned-out, moth-eaten coat. I'd beg him to let me sleep. The sun was still an hour from rising and it was Sunday.

"I got a tip from an old student." He'd shove the netted sack in my hand. "Delivery in fifteen minutes."

We walked the dark streets like thieves. The snow crunched under our boots, the frost bit our faces. No light in any window, and not a soul. Not even the dogs were out this early. The scarf on my mouth was solid ice by the time we reached the butcher's.

"*Dobrutro, drugaryo uchitel!*" the butcher would say in greeting and rush us in through the back door, lest anyone see us. "Good morning, comrade teacher!" He'd give me a playful pinch, and for a long time the trail of blood he'd smeared would burn my frozen cheek. The carcasses of two or three freshly slaughtered pigs would hang among a forest of empty hooks. The butcher would strop the knife on his belt. "For you, comrade teacher, only the best."

He'd wrap the chops in a gigantic sheet of brown paper and I would open the netted sack. "Let me throw a chop on the grill," the butcher might say. "You sit in the back and get warm."

But Grandpa wouldn't have it. "Thank you. You've done enough."

He paid the butcher and the butcher acted embarrassed, but always took the money. "Of course he takes it," Grandpa said when I asked him once. "Of course we pay. We're not ungrateful. We aren't greedy."

We'd slip out in the dark and make our way to another alley, to some other entrance in the back. A steaming loaf of bread, a jar of yogurt, a bag of milk. The netted sack swelled up with our catch. We hid it inside the school bag I carried on my back as a decoy and then, like poachers dragging forbidden seines, snuck home.

Dawn would be breaking by the time we reached the apartment complex.

"Someone's up early," a neighbor might say, and hurry

out of the elevator, buttoning up her coat, putting on her mittens, bracing herself for a few hours in the line. "Is this what you're teaching him, comrade teacher? To use the back door, while we honest people wait in lines like fools?"

I watched my grandpa's face turn red.

"We live in times of wolves," he'd say once we were safe inside the elevator. And then an hour later he might add, "A man must seek connections to other men. Wolves may be loners. Men must not."

It was this advice of Grandpa's that I took to heart during my first few years in America. So what if in the beginning I didn't speak the language? So what if at school some children mocked my home-knit sweaters, corduroy pants, tassel loafers? The language could be learned, the wardrobe replaced. No bully can bring you down, when just last year in Bulgaria you fought a grizzly on the street. His Gypsy owners, not having any means to buy him food, had shooed him off and into town. At first we fought, then we became comrades. To this day, each month I send him a jar of American honey in the mail.

I was exotic, interesting, enchanting. An heir of Olympic heroes. A cosmonaut. A weapons expert. Boys wanted to be my friends. Girls dropped little love notes in my bag. By high school no one believed my lies, but then I had no reason to keep telling any—I'd followed Grandpa's advice to a T, established strong connections, made many friends. And then I left for college, and for the first time, or so it felt, I found myself completely disconnected. No friends, pitiful grades, student loans hanging over my head like swords. Maxed-out credit cards, debt collectors calling. What else is there to say? Comrade Bear was dead and there was no one left now to receive my jars of honey.

When I was six, Grandpa took me to his native village to meet the oldest man on earth.

"I am a hundred years old and who are you?" the old man said.

"Your great-grandson," I answered, petrified, and mumbled the name we shared.

"I never liked that name," he said. He was sitting up in bed, propped on a throne of red-and-white checkered pillows. The sealed windows focused the sun on him and gave him a blinding glow. The room was stifling, but he was fully dressed—wool jacket dyed bluer than the sky; thick pants and booties as black as the fertile fields outside the village. He turned his head this way and that, bared two rows of perfect yellow teeth, and let his milky eyes fidget in their sockets. "So you've remembered you have a father, eh?" he said to Grandpa, whose palms were melting holes in my shoulders.

When he had finished signing whatever papers Grandpa had brought for him to sign, the old man called me over to his bed. I still remember the stench of naphthalene that rose up not just from the wool of his clothes but from his ancient flesh.

"You'll never live to be as old as me," he said. "Whatever you think of doing, I've already done it. Wherever you think of going, I've already been and returned. And it was nothing special."

He raked my hair, then groped my face—my forehead, nose, and chin—his hand as cold as the belly of a catfish I'd once poked. I watched Grandpa in terror, but did not dare move even when the ancient man stuck his salty fingers in my mouth. He traced the gaps where teeth were missing and pushed against the ones that rocked. Then, as unexpected as lightning in the winter, he pinched a rocking tooth, yanked it out, and ate it.

The blood never washed out completely from my shirt.

That afternoon, Grandpa took me outside the village, to see the fertile fields.

"Don't begrudge the old fool," he said. "The old are jealous of the young. The living are frightened of the dying. But sooner or later they all converge."

Stalks of plentiful wheat splashed with the wind around us. We had waded in a sea of gold. Grandpa broke off an ear and munched on the grains. His eyes watered, but he gave no sign he was ashamed.

"This land was ours once," he said. "A hundred acres."

I didn't have to ask him who owned the land now. Even at six, I knew.

But then, two years later, the Communist Party collapsed. And a few years after that, when I was a sophomore in high school, a package arrived from Bulgaria—a short letter and a box for matches. Inside the matchbox lay a pinch of soil. Our land had been returned.

It was this land, or at least my share of twenty acres, that now I had returned to sell.

· FIVE ·

THE ENDLESS THRACIAN FIELD had ended. Its flatness had been replaced by oaks in youthful foliage—tall, venerable trees keeping watch, like sentries to the mountain. There was no more sand in the air. Rusty patches were scattered across the road, which snaked gently upward through the hills of the Strandja and grew narrower the higher we climbed. The holes turned to fissures, the fissures to crevasses, and soon we crossed entire stretches where the pavement had been eroded and washed away by rain. Each time the bus sank in a fissure, my teeth buzzed. The dentures of the old men and women chattered like the bills of giant birds, and for an instant I remembered how, many years ago, all passengers, my parents and I included, had clapped when the pilot landed the Boeing safely on the Ontario runway. A moment was repeating itself. And with the chatter of teeth and dentures we entered Klisura.

I was last to step out at the small square. The sun, though past its peak, was still high above the hills. A strong gust threw the smell of smoke in my face. Even from here I could hear the wind whistling in the treetops. Up the road, Red Mustache limped toward his home, holding his cap so the gusts wouldn't steal it. Falling behind, ten, fifteen, twenty feet, the woman in black carried not just her basket but also his tarpaulin sack on her back. Two veiled, shalwared women who'd ridden the bus with us were making their way in the opposite direction, across a rusted bridge over a river whose waters I heard but couldn't see.

"I bet you are that boy," someone said behind me. The old man was smoking on the curb and with each gust the tip of his cigarette glowed brighter. The chicken flapped under his armpit and he stroked its feathers. "The one who never calls."

The bus honked. The driver had counted the ticket money, and now that all was in order, the doors swooshed closed, the exhaust pipe threw up black, cloudy vomit, and we were left alone on the square.

"There in the bus," the old man said, his eyes glistening from the exhaust, "you kept staring. Why?"

I said I'd taken him for someone else.

"For whom?"

"My grandfather."

"Maybe I am."

That was unlikely; he looked nothing like the man.

He tossed his cigarette and the wind carried it halfway across the square. "Come with me on an errand. Then I'll take you to his house."

"Why?"

"Why, why. For the thrill. For the adventure. Isn't this

why you all come here to the mountain? With your cameras and video recorders."

I realized then that the old man had started walking toward the bridge. And unconsciously I followed. I was jet-lagged, once more hungry; my head was spinning from the trip. I didn't have the energy to fight him. Besides, which way would I go to my grandfather's? And so I asked how long the errand would take us and if the chicken was involved.

"This chicken is a lie," he said. "It's for a little girl who's very ill." Without turning, he asked me if I believed in lies. That lies could cure. I said sure, maybe, I didn't know. "The girl's mother does," he said. "She begged me to bring this chicken. Also, this chicken is a rooster and if you can't tell that much, well then, you are a city fool."

I laughed. "You may be right," I said, and I think he also laughed, but with the wind in our faces I wasn't sure.

The bridge vibrated at our feet and its metal ropes creaked. Below us the river rushed muddy and wide, high from rain or snow melting upstream. A cobblestone road, which the wind had swept perfectly, took us past a flock of empty houses, the likes of which I'd never seen before. Later I learned such was the Strandjan architecture—the ground floor with walls of neatly fitted stones, where back in the day the cattle slept. The floor above—a deck with walls of wide, oak-wood planks; a covered corridor encircling the rooms, a terrace, and in one corner, the privy.

The old man led and I followed. The ancient houses alternated with modern ones—clean, lime-washed façades, shiny red-tiled roofs—and in the distance above them, thin as a knife and black with the sun behind it, the minaret of a mosque. We saw not a soul until we passed the village café. Which later I found out was also the grocery store. And the barber shop. On tables outside, men drank coffee, or lemonade from tall glass bottles. Some played backgammon, others cards. I'd never seen so many mustaches and prickly beards in one place.

"*Salaam alaikum!*" someone called. "You come to sell at last?"

The old man halted. Petting the rooster, he eyed the one who'd spoken. That man was also old. He stood in the doorframe and cleaned a glass with a towel.

"And who's the beardless beauty beside you?"

"His lawyer," someone else said, and the crowd burst out laughing.

The old man pointed to the sign above the entrance.

"It's in Turkish," he told me with a smirk. "It says Suleiman Pasha Café. You know why?"

I shrugged. I suddenly felt very thirsty.

"A hundred and thirty years ago, Suleiman Pasha, on his way to be spanked by the Russian army, stopped here to drink a coffee. And for a hundred and thirty years, these fools won't shut up about it. Listen, *kardash*," he called to the man in the doorframe, "I know where Suleiman Pasha squatted after he drank your hogwash. He didn't make it far. I'll show you and you can write a sign."

A new gust of laughter stirred the bushy mustaches. The man in the doorway waved the towel like a white flag after us—we had started up the road again. "Come back tomorrow," he called. "I've just received some of your favorite tea. We'll play backgammon. Bring the boy." The old man raised his hand as if to give a maybe.

"His name is Osman Rejep, but everyone calls him Baklava Osman. I gave him this nickname myself, when he was still a boy. Why? Only God remembers."

To this, I had absolutely nothing to say. We rounded a corner. We had arrived.

The house was of the modern kind. The mica in its plaster glistened in the sun and gave it a gentle glow. The old man slammed his fist against the yard gates and they rang like a bell. He kept on pounding.

"Why don't you slam harder?" a woman cried from inside the house. "That ought to make me run faster." The front door flew open and a barefooted girl flapped across the tiled path in the yard. She was adjusting her headscarf—a blue kerchief with blooming red carnations imprinted in the cloth—but when she recognized the old man she flung the scarf away and shoved it in the back pocket of her jeans. She was younger than me, but not by much, her hair short, like a boy's. Her face was flushed, and sweat ran down her cheeks in trickles, down her neck.

"*Marhaba*, Grandpa," she said as she opened the gates and flashed us her bone-white teeth. Then she saw the rooster and her smile expired.

"So you've brought a rooster," she said, and looked at me. "Two roosters." There was something cruel in the way she pursed her thin lips, in the way her large black eyes watched me, unblinking. Maybe that's why I was reminded of the girl from the station.

"Grandpa," she said, "tell him to pick his jaw up off the ground."

Oh, please, I wanted to say. But, knowing that my accent thickened in moments of anxiety and anger, I kept quiet. The girl was leading us across the yard when somewhere behind the hilltops the whistle of a songbird rang and then grew quiet. The old man halted and so did the girl. They listened intently, and only after another bird had answered, somewhere from within the village, did they resume. I watched her scarf wave from her back pocket like a fox's tail. Her jeans rustled with every step up, up the outside staircase to the second floor, and a new kind of uneasiness flooded my head.

The stench of something burned slapped us at the threshold. In a flash, I saw my mother helping me plant candles in a church sandbox, for the dead. Careless, still a child, I'd held the candle much too close. The stench of burned hair had haunted me for weeks. It was this smell I tasted now as the girl led us through the dark hallway.

For the first time I thought of the sick girl we were about to meet. What was her illness and how were we supposed to help her? And gradually, all sense of adventure left me. Listen, old man, I was about to say, but then the rooster crowed. It flapped its wings as if behind the door we stood by was rising the morning sun.

"All night, Grandpa," the girl said. "All night Aysha jumped and danced about the room. So Father tied her down to the bed, but even then she kept on wailing. When the sun rose, she wailed louder. So we covered the window, like you told us to, and only then did she fall asleep. But I couldn't sleep. I couldn't study. And I can't fail another exam."

Clumsily, the old man petted the girl's head. "Elif, Elif," he said. Then Elif pushed the door open and led us in.

The room was pungent with the stink of soot. Dressed in a white gown and tied to the bed with a thin rope lay Aysha, the sick girl. Her face was pale in the gloom and perfectly still, like a frozen puddle, and only her eyes flittered under her closed lids. She looked ten, no older. The rope snaked over a red pillow on her chest, a pillow on her thighs, a pillow on her ankles. The soles of her feet were covered with blisters so deep I couldn't bear to look.

"Grandpa," someone called, and from a rug in the corner a third woman rose, older than the others. A green scarf whose edges were dark from sweat framed her flushed, tired face.

"She's slept all day," the mother whispered. "But we're afraid to untie her." She leaned forward and kissed the old man's hand. "Help us," she said. Her eyes shone feverish when she looked up at me, and I understood that this woman too was sick.

"Elif," the old man called to our guide. "Fetch me a washbasin and a knife."

The first thing he cut with the knife was the rope. He threw the pieces to the floor in disgust. I noticed a large scorched circle, which the rugs could not hide fully, as if someone had built a fire in the middle of the room and let it burn. Sweat was pouring down my back and my throat burned thirsty. A motley rug covered the window and the sun shone muffled behind it. The yellow, the orange, the red bands glowed brightly; the others were black. Across the rug, on a nail in the wall, hung a braid of garlic.

"And how are you, *kazam?*" the old man asked the woman. He readjusted the rooster under his arm and, still holding the knife in the other, touched her forehead with the back of his hand.

"I've been burning, Grandpa."

Gently he raised her chin to have a better look. Gently he brushed his fingers across the bruises of her cheek. "I see the imam has opened up the slap factory again," he said.

"He worries, Grandpa. His hand is quick to slap, but he means well."

"And where is he now?"

"Where can an imam be?"

The old man grumbled. "Let's get this over with," he said, and motioned me to join him by the bed. I didn't have time to hesitate—he'd already shoved the rooster into my hands. Beside me, Elif embraced the metal basin.

We watched Aysha sleep. As if our eyes had tickled her, she stirred. Her mother followed the old man the way a hungry dog follows the butcher.

"Saint Constantine," the old man whispered, "are there no Christian girls for you to take? Or are the Muslims sweeter? Go to the Greeks. The Greeks love you."

He reached over and removed the tarpaulin pouch from the rooster's head. The rooster's chest expanded and, feeling that it wanted to flap, I gripped it tighter. Then came the crowing—so loud and piercing I almost dropped the bird.

As for the rest, what's there to say? Aysha woke up startled and began to cry. Her feet took tiny steps in the air, and her heels knocked against the bed. The old man ordered me to hold the rooster tightly, and, eyes closed, I did. I could hear the sound the blood made splashing against the basin. The air thickened with a metallic stink. The rooster thrashed, kicked, and so did Aysha. The whole bed shook and creaked. "Vah, vah, vah," she cried out, like the old woman at the station. Then she was still.

The old man had painted crosses of blood on her cheeks and forehead. A big, content smile stretched her burning lips. He painted crosses on her mother's cheeks, and on Elif's. He dipped his thumb one last time in the foamy blood and asked Elif to carry the basin out.

"Grandpa," I said after he'd drawn a cross on my forehead. "I haven't seen you in fifteen years and this is how you greet me?"

He called the mother over. He said, "This is my boy, my grandson from America. The one who never calls."

"Oh, please," I started to say, but now was hardly the time for confrontation. The woman smiled. She lowered the rug and pushed the window open. At the ledge, I filled my lungs with fresh air, gulped it like water. I let the sun above the hills burn itself upon my pupils and listened to the wind in the treetops. The imam began to sing from the mosque.

Most likely the old man was right. How odd this whole situation seemed to me now. How bizarre that after fifteen years, I would meet my grandfather without an official moment of recognition, without an affectionate embrace to mark the instant of my return. And then I understood that we reunited the way we'd drifted apart—gradually, over time; that I returned the way I'd left.

· SIX ·

MORE THAN FORTY YEARS AGO, as a punishment for his scandalous membership resignation, the Bulgarian Communist Party had exiled my grandfather to the village of Klisura. A schoolteacher, he had taught the Klisuran children for four years before returning to civilization. This was all I knew, all I had learned from my father.

To claim that Grandpa despised the Communist Party would be an understatement of great proportions. And yet he never showed his contempt. To say that he expressed joy when the Party fell would also be inaccurate. "The wolves have retailored their coats," he once said, regarding the new democratic leaders. "Woe to the lamb who thinks the wolf his guard dog." In short, Grandpa claimed to give the Communists no thought at all. He wished for them what he considered the ultimate curse—the Cup of Lethe. "May no one remember them in fifty years," he told me once, during my senior year in high school. I was writing a paper on Communism and he had shut down my request for help. "May their children forget them. I certainly have."

But wasn't short historical memory a dangerous thing? I asked him.

"You muttonhead," he said. "People don't write history books so others can learn from their mistakes. They write them so they will be remembered. And I for one will *not* remember." For years I was convinced that his animosity toward the Party stemmed from the fact that in 1944, along with the reins of Bulgaria, the Communists had seized our family land. But when, upon Grandpa's sudden disappearance from our lives three years ago, my father spoke of Klisura, I realized that the old man's hatred must stem from some deeper, darker place. I decided that Grandpa's punitive exile to the Strandja Mountains had brought him much suffering and pain. But if I was correct, why had he returned?

"You had no right to disappear like that," I said. We were eating dinner on the covered terrace of his Klisuran house, some bread and cheese Elif had given us on the way out. Silently we had crossed the bridge, the small square. Silently we had followed the eroded cobblestone road. Every now and then Grandpa would pinch the scruff of my neck.

"Look how you've grown," he'd say. "Had I known you were coming, instead of a rooster, I might have bought a lamb." Then he'd tousle my hair as if such playfulness could mask the truth—neither I nor he knew where to begin. And yet we had to, somewhere.

"We were worried sick. We thought you were dead."

He shook the crumbs from his sleeves. "Good bread, this," he said. He reached for his jar and for a long time gulped water. Then he picked on the crumbs stuck to its sweaty walls.

"Grandpa," I said. He pushed the jar away and the newspapers we'd spread on the table rustled.

"Quite frankly, Grandson, I didn't think you'd notice."

I begged his pardon.

"Beg all you want," he said. "For all I know, you have no grandfather. You certainly acted it for years."

"I was busy with school. Preoccupied. But I always made time to call you."

"My erections are more frequent than your calls."

What very useful information, I said. I asked him if it was daily reports he expected. He asked me to repeat myself.

"This mumbling," he scowled, "this so-called Bulgarian of yours. It's pitiful."

He'd dealt me a low blow. I bit my tongue, then chewed it as if it were to blame. All the accusations, the powerful, dramatic speeches I'd been preparing for months rang perfectly clear in my head even now. But the moment I opened my mouth the words rolled out crippled.

Grandpa picked up the jar and drank it dry. "I'm thirsty like a rabid dog," he said. "And maybe I *am* rabid. Maybe that's why I came here. Did you think of that?"

I nodded. Insane, unstable, terminally ill—all these were scenarios my parents and I had considered at length.

"Listen, my boy," Grandpa said gently, and spread his palms open. "We're both tired. We'll talk tomorrow."

The newspapers on the table flapped and, zipping up my jacket, I stretched back in the chair. I really was tired. The wind had grown cold. The sun had dived behind the hills and though the sky was bright in that direction, it was indigo to the east. From our vantage point, high on the terrace, I could see the bridge, the river, and on the other side the Muslim houses with their red rooftops, the thin minaret of the mosque. On our side of the village was desolation—crumbling stone walls, yards overgrown with thorns and dead trees. And on the chimneys of the ruined houses—like large, unblinking eyes that watched me in the dusk—dozens of stork nests.

"Does every house have a nest?" I asked Grandpa a few days later.

"Some roofs have two."

But why there weren't any in the Muslim hamlet he couldn't say.

The nests were still empty. Though it was time, the storks had not arrived yet. Two more weeks would pass before the first birds—the scouts, as Grandpa called them—spun their belated wheels in the skies over Klisura.

"What's that?" I pointed toward the end of the village, where, as a grotesque counterpoint to the white minaret, stuck up an ugly black metal frame.

Grandpa groaned in disgust. "There is the Babel Tower," he said, "there is the Eiffel Tower. That there is the Tower of Klisura. A world fucking wonder. If you permit."

A few months back some genius had started building a wind turbine and then abandoned it mid-construction. And that was that.

He lit up and the plume he exhaled hung between us, changing shapes. The wind whooshed through the treetops and carried the smell of budding leaves, of wet, damp earth, which mixed with the stench of the tobacco. I cowered in my jacket. The cigarette burned red, redder in the smoke, like a living coal. The smoke drew a wing, the wing morphed into a woman's face.

A hand shook my shoulder. "Wake up, my boy. Listen. Hear!"

How long had I dozed? Night had fallen. Somewhere in the dark, behind hills I couldn't see, a bird was calling, its song melodic, mournful. And like today, another bird answered it from the Muslim hamlet, where now timid lights shone behind the curtained windows.

"It's from across the border," Grandpa said. "A man has died. They're letting us know."

"Who is?" I perched forward and listened to the whistling song.

"The people of his village. That's how they cross the hills. They've learned to speak like birds."

I'm not sure how long I sat in my chair mesmerized. The song had dissolved in the night and silence had returned to the village—crickets cried in the yard, dogs barked, the treetops rustled.

"This man," I said at last, and my ugly accent startled me. What beauty, to speak unburdened like a bird. "Did you know him? Was he a good man?"

"What difference does it make?" Grandpa asked. "He's dead."

I woke up with thunder ringing in my ears. Sheets of rain slapped the window and the glass rattled in its frame. The whole house had come to life—walls, floors, beams in the ceiling. Caught in jet lag, I listened, dozed off, came to again. Then, sharp as the bolts of lightning that flashed over the hills, a man's voice echoed. Someone was calling down the hall.

I turned my flashlight on and for a brief moment did not know where I was. The beam illuminated a tiny fire truck on the floor, a whipping top. A small desk in the corner and on the wall above it a map of the ancient world. My childhood room re-created piece by piece.

"I moved it here exactly as it was," Grandpa had said a few hours earlier when he led me over the threshold. "Once I sold the apartment, I had a decision to make. I couldn't throw you on the trash." The tiny bed, which at the time had seemed so giant—a pirate galleon, a rocket ship—and the chair by its side, in which for nights on end Grandpa had told me goodnight stories of khans and tsars and rebels. He'd brought them here to the village.

"Grandpa!" I called now in the hallway. The voice had not echoed again, but in its place I heard the smashing of a hammer. Light flickered around the frame of his shut door. I knocked, then entered.

Grandpa was writing frantically behind a desk. The storm had thrown the windows open and banged them against the walls. A curtain flapped heavy with rain, which pounded the room with every gust. But the old man wrote unfazed. His drawers, his hemp shirt stuck drenched to his body. Sheets of paper were scattered across the desk, where a gas lamp flickered despite the storm. How he had not set the room on fire, I didn't know. And there were yet more papers, spilled wet on the floor.

I slammed the windows shut, then laid my hand on his shoulder.

"You're shivering," I said. I could see my breath escape in a cloud and his breath when he stammered.

"My boy. I was just writing you a letter."

His eyes were muddy. They darted across my face like frightened things.

Gently I helped him up and led him across the hallway to

my bed. I took the drenched clothes off and rubbed his body under the thick Rhodopa blanket.

"You are that boy, aren't you?" he muttered once. And once he said, "My boy!" Then he was quiet. He watched me terrified. I tried to calm him with gentle talk, but I was anxious, myself frightened, and so my accent had worsened. I don't think he understood me.

Earlier that day, on our way back from the sick girl's house, like a man who wanted to fake a careless disposition, Grandpa had started whistling a tune. The tune had sat on my tongue all day, familiar yet out of reach. But now, to my surprise, I pursed my lips and whistled, a song Grandpa had sung for me goodnight. He closed his eyes. The storm had passed. Far across the border, in Turkey, its thunder still rumbled.

The words to the song too returned. But I ignored them.

· SEVEN ·

I WAS ON MY THIRD KNOCK AT THE GATES when, in the window overlooking the road, a curtain stirred just enough for Elif's face to peek through. Her expression didn't change when she saw me. The curtain fell and for a long time I shivered in the morning chill. Then the window opened, but the curtain remained drawn.

"What do you want?" she said. And after a while, "I know you're there. I can hear you breathing."

I focused all my faculties. I'd come to return the towels. The towels in which she'd wrapped the bread and cheese. And would she let me, allow me to use their phone?

"Look up the street," she said. "Is there a window open?"
There was.

"And a hag hanging out the frame. Staring at you?"
She was.

"Well then, we might as well." Her white hand parted

the curtain and slammed the window shut. A minute later she was shooing me in through the gates.

"Good morning, Aunt Nadiré," she called to the woman up the street. "Don't tumble over and break your neck now!" And then to me, "The phone's in the living room. When you're done come back outside. I'll be here, waiting."

Sand dunes as wide as oceans and camels in long, snaking caravans. A flock of storks against a blazing sun and an oasis where men in white gowns and turbans had stopped to quench their thirst. A placid lake. A calm blue sky. I'd entered not a living room, but an entire world of magic.

Besides the murals, the room was plain. Red rugs covering the floor from wall to wall and cushions around a low rectangular table. A large chest against one wall and on the chest the phone. No TV set, no books other than a single leather-bound volume on the table.

I stuck my finger in the rotary and dialed the number on my calling card. Six times before I connected. *Enter your twelve-digit PIN*, the automated operator said. I turned the rotary, but by the fourth revolution the operator had asked for the PIN again. I watched the camels make their way through the desert, immense riches locked in the chests on their backs. I watched the men about to drink from the lake and wondered if it was in their power to turn tone into pulse so I could call my parents and tell them I had arrived.

I hung up and would have stepped outside if not for some sudden burst of curiosity. The sick girl's room was empty and air blew through the open window in cool, damp gusts. The bed was neatly made. The burned spot on the floor had been covered entirely with rugs, but there was still soot on the ceiling above it. I lifted the rug and touched the spot. I sniffed the char on my fingers.

"My sister starts fires here," Elif said from the threshold.
I leapt up, stuttered an apology.

"Each spring, three years in a row. She dances barefoot in
the coals and barks like an owl. Vah. Vah. Vah." She pulled
out a cigarette and lit it. "It's really sad the way her feet blis-
ter. The way my father treats her, like she's a leper. The way
he treats me, like I'm his sheep. Would you believe he pays
that hag across the street to spy on me day in, day out? A jar
of honey every month."

She forced a blast of smoke through her nostrils, one
stream thicker than the other. "You need to loosen up, *amerikanche*," she said. "I need to loosen up." She watched me for
a moment as if she was sizing up my weight and finding it
unsatisfactory, much too low. "I know this place outside the
village where back in the day the Christians danced. Where
the storks nest. Where the weed hits you at least twice as
hard. Don't look so scared," she said, and seized my hand.

· EIGHT ·

EVERY YEAR, for thirteen hundred years, the *nestinari* dance. Come spring, come May, come the feast of Saint Constantine, the feast of Saint Elena. They build tall fires; three cartloads of wood are torched and burned to embers. And then, barefooted, they take the saint's invisible and holy hand and plunge into the living coals. They spin, they wave their sacred icons in the air, they rush first in, then out. They feel no pain because the saint protects them. A week, two weeks, a month before the dance the saint descends upon the ones he's chosen. The women swoon, their eyes like popping chickpeas under their flaming lids. The men blaze up in holy fever. Their temples split; their lips bring fire to everything they touch. And yet, despite the fever, a deep freeze chills them to the bone. Feet come alive, take quick, rushed steps. The muscles spasm, the bodies shake and seek the flame. An owlish cry escapes the throat. Vah. Vah. Vah. And only dancing in coals can bring relief. But if the chosen push away the hand that leads them, if they refuse both dance and saint, their sickness worsens, their blood transfigures into liquid fire, which then incinerates their bones, their hearts and souls. Come spring, come May, come the feast of Saint Constantine, of Saint Elena, the *nestinari* dance. And it has been like this for thirteen hundred years, here in the Strandja Mountains, and nowhere else.

Such was the yarn Elif was spinning. We walked the bushy bank, upstream and out of Klisura. The river rushed muddy from last night's rain and so loud I struggled to hear all that she said. The mist through which I'd left Grandpa's house that morning had rolled away and a warm sun was climbing the sky. The bushes here were in bloom. White and yellow flowers danced before my eyes as Elif pushed twigs and branches out of her way with fury.

"It started three years ago," she said. The branch she released whipped me across the chest and I sneezed from the pollen. "My sister was coming out of the mosque when she first fainted. A perfectly insolent little creature!"

For two days Aysha thrashed in bed. Her feet twitched, her teeth chattered. A doctor came from town. "I measure no fever," he said. "She should be fine." And yet she wasn't. "Keep her hydrated," the doctor ordered. Who knew, perhaps it was the flu? After all, six other girls were sick in the village.

But the old women knew. They'd found the cause long before the doctor's visit. Black magic? The evil eye? What monster could have the heart to hurt the seven little darlings? "Don't be afraid, my dears," a woman from the Christian hamlet said. It was Saint Constantine who'd claimed the girls.

The pieces of the puzzle fell into place. A week before, Aysha and her girlfriends had gone to the river to watch the baby storks. They played in the mud, splashed in the shallow pools, then snuck into the abandoned *nestinari* shack. This was a hut down by the river where once upon a time the fire dancers kept their icons and their holy drum.

A week went by. And then two of the girls lay down with fever.

"There will be more," the hag from the Christian hamlet said. And she was right. Before long, Aysha and the remaining girls were also sick. The hag came to Elif's house. Their father was furious at first, but he was also worried and so he let her in. They sat her down under the trellised vine and brought before her the seven sickly girls. The hag fished out a clove of garlic from her apron and popped it in her mouth— she ate garlic, Elif told me, like it was bonbons. Then she ordered the fathers to fill up a trough with water and the seven girls to stand around the trough. Their feet took tiny, frenzied steps. Their eyes rolled white, their teeth chattered. The hag waited for the water to settle and for a long time studied the faces reflected on the surface. That's how bent she was, Elif said, unable to stand up and look you in the eye. But there was more to it, the women whispered. Only in water could the hag see the things she sought to see. "Don't be afraid, my dears," she said at last. "Rejoice!" It was Saint Kosta who held the girls like sugar cubes under his holy tongue. His feast was coming near. "Build a fire, spread the coals. Give the girls icons and let them carry them across." Only then would the saint be calmed. Only then would the fever go away. "Lucky, lucky doves," the hag said. "What I would give to have him claim me one last time." And tears rolled down her cheeks.

Bitter indignation choked the parents. "Our daughters kissing Christian icons and worshipping a Christian saint? For shame before Allah!" Each father seized his daughter's hand and dragged his sickly girl back home. Windows were sealed and doors were bolted. "I'm the imam," their father told Aysha, "and you are making a mockery of me. A mockery of God." And then he smacked the little girl, bloodied her lip.

For seven days and nights Aysha stayed imprisoned in her room. Twice a day Elif was allowed to bring her meals, to empty out her chamber pot. How she wished she could forget that stench. Shit and piss, and her little sister, shaking on the floor and chewing the tresses of her hair. No, she would not forgive this man. As long as she breathed, she'd curse her father's soul.

The feast of Saint Constantine arrived, and with the feast, just as the hag had told them, Aysha began to howl. She jumped behind the bolted door all night. Then in the morning she was calm, slept through the day, and woke in peace. Elif and her mother washed her gently, combed her hair, and when she asked them why all this kindness, they burst into tears.

Last year the sickness once again returned. Three weeks before the feast Aysha built a fire in her room. The hag had warned them many times that such a thing might happen. Aysha burned a handful of sticks down to embers, and it was because of her shrieking that Elif found her, jumping on the glowing coals. Who knew how badly she would have hurt her feet. And what if the house had caught on fire?

Again their father locked up the little girl. But a few days later Aysha was once more dancing in the fire. At first, Elif couldn't see how her sister had snuck out, where she had found the sticks and matches. Then she understood. Their mother had helped her. Their mother too was burning with the Christian flame.

And this year, Elif told me, the fever had turned to madness. "You saw how Father had roped Aysha down. You saw my mother's blackened eye. What else is there to see?"

· NINE ·

WE HAD WALKED as far out of Klisura as the bank allowed us. From here on, the bushes were too thick. Blooming branches crisscrossed over the river to form a tunnel through which we had to pass. Sitting down on the grass, Elif removed her headscarf and stuffed it in her pocket. She tousled her short hair, then slipped her sneakers off and began to roll up the legs of her jeans.

"Hey, *amerikanche*"—she had taken to calling me "little American"—"you can't imagine the fight I had to fight with my father so he would let me walk around in jeans. The things he'd do to you, to both of us, if he found us together here, alone. If he knew you could see my toes and feet. You like them?"

I think she laughed. Sheep bells were ringing up the hill or maybe closer. I pictured a shepherd, resting on his crook, watching us and twisting his mustache. The shepherd would speak to Elif's father, who then would come for me. I sneezed.

"I've seen goats faint when they are scared," she said, "but never a man sneezing when something spooks him," and, laughing, she splashed upstream. Shoes in hand and trousers rolled up, I followed. The water sliced me, knee-deep and razor-cold. Elif was crying in pain or pleasure. I couldn't tell. We walked the tunnel, twisting, turning, brushing away the blossoming branches overhead. My nose ran, my eyes smarted, and every other step I sneezed.

At ten sneezes, Elif began to count them. At twenty she was laughing so hard, she had to stop and catch her breath. She told me to splash my eyes with water, which helped a bit. At thirty sneezes, the tunnel had ended and we were out in the open.

What spread before us was an island, a perfectly flat meadow, as wide as a baseball field, which split the river into two turbulent streams. One stream came from Turkey. The other was Bulgarian. They merged here and together they flowed eastward to the Black Sea.

Where the two streams met, the water was black with mud. It churned dry leaves and twigs, like a giant centrifuge, but because the basin was so wide, the water never reached above our knees.

And in the meadow I saw a tree. A giant, whose trunk a dozen men would not encircle hand in hand. Each of its lower branches could be a tree itself. It reached so high I strained to see its top. I felt at once protected and exposed, completely at its mercy. The tree was dead. But all the same, it bloomed in massive charcoal blossoms that weighed its branches down, from top to bottom.

"Stork nests," said Elif beside me. Each year, on their way from Africa to Europe and then back, the storks passed over the Strandja Mountains. The Via Pontica, she said. Once, as a little girl, she'd tried to count the nests on the tree. At fifty, she'd lost track. But there were more. Not just in its branches, but in the oaks along the banks as well.

The giant was a walnut tree. As old as Klisura and maybe older. Under its branches once upon a time the *nestinari* danced. Look, can you see the soot on its bark? And there by its trunk, in the mist, can you see it? A tiny hut, its roof covered with stones from the river? The shack of the *nestinari*.

"I was inside it once. Found nothing. Except a twisted saint who tortures little girls." She laughed. We sat on the ground and rubbed our feet to warm them. Mist still floated here in the meadow and the sweet stench of rotting grass filled my nostrils. At least I wasn't sneezing.

"You're shivering," she said with a laugh. I nodded. I had told Grandpa the same last night and now I wondered if he was still in my bed, if he was feeling better. I wondered what he had felt when inevitably, many years back, he'd first seen the giant tree. Who had stood by his side then, the way Elif now stood by me?

"Look, see," she said, and dug her fingers in the ground, scooped up a handful, and pulled it out of the mist.

"Feathers. The whole field is blanketed with them. Tell me, is there a thing sadder than feathers rotting in the ground? A thing more pretty?" She tossed them behind her back and dusted off her palms. "Let's go get high," she said. She put on her shoes and, as if she were a little girl, smacked me on the neck. "You're it," she said, then jumped up and, laughing, sprinted toward the tree. "I'll race you to the top!"

Her yell carried across the meadow, bounced back in the

oaks along the banks, and drowned in the mixing rivers. I watched her through the mist, a little speck against the walnut that stretches its arms and legs, somehow connects with the bark and climbs it. Up she went, up beyond the lower branches, in a straight line, quick and assured. Ten, fifteen meters into the air. She straddled a branch and, with her feet dangling on either side, moved toward a giant nest in its middle, where other branches crossed into a firm foundation. She threw herself into the nest, the way she must have done a thousand times before, and for a moment I lost her from my sight. When she reemerged, she was waving her motley scarf. The scarf slipped from her fingers and spiraled down, down through the mist.

I remembered the storks that gathered in my childhood town in August, wheeling high above the rooftops of houses, blocks of flats, catching warm currents in the air, their cartwheels growing larger, thicker with every new arriving stork. And I remembered how we had watched them from our balcony, and Grandpa asking, "My boy, which stork are you?"

· TEN ·

THERE WAS A VILLAGE once upon a time that would have lain some fifty miles south of Klisura. Today this land was in Turkey and two hundred years ago, not just this land, not just Klisura, but all of Bulgaria belonged to the Ottoman Empire. In this ancient village, the Christians—some strange mix of Bulgarians and Greeks—were allowed to build tall churches, to worship their god with the kind of freedom Christians across the empire did not enjoy. Why the sultan allowed such liberty to a handful of his *rayas*, Elif couldn't say. Nor could the hag who had told her this story. One night three years ago, intrigued by her sister's affliction, Elif had snuck across the bridge into the Christian hamlet and sought the hag who had examined the sickly girls. And in the cloak of darkness, the hag had told her the story of how the fire dancers had first set foot in Klisura.

We were sitting in the stork nest now, our bent legs almost touching at the knees. The nest walls were sticks entwined and balls of straw and wool and feathers. The sticks poked me, but I didn't mind. Sheltered from the wind, I was no longer freezing.

Elif had fished a nylon pouch out of the hay that lined the nest's bottom and was rolling a joint. Her secret stash, she called the baggie. Her happy place, this nest. Ever since she was a little girl she'd hide here from her father, from all the troubles in her life. She'd carved steps in the tree trunk, built herself a stairway. "I'm a hot-air balloon," she said, and licked the edge of the rolling paper. "My troubles are the sandbags I throw out one by one. Up the bark I climb until at last I'm lighter even than air itself."

She lit the joint and took a drag. The stench of pot, of rotting hay mixed in one noxious fume. "I go to the university in Burgas," she said. "I get some money for my good grades and this is what the money buys me." She passed the joint, which I refused.

"Suit yourself," she said, and leaned her head back on the entwined sticks. Through an opening in the hedge I could see the shack of the *nestinari*, rainwater pooling on the flat stones of its roof. The pools glimmered with sun, which had tangled midway in the dry branches of our tree. The rivers boomed and Elif began to speak.

For centuries that ancient village prospered, protected by the great sultan himself. There in this village the first *nestinari* danced. Bulgarians and Greeks alike, living together, speaking a language of their own. Each May, Saint Constantine descended upon the peasants like a storm, and after him, like light spring rain, merciful Saint Elena followed. Each May, for centuries on end, the *nestinari* built tall pyres and danced in their coals. Until, one day, the Turks burned down the village and slaughtered as many fire dancers as they could.

"Why, Grandma?" Elif had asked the hag. "Why, why!" The hag had answered, "Does the dog need a why to suck the marrow from a bone? Does the Turk need a why to slaughter the Christian? They weren't pretty like you, my dove, the Turks back then. Back then the Turks were ugly hunchbacks with wolf teeth, thirsty for Christian blood."

"That's what she said." Elif laughed and sniffed the burning joint. "Hunchbacks and with wolf teeth at that."

The village had been torched and ruined. The *nestinari* nearly wiped out. Only a handful had survived, taking their icons, their holy drums into the thick oak woods. Fear not, my children, a man had cried, their leader, the *vekilin*. And it was this *vekilin* who led the survivors north through the Strandja Mountains in search of new land to call home.

"But no one would have them, my dove," the hag told Elif. They would come to a village, ruined and in rags, their stomachs churning, their lips cracked and bloodied. The village nobles would gather at the square and the *vekilin* would fall before them on his knees. "Give us some land from yours," he'd beg them. "It could be stones, thorns, nettles, we aren't picky. Let us call it our home." But when they saw the icons with the tails, the drums, the bags of bones these people carried—because the *nestinari* also transported the skulls of their dead—the villagers grew frightful. The madness of the fire dancers scared them, the grip of Saint Constantine, the wrath of the sultan, who had suddenly slaughtered the very people he'd protected for centuries on end. And this past protection too made every village angry. "Why should we help them?" the peasants fumed. "While the Turks trampled on us, these dogs were dancing. While we cried, they burst with laughter. It's their time to weep now, and ours to be merry. You holy lepers, scurry off!"

For weeks the *nestinari* roamed the Strandja Mountains, until one day they reached Klisura. Even back then the village was split in half—Bulgarians on one bank of the river, Turks on the other. "Brothers, we're perishing," the *nestinari* begged. "Give us some land." And like before, instead of land it was a curse they received.

But Saint Constantine is a merciful saint, the hag told Elif. And lo and behold the Turkish aga, ruler of Klisura, allows the *vekilin* to bow before him and listens to his plea. Sitting on the balcony of the *konak*, the aga smokes from his long *chibouk*, and his meaty fingers play with a rosary of red amber. He's heard how terrified the *rayas* can get of these newcomers and so he wants to spite them, his little slave lambs, he wants to keep them full of fear. Besides, he's not afraid of the sultan. He even has a bone to pick with him. "Why not?" he says to the *vekilin*. "I'll give you land in the Bulgar hamlet. Build your village there if you will."

"But the aga was a Turk," Elif said. Her eyes had turned watery and red now, and they glistened like the pools on the shack's roof down below us. "A Turk, like me. And therefore a wretch. Or so the hag told me. The aga, she said, couldn't just give the infidels what they wanted without receiving some pleasure in return."

So the aga orders his soldiers to gather up all male *nestinari* in the courtyard. No more than twenty—young and old, beaten from the road, barely standing on their feet. As for the women and children, the aga lines them up against the stone wall so they may watch the circus that is about to unfold. He calls for his favorite *zurla* player. "Do you know what a *zurla* is, *amerikanche*? Like the oboe, but cheerful and much louder. He calls for the *gadulka* player." Elif made a motion with her hand, driving an invisible bow across a set of invisible strings. "The players gather, ready to play. All men back then, they wore sashes. The older folk around here still do. Ten, fifteen elbows of cloth wrapped around their waist. So the aga orders his soldiers to hold the end of each sash and pull. The sashes unwind and the men spin like tops. The *zurla* fills the yard with shrieking and the *gadulka* joins it. That's how I imagine it at least. The poor things spin across the yard like mad, hardly able to stand on their feet as it is. The soldiers whip them with their whips. By now the children are crying, the women are screaming, and the aga, that wretched Turkish dog, stands on his balcony, laughing, throwing his own whip about, urging the soldiers to lash the men faster, harder."

Some of the men spin left and tumble to the ground on one side of the courtyard. Some fall on the other. Half and half, more or less. "You on the left side," the aga booms, laughing. "I'll give you land. Keep your women, keep your children. You on the right, I have no use for you. So scurry off."

The *nestinari* were split in half. But so they wouldn't forget each other, the *nestinari* exchanged their icons, their bags of skulls. One group would safeguard the saints and ancestors of the other, a holy bond. They gave an oath, to reunite each May, on the feast of Saint Constantine, and dance together over the burning coals. One year in Klisura, the next in the village where the second group would settle, no matter how far away that village lay.

"Where did the rest of them settle?" I asked, and Elif shrugged.

"Across the Strandja somewhere. Some village that even today is part of Turkey. The hag told me, back then it had been Greeks who lived there, Greeks who'd taken pity on the *nestinari* and given them some land."

I struggled to wrap my head around this story. An ancient village, home to the first fire dancers, part of Turkey, in which the peasants were neither fully Bulgarian nor fully Greek, but a mix of the two. And Turks in what was now Bulgaria who'd given shelter to half the refugees and chased away the others. And Greeks in what was now Turkey who'd sheltered the rest.

"As clear as springwater," I said, and Elif asked me which spring I meant—the one that came from Turkey, or the one that was all Bulgarian? We burst out laughing and laughed too long. It could have been the smoke she blew my way.

"So did they meet?" I said. "Each year?"

"For centuries they did. The hag saw the Greeks. She traveled to their village and danced with them, back when she was still a girl. Back when Saint Constantine was kind enough to claim her. I wish you'd seen her, standing before the sickly girls. An eighty-year-old woman, bursting at the seams with jealousy. Over some saint. I wish you'd seen the longing in her eyes. I told myself, this hag and I, we are the same woman. Her breath stinks from the garlic and mine from spite. She hates the girls, I hate their parents. We both want something we'll never have."

"What do you want?" I said, trying my damnedest not to laugh.

"Freedom, my American friend. Not just here in the nest, but down below. I'm not free, and I want to be. You understand? And I don't think I'll ever be."

I understood then that she had begun to cry. Her shoulders rocked; she cowered into herself. And then, like that, she'd blinked away the tears. "I'm such a vile thing," she said. "I despise my father, which is a huge sin. God sees, I know. And I despise Him too—my god." She snatched out of her pocket the headscarf I'd collected from the ground and threw it carelessly across the nest. "I renounce Him day after day. Each day in jeans, each day hiding the *shamiya* like a knife in my pocket. My friends in the city, they don't know I'm Muslim. I'd kill myself if they found out. And yet, I love my god. I love my father. And yet, I hate them as much as a living heart can hate."

Her father, she began to tell me, was the village imam. His father had been the village imam, and then before him his father's father had been the village imam too. A great spiritual tradition ruled over her bloodline, and so when she herself was brought into this world a girl, her father grew sick at heart. For a whole month after her birth he did not leave the mosque, praying to Allah for forgiveness. "I am a sinful wretch, Elif," he'd often told her when she was still a child. "Why else would God punish me with someone like you, a girl?" He never hugged her, never gave her a kiss, not when she fell and bloodied her knees, not when she suffered, feverish and sick.

And when her sister was born, her father, upon hearing the baby's girlish cries, lay down, closed his eyes, and had a stroke right there on the floor of the birth room. Entirely out of spite. An ambulance picked him up and he spent a month, this time in the city hospital, licking his wounds. Because of the stroke, his mouth froze forever in a frown and twisted like a dagger every time he spoke to his girls. Which he did rarely. At dinner, they ate their meals in silence, the only noise that of his lips smacking and of his hand wiping grease from his mustache and his beard. Some days the only time they heard their father was when he climbed the minaret and summoned everyone to prayer. There was no muezzin in the village.

"When I was little," Elif said, and filled her lungs with smoke, "I'd watch the minaret from the yard and listen to my father singing, his voice so pretty, deep, loving. And I'd imagine he sang not for Allah, but for me. I was a really stupid girl."

No television, no radio, no books other than the Qur'an. Only a handful of girls were deemed decent enough to be her friends. No boys allowed. She was sixteen before her father let her travel to the city, and even then he came along to guard her. "For sixteen years," she said, "I hadn't set foot off this mountain. Can you imagine this?"

No. I could not.

"I have become a master of retaliation," Elif went on. "I know exactly how to get each little thing I want."

Her first pair of jeans? She cut herself for a whole month before her father caved in. That's when he took her to Burgas. They walked into a Levi's store—oh, how people looked at them. Their jaws on the floor. Elif in her colorful shalwars, a scarf on her pretty little head. In the dressing room, she hung the shalwars on a nail and watched them the way the snake must watch the skin it's shed. She stared at the cuts on her thighs, on the insides of her arms, and wondered if it was really worth it. Then she put on the jeans and absolutely hated how tight and coarse they felt. And absolutely loved this tightness, which only gave her wings. Oh, it was worth it. Dear God, was she beautiful in that mirror. Did she feel strong, invincible. All right, you old fool, she told herself. I got you now. In the palm of my hand, under my thumb, just where I want you. And when she walked out, her father could see it in her eyes. For the first time he'd lost a battle, and then he knew—the real war was only now beginning.

It's here I burst out laughing. I slapped my knees. I doubled up. None of what Elif was telling me was even remotely funny. And yet it was, incomprehensible, surreal, so far removed from my own life that I could think of no other way to deal with it but by laughing.

"You little prick," she said. "I'm glad you find my misery amusing."

But by the way she watched me I knew she was pleased. I had surprised her with my laughter.

"I got a thousand other jokes like this," she said. "Get this."

Her father had planned to marry her off right after high school. He'd found her a husband. This boy, a good kid really, from a village two hills east from here. But on the day she collected her diploma—this was three years ago, early May, just before her sister started burning with the saint's fever—Elif went to the mosque. Her father was in his little room, getting ready to call out the *adhan*. "Father," she told him, "I'm going to Burgas." She would enroll at the university and in the fall she'd be a student there. She'd find a roommate, rent a room, and get a job. She wouldn't bother him for money. But she was going, no matter what he had to say.

Her father walked right past her, as if she hadn't even spoken. Stepped out for his prayer and shouted at the top of his lungs from the minaret for everyone to hear how great Allah was. All right then, Elif told herself, Allah *is* great. And for six days she did not put a morsel to her lips. Drank water only once a day. Her mother would not stop crying. "Why are you doing this?" she'd say. Elif would answer, "I'll let the earth eat me before I eat a bite." On the fifth day of

Elif's strike, Aysha started burning with the Christian fever. In her room, Elif fell on her knees. Thank you, Allah, she said, ashamed that her baby sister too had to suffer because of her. Grateful that the Merciful had picked her side in the war.

All this was more pressure than her father could bear. At last, they struck a deal. She could study in Burgas, but not live there.

"And so," Elif said, "each morning I take the bus to town for sixty kilometers. Two hours on a good day. Each afternoon, when my classes are over, I run to the station and ride the bus back home. Four hours of my life, each day, squandered."

Elif, Elif, her friends would say at first. Come watch a movie with us. Come to a party. Walk with us by the sea. But she would tell them, no, I can't. Her mother was sick, needed her home. Poor old Elif, her friends would say. And then one day they simply stopped asking.

"And no one knows where you live? That you're Muslim?"

She shook her head.

"Not even your boyfriend?"

She closed her eyes, leaned back. "What boyfriend, *amerikanche*?" she said. "And now Aysha is sick again and I have so much to study. I have exams, and if I fail . . . It's all for naught. And nothing really matters anymore."

I shifted in my seat. "Why are you telling me all this?" I asked. Maybe from the smoke, my accent had gotten lighter. Or maybe I didn't mind it now. "If you've never told anyone, why are you telling me?"

"You weren't here two days ago," she said; "you won't be here tomorrow. Our lives are not connected, nor will they ever be. What difference does it make?"

And really, what difference did it make? Tomorrow I would be gone. This moment was already slipping through our fingers, like four hours lost on a bus. Tomorrow I would be elsewhere, while Elif remained, fighting one little battle after another. She'd win some, lose some, but in the end she'd stay, chained to her father, to Klisura, to the mountain. I've fought enough, she'd say one day. Tired, she'd marry that promised boy and bear his children. She'd grow old and watch them scatter and through her offspring she would pretend to know the taste of freedom. Only her heart would keep the bitter truth.

"They think they have me figured out," she said, and her voice dipped, raspy and low from the smoke. "My father. My mother. All of Klisura. But they don't know what I've cooked up. The little plan I've plotted out." She leaned in closer and whispered, her eyes bloodshot and swimming, the pupils themselves as large as stork nests. "The day I pick up my university diploma will be the day I disappear. Like smoke in air, like flame in wind. I'll vanish without a trace. Without a note, without a word goodbye."

Her voice, the stench of her breath, the enormity of her pitch-black pupils suddenly frightened me. And maybe it was out of fear that I asked, "And you don't think that's cruel?"

"Cruel," she said. "What do you know of cruel? With your pockets full of gold, crossing the ocean in less time than it takes me to go to school. Cruel," she said, and then was quiet. Her skin had turned the color of the rotting hay and I realized she had finished the entire joint—much more than she had intended or wanted to smoke. "I'll give you cruel," she said. "My sister makes me love her, and then she hangs around my neck like a stone. She is the anchor that won't let me sail. Each night I pray to God. I say, Allah, my sister is the rope that chokes me, so sharpen my knife and let me cut her clean. Allah, you've stuffed my heart with hatred—I hate my father, this village, I hate myself. So make me hate my sister too. Make me despise her. What should I care that she needs me? What should I care that she will suffer once I'm gone? And each morning I love her more, and hate myself more for the pain I am about to cause her. My God," she said, and held her face in her palms. Her shoulders rocked, this time with laughter. "You're right to laugh. I'm such a mess. A hunchback with wolf teeth thirsty for Christian blood. Run away, my boy. I'll gnaw your bones. I'll eat your heart. Run while you can."

I wanted to tell her that she was wrong, that problems in life sometimes had an almost miraculous way of resolving themselves if only we'd bear the suffering a little longer. Or so I'd heard. But then I thought of my own loneliness, depression, financial debt. Wasn't this why I'd returned? To sell my land and see my problems solved. Or had I merely run away?

"When I was very little," she said, "my grandmother, Allah rest her soul, taught me a trick for wrestling with demons. All her life, my grandfather had kept her well under his thumb. 'A woman is like the mule, *kazam*,' she told me. 'She has to learn to take the weight of her master and then his whip. But sometimes, darling, the whip opens burrows in your heart. And in these burrows, the Sheytan lays his evil eggs. When at night a woman lies in bed and dreams of cleavers, of slicing her husband's throat like a he-goat's, end to end, it's the eggs of the Sheytan that she can hear hatching. I've dug a hole, *kazam*, behind the house. When an egg is about to hatch, I lean over the hole and I spit right in it. Every woman needs a hole in which to lay her evil eggs.'"

Elif was watching me with a mournful smile. "You want to see the hole I dug?"

Before I could answer she was already rummaging through the straw, the sticks, the tufts of white hair I had seen lining the nest. She pulled out a bundled towel, black, with a single red thread that zigzagged through the cloth.

"For many years the Bulgarians on the Christian bank and the *nestinari* didn't mix. So great was the peasants' fear of the fire dancers that they wouldn't even let them bury in the village cemetery the skulls they'd brought. That's what the hag told me anyway. 'Bury them in the water,' the peasants had shouted, 'bury them in the clouds, for all we care. But not beside our people.' And so the *nestinari* buried their dead in the air."

Gently she laid the bundle between us on the hay, gently unwrapped the towel.

"This is the hole in which I whisper," she said, "my *kazam*, my darling."

Inside the towel was a human skull. Perfectly preserved, except for a few teeth on the side, which shone like pearls. "They buried them up in this walnut tree, up in these nests. At least a hundred skulls I've found scattered about, some wrapped in towels, others not. The storks don't touch them. They lay their eggs beside them, and the babies hatch right by the skulls. And ever since I was a girl, after a fight with Father, I'd climb up here, and take my darling, and bring her to my lips like so. And I would whisper into her hollow eye the pains that ate me. And she would grow heavy with my devils, and I would grow light." She held the skull now and watched it with a tenderness I hadn't seen in her before. "My *kazam*," she said, "my darling. The things her eyes have heard."

And she laid it gently back in the towel, wrapped it, and hid it in the hay.

We sat in silence after this. My heart was pounding, but gradually I grew calmer. Only once did Elif speak. "What you did yesterday, I thank you for it. Your grandpa is a good man. He was back in his day a teacher in Klisura. But that's not why my mother trusts him. Back in the day, or so the hag told us, your grandpa was the *vekilin* for the fire dancers. They'd chosen him for that themselves."

Then she was quiet. A warm, light rain had begun to fall and I let it wash my face and listened to its gentle rustle. I thought of my grandfather, leader of the *nestinari*, and wondered why he had never told me the story of this before. But then, he'd never spoken of his life in Klisura. The branches above us glistened; the sun was blazing higher in the sky. I turned to Elif and watched her, her eyes closed, her hair, her face, her whole body shimmering with raindrops like glowing embers. And Saint Elena, I remembered her saying, like light rain following behind.

On our way out of the village, elbowing through branches and grass, Elif had suddenly stopped to face me. "You had the world to choose," she said, "and you came to Klisura." Not wanting to speak of my plans to sell the twenty acres, I told her nothing. "What are you looking for here?" she'd asked, and I'd kept quiet. But now, if she were to ask me again, I would know what to say.

PART
TWO

· ONE ·

THE YEAR WAS 1866. And in Klisura, on the feast day of Saint Constantine, a boy was born. As was tradition, they named him Kosta, after the saint. When Kosta was twelve, the first wave of exodus spread through Eastern Thrace and through the Strandja Mountains. Russia was invading the Ottoman Empire. To free up space for the countless Turkish refugees pouring down from the north, the Ottoman army drowned entire Christian villages in blood. Hundreds of thousands fled and so did Kosta. He ended up in Sofia, where in time he began his studies in the Military University.

When in 1885 Serbia attacked, Kosta, by then a young cadet, interrupted his schooling and joined the Bulgarian army. He fought at Slivnitsa, the decisive battle. There he was wounded in the foot, from which an awkward limp remained until his end. There he saw the invader stopped and pushed out.

For fifteen years after graduating from the university, Kosta served as an officer in the army. He became a captain; his soldiers feared and respected him in equal measure. "His blood is packed with gunpowder from Slivnitsa," they said. "Don't bring a match too close and you'll be fine." But in 1903, despite his promising career, Captain Kosta discharged himself and returned to the Strandja. He had joined a network of rebels who had been plotting a massive uprising. Soon enough, they hoped, Macedonia and Eastern Thrace would be part of a new, large, free Bulgaria. Kosta did not ask for a leadership position based on his military rank. He followed orders humbly, without much talk.

The spring of 1903 the captain spent training the Strandjan peasants. He taught them battle formations, hand-to-hand combat, how to shoot the old Russian rifles. One group, he was heard saying, he would trust with his life. Another he would be proud to stand beside in battle. But a third group he wouldn't even ask to mix his evening porridge, to tie the laces of his boots, to pick the lice from his head.

On August 19, 1903, the day of Christ's Transfiguration, the Strandja Mountains rose in arms. For days the smoke of battle covered the sun, and when at last the wind blew it away, like the veil off the face of a *hanama*, the Strandja was free.

Two thousand years ago, on top of a mountain, Christ had spoken to Moses and Elijah. On top of a mountain the human had met the divine. Christ had been transfigured and so now was the Strandja. This was what Captain Kosta was telling the peasants in his native Klisura, standing tall on a barrel of gunpowder, bandoliers across his chest, two pistols in his sash, a saber in his hand. And his mustache like smoke gushing from the nostrils of a dragon. "From this day on," he shouted, "until we unite with Bulgaria, the Strandja is its own republic."

For twenty days the Strandjan Republic existed free. But what is a republic without a symbol of its freedom? And so, Captain Kosta decided to build a school. "As big as those in Thessalonica and Edirne. Three stories tall. And with a cross on the roof. Like a church. No, three crosses, like a monastery!"

For fifteen days and fifteen nights the people of Klisura built, assisted by people from the villages nearby—Bulgarians and Greeks alike. For fifteen days they tasted of this freedom. In vain, Captain Kosta's rebels looked for help across the hills to the north. In vain, they waited for reinforcement from other Thracian regions. "Let them build," the captain would say to his men. "More sweat on their brows, less time to think, less time to fear."

By the fifteenth day the roof was covered, the crosses were affixed. And though by any standard the building was shabby, pitiful even, in the eyes of the Klisurans it rivaled the sultan's palace in Istanbul. "What should we name it?" someone said. "You have to ask?" answered another.

The first school in Klisura, Saint Constantine and Saint Elena, stood tall for seven days. Until the Ottoman army burned it to the ground.

I found the pages still drenched in rain, scattered across the floor around my grandfather's desk. I pulled them out of every drawer, where they were pressed tightly between the covers of shabby but carefully labeled binders. *History of Ancient Egypt. The Old World. The First Bulgarian Empire. Grades Fourth and Fifth. Grade Eleven.* The ink fading, the pages turning yellow, and the red of Grandpa's pen like dried-up blood across words his students had written a quarter of a century ago. These old exams were the scrap paper on whose back he wrote.

To me. To himself. To no one in particular. To all of us at once. The day after his nighttime episode I gathered up the scattered papers and spread them out in the yard to dry. He watched me weigh them down with pebbles against the wind, without offering me an explanation. That evening in my room, I read.

War. Struggle. Freedom and death. It was the Strandja Mountains that Grandpa was writing about. Hand-drawn maps. Meticulously calculated numbers. This many villages reduced to ash. This many killed, this many exiled. But in my mind the picture burned too brightly and would have left me numb and blinded if not for the story of a single man. I found it trickling in the margins the way cold water flows more slowly beneath a turbulent and boiling stream.

They said his father, he too a mighty rebel, had wed him to the Strandja. He'd slashed the boy's palm and the boy had thrust it inside the Mountain so his blood might take root in her.

They said he'd never spoken to a woman and never would. The Strandja was his woman. He'd give his life to free her from the Turks.

They said his father had taught him the old tongue, the bird language. When he whistled, wings grew from his shadow. A bird's shadow, an elohim's. And the Mountain, they said, would answer.

"His name was Captain Kosta," Grandpa told me out on the terrace. The words left his lips with effort, as if each one brought him physical pain. And yet I felt as if, despite the pain, he was relishing the chance to share a man he'd thought would never leave the page.

"He looked like Nietzsche," Grandpa said. "Or so one of his *chetniks* wrote of his sullen disposition, of his bushy, curved-down mustache. Or maybe no *chetnik* ever wrote such a thing. Maybe that's just the way I see him."

And so that was the way I saw him too. This captain who for some reason had captivated Grandpa's mind. At night I thought about them—Kosta, returning to the Strandja after many years to set her free. And Grandpa, coming back to Klisura, for reasons yet unknown. The more I thought, dizzy with jet lag, the closer the image of the two came in my mind. And in the end, I wasn't certain where the captain ended and where my grandfather began.

Up from a hill Captain Kosta watched the school burning. His rebel squad had been destroyed, and so were all other squads across the Strandja. And now it was the Christian peasants who met the Turkish wrath.

Earlier that day, the elders of Klisura had bowed before the Turkish pasha who'd led his troops into their village. "*Pasha efendi*," they'd begged at the hooves of his stallion, "here in these bundles is the jewelry of our women. Take the gold, but don't burn down our homes."

The pasha seized the bundles. Then he ordered his soldiers to get the torches ready.

"*Pasha efendi*," the elders begged, "these are the costumes of our grandmothers. Take them, but don't burn down our homes."

The pasha seized the handfuls, then ordered his soldiers to light the torches.

"*Pasha efendi*," one Klisuran said, an old man, tall and wiry. "This is the icon of our saint. His hands are cast in silver, so cut them off and take them with you. His feet, so he may walk on fire, are cast in gold. Chop them off, *efendi*. Strip the gold. Burn down our houses if you must. But spare our school."

The pasha snatched the icon, took a torch, and with his own hand set the school on fire. He threw the icon in the flame. "You fools," he said to the peasants. "You cannot bribe me with what is mine already."

It was these fires that Captain Kosta watched now from the hills. For years he would limp across Eastern Thrace, in vain struggling to spark up new uprisings. Only death would show him kindness. Captain Kosta died defeated, alone, in complete poverty, two weeks before the start of the Balkan War. Merciful death spared him. He would not see the absolute destruction of his Strandja and of Eastern Thrace.

Pages and pages, chains of words. Stories of exile and of death. Bulgarians, Greeks, Armenians, and Turks. The Strandja burned time and again, reduced to coals, to ashes. And then it rose, time and again, the Strandja itself a fire dancer, a *nestinarka*.

Five times the people of Klisura rebuilt their school. Five times the school was burned down to the ground. It was a pile of ashes Grandpa found in its place, upon his first arrival, himself an exile. He rebuilt the school almost entirely alone—the ground floor for his students, the second for himself.

It was to this school that he had moved three years ago. It was in this school that we lived now.

· TWO ·

BACKGAMMON IS A GAME of chance. You cast the dice and pray to Fortune. That is, if you're a fool. If you're smart, backgammon is a game of odds, of calculations, and of patterns. A game of vision. Only the wise man knows the truth: like life, backgammon is a game of luck; like life, a game of skill.

Or so Grandpa was trying to convince me. Every evening after dinner, we sat outside on the terrace and spread open the board. Two little bone-colored dice and fifteen checkers. Move all your checkers around the board and bring them home. Then bear them off faster than your opponent has borne off his and laugh in his face, a victor. You see, old man? Who is the fool now?

I was. In every single game we played.

The day after his nighttime episode, Grandpa was sluggish, visibly tired. But he was stronger a day later, and from then on—as strong as a bull stud. No, *stronger* still. At least that's what he claimed. Unable to phone my parents, I wrote them a letter. I told them that overall Grandpa appeared in sound condition, but that he had grown old and sometimes showed his age.

Out on the terrace, I asked him if these episodes were a frequent occurrence.

"What are you, a doctor now?" he said, and the topic was closed.

I've yet to find out the reason for his return to Klisura, I wrote in my letter, but did not write that it was out of shame I delayed asking. To my surprise, Grandpa too asked me nothing. Why had I come back? What did I want with him? The dice chattered against the board, the wind whistled through the planks of the house, and the silence around us grew so oppressive that I was entirely convinced: the old man was hiding something.

Even the story of Captain Kosta, which he spun before me when the silence got too heavy, soon began to feel like a diversion. Or was he using the story to tell me things without addressing them directly? I was overthinking to exhaustion. *He seems guilty*, I wrote to my parents. *His eyes won't look in mine and his fingers rap on the table suspiciously.*

A few afternoons we went down to the Pasha Café, where Grandpa played backgammon with the owner. He won some, lost some, quarreled, and sulked. Always in jest, he insisted, but I wasn't always sure. I stood by his shoulder while old men surrounded the table like buzzards around buffalo carrion, tugged on their mustaches, rubbed on their beards, quarreled, and sulked, always in jest.

It was on one such afternoon that Elif walked by the café, returning home from the university. A green military pouch bounced on her back, full of textbooks, I assumed. She cast a guarded glance at our table, but when I waved, she hurried to look away and strode faster up the street. I thought of her often, mostly at night when I was too jet-lagged for sleep or reading from Grandpa's papers. Five times a day Elif's father sang from the minaret—his voice so full and deep it carried well beyond the Muslim quarter—and I wondered, how could a man who sang so beautifully be so full of malice?

A few times, in between the games on our terrace, I asked Grandpa about the fire dancers. But every time he waved his hand. "Don't bother me with crazy fools," he'd say. I asked him about his youth in Klisura, about the school. "What's there to tell? I quit the Party and the Party crushed me. I came here in the spring, ready to teach, and I found a pile of charcoal in place of the school. Let's build it, I told the peasants, and they started crossing themselves as if the Devil had arrived to pull out their canines. Every time we rebuild our school, they told me, someone comes by and burns it to the ground. And with it burns Klisura. They'd tell me the stories of Captain Kosta, of how he'd built the first Klisuran school only to see it turn to ash soon after. So in the mornings, I taught the children in a cherry orchard outside the village, and I built for the rest of the day and sometimes at night, by the light of the gas lamp. The priest helped me. And the village idiot. Vassilko. He was a good boy. This terrace was all his idea, high and jutting out, so that when a maiden passed by we'd ogle her unseen. Eventually the school was built, but even then the parents wouldn't let their children cross the threshold. For a whole month I begged them, the superstitious fools. How could I imagine that they were right?"

"In what way were they right?" I asked, but Grandpa waved his hand. Another topic had been closed.

On the fifth evening of my stay, after I'd lost a game to gammon—that particularly humiliating kind of defeat in which you fail to bear off even a single checker—I seized the dice. "Let's play an American game," I said. He'd throw one die and I the other. "The higher value wins. The loser chooses—truth or dare."

I rolled a four. Grandpa—a six.

"There is a jar of rainwater down by the well," he said. "Go drink it."

I told him this was silly. It hadn't rained in three days.

"You suggested a game," he said, "I'm playing it." He laughed long after I'd gulped the lukewarm sludge.

"Are you dying?" I asked him as soon as I'd won my throw. This was the question whose answer I feared the most. Had he been diagnosed with a fatal illness?

"Exceptional virility," he said. He'd been diagnosed with it back in the day, and on a few occasions it had proved fatal.

"Must all your jokes be sexual in nature?"

He shrugged. He could joke about death if I wanted. Here was a cracker: all his friends his age were dead. But no, he wasn't dying from a fatal illness.

"Then why did you disappear like this? Selling the apartment one day and vanishing the next?"

He shook his finger at the dice. I hadn't won my turn. We cast. It was for him to ask.

"Why are *you* back? And listen, I want an honest answer."

Slowly the night was rising from the soil. It crawled up the Strandjan hills, dark at their base and brighter up above, where the sky was still bluish. A warm wind from Turkey carried the smell of grass in bloom and made me sneeze.

"I was worried about you," I said. I had begun to slur my speech. Like electricity, the right words buzzed through my tongue, but in English. In graceless, chopped-up sentences I told him about my failed studies in America, about my lost scholarship and hefty student loans. How if only I could get back on my feet, pay for the remaining credit hours and finish my thesis . . .

He watched me unblinking, a chunk of rock in the gloom. I wasn't even sure he breathed. Until he raised his hand. "You have returned to sell your land," he said.

I gave him a timid smile. He'd guessed it right. The prize was his.

"What prize?" He looked disgusted. "The nerve on you! To kid!"

He pulled out a cigarette, brought the gas lamp to his face, and lit up. The flame regaled him with a scarlet glow, and when he glanced up, his eyes burned red.

"How much are you in debt?"

I gave him a ballpark figure. "Ballpark?" he asked. An American expression. In baseball— He cut me off. "It doesn't translate." And neither did the thought—that his only grandson, his flesh and blood, would be so arrogant, so impudent, so brazen-faced as to even consider . . . Did I know what my great-grandfather had gone through to earn for us that land? The blood he'd spilled? The sweat and tears . . . He rattled ferociously like this. Until I raised my hand.

"We no longer own that land, do we?"

It was his turn to grace me with a smile. "The prize is yours."

I gripped the edge of the table. The twenty acres *were* my prize.

"Well, now they're gone. And your father's share. And mine. I sold it all."

For a long time I sat speechless. Beside us on the wall our shadows danced, enormous, monstrous, disfigured. I felt weak and dizzy and a pungent, noxious taste climbed up my esophagus and washed the roof of my mouth. No, it wasn't from the murky sludge I'd drunk. It was the taste of Grandpa's betrayal, the bitterness of bank loans I'd now be helpless to pay off. The absurdity of my plan came to me as if for the first time and I grew livid not just with Grandpa for selling our land, but also with myself. For seeking an easy and dishonest fix, for allowing myself to fall into this position in the first place—broke and in debt, crossing oceans to chase after what wasn't even there. Thick and sticky, the night spilled around us and filled my lungs like swamp water with each new gulp of air.

"Where is the money now?" I said at last.

"Completely spent."

"What did you buy?"

"This house."

"The village school? This place is shit!"

"The house across the road."

"That one is even worse. What else?"

"The house next to it and the house next to that one . . ." He waved his great hand through the dark, like an Indian chief marking his plains before the white man.

"You bought Klisura, then?" I said. But he wasn't joking.

"Only the Christian part. And if you're kind to me, my boy, and if you play the dice and checkers right, one day this kingdom will be yours."

"But why?"

For some time he struggled to pick up a white checker from the board. The checker danced in his fingers and he placed it alone on a point. "What do we call this?" he said. A blot, I answered. The blot was unprotected and any minute your opponent could hit it with a checker of his own.

"And how do you protect a blot?"

Though I was no longer in a mood for games, I picked up another white checker and covered the first. "You make a point as soon as you can. One checker protects the other. The two are safe."

"You make a point," he repeated. "As soon as you can. And how do you block your opponent?"

"With a prime." Make six consecutive points in front of your opponent's checkers and prevent him from getting past you.

"And what's the final goal?"

Bring your checkers safely to the home plate. Roll favorable dice. Bear them all off.

"Bear them all off," he said. "Now then," he said. "Where you see a house, this house, I see a blot. An unprotected checker. And the opponent can hit it any minute. So to protect it I purchased another checker. And then two more, six more. I made a prime. And now my opponent can't get past me."

I told him I didn't really follow.

"My boy," he said, "Klisura has been transfigured into a backgammon board. The Christian hamlet is the inner table. The Muslim hamlet is the outer. The river that divides them is the bar. I play to save my checkers, and my opponent plays to hit them."

I watched him smoke his cigarette down to a butt. I was angry with him and with myself and suddenly this anger weighed down on me, horribly exhausting. The wind had changed directions and gusted cold through the terrace. So cold I zipped up my jacket. "And who is your opponent?" I asked to humor him a little more. He gave me a cunning smile. Then waved his hand.

· THREE ·

OF ELIF'S FATHER I first noticed not the eyes, black and warm,
one opened wide, the other almost hidden behind a droopy
eyelid; not the beard, short, graying, hungry to consume
the face from cheekbones down to throat and even lower
into his sweater; not the lips, like a sickle curved downward
in one corner; not the flat-brim hat or the black coat, slack
at the narrow shoulders, loose at the sleeves, and tied around
his waist with a black thread; not the smell of sweat and of
tobacco when he came near; not the heat of his hand when he
shook mine firmly; but his voice. It seemed to me at first he
didn't speak. He sang.

"The acorn has reunited with the oak," he said, and
crossed our threshold smiling. "May the Almighty send you
peace. Look at you, Grandpa, a happy man."

It was the day after Grandpa and I had spoken of checkers
and backgammon boards. We were drinking coffee on the

terrace when, from the roar of an engine, the sparrows scattered, screaming out of the bushes. Down the road, with its top shining like a war shield, a blue Lada flew our way, the kind of Russian car I hadn't seen in many years. Behind its wheel was a small girl, her head covered in a scarf. The Lada parked at the gates and as a greeting the girl punched the horn. Out the door she emerged and I realized that this was Aysha, Elif's little sister, and that the man who carried her, and in whose lap she had been sitting, was their father, the village imam.

"The wind spells trouble," Grandpa said, and I followed him down the stairs.

"So this is the American, eh?" the imam was saying. "He looks it too. His neck is thicker, like a wolf's."

He carried Aysha in the crook of his left arm, and so he offered me his right.

"How do you do?" he said in English. "That's all I know, all I can say. Like a parrot. *How do you do, how do you do.*" He tossed Aysha lightly so she wouldn't slip and she laughed. "Come on now," he told her. "Greet our friends."

But she wouldn't. Her cheeks like red apples, she tugged on her headscarf, pulled it down and over her eyes.

"As shy as a hedgehog," the imam said. "Touch it and it rolls into a ball."

It was then that I noticed the bandages on her feet, yellow at the toes and soles from the ointment. "Third world business," the imam said when he saw me looking. "Old grandmas' remedies. Klamath weed. Not like in America, hospitals like seraglios. Do you think, Grandpa," he said, and turned to the old man, "they have Klamath weed across the ocean? Devil-chaser, we call that herb. Christ's blood. Don't we, Grandpa?"

I listened very carefully for something vile. But his song

was pleasant, even warm. Grandpa too, it seemed, was listening for trouble, because not once did his lips stretch in a smile. We invited our guests under the trellis, which had not yet budded green but hung like a dry, sad mesh along the rusty frame above us. I brought more coffee to a boil, and Grandpa sent me down to the cellar to search through the fern leaves on the floor and fetch some fruit for Aysha.

"What do you say?" the imam asked her, after I'd given her an apple as firm as the day it had been picked.

"Thank you."

I nodded and joined Grandpa on the bench. We watched her small teeth sink into the juicy fruit and I thought that she looked healthy, fine. The imam finished his coffee in a few sharp, loud slurps. From his coat he pulled out a red leather pouch and a pack of rolling papers, the same kind Elif had used up in the stork nest.

"A noxious habit, this," he said. "Years ago, when I'd just married, I promised my wife to quit. I told a friend about my resolution. 'I'll more readily believe in a beardless imam,' he told me, 'than in an imam who doesn't smoke.' Since then, for twenty-odd years, he sends me every month, regular as sunrise, a pouch of his finest tobacco. 'When I die,' he tells me, 'I'll stand before Allah and look Him in the eye. You scoundrel, Allah will say, you've sinned a great deal. You ate well, drank much too well, and fooled around with other men's women. Tell me one reason why I shouldn't cast you down in the Jahannam. And I will tell Him: Almighty, for twenty-odd years, each month, regular as sunrise, I have been saving an imam's soul.'"

The imam laughed. "He is a good man, my friend. May Allah keep his heart simple and his tobacco coming."

In Turkish he spoke to Aysha and she spread open her

palm. He laid in it a sheet and sprinkled the sheet with to-bacco from the pouch. When he had rolled a cigarette and licked the edges, Aysha fished a matchbox from his coat and struck a match. A long time she stared at the tiny flame, and right before it touched her fingers she blew it out. Her father scolded. She dusted the tobacco flakes from her sweaty palm, and when she looked up at me, I recognized the fever I'd seen in her sickroom.

A thick smell rolled through the yard. Smoke gushed out of the imam's mouth, and when he drew some back in through his nose, his nostrils quivered. He looked at us the way Elif had looked at me, as if to measure our weight to the gram.

My grandfather stirred. "Mehmed, why have you come?"

The imam moved his eyes from Grandpa onto me. The droopy eyelid twitched; a sharper curve twisted his lips. From the smoke his voice had dropped, but it was still as smooth as singsong.

"There lived a man during the rule of our great Sultan Ahmed the Third, three hundred years ago. His name was Manol, the son of a miller, a pious Christian, a good Bulgarian, like the two of you. Manol was in love with a beautiful girl, but two weeks before their wedding the girl went missing. That evening in the tavern, one of the Turks, the aga's nephew, drank too much *rakia* and started babbling. He had been thirsty, he said, and the girl had refused to give him water. Manol's sweetheart. They found her body outside the village, at the bottom of a well. The aga promised to put his nephew on trial, but by sunrise the nephew had vanished from the *konak*, on a white horse to Istanbul, it was rumored.

"Manol stuck a knife in his sash and took to the mountains. He joined a gang of bandits, became a *kardjaliya*. They lay in wait at the passes, these bandits, ambushed the Turkish caravans, killed the merchants, and robbed their riches. At night they raided Turkish hamlets, set them on fire, raped women and left them widows, and their children they left orphans.

"The great sultan himself dispatched a janissary unit to hunt down this evil. One dawn, the bandits were sleeping in their lair, exhausted from last night's pillage. They had just burned a small hamlet to the ground, slashed many throats, left behind many widows. Hungover and so unable to sleep, Manol had gone to a stream not far from the cave, and was quaffing water like a buffalo, when he heard the first gunshots and the dogs barking. He set off through the bushes, but how could he outrun the janissaries and their bloodhounds? His stomach was heavy, his head was spinning, his knees were giving way. He found himself out of the woods, and on the mountain path before him there came a little donkey, and by the donkey a Turkish priest, an imam. The dogs were barking, closer with each bark, and without thinking, Manol flung himself upon the imam, broke his neck, undressed him, threw the body off the cliffs, and donned the holy garment.

"In a cloud of dust the first janissaries appeared and called off the bloodhounds that had already surrounded Manol. '*As-Salamu Alaykum, hodja*,' they greeted him, and he tried to smooth over his beard, which was maybe a bit too bushy for an imam's. 'Have you seen any bandits running?' one janissary asked him, and in Turkish Manol answered: If he had seen them, would they have spared him to tell the story? 'Don't look so scared, *hodja*,' the janissary told him. 'From this day on, the mountain breathes free again.'

"And really, down the path Manol saw the rest of the janissaries coming, giant on their horses, and roped by the ankles, dragged naked through the dirt, he recognized his dead comrades. 'We'll drag them across every hamlet,' the janissary said, 'so every widow may spit in their faces, so every orphaned boy may piss on their bones.'

" 'Allah is great,' Manol said, and, as was expected, spat on the corpse that just then was being dragged past him—the body of his beloved captain. After that, all thought left him. The janissaries vanished; the sun gashed like a wound in the cloudless sky. One moment he found himself deep in the woods; the next he was standing on the path again. One moment he was petting the donkey; the next the donkey had gone. He was dying of thirst, but when he came to a stream, he crossed it without stopping. I'll kill myself, he decided, but kept on walking.

"The sun was setting when he reached a hamlet. Women sat outside the ruins of their smoldering houses and watched him pass, their eyes red and puffy. There were women around the village well, weeping, pulling buckets of water and splashing it on the ground to cool it down a little, to wash away the stench of smoke and broiled flesh that hung in the air.

" 'Our souls are burning, *hodja*,' they cried out when they saw him. 'Do something so our hearts won't burst with sorrow.'

"He watched them and thought of their husbands' throats he'd sliced open the night before. He watched the well and remembered how in another lifetime the men in his village had lowered a tiny boy, to tie a rope to his sweetheart's ankles, so they could pull out her body.

" 'Sisters,' he said to the women, and wanted to tell them—

I'm not an imam. Instead he called them to gather around him, dropped a bucket in the well, and filled it with water. He washed his hands, mouth, nose, arms, and face, hair and ears. He washed his feet. And he felt blood and death flow away from him in a muddy trickle. Then, after each woman had performed the ablution, he began singing. What he sang, he didn't understand. How he knew the verses, he didn't care to consider. All he knew was that Allah held him in His mighty palm. Allah had thrown him in darkness, had led him along a steep path. And all that had happened had happened on purpose, so he could draw water from this well, console these women, and sing in the name of the Everlasting, the Resurrecter."

For a long time we sat frozen. In the distance the door of a ruined house was slamming against its doorframe and a dog was barking somewhere in the Muslim hamlet. Wind blew in the mouth of the well beside us and I thought I could hear all the wells in the village, howling.

"From that day onward," the imam said, "Manol was known as Mehmed Abdullah. And he, Mehmed Abdullah, became the first imam of Klisura. When he returned to dust, his son became imam, and then his son after that. For three hundred years, Mehmed Abdullah's sons have summoned the righteous to prayer across the hills of the Strandja. For three hundred years, their wives have borne them one boy after another, a holy bloodline. It is this line," the imam said, and gently smoothed Aysha's headscarf, "that ends with me here. As willed by the Ever Relenting, the Watchful, glory be to His name."

He had forgotten his cigarette and the ember had gone out. With a shaking hand he struck a new match and from the heavier stench his eyes watered. But he smiled a serene smile.

"How much I prayed to Allah," he said, "when my wife was first pregnant that He should send me a boy. And He did, the Merciful. A beautiful boy." He puffed on the cigarette and exhaled carefully away from Aysha. "The boy died a baby." Then he smoked, deep in thought, and all I heard was the smack of his lips after each new drag and the tobacco crackling. It seemed that the memory of Mehmed Abdullah had awoken in him other memories, one linked to the other, and when he spoke again I thought I could hear the links of the chain rattling, if only for a second.

"That darkness, I don't wish it upon my worst enemy. I don't wish it upon you, my American friend. Allah, I said, weak, full of doubt, having just buried my boy. Why are you wounding me like this? But I bowed and worshipped and soon my wife was pregnant again. Send me a son, Allah, I prayed. Instead, He sent me a daughter. How I hated her that day, how I hated my wife, myself, my God. Why, I asked Him, are you wounding me like this? But soon my wife was pregnant a third time. Surely, I thought, the Almighty will have mercy. Surely, He won't allow Mehmed Abdullah's bloodline to end. Then this little hedgehog was born," he said, and leaned forward and kissed the back of Aysha's head. "And my heart was filled with a thousand needles. And when we found out that my wife could have no more children I fell before Allah, defeated. Almighty, I said, I shall never know why you wounded me like this. But I accept it. You expect me to hate my daughters, like any father in my place would, but instead, I vow to love them. And because I love them, I know You'll try to hurt them. And so, I vow to raise my daughters so they may protect themselves even after I'm gone. Do you know, my American friend," he said, and looked straight at me, his voice low and his eyes unblinking, "how you raise your dog to be a wolf-killer? You start her off early, from a little puppy, and you never spare the stick. You starve her, even when her howling at night plants daggers in your skull. You never let up. And when the wolf arrives, she snaps his thick neck like a twig.

"A few days ago," he said, and stubbed out the cigarette on the leg of the chair, not even looking at me, "you told my daughter a person ought to have the freedom to choose her own path in life. You spoke to her about rights and liberty and free will. This is why I in turn told you the story of Mehmed Abdullah, and then my own. You want to speak to her again, that's fine by me. But know this much: for every thing you tell my daughter, I'll deal her one blow with the stick. I'll hit and she'll grow feral and finally she'll gnaw your throat. And if she speaks to you, I'll turn the stick on this little one in my lap," he said, and kissed Aysha again, and she smiled and blinked her feverish eyes. "And you too, Grandpa, stay away from my house. I've told you before, but I won't tell you again. Keep away your curses and your saints, or else my little wolf-killers will spill their guts across the Strandja, hill to hill."

And then he watched us with a smile and I could feel my throat pulsing long after they'd gotten back in their Lada and driven it away. For a long time Grandpa and I sat quiet under the trellis. The hills grew dim. The roofs of our ruined houses burned with slipping sun. Over and over again, Grandpa turned my coffee cup in his hands. Over and over again, he licked his chapped lips. At last he spoke:

"Do not believe a single word he said. About Manol, the janissaries, his holy bloodline. Hogwash. All of it. And don't believe it's your fault that he will hurt his daughters. It's not theirs either. It's mine." And then in one swift motion he hurled the cup at the well and shattered it to pieces.

· FOUR ·

ONE EVENING THREE YEARS AGO, when the snows had just begun to melt, the phone rang in Grandpa's small-town apartment. "Comrade teacher," the voice on the other side said, "I know some things you too should know." The voice belonged to an old student, a "motivated, driven young man" whom Grandpa had once tutored for university exams, without accepting payment and out of his own goodwill. Since then, the student had done well for himself, climbing up the ladder to a position in Sofia, in the Ministry of Environment and Water. And now he was calling to repay his debt.

Here was the scoop: a company from Turkey was getting ready to obtain some Bulgarian land and build on it a wind farm—a series of turbines for cheap, green electricity. The land, in a protected area—a nature park—was not itself protected. And it could be bought dirt cheap; that is, if the real estate agency that owned the rights did not get a whiff of the planned construction.

"Now, comrade teacher," the student said, "this is where you come into play."

The land in question was Klisura. While examining the cadastre, the student had, to his great surprise, stumbled across Grandpa's name. And so, without delay, he'd phoned him up. "We're recruiting, very discreetly, a handful of trusted men." Each would purchase a Klisuran house—some claiming it as a vacation home, others as a place to live out their retirement years. It didn't matter that demand would drive up the prices. The deals would still be bargains. All Grandpa would have to do was sign a few papers. The money would be provided in full and once the house was in his name, with a quick signature, Grandpa would turn it over to the Turkish developer; or rather to their Bulgarian representative. It was easy. There was no risk. And the reward was hefty: for his troubles Grandpa would receive—

"Why are you doing this?" Grandpa asked his student.

"Comrade teacher, you've done so much for me. I'm forever grateful. Why grease up a stranger when I can put the money in your pocket?"

Yes, that was true, Grandpa said. And kind of him. "May I think it over?"

"Two days," the student answered. After this, he would look elsewhere. But he trusted Grandpa wouldn't squander this golden chance.

That night, Grandpa didn't sleep. His shut eyelids were silver screens on which he saw Klisura—the houses of his youth razed to the ground and in their place the skeletons of spinning turbines. He thought of all the men and women he'd known, the village mayor, the priest, the idiot Vassilko, their graves covered by a farm for winds.

Within the week, Grandpa had contacted the Strandjan real estate agency and finalized a swap that only a Vassilko could conceive. Almost a hundred acres of first-grade, arid land in the Danube plain—the same land I had returned to sell—for a handful of ruined houses, rocks, and brambles up in the godforsaken Strandja Mountains.

For days on end his phone rang unanswered. "I give you my hand in friendship," his student barked when at last Grandpa picked up, "and like a dog you bite it to the elbow!" But if Grandpa thought all profit would be his, he had another thing coming. "A signature, comrade teacher, doesn't mean a thing!"

"Of course it does," Grandpa told me now on the terrace. "But a man needs to lawyer up first." He rolled the dice: four and two—a point. We had just finished dinner—potato stew he'd cooked on the open fire with paprika and too much salt— and I was quaffing jar after jar of water.

Five months after Grandpa purchased the houses of Klisura, the Turkish company began construction of the first wind turbine. "He simply had to brag," Grandpa said. "The cocky fool. He called me up one night. His ministry had approved the construction and there was nothing I could do to stop them. And so I told him—a signature doesn't mean a thing."

To pay for the lawyer Grandpa sold his apartment, packed up, and moved to Klisura. And why not? We weren't calling him; we weren't making any plans to visit. Why shouldn't he enjoy fresh air, a scenic view?

"You have no shame," I said. How many times in the

past ten years had Father begged him to come and live with us in the U.S.?

"Three. And four." He read the dice and hit one of my unprotected checkers. "And what will I do in America exactly?"

Once in Klisura Grandpa made "a real stink." He contacted two newspapers, three radio stations, a TV channel. An old man protecting a historic village, fighting the greedy politicians to the death. It was a compelling story. Besides, he had a lawyer now to help him drive the point home: the land was his, regardless of how many permits the government had issued. And the hasty construction of what he referred to as "that phallic piece of junk the Tower of Klisura" was promptly stopped.

"All right," I said. I rolled a five and reentered with the hit checker. "If this Turkish company is so well connected, why not build their farm right there on that hill? Each turbine a middle finger in your face?"

Grandpa shook his head. That hill was part of a nature park. And so was the hill next to it.

Then why not in another village? Surely there were others in greater ruin than Klisura?

He leaned back in his chair and lit a cigarette. The warm gust picked up the smoke and carried it toward the house. *Klisura*, he said with a wink, as I no doubt knew already, was Bulgarian for *gorge*. The hills stretched on both sides of the village and formed a tunnel through which a current blew—not ferocious, but constant.

"The perfect spot," I said.

"*A* perfect spot," he corrected. "I have been told that there are turbines across the border, from here all the way to the White Sea. Like Klisura, ghost villages transfigured into wind farms."

For three years now, Grandpa and the Bulgarian contractor had waged a lawsuit. Just last week, the day I met him on the bus, Grandpa had been to town. But once again the hearing had been postponed, this time until the fall. "They prance me about like a circus bear. Every time I go to court they find some new reason to postpone. I pay my lawyer, I pay the court fees. Then the charade repeats. I'm bleeding dry. And now they've started coming here to put the screws on me."

"Elif's father?" I said. "How is he involved?"

Without giving it much thought we had both brought our checkers to the home boards. A curious battle was about to unfold—whoever rolled the better dice would bear off first. No strategy or skill—just luck. I rolled a one and a two, collected the measly checkers. Grandpa rolled a pair of threes, grabbed a handful, then rolled again. In no time he'd borne off half of his checkers. And in no time I'd found myself, once more, behind.

The imam worked for the contractor. Not officially, of course, but he had been paid. His job was to put pressure on Grandpa, to get him to sign an agreement. The Bulgarian hamlet was full of ghosts, the imam had said, but the Muslim quarter was full of the living: men, women, and children. The wind farm would bring investments to Klisura, a fresh, new life.

"And he is right," Grandpa said. "The people of Klisura will benefit from the farm."

"But you don't care for the people?"

"My boy," he said through his teeth. "I don't expect you to understand."

I really didn't. Besides, what was there to understand? He'd swapped our land—beautiful, fertile fields that could have delivered me from debt—for heaps of rock and bramble, for desolate and ruined houses. And why? To save the memory of people long dead—the idiot Vassilko, the mayor, the village priest. I didn't know these men. I didn't care to know them. They were strangers whom Grandpa had chosen over me, his flesh and blood. He'd preserved the dead and betrayed the living—and not just me, his grandson, but also the people of the Muslim hamlet, who stood to profit from a wind farm.

My heart was racing. I picked up the dice and rolled a pair of sixes. Grandpa blinked in disbelief while, with a shaking hand, I bore off almost all of my remaining checkers. I was an inch away from beating the old man. My rightful indignation was manifesting itself, if not in real life then at least upon the backgammon board. I rolled the dice so hard one popped out on the table, hit the jar, and bounced back. With a magnanimous wave, Grandpa allowed me to roll again. I did: an unfavorable value. I moved two checkers, but bore off none.

"They're all waiting," he said. "Hoping for me to die so they can seize my land. So let them wait." A large, contented grin stretched his lips and quickly turned to laughter. He had rolled a pair of sixes. The game was over. He'd won again.

I grabbed the jar and drank it dry. Another loss, another disappointment. And while I was refilling the jar from the earthen jug at my feet, the imam began to sing for the evening prayer. His voice enveloped Klisura like a fishing seine and I could almost feel its knots thick, inescapable against my skin.

Lightly Grandpa closed the board; lightly he took my hand. His was as cold as well water. "My boy, with your arrival a favorable die was cast. The question now is who will play it?" Then he lit a new cigarette, stretched back in his chair, and smoked.

· FIVE ·

TWO WEEKS AFTER I first set foot in Klisura, the storks returned.

I was dreaming of America again. In my dream I was back in my apartment, back in my bed. I wanted to sleep but couldn't. The tree outside my window was heavy with chirping birds, and the harder I pressed the pillow against my skull, the louder they screamed. "A good man has died," someone said in English beside me. "They're letting you know."

It was the girl from the station, the one who'd cut her wrist. She was naked, except for her face, hidden behind the sheet as if behind a headscarf. Beautiful roses began to blossom across the sheet, each petal the color of dark blood. "Who is the man?" I asked her. "Who has died?" She started laughing. Her voice was muffled, as if coming from deep underground. I knew I'd made a mistake. She wasn't the girl

I thought she was. "You know the man, *amerikanche*," she said in Bulgarian. "Now hear the birds."

I awoke startled, with the sun in the top corner of the window. The room was stuffy and the Rhodopa blanket soaked with my sweat. For a long time, eyes closed, I tried to shake off a dream so vivid I could still hear the girl's laughter, the screaming of the birds. A dull, anxious heaviness settled in my stomach and I rushed out for Grandpa.

He was smoking on the terrace, leaning against the banister. "Good afternoon, sleeping beauty," he greeted me, but didn't turn. "Don't you know there is no memory from sleep?" Then he pointed the tip of his fuming cigarette at the sky. In his mind, this moment allowed no room for words.

High up above the ruined houses, a dozen storks spun their wheels. Some glided clockwise, others counter. They called to one another, shrill, loud screams.

Grandpa kept quiet. He smoked his cigarette and watched the storks and I couldn't tell if his old, tired face showed joy and pleasure or worry and regret. But when he turned to me his eyes glistened like a child's.

"The storks are here," he said.

He'd brought a bottle of *rakia* and two small glasses, which now he filled to the brim. "I've lived to see them one more year."

We drank bottoms-up, to welcome.

These were the scouts. The first of a giant flock of white storks that would arrive in waves. It was the old birds who returned home first. The males. Then came the females. And finally, a few days later, arrived the young.

Their home was here in Europe; here were the nests in

which their babies hatched. But when the end of August neared, the storks flew south to Africa, where they waited out the winter months, from Egypt to Cape Town. Once it was time to fly back home the storks gathered in the savanna and in flocks of thousands headed north. Some chose a western route, but most took the eastern: they tracked the valley of the Nile, traversed the Levant, and crossed the Bosphorus from Turkey. And then it was the Via Pontica they followed—that ancient Roman road along the Black Sea, which started in Constantinople and continued north into Bulgaria: the towns of Sozòpol, Burgas, and then Nessebar. It took the white storks fifty days to make their journey.

Why didn't they fly over the Mediterranean? To conserve their energy, the storks depended on thermal columns, and thermal columns formed only over firm land. The sun warmed the ground, which in turn warmed the air above it. The warmer air expanded and rose and with some steady wind these thermal columns aligned in rows to form a highway. It was these thermals the storks used as lifts, this highway that they traveled. Three-quarters of all European white storks flew over Bulgaria. Two hundred and fifty thousand birds.

They flew the days and rested at night. There was this place near Burgas, Poda—caught between the sea on one side and three giant lakes on the other—that Grandpa had gone to visit last year. By the time he completed his hike the sun had set. All night, huddled in a blanket on the ground, he heard the clattering of bills, could hardly sleep from the excitement. He saw them with the dawn. Hundreds of thousands of storks and pelicans and cranes and herons and ibises and egrets and other birds whose names I'd never heard before. When the storks rose, the sun vanished, the sky disappeared, the earth dissolved, and only sound remained.

By that time Grandpa was weeping like a little girl with fury. Furious, he threw his peaked cap to the ground; furious, he stomped on it. To hell with this life, he told himself. How many years had he lived and never seen a thing so pretty as the sound of rising storks at dawn? And how many other beauties would go unseen?

Now on the terrace we watched the sky. Before the day was over, three more waves of birds had arrived like a chaotic school of fish, spinning in opposite directions, passing so very close to one another. Some were here to rest; others had returned to their homes. One after another the nests on the ruined houses were filled with storks—a single bird for every nest. At once the repairs began: the sticks were re-woven and new ones were brought to reinforce the walls and bases. I felt the need to tidy up our yard.

It was nighttime when Grandpa leaned against the terrace banister. The dark was alive with the flapping of wings, the clattering of bills. I could discern the white coats of those storks that rested in our yard, five, maybe six motionless birds. For a long time Grandpa watched them; then he brought two fingers to his mouth and whistled. His singsong carried across the rooftops and the nests, across the hills. The storks in the yard startled. A few took off, rose as high as the terrace, and I felt on my face the cold whiff of their wings. But when the storks had settled once more near the well, Grandpa whistled a second time. Quietly we waited. I didn't have to ask for what.

"I'm telling them the storks have made it safely," Grandpa said once I had joined him by the banister. "*Thank you*, I'm telling them, *for giving the flocks a place to rest.*"

We listened. An eerie anticipation pounded in my chest and somehow I started thinking of Captain Kosta. People said that he alone could speak to the mountain. That when he whistled, wings grew from his shadow and the mountain spoke back.

The night smelled of damp earth, and sweet—the way the field of rotting feathers had. Silent, we stood and waited, and just when I was ready to say goodnight, a singsong reached us from afar. The old tongue, the bird language.

"What are they saying, Grandpa?" I asked him.

"They're saying: *Thank you. And don't forget to send them back.*"

I didn't know yet that the village with which we spoke in whistles was that same village Elif had told me about—the place where centuries ago the rest of the exiled fire dancers had settled. And I didn't know yet that the *nestinari* and the storks were tied together with a sacred rope, that they were one.

· SIX ·

WITH THE STORKS CAME SPRING to the Christian hamlet. Trees that I thought were dead blossomed white, yellow, pink; the brush sprang leaves; the vine in our yard budded green. And with spring came the mosquitoes. Insolent, bloodthirsty they rose from the puddles by the well, from the old buckets of rainwater near the hedge, and then in thick flocks from the river. They stormed our terrace at dusk, as if the smoke of the repellent spirals were for them an offering, as if the frantic flapping of my hands invited them, like a sacred dance, to bite us deeper. My neck, my ankles—in short, every exposed spot on my body was soon swollen, itchy, and in pain.

"You're like a female," Grandpa would say, watching me sweat in my jacket. And in his sleeveless shirt, with the tenderness of a mother nursing her baby, he would watch a mosquito suck blood from his wrist. "When you're as old as

I am," he'd say, "you can't begrudge the vampire. I'm happy he considers me alive. So let him drink."

Grandpa was alive. But he wasn't well. The episode on the night of my arrival soon proved to be a regular occurrence. A few times I caught him wandering through the dark house, confused, not knowing where he was. Sometimes in the middle of a sentence he would hang and stare at me a long time and I was certain, by the way his eyes darted, that in these moments he knew not who I was. Such episodes left him sluggish, tired, and gradually an eerie feeling filled our days, the fear that night would bring something worse than the one before, something from which he wouldn't emerge unscathed.

It was the premonition that he had little time left to live that had first prompted Grandpa to start writing. At night in bed, swimming in my own sweat, with the window tightly shut and the mosquitoes slamming against the glass and crying for me to let them in to feast, I kept on reading.

"Tell me your stories," I said one evening on the terrace. "I'll write them down for you."

For some time Grandpa smoked and watched the green coil smolder on the table.

"The old folks say you die two deaths," he said. "Once when your heart stops beating, then a second time when you vanish from the memory of those who knew you. But I don't believe this to be true."

I swatted a mosquito on my neck and scraped off its mangled remains with great pleasure. Then I blew against the green spiral to stoke its ember.

"At first," he said, "I wanted to build the people of the Strandja a monument with words. A monument not to their greatness, but to their existence. I wrote so as to keep their second death at bay. But then, one night, I was reading what I'd written, and my stomach was churning with hunger, and I had this funny thought: Why do the living eat?"

"Because they're hungry?"

He nodded in agreement. "And why do they remember things?"

I shrugged.

"Because they're afraid." Afraid that they themselves would be forgotten. The Cup of Lethe. But a dead man knew no hunger; a dead man feared nothing, so why should the dead care if someone remembered them or not?

"It was a monument to vanity I was writing. My own monument, not theirs. And after that—I dropped the pen."

Yet he had picked it up with my arrival. Never mind the numbers—this many killed in war, this many exiled—I wanted him to tell me about the people of Klisura. Vassilko the idiot, the priest. The maidens he'd ogled from this terrace. The whistles with the distant hills. The fire dancers.

But he would not. *He's hiding things*, I wrote in another letter to my parents, not yet realizing that for Grandpa to remember the past would mean to relive it and so to suffer it again.

In my letters, I wrote with great pride of how I'd tidied up the yard—despite Grandpa's protestations that, historically, fixing up the school had always brought the village bad luck—of how I'd hoed away the weeds, dug up beds for beans, carrots, tomatoes, cucumbers, and squash. How I'd whittled sticks with the adze for the beans and tomatoes, constructed a framework along which to tie the cucumbers when they were ready. How I'd fallen knee-deep in dung when Grandpa took me to the neighbors' to gather two buckets of fertilizer for our trees—apples, plums, and peaches. *I cut my thumb, bloodied my knuckles, stubbed my toes, but I've never felt as good as now. I'm like a brand-new man.* And the neighbors too could see it. Baba Mina—the grandma in black from the station—and Dyado Dacho, her husband, Red Mustache.

"You've corrected yourself," Grandma Mina told me on one visit. I'd looked as skinny as a beanstalk when she'd first seen me, but now my cheeks were filling out nicely. Then she pinched them.

That too went into my letters. The only thing I never mentioned was Elif. And day after day, she seemed to be the only thing I thought of. In my thoughts I kept returning us both to the stork nest; I kept embracing her gently and kissing the beads of sweat on her neck. *Why don't you come with me to America?* I'd tell her in my thoughts and she would seize my face in her palms as if to make sure I wouldn't disappear.

I wrote my parents a letter a day. Then in the afternoons, even when he was reluctant, I walked Grandpa down to the Pasha Café so he could play backgammon with the owner. Around the fifth game, I always excused myself, crossed the bridge to the square, and waited for the bus from town. At a safe distance, I watched Elif carry her military bag down the stairs and make her way to a bench outside the municipal building. Then I would run to the driver and shove the letter and some money in his hands.

"I'm not your mailman," he'd say, but always pocket the cash. Every so often he too went to the Pasha and played backgammon. Rolling the dice against Dyado Dacho gave him the most pleasure. Their games often stretched into the night, past closing hours, but the owner never chased them. Instead, he would lock them up in the tavern, drinking and playing, only to find them peacefully asleep on a bench in the morning. "I can't drive the bus drunken," the driver told me once, when I asked him how come he stayed the nights there. "I'm no longer a young buck. But my blood is hot and I might be tempted. So it's best they lock me up until morning."

And how come he left the keys in the ignition on his way to the tavern? Wasn't he afraid the bus might get stolen? "And who would steal it? Dyado Dacho? I'm more afraid the key might fall out of my pocket. It's happened twice before."

Within a week he'd doubled the fee I was paying him to deliver my letters.

"Dyado Dacho's been winning," he said, though I knew their bets were symbolic. "And who are you writing to so much anyway? Have you got yourself a damsel?"

"The CIA," I told him. He snickered.

"So your mommy and daddy are secret agents, then?"

"I think he reads my letters," I told Elif that day, and sat on the curb a few feet from her bench. But as always she said nothing. Day in, day out, that's what we did—for fifteen minutes she would sit on the bench on the square and I on the curb in silence. I faced one way, she faced another, and yet it didn't matter that we kept quiet. At last she stood up and headed home, and some time after, I followed in her steps and took my seat in the café, next to Grandpa, who rolled dice after dice.

"You be careful with Elif," he told me on more than one occasion. "People are starting to talk."

I feigned surprise. It was the letters I needed to send. My parents were worried.

"As am I. You stay away from that girl."

But I couldn't. These fifteen minutes of mutual silence were all I looked forward to, awake or in my sleep. And people would always talk. The feast of Saint Constantine was coming near, they said, less than two weeks away. And once again the little girls had started burning with the fever. The imam had locked up his girl in her room. *It's a bad year*, someone said in the café. *It's May already, but it's cold and humid like October. The grass is rotting. And my chickens aren't laying eggs.*

"What do the chickens have to do with things?" Grandpa asked me later, but I could tell that the closer we got to May 21, the more restless he grew.

It was a week before the feast when Grandpa took me to the river. It had rained all night and a thick mist rolled over the ground. The road was muddy, and so were the banks and the river. Up above us a few storks flew in the cloudy sky, but most of them watched us passing up from their nests in the oak tops. Every now and then a male stork would balance himself atop a female, rub his long neck against hers, clatter his bill, and flap his wings. For a week, I had watched them mate from the terrace, and I watched them now, walking the muddy bank.

"Where are we going?" I asked, but Grandpa wouldn't tell me.

"Must you always ask so many questions?" he said, then urged me to walk faster; we didn't have all day.

We reached the giant walnut of the *nestinari* just when the sun was peeking from behind a break in the clouds. The nests in the branches were heavy with mating storks. But these storks were smaller than the others in the village. And they were black.

This was their tree. The only place in all of Klisura where black storks gathered. We watched them for some time— the males climbing the females, some flying away, others returning to their nest, a snake, a frog, a rodent in their bill.

My eyes drifted to the nest where Elif and I had sat, where now two storks rubbed their long necks together.

"I try to come here every now and then," Grandpa said, and tightened up his coat. "Especially once their babies hatch."

A gust blew through the meadow and I too zipped up my jacket. Such cool weather, Grandpa told me later, was odd, uncharacteristic. The cold was bad for the storks, bad for their babies and for their food. But secretly I cherished the cold—like garlic does a vampire, it kept the mosquitoes at bay.

"What's wrong with you?" Grandpa asked me, and pinched the scruff of my neck. "Did all your sailboats sink or something?"

"I'm cold," I lied. "Let's get warm in the *nestinari* shack." I started toward the little hut under the tree. But Grandpa wouldn't follow.

"I'd rather let the frost bite off my balls," he said, "than set a foot inside their shack. The crazy fools." And then he clapped his hands so as to spook the mating storks.

· SEVEN ·

THUNDER ROLLED across the hills of Turkey. Out the open window I watched the shapes of black trees sway in the yard. The house was quiet. The wind smelled of rain.

How weary I had been, a few weeks back, walking out of the airplane in Sofia; disconnected from the world, fed up with my life as a failed graduate student. And how distant this weariness felt now. The rain nourished me, my feet burned, my fingers itched, and I could almost hear the roots sprouting out of them and spreading through the soil. Grandpa and Elif, her father, even the ruined houses of Klisura, were nothing but bricks in my foundation. And yet the bottom line revealed a terrifying truth—this trip, like so many of my other endeavors, had proved a failure: I was still broke and still in debt.

The Tower of Klisura stood tall over the quiet village. A pair of storks had started constructing their nest atop the metal frame and I imagined them now in the dark, huddled against the wind. How much would we make, I wondered, if we turned that section of Klisura into a wind farm? How much would the Turkish company pay us for a few empty lots?

After two decades away Captain Kosta had returned to the Strandja to fight for her and bring her freedom. After fortysome years away, Grandpa too had chosen to come back. Now he too was waging war for liberation—that of Klisura and probably his own. How could I ask him then to sell what he was fighting so desperately to preserve?

My thoughts turned like concrete in a mixer: ancient skulls mixed with stork eggs, with muddy rivers, with fire dancers and janissaries slaying Christian bandits and dragging them by their ankles through the dirt. Captain Kosta watched me, atop his cask of gunpowder, his face black with the smoke of battle, his face the face of Grandpa. The imam sang somewhere in the village, or maybe I only thought I heard him singing. My great-grandfather picked my teeth and ate them, one by one, as if they were sweet grapes. "Whatever you think of doing," his raspy voice echoed, "I've already done it. And it was nothing special. Now bring the papers so I can sign. The land is yours."

And through these visions, like a knife smoothly sliding through a block of cheese, Elif's headscarf was falling down, down, down. A flash of lightning revealed before me the walnut tree. A black wing slashed it like an ax and where the tree had stood I saw a dark shape grow thicker, darker. I heard the growling of wolf-killing dogs and with the growling an ugly thought rang in my ears: That which will be demolished must first be built. That which will be taken must be given first. The giant walnut swayed, Elif's closed lids flicked open, and raindrops glistened on her neck. "Merciful Saint Elena," I heard her tell me, "has come to our yard." It was raining. Soft rain, which turned to hail. The hail slammed against our roof, against the side of our house, against my window, and into my room.

"*Amerikanche*." I heard Elif call me and only then did I realize I was no longer in a dream. The hail was no hail, but pebbles she chucked from the road. And there in the road, I recognized the sharp hump of the Lada, its high beams flickering, the engine roaring. "Come on, my American friend," Elif called, and stepped on the gas. "Let's go before I've woken the dead."

· EIGHT ·

WHEN I WAS STILL A LITTLE BOY, Grandpa often told me stories of khans and tsars, of great heroes. Sometime in the tenth century, a scribe recorded the lineage of the first Bulgarian rulers in a codex, which lay forgotten between the pages of a Slavonic Bible until a Russian historian stumbled upon it a thousand years later. This codex, now famous as the Nominalia of the Bulgarian Khans, began with Attila, also known as Avitohol, then spoke of his son Irnik, of Gostun, Kubrat, and of his son Asparuh, the white horseman, who with his tribes crossed the Danube, allied with the Slavs, defeated the Byzantine Empire, and founded Bulgaria in 681 A.D.

Many a night I had lain in bed imagining the glorious battles, my head turning the way any boy's would when he believed the blood of Attila and Asparuh coursed through his veins. The stories Grandpa told me were only loosely based on historical fact; at my persistence he invented wildly, a codex of our own. We called it the Nominalia of the Imaginary Khans.

"Perun was the main god of the Slavs," Grandpa liked to tell me in one such story. Master of thunder and of lightning, atop the highest mountain, he presided over many children, while Veles, the dark nether lord, controlled the underworld.

Of course, Perun loved all his children. But none as horribly as Lada. Lada was beauty, endless joy, eternal youth. Lada was love. Thick stalks of golden rye? The lashes of her eyes. The eyes themselves were humus-chernozem. White flour for steaming bread? This was her skin. Her teeth were bushelfuls of wheat. Her hair—a river.

So frightened was Perun of losing Lada that on the day the girl was born he seized her hair. Each year Lada's hair grew longer, and each year Perun wound it around his fist a new revolution to keep her in his sight. But at his feet Lada faded. Her lips withered. Her breath turned rotten. Without Lada's beauty, Dazhbog grew tired of pushing the sun across the sky. Cold sleep took possession of Zornitsa, and dawn no longer broke. Veles, the nether god, looked up, saw night, and climbed out of his domain. Snow, ice, and darkness ruled the land for ten thousand years.

The gods convened and, weeping, collapsed before Perun. "Almighty Father," the twinkling Dawn begged him. "Your love for our sister has turned to poison. Your fire has turned to stone. Her beauty—to carrion. Look at her, black with flies at your feet, white with maggots. Let her rise so that her beauty may blossom. Set her free so that the land may be born again."

This plea moved Perun. Reluctantly he unwound Lada's hair a thousand times, two thousand. Her hair fell free. It gushed out of the mountain, down its slopes—a river, which swept all ice, snow, darkness in its way and left behind meadows and fields for plentiful harvests. Veles retreated underground and spring was born again, and spring extended as far north as Lada's hair allowed.

But oh how Perun suffered without his beloved daughter. Nothing gave him repose. He thundered, threw fire and lightning, torched, ruined. At last he wound her hair around his fist a thousand times and summer came; two thousand times and it was autumn; three thousand times and Lada was back at his feet, and out into the world winter ruled.

I had remembered this story unexpectedly one night, sitting on the windowsill and thinking of Elif and of her father. And now again I thought of this story, if only for a moment. Perun, the god of thunder, roared around us. My head bobbed, my teeth chattered, and with the stench of burned oil and exhaust, Lada, the goddess of youth and beauty, rushed us in her palms up the Strandjan hills.

Beside me, Elif was shifting gears, barely releasing her foot from the gas. *So this is how death arrives?* I wanted to cry out, but couldn't. All I could do was squeeze the door handle and dig my heels into the floor, like that would halt us. The high beams bounced up and down, revealed now cliffs, now bushes and branches, now ruts in the dirt road. It wasn't raining, but the wipers flapped; the gears grinded and from a hoarse, pathetic stereo Metallica's James Hetfield commanded us to give him fuel, give him fire, give him all that he desired.

"That was the first time I ran away from home," Elif said, and she even looked at me, for effect. "Metallica in Plovdiv. June 11, 1999." Having no money for tickets, she and her friends snuck onto the roof of an apartment complex near the stadium from where all they saw was this tiny sliver of the stage. The music reached them doubled up in echo, which was about the same quality as most of her bootleg tapes anyway. And the bastards didn't even play "Seek and Destroy." "But who cares, *amerikanche*? Best night of my life to date."

At that, she floored the gas. We had emerged from the wide curves of the road onto a fairly straight stretch. A hundred meters ahead, the stretch ended in a thick mass of trees, which swayed in the beams. I think I yelled, but how could I be certain with the tires screeching, the engine roaring, the clattering of metal parts? Elif had slammed the brakes and we were skidding sideways. My head smashed into the ceiling, then into the headrest—a hard, rubberized plastic the car's Russian constructors must have invested with a dual function: to stop your neck from snapping while simultaneously halving your skull.

Then we were no longer in motion. The wipers scratched the dry windshield with a noise that raised my arm hairs, and Hetfield screamed for fuel and for fire. In sync Elif banged her head, in sync she joined him in the scream. "Yeah, oh yeah," she hollered, and when she looked at me, the black of her pupils had swallowed up her red eyes. "I have no idea what he's saying and I don't care. But I relate."

We abandoned the Lada and sank into the forest. A rusty circle of light showed us the way—an ancient flashlight that danced in Elif's hand. She held mine and pulled me forward, her palm burning and so sweaty that a few times I slipped from her grip.

"Where are you taking me?" I asked, and when she answered, the lightness of her voice sent shivers down my spine: "Across the border."

The wind howled in the treetops and with each gust the rain in their leaves fell to the ground in whooshing sheets. My soles picked up chunks of mud and so did Elif's, but the heavier our shoes grew, the tighter she pulled me forward and the faster we walked.

"I don't have my passport," I told her, and for a long time her laughter bounced through the trees and in my head. How many times had I fantasized about finding myself alone with her, away from other people's eyes? Of holding her hand? But not like this. Listen, I wanted to say, and plant my heels in the mud and demand an explanation. And yet all I did was follow wherever she led, just happy that she was near.

At the edge of the forest she turned the flashlight off. A half-moon broke through the clouds, then disappeared, but I could see ahead of us a clearing split by a tall barbed-wire fence. There were gates in the fence, for people and vehicles to pass, and large, rusted warnings that trespassers would be shot on sight.

Elif stood on her toes and whispered in my ear, "Right there, a hole," and pointed, as if I could see a thing. Her breath was vile from what she had smoked, but nonetheless to feel it so warm on my cheek made my knees go slack.

The opening was where she said it would be. She lifted the fence for me, and once I'd crawled under, she followed with great agility. Like that, we were in Turkey. And not a soldier was around to deny us passage. Once again we hid in a forest; once again we emerged in a clearing. A few shepherd huts stood in our way, abandoned, desolate—an old Turkish hamlet; and to one side wooden frames for hay, bare and sticking up in the dark like Inquisition stakes.

My heart was pounding, but now, with the adrenaline, all fear had turned to excitement. I pulled Elif closer. I whispered, "We snuck across the border!" She laughed, once again loudly, not afraid we could be heard. "Go, go," she said, stuck the flashlight in my hand, and nudged me forward. Now *I* was leading and she followed. It felt good to be in charge even for a short while. Finally, here was the kind of romance I had dreamed of.

"Where now?" I turned to ask her. "Elif? Where now?"

But she was gone. I waved the flashlight—at the collapsed earthen wall of a hut, at the tall grass that flowed with the gusts, at the ugly stakes, and at the forest from which we had emerged.

"Elif?" I called more loudly. "Elif!"

My heart turned inside out. My feet and fingers grew deathly cold. But I wouldn't have the chance to wander—the roar of an engine exploded in the night, and soon a globe of blinding light had locked me in my tracks, like a hare.

"Stay! Don't move!" someone yelled in Bulgarian. I couldn't lie on the ground, though I wanted to. I couldn't even hold my hands up like the voice commanded. A giant man stepped from the light, an entirely black figure that grew larger the closer he neared. Captain Kosta, I thought, in my terror, in my confusion. "On your face," the man screamed, and I recognized, undeniably, the Kalashnikov he carried. And so I took a bite of the mud, my nose an inch from the tips of his boots, and could say nothing, nothing at all, no matter how angrily he screamed.

Like a feather he picked me up; like a feather he carried me to the idling jeep. He leaned me against the back fender, and now that the light was not in my eyes I saw him better: a young man, a border soldier in full combat uniform and gear, his face running with sweat and mud in a grotesque mask. With each wipe of his hand, the mask twisted, changed form so that it looked like he was wearing many faces. "Who are you?" he was saying, pointing the Kalashnikov my way. And then the sound of laughter from a hut made him freeze. He turned. "Come out," he yelled. "Hands in the air. Come out or I'll shoot!"

The laughter chimed with the clarity of crystal glasses shattering to pieces. The sound of clapping hands drowned it momentarily and Elif stepped out from behind a ruined wall.

"Halt or I'll shoot!" the soldier screamed, but she laughed and clapped and neared. And so he fired, *rat-tat-tat* right at her feet, and the mud boiled with the rounds. And then he seemed to recognize her; she laughed louder, and before he knew it she was hanging on his neck and kissing his lips.

"Elif, you little shit," he yelled in Bulgarian, and pushed her away so hard she almost plopped on her back. "You little, little shit," or something to that effect.

But she was in his arms again.

"It's good to see you too," she said, and faced me. "You were adorable," she said. "So cute!"

I tried to move, but couldn't. The soldier had handcuffed me to the jeep and I hadn't even noticed when.

· NINE ·

THE MATCH IGNITED and its tiny flame spread through the pile of sticks and straw. Our lungs filled up with smoke and, coughing, we huddled by the fire. Light pushed back the night, and heat spread through my bones, slowly, the way a snake devours its prey. We were sitting on solid rock, surrounded by boulders and remnants of ancient walls—I on one side of the flame, Elif and the soldier on the other.

"I could've shot him dead," the soldier had cried out only a few minutes earlier. "Damn it, Elif, I could've shot *you* dead!"

"What luck that'd be!" She'd reached for his rifle, but he had slapped her hand away. "Get in the jeep!" Unlocking my cuffs, he'd asked, "And you? Have you no head on your shoulders? Or do you do all that she says?"

"We came to see the ruins," she told him later, from the front seat. We were flying through the brush and in the back

I felt as though we'd thrown ourselves, voluntarily and irrevocably, toward the bottom of a dried-up well.

"And here I thought you'd come to see me," he said, and stepped on the gas harder. She put her hand on his, switching gears, and rubbed his knuckles.

"No way," he said. "Do you know what'll happen if they catch me off my post? No way. I hate that place." But then he yanked the hand brake. The jeep skidded and we flew in a different direction.

"Get out," he ordered once we reached the bottom of a cliff face. And after that we followed him uphill, without the flashlight, the sky still plastered, but the clouds thin and radiant with moonlight. The cliffs had softened in their edge; the wind blew colder the higher we ascended and tossed at me now the smell of damp earth, now that of the soldier's sour sweat. The path was slabs of rock, and in the distance atop the hill were boulders, like the rocks at our feet, arranged artificially, remnants of what most likely had once been a Byzantine fortress.

"So who are you?" the soldier asked me now by the fire. The mud on his cheeks had dried and fissured and made him look as ancient as the rocks, and tall as he was, he seemed himself to be a boulder.

I told him who I was. He told me he would have never guessed.

"You speak well," he said, "no accent," and Elif snickered.

His name was Orhan, he said, and he was in the third month of his twelve-month mandatory army service, in case I wondered. He lived in a village a couple of hills to the east and he'd been lucky to get a post here on the border.

"Luck in the form of seven rams," Elif said, "which his father slaughtered for the members of the draft committee."

Orhan laughed a hearty laugh and raked the fire with his army knife. "My heart still hurts. What loss!"

"You think he's joking," Elif said, though I was thinking nothing of the sort. "But this boy loves his sheep. Tell him about your *dreams*!"

Orhan shifted on the ground. He poked the fire some more, turning the blade, blowing the sparks away from his face and from Elif's.

"They aren't really dreams as much as plans," he said at last, but softly, like he was afraid that merely uttering the words would ruin things. "I'd like to close the cycle, you know? Not just herd the sheep. I'd like to apply for European funding and with the money build a proper farm—a large roofed space for the animals, a feeding belt, machines to milk them . . ."

"And that's his dream." Elif laughed.

"More like my plan," he said, and stabbed the flames some more. "Hey, now," he said suddenly with a smile. "It's a good plan. And if it works, Elif, I'll bathe you in milk. I'll roll for you the softest bed of wool."

"Wool makes me itchy," she said. "And I get bloated from milk. But I might take you all the same." She leaned her head against his shoulder, her eyes on mine. A stick crackled; the flame loomed taller and seemed to lick her face.

"As if I want someone like you," he said, laughing. "A hedgehog in my pants."

There was a reason Elif had brought me here, beyond the prank, beyond just showing me some ancient rubble. I watched her, prettier than she had ever seemed now that her cheek was on his shoulder, and something hurt, deep in my jaw and in my teeth, the way it hadn't hurt for any other girl. And I was certain she read my hurt, because a smile had forged of her lips a sickle.

"My American friend," she said, still leaning. "I've got the medicine for you." And then she fished a plastic Coke bottle, sixteen ounces, out of her jacket and tossed it through the flame. I took three hurried gulps of brandy that set my throat afire and kicked my mind off the hurt, if only for a while. I tossed the bottle to Orhan, but he allowed it to bounce off his chest into the flame, from where the yelping Elif pulled it out barehanded.

"I don't drink," Orhan told me, while she was cursing that the *rakia* had gone to waste.

"Orhan here drinks only milk and water," Elif said, dusting off the ash from the bottle. Its label had melted, and its sides had morphed into an odd shape, half girl, half something else. "The flesh of pigs disgusts him. He prays five times a day and once, during Ramadan, he swallowed a fruit fly by accident and then was sick with guilt for a year. Spent it in the mosque, with my father, chatting about the greatness of Allah. I bet my father wishes Allah had sent him not me but Orhan for a child." She spoke like this for a while, trying in vain to unscrew the cap, which the fire had sealed. And when she'd gotten tired, she snatched the knife from Orhan, stabbed the bottle in the throat, and cut the top away. "See what you did?" she said, and I wasn't sure if she meant me, or Orhan, or both of us. "See how you left me no choice? But we will drink it all." Then she tossed the cut-off plastic into the flame and, in a veil of fuming blackness, brought her lips to the jagged rim. "Hey, Orhancho," she said, "I love you, but why you have to be so crazy?" and then, dropping the knife on the ground, she handed me the bottle through the flame. Some of the liquor sloshed when I took it; the fire hissed and thicker tongues shot up at the sky.

"Yeah, oh yeah," Elif yelled, her voice bouncing distorted in the boulders. With a simple smile Orhan watched her run toward a rock and attempt to climb it. She threw pebbles at another rock, then tried to stride the remnants of a wall, flapping her arms on either side for balance.

"I worry that she will make a bad wife," he said when she had sunk into the night, and only her yelping could be heard. I was just having another sip and after that I had another.

"Pardon?" I said in English, but he didn't seem to hear.

"I feel it is my duty to correct her. To save her from the Sheytan. But still I worry she is more trouble than it's worth."

· TEN ·

MORE THAN TWO AND A HALF MILLENNIA AGO, the priest-esses of Dionysus tore piece by piece their sacrificial prey. "Right where you sit," Elif said, and leaned closer to the flame so that her face ignited orange. "But there is more."

Of course there was. And now that the *rakia* had untied her tongue she let it out with gusto. The year was 1981 and Bulgaria was celebrating thirteen hundred years since its founding. The Ministry of Culture, headed by none other than the daughter of the general secretary of the Commu-nist Party, was proudly unveiling one monument after an-other, new palaces, new buildings all through the land. One day, amid the frantic celebrations, a man from the Strandja Mountains showed up at the ministry's gates. "Take me to the minister," he demanded. "I've got something she must see." And though his face was scrubby, his clothes ragged, dusty from the road, they rushed him right in. This man was

Mustafa the Treasure Hunter, a man who knew his way not just through the hills of the Strandja, but also through her past; a man who'd helped the ministry discover more than a few cartloads of Ottoman and Thracian gold.

Now before the minister, behind the locked doors of her office, Mustafa pulled out a piece of cow hide. A map to a treasure the likes of which they'd never seen before.

"Ottoman?" the minister inquired. Mustafa shook his head. "Then Thracian?"

He shrugged. He wasn't certain, but if the men from whom he'd bought the map could be believed the treasure was older still.

"Older than the Thracians?" The minister sneered.

"If the men can be believed."

She didn't bother asking what men these were. So that the treasure hunter would lead them to the ancient secrets, he had to be allowed to keep his own.

"She was a fine lady," Elif said now of the minister of culture, and slurped *rakia*, half of which we'd already killed. "Even my father won't say a bad word about her and when it comes to the Communists he doesn't spare his curses. A cultured woman, he says. But her head, he says, wasn't well screwed onto her shoulders. She was into that mysticism stuff. Flying to India; meditating days on end in a cave. Imagine this, the daughter of the general secretary of the Communist Party, eating nothing but bean sprouts and chatting with gurus? She was a rebel, like me. That's why I like her."

At this Orhan grunted. But he said nothing, only raked the fire with his knife and blew on the flame.

So what the minister of culture did with the treasure map was only the most logical thing she could do.

"She took the map to Baba Vanga. You know who Baba Vanga was, don't you, *amerikanche*?"

Of course I did. What Bulgarian didn't? One day when Vanga was a little girl, just after World War I had ended, a sudden twister of red desert sand picked her off the ground outside her village and carried her the way a thermal column carries a migrant stork. The peasants found her in a field, blind from the dust and sand. But though the twister had taken Vanga's eyes, it had given her a different kind of sight. For decades, Baba Vanga was Bulgaria's—no, Eastern Europe's—most renowned clairvoyant. And so, quite naturally, the treasure map was brought for her to see.

But Baba Vanga refused to even touch the piece of hide. "It's very bad," she told her high-ranking visitors. A long, long time ago tall, strapping men had crossed the sea from Egypt. Men with black hair, and gold masks on their faces, and many slaves. The slaves dug a grave and buried in it a royal woman, and then were all put to the sword. The tomb was sealed and hidden. Inside it, to this day even, were chunks of gold and awesome riches, and in her coffin the royal woman lay. She held a scepter and rolled at her feet was a papyrus, which spoke of how things had been thousands of years back and how they would be, thousands of years in the future.

"Who was this woman?" I said. The wind had turned colder and so I huddled closer to the flame.

"Bastet," Elif whispered. "The Egyptian goddess of cats." She watched me a long time, without a word.

"Fuck off," I said. "Get out of here."

Orhan stirred. "It's true. I mean, the Communists believed it true." He looked about and over his shoulder, as if to make sure no Communist was there to hear him. "They started digging, right here in the ruins. My uncle told me of how the soldiers who dug the hole all got really sick. Their hair was falling off in handfuls."

"And did they find anything?" I asked, so close to the fire now my eyes watered.

"Death," said Elif. I tried to see if she was joking, but her face betrayed only pleasure—from being here, with me and with Orhan, from saying the things she said and watching me absorb them. "A month or so after the digs began, the minister died in suspicious circumstances. A number of key officials involved in the excavations took their lives. And those who didn't die, the Committee for State Security locked away, for good."

"After this the hole was sealed," Orhan said. "My uncle tells me they poured concrete in it for fifteen hours straight. And that was that. Goodnight, I say, sweet dreams. Now let's go back, before they've caught me off my post."

But when he tried to stand, Elif pulled him down by the lapel.

"A coward," she said. "That's what you've always been. Learn from the American. He's not afraid."

"Oh yes, I am," I said. But not because of her gibberish. And if she had caught the flash in Orhan's eyes, she too would have grown fearful. Instead, she gently swept her palm across the rocky ground.

"I wonder what she looked like, this goddess of cats. I bet she drove men crazy with just the flitter of her lashes, the flick of her tail. Imagine, to be buried with such high honors. And then the slaves who dug your grave—all put to the sword. I bet it was the goddess who drove the Thracian women mad. I bet they came to dance here not in honor of drunk Dionysus, but in hers."

Right there, could I see the trough the Thracians had

dug in the rock? That's where they mixed their sacred wine, and then they drank it, the naked, mad priestesses of the demented god. And tore to pieces the sacrificial goats. "And even men," Elif said, and her eyes glistened. If the men were stupid enough to spy on their dances. "I bet you two are dumb enough," she said, and laughed. "I bet you two would have been first in shreds."

I guess by now she was pretty drunk. But so was I. Or else I would have told her to stop, if not for my sake, then for Orhan's.

"My head's started to hurt," he said abruptly. "American, is your head hurting?" But he didn't wait for my answer. "I hate this place. Never once have I seen a snake in the stones, a bird in the bush, a beetle in the dust. All living things hate it and stay away."

"Well, I love it," Elif said. "And you, like your whole family, are a coward."

"Let's go," I said, and tried to stand up only to plop down on my ass again.

"We're going nowhere," she said. "You don't have to act so that the coward may seem less like a coward. That's what you are, Orhan. A mouse-heart, like your father."

At this, he slapped her, a backhand slap that sent her tumbling to the side. Her lip glistened in the light of the fire and hungrily she licked it. "Big man you are, taking a girl like she was a sheep for bribes. I bet that rifle of yours, I bet you don't even know how to shoot it properly."

Oh yeah? he said, and grabbed the Kalashnikov. Oh yeah, she said, and waited for him to spring up to his feet. I watched them, hypnotized—him on one side of the fire, her on the other, their faces bloody with flowing flame. "American," she called, "wake up! Where is the bottle of *rakia*?"

I pointed, not quite sure my finger was showing her the right direction. But all the same she found the bottle on the ground, and when she bent down to take it, she stumbled and fell. She dusted off her clothes, then picked up the bottle, in which some drink still remained.

"I'll count ten paces," she said. "One, two, ten. Then you shoot the bottle off my head. The real man you are. The brave."

You think I won't? he said. I think you can't, she told him, and so he said, balance the bottle on your head and I will shoot it off, clean as a snowdrop. The safety of the rifle clicked, and while she was struggling to balance the bottle on her head, swaying this way and that, a deathly chill spread through my back and held me in its fist.

"The bottle is crooked," she cried.

"Or are you afraid?"

Her laughter set my ears to buzzing. "Okay," she yelped. "I'll hold the bottle up. Like this. You shoot it off my hand."

She held the *rakia* high, took tiny steps to counter her swaying; the soles of her shoes crunched against the sand and rock, the drink sloshed at the bottom of the bottle. Orhan jabbed the Kalashnikov against his shoulder and fixed his gaze through the sight.

"I bet you—" Elif began but didn't finish. The rifle had expelled a single deafening bang that smashed the ruins, bounced back at us, then rolled off the cliffs and into the valley in waves of unfolding echo. The bottle was no longer in Elif's hand. Her hand, however, was luckily still there. Spilled *rakia* glistened on her sweaty face and on the short locks of hair.

I called her, but she didn't hear.

Anyone could be brave, she said, rubbing her eyes, when

he was on the safe side of the barrel. Let's see how he braved the death side. Oh, was that right? Orhan called. They'd come face-to-face now, and he shoved the Kalashnikov in her hands.

"I hold my canteen up and you shoot it. Five paces!"

"Ten," she said.

"Make it fifteen!" He unlatched the canteen from his belt and held it up, like a conqueror toasting a victory. "American," he barked, "she's too drunk to count. Count fifteen paces for her."

"American, don't move!" she ordered. "I can. Alone."

One, two, three. He held the canteen up while fifteen paces away through the night she stabbed the rifle against her shoulder. She swayed this way and that and I'm certain she would have shot him dead, if it weren't for me stifling her in my embrace.

There was no *Let me go! Get off of me!* Instead, she closed her eyes serenely and pressed her cheek against my shoulder. A light burning breath fled her lips and we swayed together in the dark silence before her laugh. Next I looked, Orhan had snatched the Kalashnikov and locked the safety.

He too was laughing. "American, I owe you one." From this day on, he said, he was forever bound to me. Whatever I asked of him, no matter how daring, he'd do it.

I swung to square him in the jaw, to drop him to the ground, to knock him out. Instead, I buried my nose in the dirt and they were laughing. The kind of hate I felt for him, for her, was new, unfelt before. And for a fleeting moment, I think I liked it.

"Hey now," Elif was saying. "It's all a joke. We do this every time."

"For shame we do," Orhan agreed, and took her in his arms. From my vantage point in the dirt, I watched her snuggle against his chest, the way she'd done with me, and couldn't bear it. Back by the fire I curled up into a ball and prayed the heat of the flame would burn away my hate. I couldn't reason this in so many words, but I knew it with my teeth and nails, and in my heels—for weeks my pining over Elif had inched me closer to an awful point of no return. But only tonight, among the sacrificial altars, the troughs for doctored wine, the walls of strongholds that were, for shame, no more, had I crossed this point and plunged myself, irrevocably, toward the bottom of the dried-up well.

When next I opened my eyes the fire had died and a thin red line bloodied the horizon. The rattle of the Kalashnikov shattered the air: Orhan—no, Elif—was shooting it into the dawn. Then in the valley below us, a louder rattle boomed. *American, get up and try it!*

I squeezed the trigger and the rifle wriggled, a biting snake in my arms. *Rat-tat-tat.* The echo answered, *tat-tat-tat,* a thousand clacking bills. We stood atop a ruined stronghold, and down below us in the valley a thousand white storks clacked their bills. A thousand wind turbines spun their propellers, in neat and endless rows.

"The storks speak with the gun," Elif whispered in my ear, "as if the gun were one of them. Do it again," she said. "Speak with the storks."

Eastward, the sun was rising from the Black Sea. I pulled the trigger and spoke with the storks.

· ELEVEN ·

THE GODDESS LADA had reached as far north as she could and now her father, the god Perun, was reeling back her hair from his mountain. She knew his pull could not be stopped, but still she fought him. That day, while he was resting, she planted her heels deep into the soil to bid farewell the land she was departing. Darkness awaited inside her father's cave, uneasy slumber at his electric feet. Farewell, my brothers, she told the stones of many sizes. Farewell, sweet, fragrant sisters. Thick, frosty moss tangled the stones; the flowers withered. And just when Lada was about to go, she saw through her tears a cloud on the horizon, a pall of black smoke creeping near, flashes of lightning boiling in its bowels. This was, she understood, a multitude of riders the like of which no Slavic god had seen before. And at their front, she saw a man whose head was shaven cleanly, a man who pointed a shiny saber as though at her. His madness took hold of Lada's heart, like a worm in an apple. She tried to run and meet him, but how could she escape the shackles that weighed her down? She tugged, she chewed on the tresses, yet nothing helped. So then she wept in greater anguish still.

But suddenly the riders halted. The man who led them brought his horse her way. Thick rags of soot were falling from the sky now that the hooves no longer raised up dust and ash from pillage fires. In ashen rain the young man watched her, without a word.

"Are you a god?" she asked, and so he told her: at first he'd been a solitary rider, but then his lust to gallop on and on and pillage had sucked into its vortex a multitude of restless tribes. He was their leader now. Attila. But god? There was a single god—the great, vast sky whose life force was coursing through his veins.

She laughed. "When mortal men look me in the face they see a river."

"I see a girl," he said.

And so she begged him. "Take me with you. I want to ride free by your side."

"So ride then." He turned to leave, but didn't move. She had expected this, of course.

That night the Huns camped by the river, their horde extending as far back as the human eye could stretch. The sky was merciful and opened up. Rain pounded down the cloud of ashes and blackened Lada's hair. She knew her father would soon wake up and start his reeling.

"Tell me," she asked Attila, who, tangled in her tresses, was sharpening his saber on a deer hoof. "Where have you been? What have you seen?"

He was afraid to look her in the eyes. He'd never felt like this before. He said, "For ten thousand days I saw nothing but steppe and sky. Then I saw a city of silver. I thought of stopping there to drink its water, to eat whatever food its king would give. I thought of lying under the shade of silver trees. Instead, I slew the king, and burned the city, and turned it into a silver lake. I rode ten thousand days through steppe and sky and came upon a golden tower. Inside the tower, like storks in a cage, a thousand women slept—a woman of every human tribe. I thought of climbing up the tower to look at all the world. I thought of bedding the women so they might bear me one thousand sons. A son from every human tribe. Instead, I brought the tower to its ruin. The women we trampled with our hooves. Our hooves are golden now.

"Three hundred years without repose," he said. "I cannot stop. I must ride on."

"Take me with you," she begged again. And then she told him of her hair and of her father, the great, almighty god.

"There is one god," he said, jumping to his feet as if to prove it, and brought his saber down. In vain, he hacked at Lada's hair. In vain, he tried to slash it.

"You fool," she said. "I am a god as well."

"There is one god," he said a final time, and sprinted to his horse.

At this point in the story, Grandpa usually paused and leaned closer, his whisper hoarse from all the talking, his breath scathing my ear. "An ancient scribe once wrote of how the Huns made the Yantra River disappear. *So horrific was the multitude of Huns who crossed the Yantra River*, the scribe wrote on his parchment, *that by the eleventh day of their crossing, their hooves had severed the river in two. By the twentieth day the Yantra was flowing backward, and by the twenty-fourth, it had disappeared whence it had come.*

"No ancient scribe can tell you why all this happened,"

Grandpa would whisper, "but I can. Imagine, the golden hooves pounding the riverbed! A hundred horses, then a thousand. A hundred thousand. By the fifth day Lada's hair was starting to split, tress by tress. By the eleventh the Huns had severed it completely."

Perun awakened. He reeled, and gathered Lada's hair back to his mountain, the way one gathers a fishing seine. What horror the old fool felt to see no Lada where the tresses ended.

Lada was free. Short-haired, she flew behind Attila and on her wings flew Spring and Beauty. Where the Huns passed, beautiful death followed. And from the funeral pyres, bright peonies bloomed.

PART
THREE

· ONE ·

AND AFTER THIS IT RAINED, melodramatically, for many months. Or at least it seemed so from underneath the stifling Rhodopa blanket, which scratched my cheeks each time I tossed and turned. Quite frankly, I felt ashamed. Quite frankly, I couldn't help it. Beyond the window glass rippled with age, over the hills in the distance, black waves were clashing with blacker. Greek clouds tore into Turkish and battled with our own. Back in the day, Grandpa told me, on the eve of the first Balkan War, even the clouds here had been forced to pledge allegiance to a single nation. "It's raining Turkish rain today," he'd say, then sit at the foot of my bed and force me to drink a cup of *mursal* tea. "Only Turkish rain touches this softly. And Turkish girls." He'd laugh in an attempt to cheer me, but I would stare into the steam.

"Get up, my boy," he'd cry an hour later, and throw the window open. "Two days is plenty to toss about in bed.

Come help me tie the tomatoes. The wind's knocked over some of their poles." Instead, I buried myself in the blanket and waited to hear his fading steps.

Each day he worked the garden, went for bread and yogurt to the Pasha Café, even rode the bus to town—a business trip, he told me, which would have been a great deal more bearable with my pleasant person by his side.

"A sacrilege! Three days in bed!"

"My boy, how can I say this nicely: you stink like a widowed badger. Run and shower in the rain, then help me fix the frame for the cucumbers."

"Five days! A heart of briar jelly would mend itself in four!"

Each time he came to my room, I wanted him to leave. Each time he left, I wanted him to barge back in. What a tragic waste of precious time, I thought, and watched him act the clown, shoulders slouched at the foot of my bed. For shame, I told myself. Get up. There is no time to waste with broken hearts.

"It lashes bad," he'd say some days. "It stabs like a dagger to the back. Greek rain." He would expel the words like spittle. A long while he would watch the stork nest on the roof of the house closest to ours: one stork braving the sideways-falling rain, brooding the eggs, the other fetching mice, frogs, little snakes; the two switching places. Grandpa would tick his tongue. "If it rains another week like this . . . ," he'd say, but never finish.

On the sixth day of my self-imposed home incarceration Grandpa rapped on the door and, completely disregarding my cry to wait, stormed in. He held a nylon sack of bread and with the same hand struggled to close his umbrella. "It's stuck again, the brute," he muttered, without once looking up, shaking the umbrella and spraying water on me, on my desk, on the map of the ancient world behind me. Then, almost as an afterthought, he added, "Look who I found outside, standing in the rain, afraid to knock."

"Grandpa," I started to say, but still fighting the umbrella he stepped aside to let Elif pass through. She appeared in the doorframe so drenched, so shrunken in size, so despondent with her headscarf glued to her cheeks, with the sleeves of her jacket soaked and droopy, that I have no idea from where that burst of sudden laughter came.

"Yes, laugh," I told her, standing helplessly naked in the middle of the room, the pair of clean boxers I'd meant to change into treacherously far away in the wardrobe. "You too, Grandpa. Laugh it out."

A joyous grin on his face, he handed me the open umbrella. And while I hurried to cover up he spoke to Elif, still grinning, predictably as coarsely as he could. "Chilly rain today, Elif. Bulgarian."

· TWO ·

HER TEETH CHATTERED; her shoulders rocked. Water dripped from her jacket and drummed on the carpet, yet she refused to take it off. I offered her a blanket, but she said no, she wasn't cold. "Nonsense," Grandpa said, back from the kitchen, and ordered me to look away. When I looked again, Elif's jacket had been stretched to dry on the hanger in the corner and she was wrapped in a cocoon of wool. The old man shoved a steaming cup into her hands, and as she brought it to her lips some tea splashed on the headscarf, now spread in her lap. "With extra honey," he said, and did not move until she'd taken a few small sips.

At the threshold, he stopped. "I have much work to do," he lied, "and will be in my study. If you want more tea, the boy can brew it." He hesitated, then at last chose to leave the door wide open.

By now, some color had flushed Elif's cheeks and the

purple of her lips had begun to turn scarlet. She steamed under the blanket, the stench of wet wool mixing with the reek of my six-day sweat and fogging up the window so that I no longer recognized the yard, the rooftops, and the storks.

"Nice fire truck," Elif said, and nodded at the toy by my desk. I told her the ladder was telescopic, meaning it expanded when there was need, to which she said, "I know what 'telescopic' means." And then, "I bet it does."

She looked about the room in silence. "Orhan has been detained," she said at last. "Locked up in solitary confinement. But his father will slay a ram and grease up the right people and he'll be out before his beard has grown in length a third of yours."

"And you find this amusing?" I asked, disgusted, and in embarrassment scratched at my scruffy face.

"I find it hysterical. Like the rest of my life, which is so packed with jokes."

Here was a good one—she was no longer allowed to see her sister. Aysha was now alone, locked up in her room, and there were not enough rams in the whole wide world we could slay to bribe her father. "He is the only one allowed to see her. He feeds her, bathes her, in her room. And I won't be surprised," she said, "if my mother joins them shortly, the way she's been burning with the Christian flame."

Other girls in the village were burning too. It was a proper craze now, only two days before the feast of Saint Constantine and Saint Elena.

"I wish I too were burning," she said. "I'd grab this Saint Kosta by his beard and then—hold tight, Elif!—either he lifts me up to the clouds or I pummel his mug into the dirt. There is no third way."

I watched her fuming, prettier now in her spite than she

had ever seemed before. The short locks of her hair were drying up and curling and she resembled a ball of needles I wanted, no, felt compelled to hold. Here she was, crying out for help—a cornered, ferocious little beast—and all I thought of was how softly her breath had touched my face.

"So how do I compare?" I asked her. She blinked, surprised at the question and my tone. Side by side, I said. Orhan the shepherd, the soldier whose madness equaled only hers—and me, the boring foreign boy?

"Please stop," she said.

But I kept going. He was tall, I wasn't. He was handsome, I—not so much. He was daring, and spontaneous and brave . . . Please stop, she said. Why should I? I could be just as vile as she had been. I simply had to know—

"Well!" she cried. "You compared well, all right?" And only then did she look me in the eyes, hers feverish and frightened. "You are safe, all right? Dependable. But you'll be gone tomorrow and I'll be here."

To this I had no comment. I asked her why she'd come.

"To say I'm sorry. For a moment I'd thought—here is someone. My ticket out. But you're right. I'm crazy. And crazy people see things that aren't there."

I don't believe I've ever wanted to kiss a girl as much as I did then. I wanted to hush her, to tell her I too had seen things that weren't there, but could be. A strong imagination, I wanted to say, could wish things into existence.

She spoke. "But this is not the only reason. I came to ask for help."

I asked how I could help her and for the first time her lips twisted in something that might have been a smile. "Not you," she said.

· THREE ·

BUT GRANDPA WOULDN'T HEAR IT. "Elif," he said, and pushed away the page he was writing. "You know I care for you."

"Then prove it," she cried, yet when she spoke again her tone had softened. She did not want Grandpa to slay more roosters, nor did she want him to bloody his hands with magic fires. He had chosen to stay away from the *nestinari*, whatever his reasons, and she respected that. But he had to tell her where she could find them.

"Find whom?" I asked from the threshold.

Back in the day, sometime in the mid-sixties, most all Christians had left Klisura and moved to the city. There had been two entire apartment complexes in Burgas full of Klisurans.

"Tell me, Grandpa," Elif said again. "Where did the *nestinari* go once they left Klisura?"

He waved his hand as if to chase away a gnat. Why should he tell her?

"So I can steal my father's Lada tomorrow. So I can load my sister in it and take her to the *nestinari*. So they can cure her."

He hushed her with kindness I didn't fully believe. He told her to stop throwing oil into the fire. No one could cure her sister, because her sister wasn't sick—she was only acting. As was everyone else in the village, including her mother. "You want to help? Then ignore them."

"The way you ignored the two girls from the upper hamlet? Were they acting too, Grandpa? Convincing actresses they were, right down to their graves."

Those girls, Grandpa said, they were a different story. Those girls—

But now it was her turn to cut him off. They must have gone somewhere, the *nestinari*, some other village, and she'd be damned if she wasn't going to find them.

"You won't find them here," Grandpa stuttered, his kindness gone to rot. "Because they all crawled back across the border, the serpents. And stayed there, in Turkey."

"I don't believe you," she said. "There must be others left."

I stood between them, ready to end this quarrel. Grandpa had turned as yellow as the paper on which he wrote, and I worried for his blood pressure. But before I'd spoken, Elif grabbed my hand and squeezed it. "*Amerikanche*, you have to ask him."

"*Amerikanche*, you'll ask me nothing," Grandpa said—no, cried out in fury. "You, American, will stay out of this mess. And you, Elif, here are some points for you to mull over." He took a clean sheet and stabbed a line with his pen, as though underlining invisible text. "Your father is punishing your sister so he may punish you and get to me." He scratched another line. "You're punishing my boy to get back at your father. And for what? What will you prove?" And then another. "Or did *your father* send you here? So he may get his precious land and harvest winds for money? Leave my boy be, Elif," he said, and circled the lines. "Go home and don't come back."

By now she was crying. Her sobs were so quiet I didn't even notice when they stopped. "All right," she said, and wiped her cheeks. She shed the wet blanket to the floor like a second skin and without looking up rushed out the door.

"I can't believe you, old man," I cried. Were land and ruined houses more important to him than a little girl's life? Was he honestly refusing to help the daughters, so as to punish their father?

I caught up with Elif two houses down the road. Of course, melodramatically, it was still raining. I told her to stop, and when she didn't, I seized her hand and spun her around.

"These girls from the upper hamlet," I said. "What happened to them?"

"What do you think? They were sick with Saint Kosta's fever and then they died."

But how? If it was all in their heads, all an act for attention?

"You said it best, *amerikanche*. A strong imagination can wish things into existence."

She tried to wriggle out of my grip, but I wouldn't let her.

"I'll help you find the *nestinari*. I'll make him tell me where they went."

She shook her head. "He's right," she said, almost shouting over the slashing of the rain. "I won't bother you again."

I'm certain she had seen my kiss coming from a mile away and still she acted surprised.

"Please don't," she said, but it was only after she'd let me kiss her a second time that she broke free from my grip and sank into the rain.

· FOUR ·

"I REMEMBER I was pulling water from the well when the man called me, right there from the road. It hadn't even been a full month since I'd returned to Klisura, so three years ago, then. I remember it was noontime and the end of May, but the sun was August sun already."

"Are you the teacher?" the man called, and Grandpa told him yes, he'd been a teacher once. Come into the shade, he told the man, under the trellis. A sweatier man Grandpa had never seen. He wore a sleeveless jacket, goatskin, with white and black spots. And his mustache was as thick as his forearms. "I'm so thirsty I could drink a river," the man said, and Grandpa filled up the jar from the bucket. The man drank it and shook his head. "This isn't helping." He set the jar aside, plunged his head right in the bucket, and held it underwater so long Grandpa thought he might have drowned. When at last the man shot up, his lungs wheezed and he looked around, face flushed and mustache dripping muddy streams. "Teacher," he said, "my girls are dying and you have got to save them." He'd come all the way from the upper hamlet, right over the hill somewhere, to take Grandpa back with him to their sickbed.

"Let me guess," Grandpa told him, "your girls are burning with the *nestinari* fever?"

The man's eyes turned to saucers. "I know," Grandpa told him, "because for two weeks now, like a circus bear, I've been parading among the houses of sick girls. And not one of them is really burning and they're all acting."

But this old grandma, the man stuttered, this old Christian woman had seen his daughters and she'd recognized in their eyes Saint Kosta's fever. "This old Christian woman," Grandpa answered, "is sad and senile. She knows nothing of Saint Kosta."

"But you do, teacher," the man said. "That's why I've come to get you."

Grandpa asked the man if he'd called a proper doctor to examine his daughters and the man told him he didn't trust proper doctors. Not since they'd let his wife die in childbirth, in the town hospital at that.

"I'm sorry, *kardash*," Grandpa told him. "I can't help you."

The man watched him, stunned. He shook his head. He wasn't leaving.

"That's fine by me," Grandpa said, then returned to the bench and pretended to read his paper.

"Teacher, if it were for my sake, I wouldn't be asking you again. But it's for my girls I'm begging. If you too are a father—"

Right about here, Grandpa's fuse blew a little. It had been months since he'd last heard from me and who knew if he'd ever hear my voice again. So he shouted. He asked the man what he knew about him being a father and this and that, and overall he brought much shame to our name that day.

The man said nothing in response. He left the yard like a clobbered dog, a trail of muddy water in the dust behind him. A week later, Grandpa heard, his girls died.

I had returned to Grandpa's room still dazed from my kiss with Elif—no, two kisses!—to find him stretched in bed, his eyes closed and arms folded across his chest. "I don't feel well," he said, without looking. He'd taken some pills already, but could I please measure his blood pressure? I did. The reading was alarmingly high. So I told him to lie still and let the pills work their magic.

"I worked myself into a fury, my boy. I said things I shouldn't have."

"You think?"

For a while we listened to what had eased into a drizzle outside.

"I don't care what its nationality is," Grandpa said to break the silence. "This rain depresses me to no end and gets my tongue wild."

"You think?" I said, and was this close to apologizing, for I too had said things I shouldn't have. Instead, I went to change into dry clothes and back in his room I took his blood pressure again. Lower, but still in the danger zone.

"What you said to Elif," I asked, "about her hurting me to get to her father, about her father hurting her to get to you. Do you believe it?"

"It doesn't matter what I believe. I've been wrong more often than I care to remember."

I listened quietly, not daring to interrupt, while he told me the story of the sick girls and of their father.

"To this day," he said in the end, "I'm convinced I could have saved them. If only I'd gone to their hut. I would have recognized the fever."

I knew I should spare him the questions, wait until tomorrow when he felt better. And yet I couldn't help it. "The *nestinari* fever?"

He blinked a moment, munching on some invisible seeds. Then he pushed himself upright and, amid the creaking of the bedsprings, spoke: "Take the meter. I want to show you something."

· FIVE ·

THE CLASSROOM SMELLED SWEET, like aging books. And musty—like feet, rubber galoshes, socks that had somehow remained wet for many years. And rotting wood, and straw, and mouse urine—at least that's what Grandpa said mouse urine smelled like. I'd come down to the first floor only once before; there was nothing for me to see here besides three rows of little desks, a larger one up front for the teacher, tilted to one side with a broken leg, an ancient stove, a blackboard with individual letters still legible under the dust, and books—piles and piles like old, crooked prisoners lined up against one wall awaiting their execution.

It goes without saying that with each new book Grandpa slammed on the tiny desk before me, I sneezed. He'd collected them, one by one from the piles, with the ease of a masterful librarian. At last, he lowered himself on the chair beside me—the two of us little schoolboys ready for a lesson.

"Now take my blood pressure again," he said, and I did, a third time.

It was better, but there was still room for improvement. He nodded. "Let's start with some light reading, then," and he untied the red strings that held shut the folder before us. Dust rose, bitter like medicine.

"'Man on the Moon,'" Grandpa read, taking out a newspaper clipping. "One giant leap for mankind, one tiny article in a Communist paper. 'The Bones of Tsar Kaloyan Unearthed.' 'The Oldest European Gold Treasure Dug Up in Varna' . . . Here, read this."

"'May 1988,'" I read from a page with torn edges. "'A Fainting Epidemic in Tanzania.'" Twenty children in a school in Tabora, while taking their final-year exams, had all been stricken by a fit of mass fainting—a common occurrence for Tanzania, the article assured. There had been a great deal of crying and screaming and running while the exam unfolded, and then the fainting fits had come.

Grandpa fished out another clipping. This one from October 1983. "A Fainting Epidemic in the West Bank."

"Creative titles," I said, and he sneered. In March 1983, the article read, more than nine hundred Palestinian schoolgirls and a handful of women soldiers from the Israel Defense Forces had fainted in the West Bank. A subsequent Palestinian investigation had determined that while some instances could have been the result of an Israeli chemical agent, the majority of the cases had been purely psychosomatic in nature.

"Purely psychosomatic," Grandpa said, and traced the line with his finger for emphasis.

He waved another clipping in my face and I sneezed once more in his. "'A Laughter Epidemic in Tanganyika.' January 1962. Mass hysteria at a mission-run boarding school for girls in Kashasha." The fit of laughter had started with three girls and before sunset it had affected two-thirds of all students and not a single teacher. By March the school was closed down, the students shipped home and with them the epidemic. More schools, more girls, thousands of people—all laughing. And with the laughter pain, fainting, flatulence—Grandpa tapped the word with his crooked finger—respiratory problems, rashes, attacks of crying, random screaming.

"In Tanganyika?" I repeated, and—God help me, because I couldn't—burst out laughing.

I could see he too was fighting. To no avail. Soon we laughed together, unreasonably long, and for a moment I felt as if I would burst at my seams and all the troubles that were crushing me like stones—Elif, Orhan, the sick little girl, my sick grandfather, my student loans—would roll away and I'd be free. "We're doomed," I cried. "To flatulence and random sneezing."

"The sneezing plague of Klisura," Grandpa said, and wiped the tears in his eyes. "Saint Kosta help us!"

He closed the folder and we both gasped for air.

"Now then," he said when we had calmed down a little, and opened a book. What caught my attention right away was an illustration—or rather a reproduction of a medieval engraving—of men and women, in what I'd say was Bavarian attire, their bodies twisted in odd, unnatural positions, their faces contorted: eyes popping, tongues sticking out, and locks of hair spilling in all directions like fire.

"Like a true scholar," Grandpa said, "he studies the picture first."

A picture, I gave him the old cliché, was worth a thousand words.

"And what words is this one worth?"

I struggled to decipher the caption—Bulgarian in its old style, pre-1940s.

"The Dancing Plague of 1518," I said at last, and felt a great sense of accomplishment. But he motioned me to keep on reading. And so I tried, then I pretended to be reading, moving my lips silently as I skipped over those letters whose sounds I didn't know.

"How interesting," I said at last. There had been a dancing plague in 1518. An epidemic.

"You think?" Grandpa said, then seemed to take mercy on my ineptness. "It started in July," he said. A single woman danced feverishly through the streets of Strasbourg. For six days straight. Within a week her madness had infected three dozen people; within a month—four hundred. The local doctors called for bleeding of the sick. They thought it was "hot blood" that was causing the affliction. Instead, the authorities brought musicians, built a stage, encouraged the dancing any way they could. Only through dancing day and night, they said, would the sick be cured. Before the month was over, more than twenty dancers had died from fatigue, from heart attacks.

Grandpa traced a line of text in the book. "'They danced in such fervor their ribs snapped like sticks.'" He flipped the page to reveal another illustration: two men fighting to restrain a woman, and two more men behind them, and two more men—all struggling to contain wild, dancing women.

"The town of Aachen, North Rhine–Westphalia region in Germany," Grandpa said. "A favored residence of Charlemagne. And later . . ."

". . . the place of coronation of the kings of Germany," I finished.

He nodded. "And one of the earliest recorded epidemics. 1374." He swept his palm across the crumpled page. In short, this dancing mania was quite the fashion in medieval Europe. It affected thousands, regardless of their age or nationality or gender. It was believed that the surest way to ward off the fever was to play music while the sickly danced. But the music only attracted larger crowds.

And so I asked him the most logical of questions. "What was the cause?"

He licked his lips. "Some said bewitchment. Others believed the dancing was a curse." He fumbled through another book. "From this here holy fool."

The drawing showed a light-haired man in a boiling cauldron. A haloed martyr, no doubt, who held a Bible in one hand. A rooster perched on the Bible. In his other hand, like a scepter, the martyr held a palm leaf, or maybe a bird feather—as large as a stork's—I couldn't rightly tell.

I read the caption. "Saint Vitus."

They called the dancing mania Saint Vitus's dance. And they crowned him patron of all dancers and epileptics Europe-wide. Each year on his feast day in June, large crowds danced before his statue to seek relief and absolution from their sins. He'd died for his faith, the poor soul. The Romans boiled him in tar.

Gently Grandpa closed the book.

"They call it *chorea minor* now," he said. The rapid, uncoordinated jerking movements that affected one's face, feet, hands. "Then there is this."

He rummaged through a third tome, bookmarked with pieces of yellowed paper, until he found a new drawing, this time of seeds and spores and pollens and other peculiarities of the plant anatomy I couldn't really name.

"*Claviceps purpurea*, or ergot fungus. It grows on rye or wheat or barley when the weather is cloudy and humid for weeks on end. So the northern climates, then. You poison your body with that stuff too long and you've got yourself ergotism."

And what would such joy entail?

Spasms, mania, psychosis. Vomiting and seizures, LSD-like hallucinations. Gangrene.

LSD-like? I asked, and he said I'd heard him right. And gangrene. With great dexterity he returned to the previous book, showed me the drawing of another saint.

"They called the gangrenous symptoms of the illness Saint Anthony's fire, because the monks of Saint Anthony's order were very good at treating the condition. But not everyone was this compassionate and understanding."

Another book was pulled out of the pile. Another sneeze, another story. But this one—to my surprise—I'd heard before. In fact, I'd studied it in school, in America.

In the winter of 1692 two little girls, cousins from Salem Village in colonial Massachusetts, were seized by a strange affliction—the girls screamed, babbled, twisted themselves in odd positions, threw objects across the room. When a doctor found no scientific explanation for their illness, the rumors spread. The girls had been bewitched. Fair enough, these things happened back in those superstitious days, but who was the bewitcher? In no time more girls in the village fell prey to the same affliction. And in no time, the perpetrators had been named. The sick cousins themselves identified their tormentors—three local women who, or so the girls claimed, had summoned Satan to lock them down in a demonic spell. The women were put on trial and promptly two of them were hanged. By the end of the year a hundred and fifty residents of Salem Village had been accused of witchcraft; a great many of them had been excommunicated, executed, and buried in shallow common graves.

"Sound familiar?" Grandpa asked, and fixed me with his teary eyes.

"Well, sure. I mean, not really. Care to explain?"

He searched across the desk and flipped open another book.

Three years before the Salem witch trials an Irish washerwoman was executed in Boston, accused of bewitching the children of the wealthy family she worked for. The case, not surprisingly, gathered serious publicity, and one Cotton Mather, a very influential New England Puritan minister, even included it in his book on witchcraft and possession.

Grandpa traced a line in the book, right under the drawing of the poor woman hanging from a tree. "Cotton Mather," he said. "I've always wondered what kind of human name this is. Ivan, I can understand. Or Boris. Or Stoyan. But Cotton Mather?"

"Forget the name," I cried. "Finish the story."

"One cold January night of 1692," Grandpa said, opening another book from the pile, thinner than all the others, "the two little cousins, Betty and Abigail—now these names I can almost tolerate—were playing fortune-tellers in the kitchen."

They'd asked a slave in the house to teach them magic and were summoning ghosts in mirrors, trying to see what kind of men they'd marry when they grew up, that kind of girly nonsense. The slave—her name was Tituba and she was Indian or African or Caribbean maybe—had cooked the girls some "witch's stew" to eat. What was in the stew only God knew, but one can imagine how it agreed with the little darlings. Before the evening was over they were seeing pretty colors and dashing men and coffins in the mirror.

So, as these things often went, the two girls told their little friends about the game of magic; they most likely shared Tituba's witch's stew as well. Before long, little Betty had begun to neglect her errands, could not concentrate one bit in church, was restless at the dinner table, and when her father tried to say the Paternoster she screamed and barked like a bloodhound. Once she even hurled a Bible across the room right at his face.

"Guess," Grandpa told me, "what her poor father's occupation was in Salem Village?"

It didn't take great flights of the imagination to guess it right. He was the village minister.

"And so he thought he'd cure his sickly girl with prayer. Until the demon swallowed her whole, that is." He leaned over the booklet and read. "*From the writings of John Hale*, a witness to the affliction. The girls looked like they *were bitten and pinched by invisible agents; their arms, necks, and backs turned this way and that, and returned back again, so as it was impossible for them to do of themselves . . . Sometimes they were taken dumb, their mouths stopped, their throats choked, their limbs wracked and tormented so as might move a heart of stone to sympathize with them.*"

A doctor visited the girls. And, unable to find a scientific explanation, he labeled little Betty gripped by the Evil Hand.

"Gripped," Grandpa said, and looked me in the eye.

"Gripped," I repeated, and heard my voice dipping, my throat getting dry.

But who had bewitched the girls? Because back in those

days of Puritan New England life, witchcraft was a crime of grave proportions, and every crime must have a culprit.

"So what do the precious girls do, you think?" Grandpa asked. "The darling centers of absolute attention—in the house of a despotic father, in a village where the king of England has forbidden merriment, music, and dancing, where going to church is mandatory for three hours twice a week and only the Bible can be read, again, again, again? The girls cry out, *Tituba did it!* And at the fall of a dagger Tituba is seized. *Ay, masters, I did it, ay!"* Grandpa attempted his best seventeenth-century American slave impersonation. *"The Devil made me. The Devil is among us, here in Salem."*

To prove that the girls were bewitched, Tituba baked a witch's cake—rye meal and urine from the sick girls—and fed it to a dog. If the dog got ill, which naturally it did, then the girls had been put under an evil spell. *"Rye* meal," Grandpa said, and let that hang in the air with great severity.

And after this Tituba, herself given attention for the first time, spoke of demons who took the form of rats, dogs, wolves, and yellow birds. Of flying about the village on brooms. No doubt she too had been snacking on the witch's stew. And if Tituba was going down, why not drag the entire world with her? "I'm not alone!" she said in her confession, and pointed at one Sarah Osborne. That woman, Tituba said, was holding in her possession a devilish creature. Its head that of a girl, two long legs and wings, like a stork's.

"Yes, yes," the two little girls cried. "There are others who are guilty!" And so the naming farce began. And all across the village more little girls, and even women—lustful for attention and for power—began to fall down in demonic fits and sing the names of their guilty tormentors. Only yesterday they had been faceless and without a voice. Today they held the lives of others between their teeth. Vengeance was theirs.

For the people of Salem Village did not get along one bit. They argued about land, and property lines, and grazing rights. And the Reverend, poor Betty's father, had taken land and money he shouldn't have and he was favoring some families at the expense of others.

So they used bewitchment as an excuse to incriminate their enemies. And the mysterious witch's stew had poisoned only some of the girls (or maybe it was the spoiled rye?), while others had only acted sick, desperate for power and attention. The pieces of the puzzle were falling into place with an eerie accuracy. In the same way now, hundreds of years later, thousands of kilometers away, the poor, tortured girls of Klisura were rebelling against their fathers.

"And the girls from the upper hamlet?" I said. "What was the stew that got them sick?"

"Two years ago," Grandpa said, and searched through the folder of clippings, "I found this in the paper." He laid the article before me gently, with fear, as if he were laying down a newly hatched chick.

It had grown very cold around us and I realized the sun had almost set behind the hills. Something rustled in the corner; the beams above us creaked. Shivering, I strained my eyes to read the headline.

" 'Five Dead in Greece from West Nile Fever.' "

"Fifty kilometers from here," Grandpa said. For him what had happened three years ago was tragically simple. The girls had gone to the river to see the baby storks and gotten bitten by mosquitoes. The disease came with the storks, from Africa. One mosquito bit a sick stork, then it bit a healthy girl.

The sisters must have gotten sick with fever. But Aysha and the others didn't. And yet the rumors spread and was there ever a little girl who didn't crave attention? In a village like Klisura? With parents like these? So they started acting. And then Baba Mina came and fed kerosene to the fire.

"Grandma Mina?" I said. So she was the hag Elif had told me about? The one who'd inspected the girls, in Elif's yard, munching one clove of garlic after another? The poor old woman in black I'd seen at the bus station, whose swollen feet her husband had massaged? How many times had we come back from their house with buckets of fertilizer for our yard? How many times had she treated us to mint tea and stale cookies? Baba Mina, our very own Tituba.

"I know I could have saved them," Grandpa said, then returned the article to the folder and piled on top of it book after book. Watching him, I was reminded of something I'd learned in school, one of the cruel ways in which the witches of Salem had been put to death—the victim was crushed with stones, but gradually, each new rock carefully placed atop the one before until their collective weight grew unbearable, fatal.

"If only I'd gone with their father. I would have recognized they weren't acting. I would've made him call a doctor."

"Grandpa," I began, but stopped. What could I say to make him feel better? I reached across the desk and covered his hand, cold, like a stone. But mine was warm.

"So this explains the fire dancers, then? Saint Kosta's madness?"

He shook his head. "It explains what's happening in the village now. This ugly farce. But the fire dancers—" He stopped for a moment and his eyes drifted across the room as if he could see them, one after the other, jumping among the desks and vanishing into the walls. "They all went away, my boy. What good is it to seek them? They are no more."

"Were you really their leader?"

"I was a caretaker, yes. Never a leader."

"And who's to care for Aysha and the other girls? Who's to help them?"

He pulled his hand away from mine.

"In the Salem trials," he said, "they would blindfold the accused witch and bring her before her accuser, the so-called victim, thrashing in idiotic fits. And they would force the witch to touch the victim, who then conveniently grew calm at once. *You see*, they'd say, *the touch of the guilty hand caused the venom to rush back to the witch from whom it'd come*. My boy," he said, and stood up in the gloom, "I don't want that venom back in my blood."

· SIX ·

THE UNTHINKABLE HAD HAPPENED: the rain had stopped. I lay in bed, my ears ringing, and listened to a thousand noises that seemed so new—the scurrying of mice in the attic, the buzzing of crickets in the yard, the flapping of stork wings, and the rushing of water down the road, down the hills where trees rustled with the wind. I'd begun to compose a letter in my head—to no one in particular—hoping to give my thoughts some order. But my head was an oven into which someone was pumping gas and any minute now the spark would flash—I must help Aysha, I reasoned, because helping her was the decent thing to do. Because it was barbaric to watch the torture of a child and not interfere. Because if I helped Aysha, Elif would thank me. Elif would love me if I helped the little girl.

"What you said earlier, do you believe it?"

Grandpa spoke from the threshold. In the light of the oil

lamp he carried, his face burned like a wick; his shadow flowed behind him like a river and though he was old and wrinkled I thought of Lada, the goddess of youth and beauty, and then, once more, of Elif.

"Do you really believe I value land more than people? That I choose not to help the girls because of their father?"

"I'm a baker's shovel, Grandpa," I told him, only half as a joke. I could turn this way or that depending on whose hands held me. One moment I believed one thing, the next another. But I'm not sure he heard me.

"I first came to teach in Klisura when I was thirty-three," he said, and, cradling the lamp in his arthritic hands, he sat at the foot of my bed. "Right from my first day here, one predicament became very clear: there was no school. So I built it. And then another: there were no students. So I set forth to find them. I still remember two little twin boys. Lived up a hill with their father. Shepherds. I found them outside their hut, washing sheep bells in a trough of milk. So the bells might sing more sweetly, they told me. I sat in the grass and watched them, two boys and their father, dip bell after bell in yellow milk. I didn't ask them where their mother was. The sun was setting when they hung the bells to dry across a wooden framework behind the hut. The father picked up his boys, one in each hand, and let them shake the framework. The bells rang and their ringing rolled down the hill and up another where other shepherds rang other bells. Soon the whole Strandja was ringing, as far south as Turkey and even Greece.

"My boy," Grandpa said, staring into the fire locked behind the glass, "an old man's mind is a mountain, each memory a milk-washed bell. It's true, God holds the future, which is uncertain and unknown, so let him hold it. But the old man holds the past. The past is certain. No god can summon it before him and rearrange it at his will. The old man can. An old man walks hill to hill and rings the bells, and bids to appear in their sound the long-gone days—a day from fifty years back as loud as another not even a fortnight old. And so the gods grow jealous of the old man. They hold the Cup of Lethe to his thirsty lips. Tempted, he drinks. His feet grow weak and then he limps from hill to hill. His feet give way. Gone is the old man's strength to ring the bells.

"It's been too long a silence," Grandpa said, and closed his eyes. "I want to shake the wooden frame. I want my head to ring, from hill to hill across the Strandja."

His eyes were muddy when he blinked them open, the kind of mud I'd learned to fear.

"Grandpa," I said, "lie down. It was a hard day. Get some rest."

But he cradled the lamp and the fire and when he looked my way I knew it wasn't me he was seeing.

"I was seventeen that spring," he said. "May 1944. It had been a bad winter, so bad the Danube froze in places and a fever crawled in across the ice from Romania."

When the ice melted, the fever spread. Left and right people were burning. Children and women began to die. Whole families fled to seek shelter as far south as the Balkan Mountains. One dawn, Grandpa's cousin—he was a year older—came to his house, panting. "Pull up your britches," he cried, "and run with me to the square. They're recruiting men for heroic business." The elders from their village had met the elders from two others. They had decided to assemble a band of *kalushari* and send them from one house to another to chase the fever back whence it had come. When his cousin said *kalushari*, Grandpa's heart leapt like a kid goat. Had he not seen them as a little boy, passing outside his grandfather's house one morning on their way to cure the sick? Men like mountains. Bells on their sandals to raise a proper ruckus and scare the demons off. Their britches embroidered with silver and those silver threads flashing like bolts of lightning. Their shirts white like goose feathers, and on their chests bloodred kerchiefs like flapping wings. Daggers in their sashes, sabers and sickles in their hands, and sharpened cudgels with their bases shod in iron. Their eyes spilling fire, their jaws clenched so hard you could hear the bone crunching. And fresh herbs on their fur caps—smelling so sweet your eyes watered. One man walking in the steps of the other, grave and quiet, greeting no one and speaking to no one, not even to the little boy, running behind them. Sickness chasers, death hunters. And did Grandpa not remember how the maidens had watched them, misty-eyed, their long lashes flittering so quickly they raised the dust off the road in thick puffs? Filling their nostrils with the smell of the fresh herbs, with the men's sweat, licking and biting their red lips? And their hearts thrashing so hard under their plump bosoms that even he, the little boy, had heard their knocking and taken fright, though with pleasure?

"No girl can resist the *kalushari*," his cousin told him, as if Grandpa didn't know this already, and they flew off to the square. "If they choose me," his cousin said, "I'm taking Kera. So what if she's getting married? And that Sevda you've been pining over, she'll kiss your feet if they choose you."

"It's true, my boy," Grandpa said sweetly. "She was a beautiful girl, my Sevda. Lovely smile, eyes, bosom. But she didn't want me. 'Look at yourself,' she'd say, and her friends would giggle. 'My grandmother's mustache is thicker than the moss on your lip. A peach's moss is thicker. Grow a beard, man up a little. Then come again to ask me.'"

That morning all the boys from Grandpa's village gathered on the square. Only those older ones, who had run up to the woods with the Communist partisans, only they were missing. And the girls too came that morning, those devils, to ogle them. There was his cousin's Kera, though she was getting married, and there was his sweet, dear Sevda, eating a fresh pretzel and licking her red lips.

The boys formed a long line, shoulder to shoulder, and this giant, this colossus of a man, stood before them. His britches were embroidered with silver; his shirt was whiter than snowdrop petals. So white, Grandpa's eyes hurt to watch him. Geranium, dock, and wormwood adorned the giant's fur cap, and in his hand he brandished a cudgel, sharpened like a spear, with bells on its top and its bottom cast in copper. Three times the giant smacked the cudgel on the ground to get their attention, and three times the cudgel sang, its bells ringing.

"I am the *vatafin*," the colossus told them, "leader of the *kalushari*. My father was a *vatafin*, and my grandfather in Romania, he too was a *vatafin*. I've come here to choose six of you, muttonheads, the strongest, so we can go after the fever and wrestle her down, that serpent, and chop her three heads off."

The village elders were there on the square and so was the mayor. The gendarme had come to see if this circus was perchance partisan-related. Back then the tsarists were awfully scared of the partisans and they could sense that a bad storm was brewing. Even the priest had showed up fuming. Godless pagans, he called the people, and waved his iron crucifix in the air; but the women chased him away, the righteous, for hadn't he left their children dying?

Then the boys were given each a pick or a shovel. "Dig a

pit," the colossus ordered, and they dug a hole, one meter deep and five meters long, just like he wanted. A cart arrived full of chopped wood, and they built a fire there in the pit and when the flames burst out like so many tongues of the plague-fever, the boys crossed themselves three times, slack in the knees with terror.

"Whatever you do," his cousin whispered in Grandpa's ear, "don't shame yourself. The women are watching."

"My beautiful Sevda," Grandpa said, and his eyes moved left, right, left, as if she were skipping lightly before him. "The Fever took her three months later. Her smile, eyes, bosom—food for the maggots. We really were muttonheads, my boy, on the square that morning, standing before a pit spitting fire. Fever slayers and death chasers. He-goats with their balls bursting with pride and desire."

There, look, see the *vatafin* gripping his cudgel. See how he sprints to the pit, and pole-vaults it, right through the tall flames. His body—a steel blade, which the flames harden. Fever, he's saying, bow low before me. You can't scorch that which fire has scorched already.

One after the other, the boys take the cudgel, run to the pit, and try to vault it. One boy falls left, one falls right, one drops straight in the fire, and when the men pull him out his bottom is flaming. They beat the flames down with their fur caps, and the girls are laughing, pointing, and clapping.

"Poor soul, he's done for," his cousin tells Grandpa. And they both know it—the lame son of the miller will have a better chance of getting married than the boy with the charred bottom.

"Saint Elijah," Grandpa's cousin prays to his name saint when it's his turn to hold the cudgel. "Don't let some fire shame me." And he runs, digs the pole in the deep pit, shoots his legs forward, and lands on the other side safely, the fifth boy to do so in twenty.

One more boy left to be chosen and it's not even Grandpa's turn to jump yet. So each time someone new takes the cudgel Grandpa prays to Saint Elijah. "Saint Elijah, you're not my name saint, but if you let the fire pass me through, I'll slay my grandfather's rooster to give you *kurban*. Saint Elijah, if you make sweet Sevda love me, just once if you let me kiss those thick lips, I'll slay my grandmother's hens and chickens, the whole coop."

Then this boy, older, almost twenty, short like a pea but a strong fellow, he took the cudgel and leapt over the pit and through the fire and that was that. The sixth boy had been chosen.

"No," I cried, and threw away my blanket. There was no way this ended the story.

"From where I'm standing," Grandpa said, and nodded, "I can see the *vatafin* and the six boys, on the other side of the pit, through a curtain of fire. And the fire flows upward and turns their shapes to liquid. So I say, 'Saint Elijah, you just watch me.' And I say it out loud, so everyone hears it."

Muddy-eyed, Grandpa sprang up to his feet. Muddy-eyed, he looked about the room. He was there, on the square, a young boy ready to leap over the fire.

"Grandpa," I whispered, "watch out for the oil lamp." But he didn't hear me.

"So I dig my heels down in the ground," he almost shouted, and stomped the floor, "and I run like a *hala* and I leap over the pit and the tall flames—no cudgels, no sticks, no canes needed. You just watch me, Elijah, my arms wings and my feet carts of fire. Pull me down, Elijah, if you can. If you dare—stop me!"

"The lamp, Grandpa!" And when I pulled the lamp out of his hands he blinked, suddenly sober, and all the years came rushing back.

"So they took you with the *kalushari*?" I said, and threw a blanket on his shoulders.

"How could they not take me?"

"And did you give a *kurban* for Saint Elijah? Did you make Sevda love you and did you kiss her?"

"I gave him a *kurban*, my boy," he said, and his voice fell lower.

Day after day, he gave the saint one offering after another. He slaughtered roosters and chicks, and lambs and cows even. He burned barns and houses. He was up in the woods by then, with the Communist fighters, three months after jumping the fire. And they were raiding hamlets and sheep pens, and their brains were aflame with this new fever. And only when his cousin came up to find him, only when he said "They're burying Sevda tomorrow," did Grandpa go back to the village. But he didn't kiss her. They didn't even let him open the coffin because of her sickness. And her father came to him when it was over, when the earth had been piled up black and steaming, and said, "Weren't you with the *kalushari*? Why didn't you save her?" And Grandpa told him, "You muttonhead, that's all opium for the masses," and couldn't run fast enough back to his comrades, to give Elijah another *kurban*, bloodier this time so the saint would remember him by it forever.

What sadness overcame me to hear this. To picture my grandfather burning barns and houses. Raiding sheep pens, stealing lambs and fleeces. A Communist fighter. A bandit. Gone was the image of Captain Kosta, of the heroic rebel.

I recalled a story Grandpa once told me when I was little.

The story of how one day in the dugout he'd met a man, older than him, a schoolteacher from a nearby village. From his pocket, the man had pulled out a notebook. "You seem like a fool and fools are lucky," the man told Grandpa. "So if I die and you live, take this to my wife and children." Inside the book were letters, and between the letters the man had stuffed tiny petals of flowers, leaves of crane's bill and basil. Then he picked up a lump of black earth—it was an underground dugout they hid in—and smeared the mud on the first page. "For my children," he told Grandpa, "to see what I've seen." A month later the tsarists mowed down the man, and when that September the Communists seized control of Bulgaria, Grandpa found the man's widow and gave her the notebook. But the widow wouldn't take it. "I have no use for words and mud and dry leaves. I want a husband and my boys want a father." And she forced Grandpa to take two sacks of schoolbooks that had belonged to her husband.

Grandpa read the man's letters and then his schoolbooks. Then he hitched a ride to Pleven, walked straight to the university, never you mind that the semester was already half over, and signed up to study to be a teacher. Never you mind that he lacked a proper academic background. Hadn't he been a partisan fighter, and wasn't this more background than anyone ever needed?

Now in the light of the oil lamp, with the babble of water rushing down hills and dirt roads, and thunder booming across the border, I could see the barns burning and my grandfather gripping the torch that had set them on fire. And I wondered, was it only the shameful stories he had never told me; and if so, was this the reason he'd never mentioned the *nestinari* and the tree with their skulls in its branches?

"For a whole month," Grandpa was saying, "we had been

walking from one village to another, curing the sick and chasing the Fever."

The *vatafin* led them and so they followed in his footsteps, they the chosen ones, the *kalushari*. All day long they kept quiet, and if they spoke it was always in whispers. They didn't make the sign of the cross and when they ate a meal they didn't bless it. They marched in pairs, Grandpa's cousin beside him, in a chain that no stranger could break. They were not allowed to tread water. Why? Who could tell you? If they came to a small stream, they leapt over it with their cudgels; if they reached a river, they waited for a cart to take them across it. They sent a scout, the *kalauz* they called him, to let each village know they were coming and to look out for other bands of *kalushari*. Because such was the custom—no two bands were allowed to cross paths. "And if they do?" Grandpa asked the *vatafin*, and the *vatafin* pulled out his dagger and began to sharpen it.

"If only you could've seen me, my boy, prouder than a rooster. My chest bursting under the white shirt."

Every ten steps Grandpa would touch the daggers in his sash and rub their handles. He'd smack the cudgel against his thigh so the bells would ring, like beautiful girls calling him to their bedside. His blood was turning sour with desire. What did he care that people were sick and perishing? All he cared about was how the women looked at him when the *vatafin* led them into the house of the dying. They'd lay the sick man on a rug on the floor and gather around him, and one of the boys would blow up a bagpipe and play the *rachenitsa* so loudly Grandpa's teeth needled. They'd dance in circles around the sick man, slowly at first and then faster, and they'd hold the rug by its corners and toss the man up in the air a few times. Then the *vatafin* would break up the circle to rub the dying man with vinegar from head to toe. How the room reeked by then! A herd of rams sweating, jumping, and dancing. Then they'd leap over the sick man three times, bellowing, bleating, and braying. *Give me a woman!* Grandpa would shout, but no one heard him. And what the others shouted, no one could tell you. The *vatafin* would place a jug by the sick man, a jug full of cold water and fresh herbs, and the bagpipe would strike a new song, the *florichika*, so fast and fierce Grandpa went through a new pair of sandals every two days. They danced in circles until floor merged with walls and ceiling and the *vatafin* commanded the oldest boy to break the jug with his cudgel. And if the sick man jumped on his feet and ran out of the room when the jug shattered, if one or two of the boys fainted, that was a good sign. They'd chased away the Fever.

The sun was setting that day and they were rushing to get back to their village before the dark fell. Such was the custom. They had sent the scout ahead to make sure their passage was clear, but what good was he in their hurry? And sure enough, just at a crossroad, they met another band of *kalushari*, young boys like them, from some other village, like them armed and stupid. What really happened, Grandpa couldn't tell me exactly. Excitement overcame him. A great rush. One minute they were marching, quiet, the next they were throwing themselves at strangers, flinging daggers to slash them. Sure enough they slashed them. And they got slashed. When at last the commotion settled, when their blood cooled off a little, they sat down, the two bands together, to assess the damage. Only, one of the other band's boys wasn't moving, and when they looked closer—from his chest there stuck out a dagger. Someone whispered it was Grandpa's cousin who'd killed him. Someone else said he'd seen *Grandpa* drive in the dagger. Was it him, was it his cousin, was it another boy—who could remember? And Grandpa's head was splitting and his stomach was turning. So he retched in the bushes and his cousin followed. "If we return to the village," he said, "they'll hang us. For brigands like us, there is only one place now." And they ran through the bushes and up into the woods and they joined the Communist fighters.

After this Grandpa was quiet. The bells had stopped ringing, and he was at rest in their silence. But I wasn't; not after he'd gone back to his room, not after I'd seen dawn over the mountains. Why was my grandfather so stubborn, so reluctant to get involved with the *nestinari* again? If he recognized the whole thing as nothing but a charade, why not play along and help Aysha?

The imam sang for prayer and my thoughts swerved in a sleepless eddy. Forget the ringing bells, I muttered. Grandpa had tried to tell me something else with his story: don't bloody your hands with superstition, stay away from the madness. I tossed, turned, hid under the blanket. If I helped Elif find the *nestinari*, I was betraying Grandpa. But I was also helping Aysha. And if I helped Aysha, wouldn't Elif love me? Who in Klisura, other than Grandpa, knew how to cook a stew for witches?

· SEVEN ·

IF MY KNUCKLES MADE ANY NOISE rapping on that door, I couldn't hear it. Nor could I hear my own heart pounding, the wind gusting, and all through Klisura the broken window frames of empty houses knocking like lids of coffins, opening and closing shut. What I heard was these noises together in one big, messy loudness that grew messier, louder. One moment the moon shone and anyone could have seen me—slouched like a thief at the threshold—the next the sky was thick clouds and the world nothing but loudness.

"Open up, neighbors. It's the teacher's boy. The American."

Was it footsteps I heard on the other side or a voice calling? I couldn't be certain. So I knocked harder and then the door opened and Dyado Dacho stood before me.

"Good evening, Dyado," I greeted. "I've come to see Baba Mina."

All day before this I had been restless. And Grandpa had taken notice.

"I don't know what you're up to," he'd told me at dinner, "but I'll tell you this much: don't do it. Not for your own sake, but for Elif and Aysha's. When someone tells you his dog bites, you listen. You don't lend the dog your throat to see how deep its teeth can sink in. So now I tell you—don't test how deep the imam can bite us."

After dinner, I washed the dishes and waited for Grandpa to finish his smoke, say goodnight, and retreat to his room. Then I climbed out my window, thumped into the cassis bush underneath it like a sack of crab apples, and limped across the yard, down the road, and to our neighbors'.

"It's me, Grandpa, the American boy," I told Dyado Dacho now from the threshold, and he raised the oil lamp to see me better. The light flickered, almost went out with the wind, and he pulled it back fearfully, as if he wouldn't know how to relight the fire once he'd lost it.

"I've come alone," I told him. "Grandpa went to bed already."

I almost saw his mustache droop in disappointment, and for a moment I thought he'd shoo me away. But he coughed up a *Come in now, hurry!* with the rasp of someone who hadn't spoken in many hours, and slammed the door shut behind me.

The noise of the world shattered into its component parts. I could hear distinctly the grains of sand from the road knocking outside like knuckles, Dyado Dacho's stuffed nose whistling, and my heart beating right in my ears.

"Goes to bed with the chickens and hides like a chicken," Dyado Dacho said of Grandpa, and led me down a narrow hallway. "Maybe he'll start laying eggs soon. But I'd hide too if I played backgammon as lousy as he plays it. If I lost all my bets and never paid up."

"Does he owe you money?" I managed, following closely. The old man barked, coughed, laughed—whatever that noise he made was really.

"I don't rightly remember. But don't you dare tell him!"

The corridor seemed to grow narrower, the planks at our feet louder in their creaking. The deeper into the house we waded, the more the smells of naphthalene and mold thickened. The mold, I'd come to realize on a previous visit, was from the house, its own smell; the naphthalene was from Dyado Dacho. In every pocket of his wool jacket he kept a mothball and he bragged boldly that he hadn't seen a moth in thirty years. "Not since the devils ate up my best suit," he'd told me. His only suit. The one in which he'd gotten married. The one in which, he'd hoped, one day he would be buried. "Some people declare war on world famine," he'd told me on one occasion, "but I can't be that noble. I've declared war on the moth devils. And I aim to win it."

The room we entered was so hot, so stuffy the heat rushed at me like a bird fleeing its broken cage. A hefty fire burned in the fireplace and stretched Baba Mina's shadow gigantic against one wall. But she was a tiny thing in her chair, close by the fire, and she did not turn to see who it was that had entered. She was mumbling under her breath—words I had no chance of catching—and metal knocked on metal so crisply that for a moment I thought it was two knives she sharpened.

"She's been knitting for a week without stopping," Dyado Dacho said, and went to adjust the blanket—perfectly preserved from the moth devils—that covered her shoulders. "It keeps her busy."

Then he called her. "Grandma, the teacher's boy has come to see you." But the needles clattered so ferociously now, they overpowered even her mumble.

"Grandma," I said, and stepped closer. It was then that she looked up—her face flushed, but not a single droplet of sweat glistening in the light of the fire and her eyes shiny like a fox's.

"Ah, the teacher's boy." She smiled kindly. "The American."

I sat in the chair across from her, a chair Dyado Dacho offered before limping to his spot in the corner, farthest away from the heat of the fire. He took a sweater out of a sack at his feet and began to unravel it, pulling the strand from one sleeve and piling up the yarn in his lap.

"What are you knitting, Grandma?" I asked, for her needles had gone back to clicking.

"It doesn't matter," she told me. "When I'm done Dyado Dacho unknits it. Ah, my boy, I wish I too were a sweater. I wish God could reknit me young as I was back in those days."

Half my face was on fire and the other was catching it and sweat ran into my eyes and hurt them.

"Listen, Grandma, I've come to ask you about the *nestinari*."

Some time passed before she answered, so I wasn't sure she'd heard me. Only Dyado Dacho grunted in his corner. But then the clicking of the needles slowed down a little and I could see that she struggled to loop the yarn a few times.

"My sweet boy, don't ask me. My feet are colder than dead bones, but when I knit, I barely notice. Yes," she mumbled under her nose, "I barely notice," and wrapped herself more tightly in the blanket.

"Forty years ago," I said, "you and Dyado Dacho, and

most everyone else in the village, moved to the city to seek a better life. Tell me, Grandma, where did the *nestinari* settle when they left Klisura?"

"Forty years," Baba Mina repeated, as if for the first time stopping to consider just how much water had passed since then. "Back when I was little my daddy had a hundred white sheep. And each night we girls sat by the fire and spun wool as white as God's beard and Mama knit us booties and jackets and hats with tassels. But Daddy is gone now," she said, and the faint smile that had blossomed on her lips withered, "and so are the white sheep. Now all we have are old sweaters and Dyado Dacho unravels them, so I can knit from their yarn new ones. That's where the *nestinari* went, my boy— after the white sheep. One by one, like unraveled sweaters. Yes, yes," she said, and began to knit faster, "one by one, like white sheep."

"Grandma," I said, and for a long time didn't know how to continue. "It's Saint Kosta's day tomorrow." And by the way she looked at me—so gently, so helplessly—I understood, for the first time, that what I was doing was terribly cruel.

"It might be, my boy. But who's counting."

Sweat rolled down my back and itched me, and my tongue had swollen up so that every word rolled off crippled and clumsy. Or maybe it was just the ringing in my ears, the blood rushing, that muddied up all sound around me.

"There is a sick girl across the river, Grandma, the imam's daughter, and I'd like to help her. I'd like to take her to where the *nestinari* are dancing so they can cure her."

"And how will you do that?" Dyado Dacho sneered suddenly in his corner. "The girl's locked up and her father guards her."

"Elif will help me."

"And when she helps you, how will you get to where the *nestinari* are dancing?"

"In her father's Lada. We'll steal it."

"Steal it?" He laughed and yanked on the yarn so hard almost a third of a sleeve unraveled. "He dismembered it, the crazy fool. The whole café went to see how he gutted it. Slashed the tires, cut the wires, threw out the battery in the garbage. He was that mad with fury."

With each word I could feel my heart sinking, my plan unraveling like an old sweater. It was hopeless then and like Elif had told me—there was no way out of Klisura. The logs crackled in the fire, the needles were clicking, and I was ready to ask forgiveness and scurry back home to my grandfather, when Dyado Dacho stopped me.

"Every spring for many years I watch this poor woman get sick without a sickness," he said, his voice barely louder than the rasp of sand grains against the window. "I'm tired of watching. I'll tell you where the *nestinari* are dancing if you promise to take her."

I hadn't even noticed when he'd gotten up from his chair and come to ours, but Baba Mina held his hand now, against her cheek, then kissed it.

"And what if you tell me?" I said. "We have no car to get there."

"Then leave the way you came here."

I wasn't sure if he meant this, or if he was trying to trick me.

"On the village bus? The driver will never take us."

Then I could see his lips stretching and his dentures shining like they were made of the fire. "Why bother to ask him?"

· EIGHT ·

IT SO HAPPENED, SIX CENTURIES AGO, that Murad the God-like One—he who first called himself sultan, he who defeated a great many peoples, seized their land, and made from his Ottoman tribe a mighty empire—fell in love with a Bulgarian maiden and desired to wed her.

Murad's armies had conquered Adrianople and turned it into their capital city. There in Adrianople, the Godlike One plotted his European expansion. The Byzantines were already paying him tribute, and their turn to meet him in battle would come soon, but it was other wars Murad needed to plot first—with Bulgarians, Serbians, Magyars. Not a fortnight before, he had sent his spies into the land of the Bulgars and now the spies were recounting—such and such strongholds, such and such armies. Only one of them was gloomy, and when the sultan addressed him, the man began weeping. "I weep for you, my lord," he said, "because I love you. You may conquer the world one day, but what good is this if you never see them?" And the spy told him: where a mighty river flowed into the Black Sea, where the sands were the color of Makassar ebony, beautiful women danced barefoot in the fire and the fire did not burn them. "No, my lord, the flame makes them so pretty it is for them that I weep now. For I shall never again see them."

For days all Murad saw were the bare feet of maidens dancing on live coals. The feet, white and puffy, raised sparks in his mind and like tired birds these sparks landed on his heart and burned it. Soon enough, the great sultan was standing aboard a fast boat, and three hundred other boats followed behind him. At the place where a mighty river flowed into the Black Sea there was a village and in no time its elders were bowing before the sultan. "I've come to see the women dancing," he told them, "so start the fires!"

A thin crescent hung in the sky by the time the wood had turned to embers. And since Murad's feet never touched land that the blood of his men had not made pure first, he waited in the boat, right by the black shore. No wind stirred the night and only the sea sighed deeply. Sorrow filled the sultan's heart. He had accomplished so little and there was still so much more that needed doing. As it happened with each nightfall, his grandfathers rose within him, lustful for conquests, and began to pull him eagerly in a thousand directions. How tired he was. How weary. And if Allah had come to ask him what he wanted, in this very moment, he would have said, "A sigh of rest, Almighty, in a boat by a black shore, waiting for beautiful women."

A drum began beating in the night; a bagpipe joined it. So deep had the sultan sunk in thought that he hadn't noticed anyone coming. And so it seemed to him now that the flame took flesh—a girl in a white robe, with her hair so long it almost touched the embers and white like the bones of the world. Then the girl gave out a loud shriek, and when she threw back her head her hair really swept the embers; its ends crackled and the stench of battle filled the air.

This was an omen, Murad knew. But good or bad, he wasn't certain. More girls rose from the fire and he watched them carry their infidel icons, jumping and thrashing, crying like flame birds from the Arabian Desert. Soon he didn't see the others—only the girl with the white hair.

He could not wait for the dance to be over. He waved to his soldiers to stop the drum from beating, the bagpipe from shrieking, and he called the girl to come near. Yet the girl wouldn't listen. She kept spinning and turning and so the sultan ordered his men to bring her over. Embers had stuck to her bare feet, to her long gown, and when she waded into the sea the water hissed and smoke rose in thick puffs.

What fool, she said angrily in his language, *dares stop my drum from beating? What fool pulls my girl out of the fire?*

For such words, many a head would have rolled already. But Murad only smiled softly. "Get in the boat," he told her, "I'm taking you with me." The girl's hair floated around her, like a thing living, and for a moment the sultan watched it. A strange feeling bloomed in his heart—that he had met this girl before, that he had always known her. When next he looked up, more girls in white gowns had surrounded his boat like jellyfish flocking.

These are my girls, one of them said to his left, and then another: *And if you want one, I'll let you have her.*

On one condition, a girl said to his right, and to his left a girl repeated, *Yes, yes, on one condition.*

They're mad, Murad was thinking, an evil jinn has

possessed them. But he could not look away from the girl with the white hair.

Give her a drum, some other girl uttered.

Give her a bagpipe, cried another, though which one he couldn't tell rightly—they all spoke too quickly.

Let her finish her dancing.

Yes, yes, don't wake her before the dance has finished.

And when you conquer the Bulgars . . .

. . . slay them all if you wish to . . .

. . . but the land my girl crosses dancing . . .

. . . you must swear to protect it.

You must allow my girls to do their dancing.

Swear it, they cried. *Swear it!*

And before Murad knew it, he, the Godlike One, the first great sultan, had sworn an oath for the ages.

"Whatever land the dancing girl crossed in her trance, he would protect it. The Christians who lived on it would be allowed to keep their churches; the *nestinari* to do their dancing. They would pay almost no taxes. And when a Turk reached their border he dismounted and his horse was unshoed at a smithy. Then he led it on foot to the other side, to another smithy, where the shoes were nailed back on. All this they wrote down in a firman. And the land the girl crossed dancing they called the Hasekiya, from *haseki*, or *the favorite wife of the sultan*. But the girl never lived to see Murad, her husband—"

"Why didn't she?" Elif whispered. We were hiding in the barn at the back of their house now because, well, what better place did we have for hiding? I had chucked pebbles at her window and she had led me across the dark yard.

"Sneeze once and my father will kill us," she'd said, and pulled me behind a bale of rotting hay.

"He might kill us without me sneezing." Then I'd told her about my visit to Baba Mina's; about Murad and the girl dancing, though not nearly in so much detail.

For seven days the girl danced in her trance, the drum drumming behind her. Not once did she stop to eat or drink water. Seven, fourteen, seventeen villages she encircled and still she kept dancing. And in his boat Murad waited for the jinn to release her. But on the eighth day a messenger reached him—the Serbian armies were marching against Adrianople. "Return at once, my lord. The men need you!"

How could he leave this beach, this girl he had fallen in love with, in the hands of a dark jinn? Despite himself, the sultan called for a white horse; despite himself he rode it across impure lands. The sun was setting by the time he found the girl, still dancing, her feet bleeding from wounds, her hair thorns and nettle. Off the ground he picked her; by his side he sat her, on the white horse.

Don't wake my girl before the dance has finished, the jinn cried, with her lips.

"But he woke her," Elif said, anticipating the end of the story.

"Where Murad left the dead girl lying," I said, "today there stands a white boulder. Wind and water have undercut it and shaped it to look like a lone tree."

I pulled out a postcard—one that Dyado Dacho had given me, old and wrinkled as it was—and shoved it in Elif's hands.

"I can't see anything," she said, and lit a lighter for only a moment. Though of course, a moment would have been plenty for the hay around us to catch on fire.

"A stone tree on a black beach," I said. That's what the postcard was showing.

"I've heard of it," Elif said. "Byal Kamak. A tiny village."

"Where a mighty river flows into the Black Sea."

"The Veleka River!" she said, perhaps more loudly than she had to.

"Where the sand is black with silt from the river."

"Dear God," she whispered. "Where the *nestinari* settled after they left Klisura!"

· NINE ·

I BELIEVE OUR PLAN was doomed from the very beginning. And I believe we all knew it. We weren't stupid. So wrote Captain Kosta—leader of the Strandjan rebels against the Ottoman armies. Or at least, so I'd read in Grandpa's papers. The poor captain had thrown himself in the enemy's jaws not because he had expected to crush them. He had done so because, in his own words, *to sit still and do nothing would bring a defeat greater and more shameful.* And so, I suppose, our plan too was doomed from the very beginning. And I suppose we too knew it.

What the plan consisted of was fairly simple. On the afternoon of May 21, the feast day of Saints Constantine and Elena, Dyado Dacho would wait for the bus at the square. "I have come to collect what you owe me," he'd tell the driver, and when the driver tried to wriggle out of paying, the old man would make him a tempting offer. "Three out of five. Double or nothing." So, seeing how there was a lot worse he could be doing than playing some backgammon, the driver would shut off the engine, and, leaving the keys in the ignition, where he always left them, he'd follow Dyado Dacho to the Pasha Café. Three out of five would soon turn into four out of seven, and so would the glasses of mint and *mastika*. And as these things so often happened, before too long the two of them would find themselves locked in and peacefully snoring on the bench in the corner.

Night would have fallen over Klisura. The imam would call from the minaret for the day's final prayer, Elif's cue to lead Aysha down to the square. Baba Mina and I would be waiting already. We'd climb on the bus, start the engine, and drive eastward—thirty kilometers to the village of Byal Kamak. All this under the premise that by the stone tree, where the Veleka entered the Black Sea, there would be *nestinari* dancing.

It's not courage that drives us. It's not madness. It's hunger for freedom. This Captain Kosta had written, a hundred years before me, and this I was repeating now on the square, behind the unlocked bus, with Baba Mina beside me. Night had fallen. The driver had eaten up Dyado Dacho's bait, hook, line, fishing rod, and all. The imam was singing. But there was no sign of Elif and Aysha.

"Are you cold, Grandma?" I whispered, then took off my jacket and covered her shoulders.

"I'll get warm soon, my boy," she answered. "Saint Kosta will warm me up."

The imam's voice flowed out of Klisura, across the hills, and the village was quiet. A dog barked far in the distance and a stork swooped down from the roof of the municipal building and spun a wheel overhead. Baba Mina clasped my waist like a frightened child.

"Don't let him take me," she whispered. "The black stork." Whether the stork was really black or only appeared to be, I couldn't tell. Nor did I have time to investigate. The metal ropes of the bridge creaked in the darkness, and footsteps echoed over the noise of the river fattened on rain. A silhouette took shape before us. And then another. And when I saw a third shape approaching, my heart leapt and I thought of running.

"It's over," I think I told Baba Mina, and in her fear she squeezed my waist harder.

But then we heard Elif speaking. The plan, she told us, had changed a little. And soon I recognized her and Aysha and beside them their mother.

· TEN ·

THEN THE KEY WAS NOT IN THE IGNITION.

"Of course I'm certain," I cried from the driver's seat. "I'm groping the ignition and the key isn't in it." It was so dark inside the bus that I saw nothing but dim shapes. Baba Mina rocked and mumbled behind me, and her seat creaked with every rock and mumble. Aysha said something and then her mother cried, "There, he's coming. He's found us!" but it was only a stork flying across the square and so she spat in her shirt to chase away the fear.

A wave of irritation washed over me. After all, I had been the one to mock the driver for keeping the key in the ignition. Now, as a reaction, he'd either taken it with him, which I doubted, considering how afraid he was of losing it when drunk, or hidden it somewhere in the cabin. So we searched, in the flame of Elif's lighter. A pair of oversized green dice hung from the rearview mirror, so I shook them, hopeful, but nothing rattled inside. Every so often, the flame burned Elif's thumb and we sat in darkness while she blew on the flint wheel to cool it. Then there was light for a few more seconds.

"Piece-of-shit lighter," she cursed at one point. "We'll run out of gas soon."

A tiny icon of the Virgin Mary was taped to the dashboard, so I untaped it and looked for the key on its back. A faded picture of long-haired Hristo Stoichkov in his Barcelona jersey. A clipping of Lepa Brena and a green pine tree that stank of cigarette smoke and naphtha. And then, just when Elif flicked on the light one final time before the gas ran out, I saw it—a dark outline, only faintly showing behind a glorious picture. Samantha Fox, patron saint of all bus drivers from my childhood. And tucked behind her magnificent bosom—the key to our freedom.

That I could drive the bus came as a surprise to Elif. So I told her: my father had taught me how to drive stick shift; for him, no real man drove automatic. And if she didn't mind, this time *I* wanted to be the one to drive us. The plan was mine and I intended—

"Watch the road!" she yelped behind me, though I had taken the turn quite nicely. We were crossing a patch of eroded pavement and that's why the bus rattled. But the farther away from Klisura we drove, the smoother the road became; the less wild the oaks on both sides, the softer the wind that shook them.

"Isn't that something," Elif sneered, because she too had noticed the world grow less feral around us. I wondered if the others too would notice. Baba Mina rocked and mumbled and so did Aysha, oblivious to the outside, every now and then stopping to synchronize her rocking with the old woman's. But Elif's mother was paying attention. Of that I was certain, though she sat in her seat as still as a stone tree.

How long had it been, I wondered, since she had last left Klisura? Ten years? Or maybe twenty? I tried to imagine what she was feeling. All her life, like a silk moth, she had weaved for herself another woman, a shell to contain her passions, hatreds, and fears. A shell in which she could hide safely. It was this cocoon that had learned to absorb a bad word, a slap to the face, a great disappointment. But in time, the shell had turned into a prison and with her passions, hatreds, and fears, this poor woman too had found herself devoured.

The road twisted beneath us, rough and uneven, and the rearview mirror shook wildly. Elif's mother sat stiff behind me, but in the mirror her reflection jumped and twisted. It occurred to me that the mirror showed her as she was truly. No shells. No prisons. Just a frightened woman, trembling with excitement. A runaway, if merely for a short while, her own, true mistress. And I knew then that beneath the stiffness this woman was fighting a giant struggle—to crawl back in the shell, afraid and defeated, or to step outside, a victor.

"Watch the road, damn it!" Elif cried again, and this time our turn was less gentle. I offered an apology, blamed the road, and was glad when soon it evened out and with it my driving. Earlier that day, I had studied my tourist map in careful detail, though in reality the chance for an error wasn't that big. The road led to the town of Sinemorets, and all we had to do was follow it to the first exit, then drive down another, smaller road that would take us to the mouth of the Veleka.

"My daddy also taught me driving," a thin voice said over my shoulder. "I too am a good driver." I realized this was the first time I'd heard Aysha speak, save for the small *thank you* when I'd given her an apple. Her voice was pretty, like Elif's, but cleaner the way springwater is cleaner than water from a river. So I let her sit in my lap and her small hands gripped the wheel and she said I too should hold it just to be on the safe side. She'd never driven a bus before, but she'd driven the Lada. And she'd never before seen the Black Sea. Had I?

"I've never seen it," I lied, and watched Elif watch me in the mirror.

"Are you excited to see it? I'm really excited."

But it was sadness I felt, not excitement. I thought of Grandpa, whom I had lied to only an hour before. He'd asked me to play backgammon out on the terrace and I'd said my head ached, that I was tired. Goodnight, I'd said, and he'd looked at me with such hurt. I know you're lying, his eyes had told me. I know you're up to something.

All this time I'd worked hard to avoid one question, but now, as the road unfolded in the light of the high beams, it was this one question I kept on asking. What the hell was I doing? Aysha wasn't sick; no saint had possessed her. She was anxious to see the Black Sea, not to jump in a fire. And if she'd seen it, as by now any girl her age should have, especially one who lived this close to the coast, none of this would have happened. And her mother wasn't sick, nor was Baba Mina, an old and senile woman. I was the sick one. And Elif knew it. I could tell by her face in the mirror. And she knew another thing—how to make me sicker.

"You two look a great item," Elif said, and came to the dashboard. She pushed the bus lighter deeper into its slot and then pressed the orange coil to the tip of her cigarette.

"Keep your hands on the wheel where I can see them," she said, "American boy," and blew out smoke from her nostrils.

At first I thought she was joking.

"I'm joking," she said. "Dear God, take it easy."

But she wasn't. She really was jealous.

"Aren't you a stuck-up bastard," she said when I refused to grace her with a smile, and going back to her seat she let out a fake laugh.

"I too would like a cigarette," someone said behind me. Even when I saw her fixing the ends of her headscarf that didn't really need fixing, I still didn't believe it was their mother speaking. "It's been twenty-two years," she said when Elif passed her the smoking cigarette. Then a cough choked her.

"American," her voice wheezed once the cough was over. "If the radio's working, I sure would like to hear it."

I fumbled with the knob, terribly excited, awfully happy for her. It was hard to lock onto a steady station. The same frequency gave us a Turkish voice one moment, a Greek the next. Even here an invisible battle was being waged—for dominion over the very air we breathed. At last I managed to capture a decent transmission—Bulgarian folk music, *rachenitsa*, fast-paced, energetic.

"Is this good? Or should I keep searching?" I asked Elif's mother.

"If you wish to," she said. Then her voice dipped so much I barely heard it, but when she spoke again, her voice was more confident, louder, and she had stepped, for the first time, outside the cocoon that held her. "Wait. I like it this way. Leave it the way I like it." And after this, she sat as before, but not at all the same.

We drove like this for fifteen minutes. Then, as the map

had predicted, we came to an exit. The new road was so narrow, a car coming in the opposite direction would have had to pull over to let us pass. The pavement had given way to dirt and pebbles and again we shook and rattled.

Somewhere close in the dark the Via Pontica stretched northward. Or at least what little remained of that ancient Roman route, a road of tsars and great armies, so efficient in its layout that even the storks followed it in their journey. How many of the pebbles below us came from that old road? How many from crumbled fortresses and ruined houses? And in the dark, somewhere beside us, parallel to our movement, the Veleka River too moved toward the Black Sea. It had moved like this for thousands of years—before us, before the tsars or their armies—and it would move, much the same way, for thousands of years after we were done and dusted. The streams in Turkey had given it birth when there had been no Turkey. The streams in Bulgaria—fresh life, when there had been no Bulgaria. And in the end, the Black Sea took it the way it took all the rivers, without concern for what country they came from. In the end, it was all water changing form— from rain to river to sea to cloud back to rain again, an everlasting motion.

I held my hand up so Elif could see it, and without words, she passed me the cigarette. How I had not realized it was a joint they were sharing, I'm still not certain. I took a deep toke and held the smoke in so it could burn me and soon my head was a bit lighter. Unlucky people, I thought, and passed the joint back. To be born here. Our balkans were fire dancers, rising from ashes to flames back to ashes. And of all the seas in the world, it was ours that was the black one. Yes, yes, I said, and took another puff when Elif offered. It was the sea I felt now, ahead in the night through which we journeyed. It was the sea that had spoken to me, like a woman in mourning, and I could not bear to hear all she was saying.

"Aysha," I said, "turn up the music."

She turned the volume all the way up and I took one last drag before I rolled down the window. Cool night tangled around us like waves of seaweed. The road lifted us up a small hill, down, up another. And when we'd climbed a high point, when I could lick salt on my lips, Aysha gave out a stunned cry and slammed the horn as hard as she could slam it. Where I'd heard a woman in mourning, she had seen the sea for the first time.

· ELEVEN ·

THE ROAD was two deep ruts now with dry grass waving between them. The oaks had given way to shorter trees, which
in turn had morphed into tall bushes. Branches scratched
the bus and lashed the windshield and so I had rolled up the
window. And just when I was thinking that we were running
a fool's errand, that we had come to a place with nothing
but thicket, a pair of brake lights flashed ahead in the darkness. In no time we overtook a row of cars parked in the bushes
and then people hiking in a thin file.

"Road gets mad from here on, bro," a young guy told me
when I rolled down the window. "But you're on a bus, you
know. It's like, what do you even care?" Then he glued himself to the door, stood on his tiptoes, and, sniffing the air, tried
to peek in. "Bro," he said, "you got room for one more?"

"Why was his hair green?" Aysha asked once we were
back in motion.

"And why are they all blowing whistles?" Elif added, because really it was whistles that sounded behind us. "Bro," she said, and burst out laughing.

Next we overtook a group of pensioners with backpacks and then more kids with colorful hair who hopped up the road like rabbits and brandished green, red, and blue glow sticks. Aysha punched the horn and giggled and again the night answered with a barrage of whistles. I caught myself thinking of the Strandjans who spoke like songbirds in their ancient language, of Captain Kosta, and then of Grandpa; of how hurt he'd looked to see me lie and go to bed so early.

The road had turned lunar. We crawled out of one crater and into another, up a hill in first gear. Lost in thought, I let the engine slip and stall a few times. Then the road was so narrow I was certain we'd keel over. The back tires sunk in a rut and spun a dead spin, but somehow we managed.

"Vah, vah, vah," Baba Mina shrieked suddenly behind me. "Here, Saint Kosta. I'm coming."

At once her shriek chased away all merriment in the air. At once, Aysha stiffened in my lap and her feet kicked a few times. "Vah, vah, vah," she repeated, "we're coming, Saint Kosta," and her teeth chattered like a stork's bill.

It was a bonfire they'd spotted on the beach in the distance—tall flames, which the wind twisted and stretched upward. This was the beach with the stone tree, the strip of land between sea and river where the *nestinari* should be dancing. The sky had clouded over and the sea was nothing but blackness, but there were boats in the river and that's how I saw it. One, two, three . . . I counted seven boats in total, illuminated by torches and lanterns and loaded with tourists.

We drove past a few parked buses and their passengers already walking. And when there was no more road to keep on, I turned off the engine and pressed the doors open. The air, until recently so heavy with salt and seaweed, now stank of grilled meat. Drums were beating from all directions, not together, but each on its own, a chaotic commotion that the sea wind tossed like sand in handfuls.

"Don't be afraid, Grandma," I told Baba Mina once the crowd took us. "Hold my hand and don't let go." She seized me as if she were drowning, as if I were a branch to the rescue. The excess of noise and color had overwhelmed me, but her it had frightened beyond words. For an instant, a thought uncoiled—it was a mistake to bring Baba Mina, a mistake to come here. But before I could really think it, the thought had flown by and into the sea of people.

"Elif," I called. "Stay closer!" And her hand burned mine when she caught me.

"I'm this close to panic," she cried, then she called for her mother to keep hold of Aysha. "Was that my father I just saw or is it the weed talking?"

Voices mixed and swept us up in a deluge—Russian, German, English. *Antonio*, someone was yelling to one side. *Bystro*, someone else was crying. A hand brushed my shoulder and I jumped, startled, but it wasn't the imam, just some French kid looking for something. My heart was racing, my chest constricted like it was wrapped around with duct tape. And from the heat of the bodies my mind misted. I thought I was seeing a caravan of riders, flowing down a dune in the distance, each holding a bright flame; riders like the ones I'd seen painted on the walls of Elif's house. Then lightning flashed in my eyes and when I blinked away the blindness I found myself not ten feet from a giant camel. On the camel, flooded with more light, a woman in a bathing suit was posing for pictures.

"Elif!" I cried. "Grandma!"

Somehow I'd lost them. I scurried from one face to another, bumping into strangers. A few times I plopped nose-down in the sand—large grains, more grayish and dirty-looking than actually black. My shoes and socks filled up quickly and with each step the sand scratched and burned me. By now the caravan of riders had gotten closer and really it was men on horses, Russian soldiers—no, tourists . . . Whistles sounded and drums were beating. I ran this way and that until at last the beach widened and the crowd spread out and it was then that I saw it. Awash with light from the bonfire, thin in its trunk, wide in its crown, as tall as a horse and its rider: the stone tree. And Elif and the others, by the fire, watching in silence.

"All it's missing are the stork nests," she told me once I joined them.

And the skulls in the branches, I wanted to say, but didn't. Baba Mina had caught me by the waist and held me tightly.

"It's all right, Grandma," I said softly, but I'm not sure she heard me. She stared into the fire, and I knew she could see something in it I couldn't. She saw herself as she had been—young and pretty. At her feet, back then, not just glowing embers but the entire world. Back then she could trample the embers and they wouldn't burn her. She could trample the world and the world yielded. Go ahead, my girl, the world told her, trample me, kick me. You're young and pretty, your whole life is before you. Why should I stop you?

The fire burned and Baba Mina held me and much the same way, Aysha hugged her mother, and much the same way the two watched the flames grow shorter. What did the flames show them, I wondered. What did they show me?

Elif, right beside us. Every strand of her short hair radiant, orange. Her face aglow. Her eyes blazing. Not watching the fire, but watching me and seeing, now for the first time, that I too was courageous and daring, a real rebel.

By now, my lips were chapped and swollen; my stomach was hurting with hunger. I had seen a vendor at some point, selling grilled meats, and I imagined how sweet a *kebabche* would taste right at this moment. Slowly the fire died down before us and embers blinked open like red eyes. Then out of the darkness three young men stepped forward. They were dressed in traditional costumes—white shirts, black trousers, red sashes—and after they'd lit a line of torches in the sand they began to spread the embers in a circle with long rakes. Each time the rakes smashed a piece of charred wood to smaller pieces, sparks flew up and the wind whirled them in thick swarms.

Their shirts white like goose feathers, I remembered Grandpa saying, though it was of other men he'd spoken. The *kalushari*, men for heroic business.

The sea boomed on one side while the river flowed silent on the other and more people gathered below the stone tree to watch the spreading of the embers. Cameras were flashing and whistles were blowing, horses and camels bellowed, and from the dark I heard the splashing of water and drunk boys and girls crying that the sea was freezing.

Then for an instant the world grew quiet: Elif had leaned her head on my shoulder.

"Thank you," she whispered, and when I looked at her, she was crying. I touched her cheek gently, warm as it was from the fire, and brushed away her tears. When my knuckles passed her lips she kissed them. She kissed my fingers. And I knew in that moment that if we were to get caught now, if we fell into real trouble, it wouldn't matter. To stand the way we were standing, together on a black shore, made all future trouble worth bearing.

It was after this that a bagpipe cut the night from throat to navel. A drum pounded to silence all others. From behind the stone tree came out the piper, the drummer, and the night turned day with all the cameras flashing.

Baba Mina tensed up beside me. "Vah, vah," she whispered, but the whisper choked her. The piper stood on one side of the glowing circle, the drummer stopped on the other, and I wondered if this was what Murad the Godlike One had seen from his boat, six centuries back, like us waiting for women to come out dancing. Was this a tree or the girl with the white hair, or was it simply a boulder that winds and tides had disfigured?

The music flowed louder; the drum beat faster and my heart tried to keep up with its beating. In the light of the torches I could see a group of Japanese tourists toying with their cameras, the lenses so long they almost touched the embers. And a few kids with colorful hair swaying with the drum, waving their hands, and scratching green lines in the dark with their glow sticks.

"What the hell is he doing?" Elif whispered, but she didn't have to point. On one side of the circle a shirtless man struggled to take off his left shoe. He'd already taken off the right one. Dirty sand glistened on his fat belly—like me, he too must have rolled on the ground a few times.

"Hey, back off," someone cried, but the man wouldn't listen. Before we knew it, he'd jumped in the embers and taken a few wobbly steps to the circle's center. I still don't know why the crowd started laughing. Maybe because his screams struck us as too high-pitched for such a big guy; maybe because he was calling for his mommy in Russian. Before long, he was out of the fire, but even after the men in the white shirts had carried him off to the darkness we could still hear him calling.

"That ought to teach him a lesson," someone said behind us.

"Fat Russian bastard," someone else said, laughing, and unexpectedly a wineskin was shoved into my hands.

"Take a sip, pass it forward," a girl told me.

"What's in it?"

"Divine nectar. What do *you* think's in it?"

It was wine—thin and sour and tasting like leaves of geranium. I knew the taste; even in America my mother had insisted on adding the herb to our Christmas Eve compotes.

"Where did you get this?" Elif asked when I passed her the wineskin. But she didn't wait for an answer. She gulped and the wine trickled down her chin and glistened.

Then her mother drank, then Baba Mina, and even Aysha took a few small sips.

"Easy now," I told her, but someone laughed behind me.

"Let her have it. It's better than milk and honey."

For a while we watched the embers glowing and white smoke rising every time the rakes spread them thinner. Baba Mina took tiny steps in her place, and so did Aysha, keeping her eyes now on the old woman, now on the live coals. But her mother stood calmly and when the wineskin made it around the circle once more she took another deep gulp. She seemed victorious now, away from her husband, liberated if only for a few hours.

One by one, the men began to extinguish the torches.

The music fell silent and we heard down the beach, where I imagined the Veleka entered the sea, the sound of another bagpipe, of another drum coming near. A shush spread through the crowd. Whispers and sighing. "They're coming," a Bulgarian said on one side. "*The nestinari*," said a woman in English, and the word sounded so funny in a language that didn't contain it.

The cameras flashed impatiently and out of their flashing the piper was first to appear. I'd never seen a bagpipe like this one: the head of the kid-goat from whose skin the bag was made preserved perfectly; the glassy eyes and black horns reflecting each new flash. *Ah*s and *oh*s moved the crowd and the cameras flashed even more greedily. The drummer followed and then the *nestinari*. Light chased darkness in a mad alternation and made their movements appear sharp and choppy. They cut through space like specters, now in one place, now in another. A young man carried a giant icon, half covered with a cloth as red as his sash. A young girl followed behind him, and in her steps another man and another girl, all carrying icons. Their bare feet kicked up sand as they weaved a circle around the spread embers.

"They're so pretty," Elif whispered, and again rested her head on my shoulder, this time without tears. The music picked up—the other bagpipe and drum had joined in. I saw that a large smile was stretching Aysha's lips and she was clapping to keep rhythm. Her mother too was smiling and clapping and neither of them seemed even remotely interested in entering the fire. Could it be this easy, I wondered, to cure their sickness?

But Baba Mina wasn't smiling. She'd stopped taking her tiny steps, and when she turned to me, her face twisted in fear. I understood that all I'd imagined—how she saw herself in the fire, young and pretty—all that was nothing but hogwash.

"Take me home, my boy," she whispered, and reached for my hand, but couldn't grab it.

"It's all right, Grandma," Elif hushed her. She put her palm on the old woman's shoulder and kissed her head through the black kerchief. "Let's watch the dancing. Aren't they pretty?" Baba Mina mumbled something—maybe the crowd had spooked her—and the bagpipe shrieked so near now that all other sound disappeared.

The first man carried his icon across the embers, his feet taking quick steps, kicking up sparks and raising white smoke. One of the women followed. The drums beat faster and the second girl jumped in the embers and carried safely across them the image of the Holy Virgin. It was a beautiful moment: the girls so pretty, the men so strong and courageous. And yet I couldn't feel this beauty. The whistles had renewed their blowing. The crowd clapped and cheered the way a crowd cheers at a football game. A bitter taste filled my mouth. It was not an ancient mystery we were witnessing, but a show for the tourists—as strange and exotic as they wanted to see it.

"This isn't right," I told Elif. My head had started to spin from the weed and the wine and the people, and I felt my stomach rising. "You watch them, I'll be back in a minute."

The beach was littered with bottles and cigarette butts and making-out couples. Boys and girls ran half naked along the shoreline and jumped in the sea, screaming. But in the darkness, the air was cooler and so fresh my head cleared quickly. How sad it was to be standing not ten feet from the sea and not see it. How awful to be looking at embers and fire dancers and not feel them. Anger choked me—not just at the drunken tourists, but at the pipers, the drummers, the *nestinari*. And I would have felt low and angry a long time if at that moment a car hadn't roared in the distance.

People yelled, others were laughing, and I watched the car, a jeep really, fly through the beach toward the dancing. Not sure why, I started running. I tripped and rolled in the sand, sprinted faster. A dull sickness lodged itself in my stomach. The jeep, like the one Orhan had driven, had stopped not twenty feet from the dancing and the crowd had broken up the circle, blinded by headlights.

I can't say I was surprised to see the imam climb out. All night, I'd been seeing him in more than a few faces. But to see my grandfather come out of the jeep surprised me. He stood by the front bumper and for a while fought the wind to light a cigarette. The bagpipes were still shrieking, the drummers still beating, and the *nestinari* kept dancing, but no one watched them. All eyes were on the imam, while his eyes were searching. He hadn't said one word even and his wife was already walking in his direction. Her head down, she climbed in the back of the jeep, inside the old, wretched cocoon. She untied her headscarf and spread it over her face to hide it.

Elbowing my way through, I found Elif and Aysha. They held hands, completely frozen in the headlights. And Baba Mina stood beside them, equally frozen. The imam was only a shadow and wind swept the sand at his feet in black puffs. Behind him, Grandpa was smoking, the tip of his cigarette a glowing ember.

"I'm not going," Elif whispered. I'm not sure if she

meant for her father to hear it, or me, or if it was to herself she was speaking. But other people heard her.

"Hey, bro," someone called to the imam, "leave the girl to do her thing."

"It's a free country!"

"I'm not going," Elif said a second time, louder. I felt like she wanted me to reach for her hand and hold it; to give her strength and courage; to pin her down like an anchor. And yet I couldn't move a muscle. And so she drifted.

"Come on, man!" someone yelled, maybe at me, maybe at the imam. Head down, like her mother, Elif walked toward the bright lights, toward the cocoon she too had been weaving for many years.

By now people were booing and even the bagpipes couldn't silence their whistles.

Then, just as she had walked past her father, just as she was but a few feet from the idling jeep, Elif turned back and sprinted. Before I knew it her lips were on my lips and the crowd was cheering. And even after our kiss was over, even after Elif had taken her seat by her mother, the crowd kept clapping.

It was a moment hard to rival. Or would have been, if not for Aysha. A woman cried and then another and I turned around just in time to see the little girl running across the embers, barefooted. At once the music fell silent, the *nestinari* as stunned on the side as the rest of us. We could hear under Aysha's feet the embers crunching as once more she crossed the circle. But before she had crossed it a third time, a man picked her up in his arms and hushed her: Grandpa, his boots kicking coals on his way out.

People were booing louder and for a second I feared a riot.

"Come on, Grandma," he told Baba Mina, and took her hand when she gave it. Then he stopped in his tracks for a moment.

"Get Aysha's shoes, will you?" he told me, without turning.

· TWELVE ·

DYADO DACHO RARELY LOST to the bus driver. But that night, the dice betrayed him. It was as though an invisible hand had interfered, he told me later, casting precisely the values that wouldn't suit him. Before long, he'd squandered his pocket money and it was still some ways to the evening prayer. He knew he had to buy us more time to get the plan in motion and so he kept betting—first his Slava watch, then his pension, and after this Baba Mina's. But the invisible hand kept rolling bad dice and sending, against all sensible judgment, for more and more shots of mint and *mastika*. Meanwhile, like never, the driver stayed sober. He was bleeding Dyado Dacho dry, that vampire, and he knew better than to allow some herb infusions to throw off his good fortune.

At last the imam sang from the minaret and the driver rubbed the cash in his beard. He tried on the Slava to see if it fit him—it didn't, his wrist was much meatier, but he still took it—and promised to come back for the pensions to-morrow. He said goodnight, despite Dyado Dacho's drunken protestations—he was now willing to bet all his chickens, his house even—and made for the bus on the square.

By the time the driver had rushed back to the coffee-house crying that his bus had been stolen, the imam was already there looking for his runaway women. It was then that the invisible hand jabbed Dyado Dacho in the ribs like a fireplace poker. So aggravated was he with losing, he simply couldn't resist spitting out some venom. "You'll never find your women," he told the imam, "and your bus," he said to the driver, "it was I who stole it!" Next thing he knew, they were shaking him down for more information. But he was dead drunk and damn glad to have ordered so many *masti-kas* and so, passed out, he told them nothing.

"He told them everything, the old fool," Grandpa said on the terrace the day after the fire dancing. I'd woken up late, my temples throbbing, and was now wrestling the chicken soup he'd cooked me. I could see my own reflection, distorted and pitiful, in the two fingers of fat on the surface—a glistening mirror Grandpa expected me to consume as a cure for my hangover.

Neither the imam nor the driver understood much of what Dyado Dacho was saying. But much wasn't needed—he'd blurted out *nestinari* and *dancing* and then *the American took them!*

"Ey, my boy," Dyado Dacho cried later when I approached him, "the hand must have made me say it." How an invisible hand could make a man say things, I wasn't certain, but I didn't press him.

"The imam came here to look for you," Grandpa said, and motioned me to hurry with the soup before the fat on the surface had turned chewy. The pitiful reflection tore when my spoon poked it. Hungry as I was, I couldn't eat a bite even.

"*My boy's sleeping,* I told him," Grandpa went on. "*He's been having a headache.* I was ready for a fistfight when he tried to wake you. Then I saw red. I shouted: *Come give him a kiss if you want to. Maybe that'll cure his headache.* I felt like a proper fool, my boy, when I saw the curtain flapping out that window." Around this time a horn had sounded from the road, and when they stepped out, the military jeep was waiting. When and how the imam had called for it, Grandpa didn't know, but the man was connected. More than a few times Grandpa had told me, this side of the Strandja belonged to the imam.

When the imam asked where the *nestinari* were dancing, where I'd taken his women, Grandpa told him he had no idea. But it was no good pretending. The imam had seen Elif's jacket in my room, on the hanger. So Grandpa said, *Get in the jeep, I'll take you.*

The rest—I had lived through it.

"You've been banned from the bus for life now," Grandpa said. He took my soup impatiently and started slurping. It was Grandpa who'd driven the bus from the beach back to the square—myself and Baba Mina drunk and sleeping, shoulder to shoulder. Why the driver hadn't come in the jeep to begin with, I wasn't certain.

"There is more in the pot if you want some." Baba Mina had given him the chicken this morning—in lieu of a *thank you,* or maybe an *I'm sorry.*

"I have no chickens to give you," I said, my eyes on the table. "Go ahead, say that you warned me."

But he asked me to look up. "You made a choice, and for

you it paid off. Besides, it was a thrill of a pleasure to see the imam the way I saw him when Elif kissed you. And then when Aysha sprinted across those dead coals."

According to Grandpa, the coals had been spread too thinly. According to him, those fire dancers were not true *nestinari*.

Walking to the bus, after the imam had driven away his women, I'd seen, or at least thought so, the chubby Russian who'd burned his feet in the fire. He had been chatting in Bulgarian with one of the men who'd spread the embers, helping him load the rakes in the bed of a pickup.

"A thin line divides them, my boy," Grandpa said, "the miracle worker from the con artist. And that line, as it often happens, lies in the eye of the one who watches."

The people we'd seen last night were not Klisurans. And the feast of Saints Constantine and Elena, it too hadn't been last night. "Wait thirteen more days," Grandpa said, "then go back to Byal Kamak." For such things, it was the old calendar that held weight in Klisura, and in most other Bulgarian villages for that matter.

I felt my blood rise to the tips of my ears. Here was a detail I'd failed to consider: while the majority of Europe had switched to the Gregorian calendar in the Middle Ages, Bulgaria had waited until 1916. Even to this day many of our older people honored dates in their old, Julian style. So not May 21, but June 3 then was the proper feast of the *nestinari* saints.

"It only hurts that it happened this way. Not that it happened," Grandpa said, and waved his big hand. "In your place, I might have done the same things. Hell, in your place, I did much worse." And for a moment it seemed like he wanted to say more. He pulled out a cigarette and lit it, his eyes on the roofs and the stork nests.

"Baba Mina was never a fire dancer," he said when a stork landed in one nest and began to feed its two babies. "Saint Kosta never took her. And after so many years, I see it still pains her. What happened, happened," he said, and took a long drag. "It's what happens next that I'm not too keen on braving. So man up. A storm's coming."

PART
FOUR

· ONE ·

THE NIGHT BEFORE the proper *nestinari* feast I dreamed of
the girl again. She was in my bed, wrapped in a white sheet
like a corpse, and when I peeled off the sheet she laughed,
tickled. She had no face and her laughter was a lark's song.
The bed had turned into a nest, the earth was moving with
a deep roar, and twig by twig the nest began to rot away. We
started falling.

I opened my eyes to Grandpa's face, blurry at first, so
close to mine, then coming into focus. The roar from my
dream had gotten louder. Deep and persistent, it rattled the
windows in their frames and it was the glass that chirped
birdlike.

For a moment I expected the Grandpa of my childhood
to throw me a netted sack. Bread, cheese, and yogurt. Delivery in fifteen minutes. Instead, he hit me with a pair of jeans.

"Get dressed. We have to go."

Go where? The sun was barely above the eastern hills. The yard lay half in shadow. By the time I was tangling in my T-shirt, a guillotine of light was touching the mouth of the well. The roar had grown so loud I made nothing of what Grandpa was saying—a curse, no doubt, at someone's aunt or mother.

We glued our palms to the windows to cushion their buzz and it was then we saw it—trampling the road on its way past our house. Burning with sun in its armor—curved blade, yellow body, clawlike tail—it resembled a giant scorpion more than it did a tank and a tank significantly more than what it really was.

"A bulldozer?" I said.

"Make it two. You slept through the first one."

The bulldozer had left behind a dry fog of its own—a cloud of dust and sand through which we marched. Once or twice Grandpa tripped in the ruts the tracks had dug, but after each falter his pace quickened. As did his breathing. "We wasted too much time," he barked when I asked him to slow down; there was no need for him to say the rest—"all thanks to you."

The roar of machines grew louder the closer we got to the ugly tower, the outermost houses, the dust bitter and stinking of exhaust. With the stench, a heaviness set in my stomach, and when the engines suddenly drowned in a different kind of boom—the rumble and roll of collapsing walls—the heaviness turned to panic. Grandpa sprinted grotesquely, like a thing wounded, and so I sprinted behind him. He shouted something and I too heard myself shouting.

Blades and rippers were cutting through the dust cloud—like shark fins and tails in waters boiling with the blood of prey; the kind of blood that stank of motor oil and of naphtha.

"The devil take me," Grandpa cried again and again, and despite the boom I could hear his jaws clenching. Making fists, he paced, left, right, left. Once, he made to enter the thick of the cloud, but I held him back firmly. And after this, we watched, fully aware that we were late and there was nothing we could do but hope the wind would scatter some of the dust so we could at least see the damage.

We saw at last—rubble where only a heartbeat before there had been a house. Slowly, methodically, the bulldozers scraped aside walls and roof, cleaned the ground and made it level. Metal screeched, wood cracked, and somewhere beyond this chaos, we recognized the flapping of wings. Two black storks swam through the dissipating cloud—the shadows of the storks above us, white like bones in the morning sky.

I knew then, as if for the first time, that this was all my fault. And I was convinced that Grandpa too knew it. But seeing him as I saw him now—wrapped in a sheet of dust, like the girl from my dream, and only two muddy claw marks on his face, where the tears were rolling, I understood something else. The houses meant nothing to him. Sticks and mud, dried-up ruins. And the land meant nothing—level or razed with bulldozer ruts. It was not because of land or houses he'd come back to Klisura.

"They had two little chicks, I think," he said.

And after this all I heard was wings beating, and all through Klisura the calling of storks.

· TWO ·

FOR TWENTY DAYS in the summer of 1903 the Strandjan Republic stayed free under the revolutionary banner. *Was it worth it, I wonder*, Captain Kosta wrote in his journal, alone and broken by poverty and sickness, a few years after the big battles; a journal from which Grandpa copied in his own notes. *To have known freedom for only a heartbeat and then to have spilled your blood under the sword and the fire? By God, I say, what does it matter, a lifetime or only a heartbeat? It matters we knew her. No. This too doesn't matter. It matters we fought to know her. By God, I say, it was worth it.*

The news that the imam's little daughter had danced barefoot in the embers spread through the village like wild-fire. And like all rumors, it spread badly distorted. In one version Aysha had crossed herself three times before leaping into the coals; in another she'd carried an icon of the Virgin

Mary and even kissed it. According to one version, it was Baba Mina who'd held the girl's hand and led her in circles; according to another, Grandpa had walked in the fire, without his shoes on. But all versions agreed on one detail—the imam's older girl had run past her father and given the American grandson a smack on the lips.

From then on, Aysha and her mother were perfectly healthy. And so were all the other sick girls in Klisura. They all thought the feast of Saint Kosta over and that knowledge alone cured them. But things with Elif were not well. She too had been banned from the bus; her father had banned her. Her school, the exams that were coming—she'd found herself forced to fail them.

Watching the jacket she'd left to dry on my hanger pained me something vicious. At times, I shook with the urge to grab it, march down to her house, and return it in person. At times, I burned with the need to take it outside, set it on fire, and pound its ashes into the ground with my bare feet. But the thought that I would first have to touch it filled me with such terror I could only watch it, where it hung in the corner, and think of the girl who'd worn it.

Grandpa was right; I'd made a choice and the choice had paid off—Elif had kissed me. What was shameful was that I'd sucked others into paying for that kiss—Elif and Grandpa, Aysha and Baba Mina. Each time I recalled the touch of Elif's lips, my heart soared. And my shame grew greater—not because I had caused trouble, but because, despite all else, I felt happy.

Three more houses were turned to rubble that morning. I shouted, flapped my arms, chucked stones at the machines.

The drivers refused to notice. At last, they took a break—in the shade of a blade, raised high as if about to take on the sky next.

"Who are you that"—one driver said, and drank water from a Sprite bottle for what seemed like an unnaturally long time—"we need to give you an explanation?" In height, he barely reached above the continuous tracks, but he struck me as the kind of man who would enjoy picking limb from limb a praying mantis. The other driver, now struggling to light a cigarette, seemed more malleable—tall and frail in his build—until he spoke:

"Yeah, pisser, who the fuck are you exactly?"

I told them I was the fucking grandson of the owner and a wave of terror washed over me, not because of them, but because of my stupidity to address them in this way.

"Maybe you are, maybe you aren't," the short one said, and finished the bottle in a series of tiny gulps. It wasn't his job to care. His job was to level the site and get it ready.

The tall one snatched the empty bottle. "You done it again. And here I am, dying for water."

"My kidney needs flushing."

"And mine doesn't?"

Behind us, Grandpa was rummaging through the mountain of rubble. Not even remotely interested in our conversation, he overturned blocks of mud from what had once been walls and shifted flat stones that had covered the rooftops.

"What is he looking for? A pot of gold?" the short one said, and his compatriot snorted, "Is he really?"

As if on its own, my hand shot up, and my finger jabbed the short guy in the chest.

"This is private property. You have no right—"

"I have the right to break your face in," he said simply,

and I'm sure he would have done it for entertainment if at that moment the boom of a car engine hadn't given him another place to look. The well-familiar military jeep was flying our way and in the passenger seat, bobbing up and down with each jolt, sat the imam. The brakes screeched, the tires locked, and the jeep drew an arc not six feet before us.

When the dust settled on our faces, the imam rolled down his window. The tall driver hurried to throw away his cigarette. The short one made an indecisive step toward his bulldozer, but gave up and froze in place.

"A coffee break already?" the imam said. The drivers babbled over each other. It was this pisser's fault. The imam raised his hand. He surveyed the site and for a long time watched Grandpa lifting chunks atop the wreckage. Not once did he look my way.

But the man behind the wheel was looking. Dressed in civilian clothes, he had no neck. His ears hung on either side of his head like an afterthought, taped there with a band of weak tape to make him seem a bit more human. He revved the engine once more and shut it and for a while all I heard was the clicking of hot metal under the hood, the storks crying, and blood thumping against my eardrums.

The imam reached over and punched the horn. He punched it a few more times before finally Grandpa spun around to face us. The imam waved him to come near and for one, two, three pumps of blood Grandpa watched him. Then he spat to the side and went on searching through the ruins.

Gently the imam popped his door open. I followed him to the pile, and so did the bulldozer drivers.

"Teacher," the imam was saying, "I regret it had to come to this." But Grandpa wasn't showing any signs he listened. He overturned a clump of dried mud, and the clump tumbled down the slope and shattered dangerously near—surely an accidental gesture, rather than one of aggression. In short, it was clear that, as far as Grandpa was concerned, the imam wasn't even present.

Then, for the first time I'd heard, the imam raised his voice. He stomped in the dust and only then did Grandpa turn to regard him, from the height of his mound, the way he would a gnat. Calmly Grandpa descended, kicking rubble down the slope. His face was black with dirt, and only his eyes glistened, like a falcon's. In that moment it was not Grandpa, but Captain Kosta descending. My heart swelled with courage.

By now the imam was smiling. For a while he had slipped; he had allowed the old man to make a mockery of him. But now it was his turn to roll the dice.

"I'm sorry it had to come to this," the imam repeated.

Grandpa patted his coat, then pointed at the tall driver. With a shaking hand the man passed him a cigarette and held up a timid flame.

From his pocket, the imam pulled out a piece of paper.

But Grandpa wouldn't take it. He puffed out some smoke in my direction.

The word flew from the imam's mouth like spittle. "The American?"

"The land is his. From now on, you deal with him."

"The land is mine," I stuttered, neither a statement nor a question. I took the paper. Stamped, signed, ratified, approved, straight from the ministry, it trembled as I read it.

"You have no right," I whispered.

"It's you who have no rights. For too long you've tried to take us for a ride. But this certificate confirms it. The land belongs to the state. Not to you."

"The hell it does," Grandpa said suddenly, and spat out his cigarette. But I was reading. According to this sheet, the village of Klisura—or rather what we referred to as "the Christian hamlet"—had been taken out of the cadastre in 1965. In 1965 this side of Klisura had been erased from the map, the land we claimed as ours stripped of ownership and annexed by the state.

"Impossible," I said once Grandpa had read the sheet, neither a statement nor a question really. For a long time Grandpa watched the imam and not a muscle moved on his blackened face. At last he tore the sheet to pieces.

The imam shrugged. "Call it a day," he told the drivers. "You've done enough. I'll send the bus to pick you up."

"We'll see you in court," I shouted to his back. The jeep started; the tires kicked up dirt and dust. When the cloud settled Grandpa was sitting on the ground—his heroic image itself reduced to rubble.

None of this made any sense to me. How could an entire half of a village suddenly cease to be a village? I tried to calm Grandpa down. We had records of our own. Deeds that quoted some earlier version of this same cadastre according to which Klisura was a village and the land was ours and—

Grandpa had turned very pale. His body trembled. "Water," he said.

"I drank it all," the short driver answered. He sprinted to his bulldozer and returned with a glass bottle full of *rakia*.

"Peach?" Grandpa asked after a sip.

"Fifty-five proof."

"Next time remove the pits before distilling."

"I told him so," the tall one said.

"I have been told."

They each drank from the bottle and when I asked to

have a sip the driver ceremoniously screwed the cap back on. And then we heard a rustle in the bushes. As though a large carp flopped in a seine. The short one went to have a look and reappeared, a black stork in his hands.

"His wing seems broke," he said of the bird, who trembled just like Grandpa. I thought it was a young chick—most likely the only one of the brood who'd managed to fly off before the bulldozers.

Large, grown-up birds watched us from the roofs of nearby houses, from the ugly Tower of Klisura. A few called when Grandpa held the chick. His shaky hand petted the frail black neck, which in the sun glistened with the changing colors of crude oil. The stork had closed his eyes and gradually his trembling settled.

"What is your name?" Grandpa asked the driver.

"Elmaz. But everyone calls me Little Shovel."

"And yours?"

"Just Shovel," the tall one said.

"Well, that's no good." And then to me: "We'll have to think of something better."

We named the stork as it was only fair, considering the feast day: Flavius Valerius Aurelius Constantinus Augustus. The First. The Great. Saint Kosta of the Storks.

· THREE ·

THAT EVENING, after he fed Saint Kosta a few morsels of soaked bread, after he squeezed water into his bill from a rag and tightened the bandage on the splintered wing, Grandpa complained of needles in his arm. Like vultures, storks bloodied with setting sun drew large cartwheels above the wreckage of houses, above their ruined nests and dead babies. Their shrieks were knives in Grandpa's leg.

His tongue tied up into a ball when the imam called from the mosque to prayer and there was nothing I could do but force him to take his pills and lay him down in bed. He had a stroke soon after.

I thought of running to Elif's. Humiliation and defeat be damned, I'd phone for a doctor. But first, how long before I reached her house? And then, how long before the ambulance made it to Klisura?

I'd never felt as helpless as I did right then. Dark all

around me and Grandpa's labored breathing, the flapping of a broken wing out in the yard. A single thought persisted— my fault. All of it, because of me.

How I wanted to throw the window open and whistle. Not a singsong call for help or pity. I wanted to whistle until another living soul answered and told me I wasn't all alone. And I suppose I wasn't. By the bed, holding Grandpa's hand, it struck me I should be grateful. We were spending this final moment together.

The night lived, grew old, and was dying. First cocks crowed from the Muslim hamlet and dawn found Grandpa still breathing, with heaviness that gradually seemed to scatter. Saint Kosta cried hungry from the yard and Grandpa's breathing quickened. He spoke as if his tongue had swollen up tenfold. "Go feed the saint."

· FOUR ·

" 'PACK YOUR BAGS and say your farewells,' the principal told me that morning. 'They're moving you to another school in another district.' I thought he was joking. Gave him a smile even. 'No jokes here,' he said, 'only Party orders. Straight from the Politburo.'

" 'Where am I being moved to?' I asked him. He had to recheck the order. 'Klisura,' he said. 'Which is where, exactly?' In place of an answer, he pulled out a bottle. 'It's this bad, is it?' I locked the door to his office and took the glass he offered. '*Naboré*,' he said, 'an apology is all the Party wanted. How hard was it to say *I'm sorry*?' We downed the drinks and refilled the glasses. I told him I wasn't sorry. 'Well,' he said, 'soon you will be.' "

More than four decades ago. Halfway through the spring semester. My grandfather on a train to Pleven. In Turnovo he took the monorail, crossed the Balkan Mountains. Rode the train to Burgas. Rocked on a bus to Sozopol, but at least there was the sea to look at out the window. Thumbed down a Moskvich at the bus stop. "There's something fishy about you," the driver told him. "No honest man goes about with two suitcases. And each weighs a ton. Open them. Books and notepads? Subversive literature, no doubt. My gut tells me I should call the militia." Ten levs convinced his gut to tell him a different story. He took Grandpa to Kiten, but no more money would make him put his Moskvich through the dirt roads that followed.

At sunset a horse-drawn carriage passed by. Grandpa rode it as far as a roadside inn and spent the night there devoured by bedbugs. Peasants were snoring all around him from their bunks and he couldn't sleep until morning. When he woke up, the sun was still rising.

"I'm a man of God," someone was shouting downstairs. "I can't be expected to handle money."

"You ate, you drank, you slept in a bed," the innkeeper was saying. "You used the bathroom even."

"I certainly didn't! Check the bushes if you don't believe me."

By the time Grandpa came down, a crowd of kibitzers had gathered to watch the circus. True enough, the man who refused to pay was a priest—but funny-looking. His cassock, black as coal, hung on his narrow shoulders like a ripped sack. The *kalimavka* was too large for his head and fell down to his eyes almost.

"And where is your beard?" someone hollered.

The priest combed his measly goatee with his nails to puff it up a little. "Lord forgive them!"

All this embarrassed Grandpa and he paid the man's expenses.

"It's not about the money," the priest said outside the inn, in place of a thank-you. "I remember my grandfather. I remember Father. The skin on their knuckles always soggy from all the hand-kissing. And they never went about hungry. Breakfast at one widow. Dinner at another. At lunch—a funeral, a christening, a wedding. And now this. Comrades and red flags." He spat in the dirt and crossed himself three times. Then he went to use the bathroom.

His name was Father Dionysus, but everyone called him "the Pope." He was three years younger than Grandpa—so thirty then—and like Grandpa he had been dispatched to Klisura.

"A troubled kind of flock," the Pope said dreamily of the Klisuran people. The two of them were riding in the back of a cart to another village, where they would get onto another cart, and so on. "Godless, the pour souls." He'd extorted some breakfast from the driver and now he set down the cheese on his belly so he could make the sign of the cross a few times. "They dance in fire there, like heretics. Like pagans." Last month, the metropolitan himself had called him over to his throne. "Father Dionysus," the metropolitan had beckoned, "the people of Klisura have lost their way. They've let an ancient heresy estrange them from the good Lord. Restore them to the righteous path."

Only later, in a moment of intoxication, did the Pope reveal to Grandpa the "truthful" reason for his relocation—a funeral, a demijohn of *rakia*, confusion in the holy chants, and a freshly baptized corpse. But in the end that too turned out to be a lie. It took my grandfather three whole years to

realize it wasn't the Christians of Klisura that Father Dionysus had been instructed to reform. It was the Muslims that
the Communist Party had sent him to christen.

Three days and six carts later the two of them arrived
in Klisura. The news that the Pope and the teacher were
coming together had reached the village long before them
and so, once they were on the square, it felt like their cart
was being dragged about by a stream of sunburned faces,
glittering eyes, and bushy mustaches. Old and young, men,
women, children, a startling multitude of hands was reach-
ing up to touch them the way Doubting Thomas had once
touched Christ's wounds.

Or so Father Dionysus told Grandpa. Fur caps flew in the
air, bagpipes screeched, a drum joined it, and voices merged
in a joyous song. For the first time in fifteen years the village
was welcoming a priest. For the first time in thirty—a school-
master. And through this sea of chaos, the voice of Father
Dionysus, fortified by the realization of his great importance,
echoed in command: "You there, with the donkey teeth. You
look like a burly fellow. Take the teacher's suitcases. And
you, with the demijohn. Is it wine for the welcome? Here, let
me do a tasting. And hold my bags, but carry them as though
a holy relic."

"Father," the people were calling around him. "Shall we
take you to the church?"

"Take me," he said, "but first to lunch. The church has
no feet to run away. But my feet are tired. I'm hungry for
banitsa and roasted hen on the spit. For chicken, *musaka*,
gyuvech . . ."

"And what about the school?" Grandpa was asking. He
wanted to see it right away, though he too was hungry. The
hands kept petting him, his head, neck, shoulders, as gently

as if he were a baby stork. Yet no one spoke. The truth shamed them. Only one boy—the village idiot, Vassilko—was not embarrassed. Above the clamor, his thin voice sang a merry song: *We got ourselves a pope without a beard. A school-master without a school.*

· FIVE ·

FOR A WEEK after the stroke Grandpa did not find the strength to leave his bed. He refused to eat, drink, or speak, and the only signs of life he showed were when he peeked out the window at the injured stork. I fed them both the same—bread soaked in boiled milk. I'd hold Saint Kosta under my armpit and force the pieces down his bill. He shook his head, tried to flap his wings, clawed the yard's stones. I'd press the spoon against Grandpa's lips and we would count the bites. "You're worse than the saint," I'd say. "He ate fifteen spoonfuls and you can't manage even ten."

Gradually Saint Kosta grew accustomed to the yard. With increasing authority, he paced between the lines of laundry—I washed the sheets often, sometimes twice a day—between the sticks of beans and tomatoes, pecked and clawed at the ground, dug up worms and beetles. In no time he'd learned how to unlatch the door to the basement with his bill and in no time he was hunting mice. "I guess he doesn't like my milk and bread," I'd tell Grandpa, and force another spoonful down his throat.

"Frogs," Grandpa said on the sixth day—the first intelligible word in quite some time. So I sharpened a stick and marched down to the river and didn't come back until I'd speared half a dozen frogs. "Show me," Grandpa said, and for the first time I helped him out of bed. He latched on to me with such fear, his body trembling like a walnut leaf, and so I said, "Don't be afraid. I'm here to hold you." He dragged his foot across the room and often we stopped and rested.

Out on the terrace, I wrapped him in a blanket and sat him down to watch. It was a proper massacre, the way Saint Kosta speared frog after frog with his bill, the way their guts splashed through the air each time he tossed them up and gulped them down. A fearsome spark ignited in Grandpa's eyes. "Food," he roared, and when I brought the bowl of milk and bread, he seized the spoon all on his own. He ate with ferocity that day, and after this he took his meals concurrent with the stork's.

At first Saint Kosta slept by the well. But one morning, after a night of heavy rains, I found him nestled up on the terrace, atop the blanket that covered Grandpa's chair. From then on, he climbed the stairs to the terrace often and so it came as no surprise that he should learn to open the door to the kitchen. I first discovered him inside, pecking through a basket of eggs, a line of yolk dripping from his bill and broken bags of flour on the floor around him. When he flapped a wing, the flour rose in a cloud into my face and onto the ceiling.

But it wasn't until he first snuck into Grandpa's room that I found myself somewhat weary. "A bit spooky this, a stork roaming the house like a specter." I had been bringing Grandpa a cup of *mursal* tea when I discovered them—Saint Kosta, perfectly still in the middle of the room, and Grandpa, equally petrified in bed—each eyeing the other, the way a predator eyes his prey.

"I have this gut feeling," Grandpa said later with some difficulty, "this stork is not at all a baby. I've seen this stork before. He's come to hold me to account."

"For what?" I asked him, amused and terrified in equal measure.

And so, it was on an evening some two weeks after the stroke that Grandpa began to tell me about his forceful relocation to Klisura. Saint Kosta had climbed the stairs to the terrace and once in a while, atop the blanket I'd left for him in the corner, he threw his head back and clattered his bill.

What a monster this Communist Party was, I thought, and listened. An omnipotent hydra with many heads and all of them breathing fire. One day you're teaching at a nice school, in a nice town. You have your own apartment, friends, loved ones, you're making plans for the future. And then, like that, all that you've built, the hydra drowns it in fire. Job, apartment, friends, and loved ones. There you are, at the edge of the world, an exile. Defeated and alone. How does a man rebuild himself, I wondered, after the hydra burns him? How does he learn to live again?

"'Pack your bags and say your farewells,' the principal told me that morning. 'They're moving you to another school in another district.'"

· SIX ·

"THE MAYOR OF KLISURA was eighty years old. Not a man, but a wild beast. Two meters tall, and a hundred and fifty kilos heavy."

He'd been born when the village was still part of the Ottoman Empire, and all his life, while great waves of people had sloshed about him, fleeing, arriving, fleeing again, he'd stayed put in Klisura. Out of spite, he told Grandpa, like a worm in a bull's heart. His skin was a living atlas of all the insurrections. He'd fought in the days of the Strandjan Republic, the Balkan Wars, the two World Wars, the two Communist uprisings. He didn't speak. He bellowed. *This scar I got from a Turk. This from a Serb. This one is Romanian and this one is Greek. And in '44, I got this scar—the worst— from my father. Sonny, he told me, you speak of Communists and dugouts one more time and I'll lash you with the poker.*

He was a hundred years old back then. May God pacify his wicked bones. And every time the mayor laughed, it was like fists were punching Grandpa in the stomach.

"You have no school," Grandpa told him on their first meeting.

"So you saw it already?" *One punch.* "That's the spirit." *And another.*

What Grandpa had seen was a pile of ashes. And that's what he told the mayor. They'd have to rebuild it.

"I like your fire. But I have no money for school-building."

"Not to worry," the Pope said later that day, and pulled out a piece of oily paper from his cassock, a pencil from underneath his *kalimavka*. He called over one of the boys who trotted behind—in those days there was always a crowd of children on their heels—and used his back to write on. "We'll write to the metropolitan. He'll give us the money."

"The metropolitan will give you nothing," someone wrote back.

"I thought they might say that," the Pope said.

"But who needs money?" the mayor bellowed. "Plenty of oaks in the forest. That's how we first built our school, when Captain Kosta made us."

Grandpa was laughing for the first time in many days. He had regained the color in his cheeks, was strong enough to hold the spoon in his right hand, and walked better now, despite still dragging his foot. Often while he spoke, his eyes drifted over the rooftops, toward the ugly tower and the pile of rubble from the ruined houses. A strange calm had followed the storm—the drivers had not returned yet and we could see now two bright lights glimmering where the bulldozers waited awash in the sinking sun.

So in the beginning there was no school. "Let that be your last worry," the mayor told Grandpa. "Here are twenty chairs from the municipal building. We'll set them up in the cherry orchard." So when the children got hungry all they'd need to do was reach up and pluck some cherries. He wasn't a great pedagogue, the mayor, but he meant well. "So what should my first worry be?" Grandpa asked him, and he bellowed, "You've got no students!"

They opened up the census books and compiled a list of all the families with children ages seven to twelve. "Even those in the upper hamlets?" the mayor asked. "And the Mohammedans too?"

"Now this is what I call a list," the Pope said when Grandpa showed him. "I think I'll join you."

For days the two of them walked from one house to another. "They look at us like we are saints," the Pope said once. And he was right. The women kissed their hands. The men offered to roll them tobacco—they had nothing of greater value to give. The little daughters, blushing, held forth dried plums and apple rinds in their aprons. "Such poverty," the Pope would say, and cross himself and bless them all.

And once they climbed outside the village up the hills—such filth, such misery and stench. Sheep, goats, chickens, babies nursing; the old ones and the young, all packed together in the same windowless huts. Thin, sickly people. Even the fires in their hearths looked thin and sickly, barely enough oxygen in the stuffy rooms to keep them burning.

My boys died yesteryear, teacher. The plague took them. We lost three girls. My son. My little daughter. Typhus. Measles. Malaria. Grippe. And all across the hills—in meadows amid the thick oak forests—little hamlets with their huts burned down in long-gone wars. Wreckage and rubble. Old trenches now filling up with earth, like jaws closing slowly, and the bones of the dead still showing white among the wild vines, the thorns, and the nettles.

The list said fifty children in the upper hamlets. Of those fifty, eleven were still living.

"Don't go farther up the slope, teacher," a mother told them outside her lonely hut. She'd lost her five children and her husband. "The plague is still alive up there." The Pope held a crucifix to her chapped lips. "Where were you yester-year, Father?" she said, but not with any accusation. "I buried them alone under the oak tree."

"I'll go to sanctify their bones," the Pope told her, and she shrugged.

"Sanctify *me*. I dug the graves."

They left her sitting outside the hut, petting in her lap a rug of goat hair, her eyes locked onto a great, invisible-for-them abyss. Once they'd lost her from sight, the Pope broke down in tears. "Who'll dig her grave?" he said. And then, "I'm going to the upper houses."

So up they went. One hut to another. Beautiful children there. Rosy cheeks and black eyes, burning. Typhus. Made the dying look so handsome. And awfully thirsty. There was a well some five hundred meters from one hut—or rather, a hole in the ground—but it had been a while since last the family had had the strength to draw water. So Grandpa filled a bucket and the Pope brought the gourd from mouth to mouth—four children, their parents, and an old grandma, all of them quaffing like wild beasts.

"You're a Christian priest," the father whispered.

"And you're dying," the Pope told him. "Gather your family. Step outside into the sunlight."

He baptized them into Christ, pouring water on their heads from the gourd. On parting, he gifted them a small icon of the Holy Virgin. The old woman was the first to kiss it.

"I was a little tiny girl," she said, "the first time they baptized me. Allah have mercy. And the Virgin."

SO WHAT if the children of Klisura were romping wild things? So what if he taught classes in the cherry orchard and had to bring the barber to shear not just their heads, but also his because of head lice? So what if the fleas chewed him to the bone and anything he ate in those early weeks gave him diarrhea? The Party had meant to break him, so to hell with the Party. That's what Grandpa told himself each night in the mayor's house, where he was lodging. If the mayor could sleep on a rug on the floor, so could Grandpa. If bread and water were good enough for the mayor, then they were good enough for my grandfather. Where did the Party think Grandpa had slept when he was little? What did they think his meals had comprised in those days when two of his brothers were wasted in the famine? And his own grandfather in the Balkan War. Punish him! To teach children, who, wild as they were, kissed his hand? Who, when he told them stories of khans and tsars and rebels, watched him as though it were a mountain of sweets they were watching? Who memorized fairy tales and poems as easily as the lark learns singsong? He enjoyed himself, my grandfather. He was even grateful. That is, until the Greeks came to the village and walked in the fire.

It was raining that night. June 2. The mayor always went to bed right after sunset, but that night he lit a lantern and took it out on the terrace. Grandpa didn't ask him why, only sat beside him, and they smoked, saying nothing. Rain fell in buckets, but every time it lightened the mayor sent a whistle into the darkness. He'd get up from his chair and pace about and curse the downpour. "You'll catch a cold out here," he'd say. But Grandpa refused to leave him. Instead, he rolled new cigarettes and they sat silent. They must have gone through an entire pouch of tobacco that night.

Then, just after midnight, the dark sent back a whistle— somewhere across the hill yonder. The rain picked up. A proper storm was raging, but out on the terrace the two men remained, waiting. Grandpa was first to hear it—the noise of feet splashing in the mud—and when a bolt of lightning flashed he saw them: pitch-black figures, in a thin file. The mayor sprinted to the gates and held them open and one by one the figures trickled into the courtyard. Grandpa lit more lamps inside the house while outside by the well the newcomers washed their feet with pails of water. Grandpa's head was spinning, not just from the tobacco but from the stench these people brought in. One by one the hoods were lowered and the room grew brighter, each wet face reflecting the light of the oil lamps. One by one they sat on the floor, muddy despite the washing. Men and women and children—twelve of them, Grandpa counted. But the thirteenth wasn't sitting yet. The mayor pulled out a dagger from his sash and slashed the rope with which the thirteenth man had fixed to his back a bundle. Inside the bundle, Grandpa found out later, were three sacred icons. But those he didn't see until the following day.

No one spoke and quickly the heads were drooping, the eyes were flittering, closing. Every now and then a boy let out a cough in the corner. Wrapped in a thick cloak, with only his face showing, thin and ashen, he sat away from the others and shivered. "Go to your room," the mayor told Grandpa, but Grandpa couldn't leave them. To see these men, the way their eyes burned, the knives in their sashes, the cudgels they propped like rifles against the wall, it set his blood on fire.

They all slept on the floor that night, together. All throughout, the sick boy coughed in the corner and his teeth chattered. Grandpa took pity on him and brewed him some mint tisane, but the boy only sank deeper into his cloak, not looking up for even a moment. Maybe it was this cloak that confused Grandpa, for the next day, without it, he realized the boy was no boy really. Her name was Lenio and she was blazing with awful fear. Tomorrow, for the first time in her life, she was to face the fire. But no one knew yet if Saint Constantine would lead her through it or if he'd let her get burned.

· EIGHT ·

JUNE 3, GRANDPA HAD GATHERED, was the feast day of Klisura, a celebration of its patron saints, Constantine and Elena.
And seeing how the parents of his students were growing ever
curious to learn the kind of tricks he taught their children,
he decided to stage a little performance. The cherry orchard
overflowed with guests that morning. His students recited all
thirty letters of the alphabet and counted to one hundred,
named the seven days of the week, the twelve months of the
year. A song was sung, two poems chanted. So wild were the
applause and whistles at the end that ripe cherries fell to
the ground and sweet fragrance chased away the smell of garlic, onions, and sweat.

"*Ashkolsun*, my boy," the mayor bellowed, and his bear
paw slapped Grandpa on the back, then on the shoulder.
Among the spectators Grandpa had noticed the strange
guests from last night—or rather, just the men, all dressed

in black, and only their jackets and their sashes the color of dirty blood.

When he awakened with the sunrise that morning, Grandpa had found the mayor's house empty—how he hadn't heard the guests rising, he couldn't say really. Later the Pope told him that the mayor had brought all of his thirteen guests to church before the rooster had crowed even once. "They woke me up at such an ungodly hour and forced me to hold a service. Three straight hours."

Now in the cherry orchard, the mayor introduced Grandpa to the Greeks—for that's what they were no matter that their village lay in Turkey.

The tallest one, whose mustache was freshly waxed and coiled upward like the horns of a wild ram, was Captain Vangelis. His single eyebrow was an eagle's wing, his eyes the color of frozen ashes. Beside him were his three sons—the oldest, Kostantinos, who wore a black headband wound so that the band's tassels fell on either side of his face like clenched fists; Demetrios, whose hair reached all the way down to his shoulders; and Yannis, who smiled at Grandpa and said in Bulgarian, "You've taught them well, teacher."

There was another captain—Elias—an old man the strength of whose hair was all gathered in his mustache so that his head shone like a boiled egg. And his two sons—the older one, Giorgios, who walked with a bad limp; and Michalis, no older than eighteen, whose smooth face betrayed his young age.

"You've taught them well," Elias repeated, but Captain Vangelis only shook his great head. He fixed Grandpa with his eyes and his jaw creaked before he spoke in his own language.

"He says it's a shame to teach in an orchard," said Yannis, the kindest of his sons.

"I say, if caves were good enough for the early teachers," Grandpa answered, "a cherry orchard is good enough for me and my students." He was referring to days long gone, when the Ottomans did not allow the *raya* to study. When people learned how to read and write in hiding.

The men nodded, but not Captain Vangelis.

"He says you have Turks among your students."

"And I say, are they really?"

"Why do you teach the Muslims?"

"I teach children who don't know how to read and write yet."

Grandpa knew well what the captain was doing. It was the same thing the leader of the *kalushari* had done a long time back, digging up that pit on the village square and filling it with bursting fire to see which boys would tumble in and which would cross it. Grandpa hadn't fallen in the pit back then, and now too he had no intention of falling. So he stood his ground, and soon Captain Vangelis too was nodding and putting his bony hand on Grandpa's shoulder.

"You teach them well," the captain said in broken Bulgarian. "But orchard is not a school." Then to the mayor he spoke, still in Bulgarian, so Grandpa would understand him. "All right. He may come."

· NINE ·

THE FIRST ONE WAS AN ICON of the Theotokos, the All Holy Virgin Mary, birth-giver to God. An icon of Eleusa or Tender Mercy; the same kind as the one the Pope had given the family they had baptized in the upper hamlets. As for the other two icons, the Pope had never seen their likeness. On one, Saint Constantine had taken a giant leap and was hanging in midair. His bare feet were cast in gold. His hands in silver. On the other, his mother, Saint Elena, was also leaping, the ends of her purple robe billowing around her like the outstretched wings of a large bird. All three icons were dressed in red cloth cases, and short wooden handles hung from their bottoms, like tails.

"That's heresy," the Pope told Grandpa later. But there in the church, surrounded by the seven Greeks, the mayor, and Grandpa, the Pope dared say nothing. He blessed the icons and chanted, and slowly the church filled up with people.

After the service they took the icons to the shack below the walnut. Back in those days, a path cut through the forest and made the walk from the village short and easy. Back in those days, walnuts weighed down the tree's branches. And in their nests, among the leafage, the black storks called sharply and clacked their bills, as if to greet both people and icons. When the mayor pushed the door of the shack open, three women, black like the storks, sprang to their feet, crying.

Welcome, welcome, Saint Kosta, and from their voices the hairs on Grandpa's back bristled. Two of the women were Greek—Grandpa recognized them from last night. The third one was a local grandma. They said she was a hundred years old, but she looked at least twice that. Her name was Baba Vida.

At first Grandpa couldn't see too well. A tiny, glassless window below the roof let in some light and then a fire was bursting in the hearth—thick oak logs the women had fixed upright. The heat was a grabbing, choking fist. The smell of frankincense was swelling and mixing with the stench of men. The walls seemed to be closing in.

Yet Grandpa was breathing in thirsty gulps. His head was turning and deep within him the *kalushari* of his youth banged their cudgels. Vassilko put down the candelabra he was carrying and from the embers of the altar lamp that the mayor brandished, Baba Vida stole flame to light three candles. The space brightened. In the deep end of the shack Grandpa saw a makeshift iconostasis, upon which the mayor arranged the holy icons, purifying each one over the smoke of his lamp, crossing himself, and paying obeisance. Strings of gold and silver coins, Turkish, from the days of janissaries and rebels. White and red damask roses. Fresh shoots from the walnut tree. The women adorned the icons, hands shaking, mumbling prayers. But no one seemed as tensed as Baba Vida. Grandpa could hear the noise her gums made slapping against each other, or maybe it was her bare feet on the wood floor he was hearing. And while this happened, people shuffled in and out of the shrine. Some brought kerchiefs and towels, some little bottles of oils and incense, which Baba Vida took with a thank-you. "Here now, buy a candle," she'd say, and the visitors dropped their coins in a chest in the corner, crossed themselves before the icons, and hurried out to make room for others.

Only one girl lingered before the image of the Holy Virgin. Her body trembling, she kissed the icon's corner. But when she came to Saint Constantine, she pulled back, as if the heat of a furnace had stung her. "Lenio!" Captain Vangelis barked from the side, and Grandpa felt the air his lips spat out lash his ears like a bullwhip. Right away he recognized her. The sick boy from the night before. But dressed in a nice dress. And two braids of black hair falling down from under her white kerchief. What hair! Make a rope of it, tie down two oxen, and watch them struggle to break free. Grandpa's heart flittered. But she was a child still—fourteen, he guessed, no older.

Terrified was Lenio when Baba Vida swooped her hand gently and led her to Saint Constantine's image. Terrified, she kissed his icon as though it were a diseased corpse she was kissing. But then she crossed herself three times and kissed the icon of Saint Elena, and when she turned to face the men, her eyes shone and she was smiling.

It was at that moment the pipers came in. And the drummer. Up on one wall Grandpa had seen a giant drum hanging, and on a nail beside it, coiled like an adder, a piece of hemp rope.

"Faster with the drum!" Baba Vida scolded, and Grandpa's heart too pounded faster to catch up with the beating. The two bagpipes came to screaming.

Narrow walls, a low ceiling. The heat boiling with the stink of incense. The men's faces gleaming, their sweat like liquid fire. Their hands on the hilts of their knives in the sashes. And the Greek women, taking quick steps around, crying "Vah, vah, vah!" like owls. The whites of their eyes flashing under the twitching eyelids and their arms flapping as though to take flight.

"Faster with the drum," Baba Vida commanded, and Grandpa could tell, by the way she was shaking, how much she wanted to do what the Greek women were doing. And yet she was too old.

In the corner Lenio too was watching the women. At once, her voice rang out like a gunshot. Her arms flapped and her bare feet smacked the floor. Faster the drum was beating. Louder the bagpipes. From the outside, two local women rushed in. They too were dancing. The Greek men joined them, howling. The women seized the icons and the music followed them out in the open. They all danced a *horo* around the walnut, the mayor waving a red kerchief in the lead, their feet black with mud from the rains of last night. The crowd clapped and cheered.

At last, the dance returned them to the shrine. The icons were rested on the shelf; the music grew quiet and then drowned in silence. Only the women spoke in whispers. And Grandpa was surprised to see that Lenio too was speaking with Baba Vida, the murmur of her voice as light as the rain that had begun to drizzle.

They said of Baba Vida that she could see what hadn't come to pass yet. And sure enough that day in the shack she pulled Grandpa to one side. "Teacher, don't do it," she whispered. "Unless you aim to wrestle Saint Kosta." But Grandpa aimed to wrestle no one. Though, strictly speaking, he told me later, before the saint there came Lenio's brothers. And then her father, Captain Vangelis, whom people also called the Wild Ram.

· TEN ·

THE DAY WAS HEAVY WITH RITUAL. As for its meaning, no one understood it fully. "Who knows what it all means, you book rat," the mayor said, and slammed his paw on Grandpa's back. "I do as the old *vekilin* taught me." That's what the mayor was—*vekilin* of the Klisuran *nestinari*; which is to say, a caretaker, the bridge between them and the people's world.

After the shack, they visited a spring in the forest, hedged in and roofed over, the *ayazmo* of Saint Constantine. There the priest was waiting for the service. "I heard there is a big lunch after," he whispered in Grandpa's ear, and let people kiss the cross and his right hand.

A fat ram was waiting in the churchyard. The mayor tied it down with the rope from the shack and slaughtered the animal *kurban*—the slaughtering hole also sacred, it too Saint Kosta's. Most of the meat they gave as alms throughout the village—the rest was taken to the shrine and cast in a cauldron over the fire. There by the shrine the mayor slaughtered one more ram and a white lamb. The parents of sick children had given them *kurban*, hoping the saint would bring a cure. As was the custom, they let the blood seep into the roots of the walnut; then they marched to the mayor's house and ate the big lunch.

Around five in the evening, outside the shack and under the walnut, an enormous pile of oak wood was set ablaze. Sparks and flames and black smoke carried up to the gray sky.

"It'll hold," Baba Vida said of the rain that still drizzled. "Saint Kosta will hold it."

At around a quarter to eight the rain picked up. The ground turned muddier and puddles pooled where the feet of the *nestinari* had sunk earlier that day. But the wood still burned with a tall flame, and a wave of relief spread through the crowd of spectators. Saint Kosta had willed it, and Baba Vida had seen it: despite the rain, there would be dancing.

It had grown dark when two men began to rake the fire with long sticks, to push the still burning stumps to one side and spread the embers in a circle. The drum was pounding faster and faster, the bagpipes were screeching, and up in the branches the black storks were crying something fierce. Yet a hush spread through the crowd when three young men stepped out of the shack with the sacred icons. Even the storks grew quiet. After the icons floated Baba Vida, Lenio and the women, Captain Vangelis and his sons, and Captain Elias and his.

And now so many years later out on our terrace, where Grandpa told me this story, I too could see them. He didn't have to tell me how the women trembled and pulled on the edges of their wet scarves. How one by one the men took the icons and swiftly, lightly carried them across the embers hissing with the rain. How Giorgios, who'd limped all day behind his brother, now hopped in perfect balance. How the mud splashed and red sparks scattered. How the rain pounded and Lenio's face ran black with liquid ashes. How terri-fied Grandpa was to watch her and feel on his cheeks the cold drops lashing each time the ropes of her hair whooshed in the dark.

I too could feel the heat of the fire, the cold of the harsh drops. I too was terrified. Because I too loved a girl and missed her.

All in all, ten minutes. That's how long the dance lasted. But those minutes seemed like many hours—the crowd awed and, by the end, exhausted. As were the *nestinari*—sitting now quietly on red pillows in the shrine, each staring into the nothing. Tired, but calmed somehow.

"May Saint Kosta aid us," the mayor, their *vekilin*, said as a blessing. A long rug had been rolled out on the freshly swept floor, and on it bowls of yogurt, plates of white cheese, saucers with young walnuts. They drank *rakia* from three small bottles and then they ate the *kurban*, for good health. Tomorrow every ritual would be repeated—this time to honor Saint Elena.

Only two souls weren't eating: Grandpa in his corner, his heart heavy, his fingers stained iodine from the walnut he was crushing into a pulp. And in her corner, Lenio, the Greek girl.

Yes, Lenio, you can relax now. Take a deep breath, have a sip of *rakia*. Fear nothing. Saint Kosta likes you. He took your hand and led you unharmed through the fire. So be merry. But take care not to show it. Your father, the Wild Ram, he doesn't like laughter. And your brothers, the cowards, they do as he tells them. So let them keep grave and quiet, the tombstones. But you, Lenio, are not a tombstone. You laugh now, the way you've learned how to—like a spring running beneath thick ice. Your cheeks red apples, your lips pomegranate. Your bare feet white as the yogurt and, only under your toenails, where no one can see it, the black ash.

· ELEVEN ·

WHEN DOES A PERSON FALL IN LOVE EXACTLY? Is it a single moment—the heart takes a beat past which there is no more turning? Or does it happen the way spring arrives, without sharp definitions?

The morning before the Greeks left for their village, Grandpa woke up awfully hungover. All night he'd drunk *rakia* with the captains and the mayor. His head was throbbing and he was so thirsty he could drain a river. He grabbed a towel and stumbled down to the well in the courtyard.

There by the well, in the blue dawn, Lenio was washing her long hair. She was fully clothed but she had let her hair fall free of the thick braids. She gathered the tresses and dipped them into a pail of water. Each time she pressed down the tresses, water splashed at her bare feet. For some time

Grandpa watched her and only then did she turn around to see him.

She wasn't startled. Instead, she was smiling. She pulled out her hair and began to wring it as if it were laundry. Then she put out her hand. She wanted the towel on Grandpa's shoulder. So he came near, his bare feet on the cool water, and he gave her the towel. When she took it, her fingers brushed his.

Had it been when he'd seen her in the shack, frightened as she was before the icon of Saint Kosta? Had it been when she'd danced in the fire? Had it been there in the courtyard, her hair dripping well water? Who can tell you? But my grandfather's heart had taken a beat past which there was no more turning.

On parting, Captain Vangelis came to Grandpa. Out in the yard, his sons were roping a bundle to Captain Elias's back—the sacred icons. By the well, some of the men sharpened their knives; some of the women wound bands of cloth around their feet to protect them from the road's thorns and sharp stones.

"An orchard is not a school," Captain Vangelis said, ready it seemed to pick up the old fight. But before Grandpa could answer, the captain pulled out from his cloak a fist of paper money. For fifteen years the *nestinari* had collected from candles and donations. To patch up the shrine if need be, and, one day, to rebuild it nicer.

"Build a real school," said Captain Vangelis.

And so, a week after they first arrived, Grandpa watched from the terrace the Greeks disappear up the road—their *vekilin*, Captain Vangelis, in the lead, then Captain Elias with the icons, their sons, their mothers, and strolling lightly at their heels, Lenio, her white kerchief last to vanish. So that was that, Grandpa thought, and after he finished his cigarette he lit another. His fingers burned where she'd touched him. Never again would he see her.

It goes without saying, he was mistaken.

· TWELVE ·

THE MONEY CAPTAIN VANGELIS GAVE Grandpa was not sufficient. And the mayor wouldn't hear of helping. The truth
came loose after much pressing—every time Klisurans rebuilt their school, the village ended up in ruin.

"So you're afraid!" Grandpa said, triumphant, for the
mayor had driven himself into a shameful corner.

"I? Afraid?" the mayor cried, then made a few phone calls.
Beams, rafters, planks, nails, lime, and tiles—he bought
them at preferential prices. And by the end of the week the
ruins of the old school had been transformed into a construction site.

"Here are your builders," the mayor said, and by his side
were only old men. It was the end of June, just as it was now
when Grandpa told me this story, and all the young ones
had gone to do field work.

"These men are good for nothing," Grandpa cried, because really, a stronger gust, it seemed, would knock them over. But, oh, was he mistaken. These men were mules. Worse yet—devils who never tired.

Each night Grandpa collapsed in his bed, a wreckage. Each morning, he woke up a living pain. Muscles he never knew existed hurt him. Bones, joints, teeth, even his scalp and hair were aching. All summer they built—Grandpa, the mayor, Vassilko, and the old brigadiers. And on September 15, the first official day of classes, Father Dionysus held a service, a *vodosvet* to bless the new school.

A school is not a Christian church, complained the people of the Muslim hamlet. And they locked at home their sons and daughters. This time, it was the mayor who came along with Grandpa, from one door to another, and tried to convince them—there was no need to be frightened.

It was the Pope these people feared. For ever since he'd first arrived in Klisura, Father Dionysus had worked like the old brigadiers—a mule, a devil who never tired. Tireless, he roamed the hills of the Strandja, hamlet to hamlet, no matter how distant, as long as a Muslim lived there. He'd grown heavier, though not in belly, but in stature. His shoulders had widened, the muscles in his legs and arms had swollen up, his beard had thickened—a great and terrifying thing, like a flaming bush it put the laity in fear. But he spoke kindly, gently, in an alluring voice. Gather around me, you poor people. I've come to tell you something. And the poor people gathered to hear his stories. How, a long time back, the Strandja had been all Christian, which was to say, all Bulgarian really. Because to be Bulgarian meant to be Christian and no one could be Bulgarian if they weren't Christian. It was, and always had been, this simple.

On and on Father Dionysus spun his stories and in them the centuries rolled by. Glorious tsars and martyrs came to life, then dust took them. Until a great danger arrived at the Bulgarian threshold—Murad the terrible sultan, at the head of a boundless army. Bravely, the Bulgarians fought him, in the name of Christ the great Lord. But the Turks were many and at last darkness overcame Christ's people, so they might be tested.

For many centuries the Bulgarians fought and resisted. Push after push, the way that oak tree right over there resists the gales from Turkey. Each time our people honored Christ, it was their own blood they honored. Each time they preserved Christ, it was themselves they were preserving. But not all trees are strong like the oak tree. And sometimes the gale fells us.

There came a day at last, Father Dionysus told them, when the Ottoman Empire weakened. Afraid of losing land and power, the sultan gave an order—turn all Bulgarians into Muslims, so they may never wish to break free. Terrible janissaries roamed the Strandja, and in their lead—black imams. When a Bulgarian refused to take off his fur cap, to renounce Christ and put on a turban, they cut his head off. Many a head rolled in those days, for great was the courage of our forefathers. But not all heads. For some bowed to accept the turban. And in this, there is no shame. Again, I tell you, not all trees are strong like the oak tree.

What matters most, Father Dionysus told them, is that God still loves you. It is never too late. Renounce the lie. Redeem your blood. Christ is the way, the truth, and the life. Return to your roots. Be born again.

And some people shook their heads, spat in the dirt, cursed the Pope, and stormed away angry. But others went home pensive, the worm of doubt gnawing at their innards. And still others, though not that many, came to the Pope, and when he offered, they kissed his right hand. And when he offered, they kissed the cross and he baptized them.

It was all this the people of Klisura feared. And even when Grandpa told them, *It's only the letters I'll teach your kids, only the numbers*, they still didn't believe him. When the mayor got angry and bellowed—*you blockheads, show some courage*—the people got quiet.

"They hate my guts," the mayor told Grandpa one evening. It was the mayor who, a year before this, had closed down the village mosque and sent away the imam. There was no need for Grandpa to ask him why he'd done so. After all, the mayor had never questioned why Grandpa had ended up in Klisura, nor did they wonder why Father Dionysus was doing all this baptizing. They both knew the reason. The Party had willed it. There was no way to defy the Party's orders.

"When I was a boy," the mayor said, "I drove an ox into a bog once. That poor beast knew the ground was boggy— he'd smelled the mud from a distance—but I hadn't smelled it. At first he resisted, but then I beat him until I broke the stick in half against his back. And so he grunted, lowered his head, and did as I told him. The mud ate him whole. I am the ox now," the mayor said, the first and last time Grandpa heard him whisper.

· THIRTEEN ·

WITH THE THREAT OF HEFTY FINES the Muslim parents were convinced to send their children back to school. It helped too that Grandpa was liked in the village. Almost every night someone new invited him to dinner—be it in the Christian or the Muslim hamlet. And to class, his students came with little bundles—now a handful of dried fruit, now apples preserved fresh under fern leaves. And after sunset, young women brought him jugs of milk, freshly baked *banitsas*, or loaves of rye bread. Afraid to be seen, they left their boons at his threshold, rapped their slender fingers on the gates, and ran into the dark with a giggle. Only one girl refused to hide. Each day, constant as the sun rising, she brought Grandpa a jar of yogurt—still warm from the sheepskins in which it had been wrapped to leaven. Each day he met her at the threshold. Each day, to show him how thick the yogurt was, she turned the jar upside down and shook it. Not once did the yogurt move. Then she would hold the jar up and make him breathe in deeply—the yogurt, alive with fermentation and sprinkling his face. When Grandpa scooped up yogurt with his finger, the girl would laugh.

"My daddy has a hundred white sheep," she sometimes told him, which was to say, There isn't a bachelor in the village who wouldn't want me as his wife, yet here I am, at your threshold.

"She loved me very much," Grandpa said now on the terrace. And back in those days, he often wondered, what would it be like to have her as his wife? Her father, the chief shepherd of the collective, the hundred white sheep, the jars of yogurt. She was a pretty girl, no doubt. She spoke sweetly and looked at him in a way that was calming—he would be lucky to have her. And yet he wasn't feeling lucky. At night, alone in the quiet school, it was the Greek girl Grandpa thought of. He dreamed of her face running black with ashes, imagined the rustle of her bare feet in the coals, felt her touch on his fingers, and sometimes, when a girl was laughing somewhere in the village, he thought it was the Greek girl, Lenio, he was hearing.

Each day at the threshold he scooped thick yogurt from the jar, guiltily, knowing full well he'd soon have to come to a decision. Take the girl and the hundred white sheep, or push away the jar before her heart shattered.

"I led her on, my boy. Day after day."

And in the end, is there a force darker than a woman with a broken heart?

"Poor Baba Mina," I said, and tried to see her, not as I remembered her, unraveling old sweaters by the fire, babbling of her father's sheep, but as Grandpa had seen her in those days, bringing him yogurt, a young and pretty girl, in love.

· FOURTEEN ·

GRANDPA'S FIRST SUMMER in Klisura was coming to an end. The storks rose in giant flocks, the leaves of the cherries dropped yellow, and the sweet smell of rot filled the air. Soon the days grew short and chilly. First snows fell, melted, then came to stay. Every morning, at the school's threshold, Grandpa collected the wood his students brought—one log per child, for the stove in the classroom. Every morning, Grandpa inspected their teeth, to see if they'd brushed them; their ears, to see if they'd washed them. Once a week, he made them pull off a stocking. To save time, he checked the right foot only. If the toenails weren't clipped, he wrote a note to reprimand the parents. *Teacher, teacher!* the children cried one day. He had just inspected Mehmed's right foot— the nails in a somewhat satisfactory condition. *Check his other foot. The left one!* Not nails, talons! His mother, the boy admitted, sobbing, was much too busy now that his father had gone away. She had not the time for clipping nails, and clipped only the ones she knew the teacher was inspecting.

"He was a good boy—Mehmed," Grandpa told me. We were taking our daily walk up the road, to the wreckage of the houses. Ahead of us, Saint Kosta was pulling something from a pile of fallen branches. "His voice was honey. I'd say, *Now children, let's sing a song.* But the moment Mehmed opened his mouth, they all shut theirs. They were ashamed to sing while he was singing." The snow falling in the court-yard, the stove bursting with flame, and Mehmed, singing sweetly. And now Grandpa stopped in the middle of the road and turned his head to listen, eyes closed, as if he could hear Mehmed's singsong.

"His father had been the village imam. A year before I came to Klisura, the militia had taken him away. Most likely to a labor camp. They never heard from him again."

It was only appropriate that at this moment, Mehmed, now grown-up, himself the imam of Klisura, himself a father, should start singing from the minaret. And yet it wasn't time for prayer. Instead, we heard the wind speeding through the dead road and in the wind Saint Kosta, gulping down a mouse he'd just killed.

The snows melted and the cherries bloomed. The storks returned. A year had gone by since Grandpa had first set foot in Klisura. And soon the feast of Saint Constantine was once more near.

"Come with me across the border," the mayor, caretaker of the *nestinari*, said to Grandpa. And he told him the story I knew from Elif—of how once upon a time the *nestinari* lived protected by the Turkish sultan. But how one day without reason, the Turks slaughtered as many fire dancers as they could and torched their village. The few survivors roamed the Strandja in search of a new home, half of them stopping in Klisura, the other half across the hills, in what was now Turkey. To keep the memory alive, each group vowed to safeguard the icons of the other and to meet year after year, once in Klisura, once there, across the hills—in Kostitsa.

"Kostitsa," I said. "The word for *little bone*?" But Grandpa shook his head. It was Saint Constantine's name that had shaped that of the village.

We were sitting out in the yard now, under the trellis, tossing back and forth a rag ball I'd made from an old shirtsleeve. We were working on Grandpa's dexterity, on his reflexes after the stroke. At first, catching the ball had been a serious challenge. But he was doing better. The day was warm. The air smelled of ripening tomatoes. As always, Saint Kosta strolled through the yard, searching for mice or moles to prey on.

"I can't cross the border," Grandpa told the mayor. After all, he was serving a punishment for his Party resignation. They'd never give him the necessary papers. But the mayor swatted his paw. Papers were for book rats.

And so, one evening with the sunset, four days before the feast of Saints Constantine and Elena, the mayor, Grandpa, Vassilko, two local men, and three women made for the Turkish border. Teary Baba Vida waved after them from the shrine's threshold; she was too old to make the journey.

"Tell me, Grandma," Grandpa asked her, "what did you mean the night of the dances?" *Don't do it*, she had warned him. But now she shrugged her bony shoulders. "If only I remembered, *sinko*, the things I saw each time Saint Kosta took me."

Father Dionysus caught up with them at the end of the village. The sacred icons were safeguarded in his church and wasn't he responsible for every candle, candelabra, lamp, and wooden box? What would the metropolitan say if he knew the Pope was allowing—

"Fine, come along then!" cried the mayor. "Just give that tongue of yours some rest."

He was a sly devil, Father Dionysus. It took Grandpa much too long to figure that out. Yes, the Party had sent him to christen the Muslims. But there were other tasks he'd been given. In the end it turned out Father Dionysus worked for the CSS. The Committee for State Security. Among other things, the Pope kept an eye on my grandfather; each month he wrote reports on all that Grandpa was doing.

"A secret agent priest!" I laughed, as if that were funny. I tossed the ball and Grandpa caught it firmly in his fist.

Sneaking across the border is and always has been a suicidal endeavor. You will be shot on sight. But back in those Cold War days, security was even tighter. Because of its proximity to Turkey, Klisura itself was then in a border zone. You couldn't just come to the village the way you did today. Back then, you needed special permission. That, Grandpa had. But crossing the border was another story.

Right away they came to a fence in the forest. The same one I'd snuck across with Elif. Like me, Grandpa found himself passing a hamlet of Turkish houses. Like me he thought, can it be this easy?

But this border was only a fake one. You were expected to cross it and think that you'd made it. You look around:

huts, a hamlet. I'm in Turkey! And just when you calm down, the guards get you.

At last they came to the real border. The moon was thin; the night was pitch-dark. And in the darkness, the tip of a cigarette glowed red. From the bushes the mayor hooted like an owl. The red ember drew an arc and shattered on the ground into a shower of smaller embers.

"You're late," the soldier whispered when they stepped out of the bushes to meet him. For the rest of the way, he was quiet. He was a local boy. What else was there to say? He let them cross. It was that easy.

Once they cleared the border, the mayor whistled again into the darkness. By then, Grandpa had learned a bit about this birdsong language. He tried to explain it now—how it was a mix of Bulgarian, Greek, Turkish; how each syllable was rendered by a different tone—but I'd be lying if I said I understood him. I trusted him, however, and that was sufficient.

Somewhere in the distance a bird answered. Someone had heard and now would pass along the message. *We're coming.* They walked all through the night, along the bank of a river—the same river that if followed downstream led to Klisura and to the old walnut. They slept at dawn, hidden in the thick of the forest. At sunset they arrived in the village.

To look at it, you'd think you were in Klisura. Even the house Captain Vangelis met them in was like the mayor's. In just a year's time, the captain's hair had turned bone-white. His sons too had grown older. And Lenio—

That evening under the trellised vine, Grandpa couldn't eat a bite. That night, in the barn where the men had bedded down, he couldn't sleep a minute. His heart was in his throat, beating.

She was a woman now. Sixteen. And promised in marriage to Michalis—the younger son of Captain Elias, that beardless boy Grandpa had seen a full year before. And he was still beardless, his face as smooth as river rock; but handsome, chiseled. They would marry them off in one more year.

That night Grandpa burned with fever. He felt better in the morning, but by the next evening he was again burning. My heart is breaking, he thought. He could barely stand on his feet while the *nestinari* were dancing. But it was only after he made it back to Klisura a week later, neither dead nor alive, his insides splitting, only after the Pope brought a doctor from town, that they realized the real reason. "Malaria," Grandpa said, and was quiet.

Uncomfortable, I turned under the trellis. Now that proper summer was upon us, the mosquitoes had come back. And since the sun was setting—

"Let's go inside," I said, but Grandpa wouldn't.

He told me to man up. And then to let him have at least one smoke.

"You're doing fine without," I said. But I could see what was eating him—Lenio, risen from the river of his mind.

"The day before we left for Klisura," he said, and lit up, "we ate a farewell lunch in Captain Vangelis's courtyard."

His fever was so bad people said his teeth chattered like a stork's bill. They too had storks there, in Kostitsa. *Teacher Stork*, the kids cried behind his back, laughing. So he mustered his last strength and dragged himself to the table. He acted well, lest Lenio think he was a weakling. He plopped himself down in a chair and this awful chord echoed, like a cat dying, and then wood splitting. Next thing he knew, Lenio was sobbing by his side, a half-crushed mandolin in her hands. "Beyond repair," Captain Vangelis said, and waved carelessly. "Here, have a *raki*. Don't sweat it."

For the rest of their stay Lenio hid in her room, sobbing. She hated his guts, Grandpa was certain. The illness would kill him and never again would he see her.

"But you were mistaken," I said while he finished his cigarette in silence. Saint Kosta had come to his side and he petted his long neck and good wing gently. "Let's go inside," he said, and when he made for the terrace the stork followed. But I stayed behind for a while, despite the mosquitoes.

Some time ago, while I rummaged through the classroom that was the first floor of our house, I'd found a mandolin wrapped in a white sheet. Half the strings hung broken; the others needed tuning.

"Where did you find this?" Grandpa said when I showed him. And when I asked if he could play it, he only waved, angered. He didn't touch the mandolin then, but a few days later I found him smoking on the terrace, staring intently at the bundled sheet across the table.

"My boy," he'd told me, and for some time chewed on his lower lip. "This thing. Get it away, will you?"

· FIFTEEN ·

IT TOOK GRANDPA MONTHS TO RECOVER from the malaria. In fact, I remember him terribly feverish on two occasions when I was still a child. He had burned for weeks, but I don't remember ever thinking twice about it. Only now, years later, did I realize that what I'd considered, in my childish ignorance, to be bouts of heavy flu had really been malarial relapses—the dormant parasite in Grandpa's liver infecting his blood again.

And who should care for him in those days of sickness if not the one girl who, even in good health, visited him daily? Grandpa didn't want her by his side, but there she was: soaking a towel in vinegar and spreading it over his forehead to extinguish the fire, bringing him thick skim from the milk, white and yellow cheese, and when he was stronger, rooster soup, grape leaf *sarmi*.

At first people were talking, then they had talked it all out.

It was no longer newsworthy gossip—Mina the shepherd's daughter, taking a tin of *banitsa* to the teacher. "So when's the wedding?" the mayor said, laughing, once, and after that, on more than one occasion, he made sure to tell Grandpa that unless he intended to marry the poor girl, he should not see her alone in his room, behind the closed door.

In October Grandpa traveled all the way to Burgas and from a store on the main street bought a brand-new Cremona mandolin. At first he kept it wrapped in its thick brown paper, but one night, smoking on the terrace, with the dark so dark, and the hills so tall and many between here and Kostitsa, he took it out and strummed it. Even the dreary noise he made was better than the silence. Night after night, he stroked the strings, each tone a syllable he sent into the night, across the border and the hills. He talked to Lenio this way.

"An instrument for females," the mayor often told him. But he began to visit Grandpa's terrace often. Eyes closed, he smoked, drank *rakia*, while Grandpa played. It was from the mayor that Grandpa first heard stories of Captain Kosta, of the Strandjan Republic.

The rebellion had risen on the day of Christ's Transfiguration in 1903, and quickly, with little blood, the Turks had been driven out of the mountain. A night of great celebration followed—songs, wine, sheep on the spit. Only Captain Kosta sat by the fire, ate nothing, drank nothing, but watched the twisting flame.

So the mayor, then only twenty years old, brought his captain some mutton, a *meh* of red wine. The captain took the meat and ate, then drank some wine from the skin. "Thank you, Petre," he said, for Petar was the mayor's name. "I forgot to eat. And drinking slipped my mind." Then he called the boy over. "Sit down and talk to me a little. I'm frightened."

Captain Kosta, the fierce voivode—he who had fought the Serbs at Slivnitsa and won; he who had just that morning stormed the Turkish *konak* at the head of his rebels and driven from there Ali Bey like a mangy dog—frightened? The mayor was smacked speechless. "What scares you, Captain?" he managed to stutter, and he felt like not just his own life but the faith of the entire world depended on this single answer.

"Freedom," Captain Kosta said. "She puts me in a fright, Petre. For in this very moment we are free the way few men before us have been. The sultan doesn't rule us. The Bulgarian tsar doesn't rule us. The tsar of Russia doesn't rule us. We are our own. We are the Strandja Mountains. And man, Petre, was not made to be a mountain."

"Man's bones are brittle," the mayor would bellow on Grandpa's terrace, usually sipping his third glass of *rakia*. "But metal too is brittle. So, to harden it, you dip it in fire and in water, you pound it with the hammer. That's how you make daggers. All my life the hammer beats me. Turks and Serbs and Greeks and Communists. Different names, the same hammer. It pounds my bones and turns them to daggers. All my life these daggers cut me. Just when one wound heals, they open up another."

But by the fifth glass, the mayor would grow quiet and listen to Grandpa stroke the Cremona. "Promise," he'd say, "when you lay me down in the earth, to play me a sweet song. Don't let that devil the priest come near."

I've often thought about the mayor's words since then—about the bones and the daggers. Whether these words were really the mayor's or only Grandpa's I couldn't be certain. But I find the idea that every hardship in our lives is a hammer-fall meant to harden our frame strangely unsettling. It seems to me that two opposing forces battle for control of our will. The body strives for ease and comfort. *Don't wound me*, it shouts, and if a dagger cuts, it fights to heal the wound, for wounded the body expires. The spirit, on the other hand, wants to be wounded. *Cut me*, it shouts, and fights to keep each wound bleeding, for in ease and comfort the spirit withers. Therein, I've come to think, lies the quandary of the man who holds the dagger—to cut himself or not.

· SIXTEEN ·

"LISTEN, TEACHER," the mayor told Grandpa that spring. "Why beat about the bush? I'm getting old and feeble. You're young and strapping. I like you. People respect you. I want you to be the new *vekilin*, the caretaker of the *nestinari*."

It goes without saying, Grandpa accepted. Hadn't he seen how the fire dancers treated the mayor? How Lenio kissed his hand? The very thought of her lips on his knuckles was enough to keep him sleepless. He'd take care of all the fire dancers in this world if that meant Lenio would be near.

So that spring, Grandpa helped the mayor patch up the shrine under the walnut, clean up the holy springs in the forest, repair their roofs and fences. When the Greeks arrived that June, Grandpa again was there to meet them. The two captains embraced him. Their sons shook his hand warmly. And when Lenio stood before him—more beautiful now than he'd ever seen her—Grandpa's heart knocked so loudly he thought the whole village would hear it. Blushing, she made to kiss his right hand, but Captain Vangelis stopped her. "He's not yet the *vekilin*," he said, laughing, and sent her to kiss the hand of the mayor.

From then on, through every ritual Grandpa shadowed the old man. He was allowed to set the icons on the shelf in the shrine, and it was Grandpa who slaughtered the sacrificial ram in the church courtyard. "Shame on you, comrade teacher," Father Dionysus said, smiling slyly. "Taking up witchcraft because of some Greek damsel. And here is Mina, the shepherd's daughter, a perfectly fine Bulgarian girl."

Somehow he knew all this, the Pope. He'd kept a close watch, his eye trained for just such details. And it seemed Mina herself had come to suspect that Grandpa was in love with the Greek girl—for during the second night of dancing, the one in honor of Saint Elena, Mina threw herself onto the embers barefooted. She burned her soles, was taken home for treatment, but never cried in pain. *To impress the teacher*, people began to whisper. *Mad, mad with love she is*, they said. *May Saint Kosta forgive her for getting his fire dirty.*

On parting, Grandpa mustered the courage to give Lenio the mandolin he'd bought her. It was an opportune moment, and one of repetition—she was washing her feet in the courtyard while inside the mayor's house the others readied for their journey.

She took the mandolin and blushed. Then, never raising her eyes to look at Grandpa, she seized his hand and kissed his knuckles. She ran upstairs, her bare feet flapping and leaving prints in the yard, a flock of black birds. Before the flock had scattered completely in the heat, Lenio's father, Captain Vangelis, emerged from the house, the wrapped mandolin in his choke hold.

"Thank you, teacher," he told Grandpa. "But she has Michalis now to give her presents."

"Teacher, teacher," old Baba Vida told Grandpa that evening, after the Greeks had gone up the mountain. "Do you see now what I once saw?"

"I see nothing," Grandpa told her, for really, there was plenty he still could not envision.

· SEVENTEEN ·

THE STORKS DREW CARTWHEELS in the skies. Harvest and vintage came and passed. The fields readied themselves for sleep and for the first time in many months they loosened their grip on the people. Children returned to school; the young ones began to plan their weddings. And in Kostitsa, across the border, Lenio too would soon be getting married. Out on the terrace, playing the mandolin, Grandpa counted the days till her wedding to Michalis.

That October, a winter chill gripped the Strandja. Ice encased the ancient oaks and from the cherry orchard there came the roar of cannons—the trees were bursting with the cold, their leaves still on the branches. At first the snow was thick and sticky, but soon the gale hardened it and even the children would not go out and play.

Two weeks before Lenio's wedding, Vassilko, the village idiot, brought Grandpa a letter. The letter had been smuggled across the border, he said, and when he told Grandpa that Lenio had written it, Grandpa raised his hand to strike the boy. But when they broke the envelope open a lock of black hair tied with a red thread fell out. The letter was in Greek, which Grandpa didn't read; and since he was afraid to take it to the mayor, in his confusion my grandfather did the only thing left to do.

"She doesn't want to marry," Father Dionysus said when he set down the letter. "She wants *you* to save her." But he wasn't smiling and his voice was low, almost a whisper.

For three days Grandpa didn't sleep a minute. He forgot to eat, drink, shave, bathe even. "Teacher," his students giggled, "show us your teeth and ears! Pull off your stockings!"

It was one week before the feast of Saint Demetrius, the feast that opened the wedding season, in the old style on November 8, when Grandpa returned to the church, panting.

"You must help me steal her," he told Father Dionysus.

Grandpa knew that since her birth Lenio had been promised to Michalis—the two families of fire dancers maintaining their special bond. What he didn't know yet was that Lenio had never intended to go through with the wedding.

For Lenio was in love with another boy, her age and from her village, a sweet talker who'd told her many lies. He would save her from Michalis; rescue her from her father. He'd made a lot of money driving sheep herds down to the Aegean. And with the money, they'd run to freedom. Istanbul, he told her, smoking a cigarette atop a pile of hay in his father's hayloft. That's where he'd take her. They'd live in a house on the Bosphorus—out one window they'd be looking at Asia. Out the other—at Europe.

Sweetly, sweetly the boy spun his yarns in the hayloft. He told her not to be afraid. It's just a little peck on the lips, he told her. All the other girls have done it. Relax now. We'll run away, I promise.

Three weeks before the wedding, Lenio snuck out of her house and hid at the end of the village, by the fountain with the seven spouts. That's where they'd conspired to meet. All day she waited. It was raining. At last, at dusk, she saw her brothers racing through the deluge. Christ, Lenio, they cried. We were so worried. We turned the village upside down looking for you.

That day, her sweetheart vanished without a trace. Never again did she see him.

She knew well what would happen the night after the wedding. What her father, the Wild Ram, what the whole village would do to her when the bedsheet was carried out into the courtyard, for everyone to see it, clean as a snowdrop. So she made plans to run away. She hadn't even reached the fountain when her brothers were hot on her heels already. *Frightened is the poor dove*, the old women giggled. Nothing was new under the sun.

They locked her up in the house and it was then that she wrote the letter. Who else was there to help but the new *vekilin*, the caretaker, the kind teacher, her last and only true hope?

"Saint Kosta bless you!" Captain Vangelis bellowed when he saw at his threshold Grandpa, and by his side Father Dionysus, their beards frozen solid. "You've shown me a great honor, teacher, coming to the wedding!"

For three days and nights the guests feasted, readying themselves for the proper wedding feast. No expense was spared. After all, Captain Vangelis had but a single daughter, dearer to him than the pupils of his eyes. Wine and *rakia*. Only they could drown his sorrow—to see her taken away by another man. Yet it was a sweet sorrow. The man was worthy. Michalis. Of a worthy kin.

On the night before the wedding, Grandpa stepped over the drunk guests scattered across the floor and forced open the door to Lenio's cell. She had dressed as thickly as she could, and he gave her the hooded cloak he'd stolen from a guest. How no one saw them sneak out of the house, Grandpa couldn't tell me. Maybe everyone there was too drunk to notice. Maybe they all thought it was a man under the cloak, not the bride, running. After all, Grandpa himself had once made that error. Maybe it was for both these reasons.

"God have mercy," Father Dionysus mumbled outside, and blessed them, and then himself, with the sign of the cross. A vicious gale was raging—sleet lashing like a whip—and growing more fierce by the minute. "Look on the bright side," Grandpa shouted over the howling. "They'll never catch us in this storm."

"God have mercy," the Pope repeated. And up they went, into the mountain.

· EIGHTEEN ·

AND SO WE DRANK, Grandpa and I. And so we got drunk on ghosts and days long gone. The more he told me of the *nestinari*, the more his head turned. The more he remembered Lenio, the hungrier the fire that engulfed his brain boomed. As for me, did I not own a head that turns? To think of nothing but Elif and hear nothing but Grandpa's story, day-time in waking and at night in my sleep? Lenio and Elif. Myself and Grandpa. With every word the borders crumbled; the territories of our hearts expanded, overlapped, and merged into one. Grandpa's longing was my own. My own sadness had become his. And that vanished youthful courage of his now flowed alive in my bloodstream, reckless, savage, impossible to weather.

I hadn't cut my hair since first setting foot in Klisura. In three weeks we hadn't shaved. Besides the sweat, we stank of onions and cheese. In short, we looked the part: the old captain with the stroke-eaten brain. The boy smacked stupid with love. The saint stork with the broken wing. A company of rebels.

"Grandpa," I cried one evening on the terrace. "We can't admit defeat like this." Elif had been taken away. The imam had begun to demolish our houses. What else was left for us to lose?

He knew exactly what I would ask him. And I in turn knew he would not deny me. But all the same, I sang it loudly, as if a rebel song.

"You have to help me steal Elif."

PART
FIVE

· ONE ·

IN MY DREAMS, I am two meters tall. My shirt is white like bones, and two bloodred kerchiefs flap on my chest like wings. Bolts of silver lightning embroider my britches; clumps of brass bells adorn my boots. Two daggers nestle in my sash and in my hand I grip a cudgel. A damask rose rests behind my ear. A sprig of wild geranium sits between my teeth. I smell of rose oil and like a man, of sweat. At my feet, the earth is singing. Wherever I pass, the air comes to a boil.

In my dreams, I need no ladders. A single leap is all it takes to climb the wall. A single push to throw the window open. "Good evening," I tell Elif, my breath pine needles. "I've come to steal you." Her face turns yogurt-pale. She wants to be taken, I can tell, but not like this, without a fight. She splinters a chair against my skull. She kicks me in the shin. And when I lay my palm to silence any screaming, she sinks her teeth down to the bone.

It's then she swoons. It's then I throw her on my shoulder and carry her off into the night. There are no complications in my dreams. No repercussions.

But this is not my dreams.

All day a warm wind blew from Turkey. All day the window frames of the abandoned houses rattled, the hedges howled, and empty tin cans rolled through our yard. Even at dusk, the wind persisted. Saint Kosta had tired of chasing the cans. Perched in his corner on the terrace, he watched us cast die after die and wait for sunset. When a half-moon rose above the Strandjan hills, we filled two small glasses with *rakia* and downed them, bottoms up.

The plan—if you could call it that—was very simple: Grandpa would ask to see the imam and while the two talked business in the living room, I'd climb through Elif's window. This was as far ahead as we had thought it out.

We locked Saint Kosta in the yard and made for the Muslim hamlet. We carried our own ladder—Grandpa in the lead, and I ten feet behind. But by the time we were crossing the bridge Saint Kosta had already caught up with us. Most likely he'd jumped the fence, which only strengthened my suspicion—his wing wasn't really broken. He was pretending; whatever the reason, he refused to fly.

As planned, we chucked the ladder over the imam's fence. As planned, Grandpa let himself in through the yard gate and knocked on the front door of the house. We didn't plan for Elif's mother to answer and tell Grandpa that, quite predictably, the imam had gone to the mosque for the evening prayer. We didn't plan for half of the ladder rungs to snap after the throw.

It soon became apparent—the window was out of reach. And so, in much less heroic fashion, I started chucking pebbles at the glass. The hinges creaked; the curtains flapped. A blue figure took shape in the night and only after Elif's voice echoed, so sweet and sad, did I understand how much I'd missed her. Nothing else mattered in this moment—selling land or keeping land. I felt that I had crossed the ocean, arrived here in Klisura, for no other reason than to be with her.

And only after her voice echoed did I realize how utterly absurd this situation was. The dream that Grandpa's stories had concocted, a dream we had both dreamed as one, was suddenly reduced to ash. I was once more awake.

"What are you doing here?" she said.

"I've come to steal you."

"As if I were a bus? Go home. You're drunk."

I wasn't drunk. It had been just a tiny glass. She was no bus, I said, and I asked her to help me up.

"Three weeks," she said. "Not once did you come to seek me out. To see if I was still alive."

"Damn it, Elif. I mean it."

But did I really? I wasn't sure and she could sense that.

"Go home, American. Get a shave. Take a shower. Sober up."

The hell I would. I spoke with resolution, hoping that a firmness of the voice would convince not just Elif, but also me—this was no joke. It only seemed to be.

But even when I told her that I wasn't leaving I could see: for her, I'd left already.

"Marry me!" I said in desperation. My voice dipped, so I repeated, I shouted it again.

"Do you mean it?" she said, and I said, yes I meant it, I meant it with all my heart.

"You are a cruel man," she said. "It's all a game to you. Go home."

· TWO ·

I CRIED A GREAT DEAL that night. I knew tears did not become a real man, but I wasn't a real man after all. I knew I was upsetting Grandpa, but honestly I couldn't help it. Over and over, I kept reliving the humiliation under Elif's window. Going there to steal her, as if she were the village bus. Then asking her to be my wife.

At last, unable to sleep, I went out to splash some water on my eyes. The sun was still behind the mountain; a mist was rolling through the yard. And by the well, Elif was waiting. She cradled a rucksack in her lap and on her face her father's slap still burned scarlet. She didn't wear a headscarf.

"Did you mean it?" she asked so quietly I thought I had imagined it. And when she said it, all doubt, embarrassment, and fear dissolved before the simple truth.

I held her tightly and she gasped for air.

"Let go, you loon!"

And then she kissed me. For the first time a real kiss. Not a stolen one, not one of demonstration before her father or the world. I kissed her back. I felt so dizzy, so weak with joy, I filled the bucket from the well and dumped it on my head. To wash the night away. To start anew. I splashed a bucket on *her* head. Her short hair was dripping rivers, there in the courtyard by the well.

"You idiot," she cried. But she was laughing.

It was then that I heard Grandpa call me from the terrace. Saint Kosta clacked his bill. What room was there for words, I asked them, for reasons and for explanations? What time was there to waste with plans? Wasn't it obvious to all who cared to see?

Elif and I were getting married.

· THREE ·

WE GOT ENGAGED in the yard that morning, Grandpa and
Saint Kosta standing witness. I filled a gourd with well water
and brought it to Elif's lips so she might drink. She held the
gourd to mine so I might drink. I broke a piece of bread and
fed her; she broke a piece and fed me. We were making it all
up, of course. A silly ritual to seal a promise that was anything but silly. We gave bread to Grandpa, then to the
stork. Elif cried and laughed, and so did I. Grandpa kissed
us on the forehead.

I said, "Let's go. This very minute. We'll sign in the Civil
Office in Burgas."

She shook her head. "I can't get married as I am. I want
to be another girl. You understand? A brand-new girl."

At first the bus driver refused to take us. Without a word,
we climbed inside the bus and left him with the ticket money.
We sat together holding hands. Every now and then, I lifted

hers and kissed it. Every now and then, she leaned her face on my shoulder. We watched the Strandja out the window— the trees astir with morning wind, the skies perfectly clear. And in the glass our own image watched us back, ghostly thin, transparent, foreign. It was as if some other boy, some other girl were holding hands, floating across the world with each turn of the bus. Now on a distant slope, now in a tree- top, now up in a corner of the sky, the boy and the girl sat together, beautiful, serene.

"Look at them," I told Elif.

"That's us," she said, and kissed me.

By noon we were in Burgas. Seeing the courthouse crowded as it was gave me a proper fright. The noise and stench of human bodies turned my head. I'd grown unaccustomed to their presence. But wherever we went, the crowd parted at our feet; when we sat down on a bench to wait our turn, the others waiting scattered.

"You look like a mountain rebel, a *haidut*," Elif said, and tugged on a tress of my oily hair. "And smell like one." And I suppose I did, and was.

At last, it was our turn to stand at the counter.

"I want to change my name," Elif said to the clerk who hid behind it. The woman nodded lightly. Her glasses slid down to the tip of her pointy nose so she could have a better look—first at Elif and then at me.

"What's wrong with your current name?" she said.

"I no longer like it."

"You need a better reason."

"I have a hundred better reasons. My father—"

"Poor child," the woman said, and slid a stack of papers across the counter. "I can't afford to listen to a hundred rea- sons." She tapped the papers with a nail, the red polish of which had all but flaked away. "Write them down. Let the court decide."

We took the papers to the side. A long time Elif chewed on the black pen. A few times she began to write, only to scratch it all away.

"Don't think too much," I told her. "The first thing that comes to your mind—write that."

I'm tired of my Turkish name, she wrote. *I'm tired of people calling me* kaduna. *Of my professors grading my exams more harshly. I'm tired of wearing headscarves and going to the mosque, of my father treating me as though I were a stock animal, like a sheep, or maybe a goat. I am a woman. My own. I was born in Bulgaria and I want a name to prove it.*

"Elena," she said to herself, and turned to me. "You like it?"

But before I could answer, she was already writing on the form.

We asked the clerk how long until a decision. She took the forms with a disgusted laugh. We may as well have asked her for the winning numbers to the lotto.

"It will be ready when it is," she said, and waved us off the line.

· FOUR ·

"LOOK HERE," I told Elif outside the courthouse, and showed her what Grandpa had given me that morning. One whole pension. An engagement gift. "Look here," she said, and took the roll her mother had given her in secret—a year's worth of savings.

"We shouldn't spend it all," I said.

"It would be very stupid if we did."

To save money we bought a pair of scissors. But it didn't feel right, her cutting my hair on a bench in the park. "Listen," I told her. "We're saving on a barber. How expensive could it be, really, to find a more secluded place?"

So we found a hotel and rented a room, a first time for Elif. The floor, the curtains, the wallpaper—everything stank of bleach and cigarettes. The TV refused to work, but there was an AC unit and that's what got Elif excited. She turned it all the way up and stood underneath the icy stream. I hugged her and, eyes closed, listened to the buzz of the AC, to her breathing, which grew sharper, more intense. It was a rush to feel her skin break out in goose bumps, to feel her shiver in my arms.

"You smell like feet," she cried, and broke loose from my grip.

She cut my hair in the bathroom and laughed a great deal in the end, though I didn't think the result was that bad or funny. When I stepped out of the shower, she threw a bag of clothes at my chest. She'd gone out shopping: a new T-shirt, pants, and flip-flops.

"Get dressed," she said, only her head peeking through the doorway. "Let's go before the sun has set."

I found her in the hotel bar, rolling an empty glass between her palms.

"It's fairly cheap," she said, and slid a shot of vodka across the counter. "For courage."

"Am I that scary?" I took the shot and asked where she would like to go.

A walk up and down the main street would be nice, she said. With the sun setting. She'd always wanted to do it, but never had.

"Never?"

"Not once. And you?"

I nodded yes. I ordered us two more shots.

Outside, the sun was setting. The tops of buildings and of trees burned red with light, yet down below we walked in shadows. We made our way through waves of tourists. Obnoxious music blared from every café, each trying to outshout the next, and floating above all this—the stench of frying fish. Elif too was speaking loudly. She was laughing and waving about, but the more we walked, the more her grip tightened on my forearm. And the more we walked, the more chaotic the world grew around us. It wasn't that the world scared us, loud as it was. It was the other way around—the world sensed our fear and spun into chaos. Or maybe it was just the vodka talking.

"Enough with this," Elif chirped at last. "I'm starving."

"There is a restaurant in the hotel."

"It's probably expensive."

"Is it really?"

It was. And very empty, which we liked. We sat at a table in one corner, and it was some time before the waiter saw us.

"Order in English," Elif said. "Ask for the English menu. Quickly!"

"That slimy bastard," she said after the waiter had brought us the new menus. "Did you see how nice he became as soon as you spoke? What's this?" she said, and jabbed a finger at the menu.

"Mackerel. But they've spelled it wrong."

"For this much money, you'd think they'd learn to spell."

We ordered a bottle of white wine to go with the mackerel.

"How *do* you spell 'mackerel'?" Elif said. "Maybe you can teach me?"

"There isn't all that much to learn."

We ate the fish in silence. It wasn't good, but we didn't care. The wine was better. We were finishing the bottle when an old woman appeared by our table. Her white hair disheveled, her clothes devoid of color, worn out, she'd snuck in from the street to sell us flowers.

"A rose for the lady?" she said, and stuck at me a basket full of somewhat withered things. None of them were roses. Not all of them were flowers. Frightened, Elif shook her head.

Was this woman real, or an apparition? A shadow that had followed us from Klisura, to hold us to account?

But then the woman smiled softly and we knew she hadn't come to judge us.

Don't be afraid, she was saying, without any words. *I bring you flowers.*

It was then that the toady waiter grabbed her by the elbow and pulled her to the side. "I told you once already," he hissed. "Don't come back."

"Wait," I said in English. "How much for the entire basket?"

"You paid too much," Elif said once the woman had taken my money and been escorted back into the street. But by the way she cradled the basket in her lap I knew she was pleased.

"Dessert?" she said, suddenly animated. "What does this say?"

"Cognac."

In Bulgarian, forgetting ourselves, we asked the waiter if we could take a bottle to our room.

"I knew you weren't English," he said. "Go across the street. Buy yourselves a bottle there. It's cheaper."

"We don't care if it's cheaper," I said. So he brought us the bottle and we paid, and tipped him way too much and took the cognac and the flowers into the elevator.

"You know," Elif said, "until today, I'd never ridden in an elevator."

"Let's ride in it then."

We punched the last floor and the elevator raced up. We punched the ground floor and we flew back down. We took sips from the cognac, sitting on the floor, her head on my shoulder and only my hand stretching for the buttons. A few times other guests climbed in and we offered, politely, to press their floor for them. We offered them cognac. "It's like the walnut tree," I said, "up in the stork nest," but she hushed me with the bottle.

"Don't talk of that. Drink up."

At last, we tired of postponing.

Back in the room, we sat down on the bed, in blue darkness, not bothering to turn the lights on.

"Don't be afraid," I said.

"I'm not." She told me to look the other way. I heard the blankets rustle and when I turned around, she was in bed, the sheet pulled up to her chin. Her lips, her cheeks had grown red from the drink and that red stood out against the white of the sheet like drops of blood against the snow of winter.

I told her to close her eyes and while she kept them shut I took my clothes off and slipped under the blankets. We lay like this, one beside the other, not touching. The heat of her hand stung me when she took mine. She guided my fingers against the insides of her forearms, thighs, legs.

"I'm hideous," she said. "All scars."

What could I tell her when for me she was as pretty as a girl could be?

I dived under the sheet. I kissed her scars—her forearms, thighs, and legs. When I reemerged she was crying. "I'm so afraid," she said. She sought my hand again and locked her fingers around my wrist like a cuff. "Don't run away."

· FIVE ·

PERUN, THE GREAT GOD OF THE SLAVS, was boiling with fury.
Lada, the goddess of youth and beauty, his most beloved
daughter, had run away. Blind wrath split his skull in half.
An avalanche of fire rolled down his mountain and scorched
all in its wake. He called his sons, his other daughters, but
no one dared stand before him. Only one goddess was not
afraid. For her, Perun's wailing was but a gentle song. She
crawled out of the swamp that contained her and when she
settled into her sled—a wild ram's rib cage drawn forth by
frogs and snakes and carp—she rushed to meet Perun.

"Her name was Starost," I told Elif, and kissed her on
the forehead, "the goddess of old age."

Elif had taken the sheet and soaked it in the bathtub and
now we lay diagonally in the sheetless bed. Only now that
all was done had she allowed herself to relax a little.

"Tell me a story," she'd said quietly, and so I did—the stories Grandpa had told me as a child. Of Lada and Attila.

Perun was startled once he saw Old Age. The hag had appeared before his throne without him realizing when. But that's how she arrived. Sneakily, like a thief.

"Why have you come?" the great god asked her.

"To bring back your girl," she hissed. "But first you'll give me what I want."

What Starost wanted was human life. "A child is born," she told Perun, "and Lada takes it for herself. And what's for me? I kiss rotten lips, while Lada kisses the lips of lads and lasses. I hold withered corpses, while Lada dandles toddlers on her knees. Why, Father, have you cursed me so? Why have you wed me to Smert himself?"

Perun feared Starost. He feared that, a god or not, one day Old Age would take him too. In a flash he saw himself weak on his last bed. He saw Smert, the white groom, take his hand and lead him not to the netherworld, where he would be reunited with his brother Veles, but to the goddess who ruled all gods. Zabrava. Lethe.

"If it's toddlers you want to dandle on your knees," Perun said to Starost, so he would please her, "let every man and woman in old age turn a toddler once again. Let them cry for their mothers and may you, mother of the old, suckle them on your withered breasts."

Old Age was pleased. On her sled she flew out of the mountain and quickly she sniffed out the trail of burning peonies, the smoke of battle.

Attila and Lada slept a dreamless sleep inside their yurt. They had pitched the yurt where, just a sunset before, a marble palace had stood. The goddess Starost dipped her crooked fingers into the marble dust and powdered her face.

For a brief second, through sleepy eyes, Attila thought it was Lada leaning over to give him a kiss.

By sunrise Attila's hair was white like bone. By noon his saber had grown too heavy for him to lift. And by the time the sun was slipping behind the Carpathian Mountains he could no longer rise from where he lay.

In vain Lada fondled his cheeks. In vain she gave him her breast to suckle. Old Age had kissed him on the mouth, and now it was Smert's footsteps they could hear rustling through the dust of shattered marble. The white groom was coming near.

Great man or not, a god or not, sooner or later the white groom comes to take you. And after that—Oblivion awaits. But Attila would not be forgotten. Lada had given him a son. A fine, strong boy who'd grown by his father's side into a man. He'd taught him how to ride his horse, brandish a saber. What else was there to teach?

"Farewell, my love," he said to Lada. But she refused to let him go.

"When you get to the other side," she begged him, "wait for me."

She knew of course she'd never recognize him there, because there, in the underworld, all human shadows roamed faceless. Her uncle Veles took every human face at the gates and wore it as his own. She knew she'd never be reunited with the man she loved, never again would feel his touch, nor hear his voice. But all the same she kept on talking.

"Down under, there is a tree," she lied, "heavy with walnuts. Wait for me in its branches. Reunited, we'll sack the netherworld and watch it burn."

Attila answered with a smile. "No more sacking, my love. It's time to rest."

Elif stirred on my chest. A shiver ran through her body and she held me tighter.

Any historian will tell you the famous story of how upon his death Attila was laid inside an iron coffin, which then was put, like a *matryoshka*, into a coffin of silver, and then once more into a coffin of pure gold. A river was temporarily diverted, and once the triple coffin was buried in its bed, the waters were allowed to return. To keep the site a secret, all men who'd dug the grave were put to death.

But this was not the story Grandpa told me.

"In order to never forget him, Lada commanded Attila's men to forge a triple coffin—of iron, silver, and of gold—and bury it in her tresses."

"And so," Elif said, and opened her eyes, for the first time, to look at me in the dark, "wherever Lada flew, Attila followed, caught in the river of her hair."

· SIX ·

"THE PARTY STARTED CHANGING our names again the year I was born. 1984. In one winter they changed one million names. They changed mine when I was two. *If it has to be Bulgarian*, Mother had said, *then let it be Saint Elena's.* Who knew? Maybe Saint Elena wouldn't mind that I was born a Turk."

We'd slept for a while and then awakened. Neither of us could fall asleep again. The night had grown stuffy. It smelled of exhaust, and sweet, of the flowers withering in the basket. Cars squeaked from the street below, and every now and then a seagull cried. The thin, moth-eaten curtain flapped out the window as if attempting to fly away. I could see the dark rooftops of houses and buildings, like scales from here to the horizon, and beyond them the thick shapes of loading cranes, with their signal lights pulsing red. Beyond the docks, I knew, was the sea. But once again, I couldn't see it.

Elif lit a cigarette. The flame of the lighter illuminated her sweaty face for just a moment, but just a moment was enough—even after she had returned to the shade, I could see her clearly, my eyes closed as I kept them now.

"Of course, I don't remember any of this," she said. "I mean, come on—1986."

But she had heard stories. How the militia and these clerks made rounds from house to house. How they forced the people to sign petitions to the court. If you cooperated, they allowed you to choose your name. But many did not comply and were given random names. Soon there were twenty Georgis in Klisura, fifteen Todors, nine Lyudmilas. In the daytime, while people were away at the fields, the militia broke into their houses; confiscated headscarves, prayer rugs, copies of the Qur'an. They'd go to the graveyard and plaster over the tombstones of the dead. Even the dead received new names. Twenty Georgis, fifteen Todors, nine Lyudmilas.

They were about to send Elif's father to a labor camp. He was, after all, the village imam. But he bribed the right people. Paid them a pot of gold coins, a treasure he'd found when digging the pit for a new toilet in the yard. No joke. You got a shovel and started digging in the Strandja, sooner or later you'd hit either bones or hidden treasures. Some pitiful refugee must have buried the pot, fleeing for Turkey. During the Balkan War, the Russo-Turkish War—god knew which war. It didn't matter. What mattered was the gold was there. A hundred years later it saved her father's life.

When the new passports arrived in the spring of 1986, no one wanted to pick them up. Just one man waiting outside the municipal building. Orhan's father. "You don't kick against a poker," he mumbled in his defense, or at least that's what Elif imagined. But then it came out that he had helped the militia cover up the tombstones. He was a wood carver, and it was he who'd chiseled in the new names of the dead. So naturally, the village men went to his house to kill him. Only the sight of his poor wife, and in her arms Orhan the baby, no doubt screaming his guts out, held them back. So they chased the family out of Klisura. And burned their house down to the ground.

How distant that name seemed to me now. How long ago, our nightly expedition to the ancient ruins. Orhan the coward. Shooting his gun a hair's length away from Elif. That's who the imam had promised her in marriage. Only later did she find out the boy's father had bought her for fifteen thousand deutsche marks. He was hoping, the old fool, that when the imam's daughter married his son, all shame would wash away from their name.

But this, Elif remembered. The spring of 1989. The storks returning to the mountain; the people of Klisura leaving. So many cars on the highway to the border, you could walk on their rooftops from here to Turkey. Mattresses and chairs, and piles of clothes, and pots and pans roped down to the cars, stuffed in the trunks, sticking out the windows. Three hundred thousand people left for Turkey that year. On tourist visas. They called it the Big Excursion. An excursion it was not.

Her family spent two months in a refugee camp, in Istanbul, in the suburbs. Thank God the merciful, Elif didn't remember much of those times. Just that she didn't understand the language. Back in Bulgaria she'd spent her days in the kindergarten. No Turkish allowed, that's for sure. She remembered dust in the camp, always. On her fingers, in her nose and hair. She remembered how much she'd looked forward to the once-a-week shower. And every evening her father coming back from work. He'd pull her to the side, behind the tent, where the others couldn't see them. He'd take out a strip of newspaper from his pocket, and wrapped in the paper—a tiny piece of Turkish delight. Every evening she ate the piece and licked the powdered sugar off the paper. God merciful, it was still on her tongue, so many years later. The bitter ink and salty dust and sugar.

According to her father they returned to Klisura because one night in the camp God told him to do so. He dreamed the mosque was burning and it was all his fault. And locked in the minaret he could hear the baby boy he'd lost. The son he so desperately wanted, calling to him, blaming him.

For Elif the reason was much simpler. They came back because they couldn't take the new life. Because dusk till dawn her father toiled away at a construction site for a salary the locals wouldn't even spit on. But after all, they weren't locals. Refugee migrants, that's what they were. Like storks.

The year was 1991. Half of the refugees who'd left for Turkey two years prior were coming back. The Party had collapsed. The Muslim names had been restored. But a different Bulgaria awaited. On leaving, many had sold their homes. To prevent speculation, local municipalities had bought out the houses at prices the state had set, which was to say, dirt cheap. Roughly seventy thousand people were homeless now.

The skies darkened. The winter stretched for years. The lines for bread and cheese—for days. A human flood swept up the streets. Where once there had been mothers, fathers, sisters, and brothers—now spilled a faceless mob.

The year was 1991. Elif was coming home from what she'd failed to make her home.

The year was 1991 and I myself was leaving.

Three hundred thousand had left for Turkey.

Four hundred thousand were leaving for the West.

I turned to Elif and watched her smoke her cigarette in silence. "At the airport in Ontario," I said, "my parents bought three Snickers bars. Overpriced, I'm sure. But this went beyond money. We'd never eaten Snickers before because we never could. And now we could. We were free.

"Halfway through, my stomach began turning. I hate peanuts. The chocolate was much too sweet. And I'd already eaten plenty of bad food on the plane. But Father wouldn't have it. He was making a statement. He ordered me to finish the entire thing and then to lick the wrapper.

"We were waiting for the shuttle when I puked. All over Mother."

"Charming," Elif said. "Made sick by freedom."

She pressed her cheek against my chest again.

"Tell me some other stories of how you've puked."

· SEVEN ·

WE STAYED IN BURGAS for five days and four nights. We never left the hotel before noon, though every morning we awoke early with the intent. By the time we finally crawled out of bed the sun was past its apex. Ravenous with hunger, we showered quickly, dressed, went out for lunch. Elif had never eaten at McDonald's. On the first day she devoured a Big Mac, a double cheeseburger, a hamburger, and a dozen Chicken McNuggets. "It's nothing special," she said, but each day after that we returned so she could try new items on the menu. They were all expensive, but we didn't care. "I wish Aysha could try this," she'd say sometimes—of the ice cream we bought in the park, of the cotton candy, of the sweet corn on the cob. "This is the longest I've been away from her," she'd say.

Sometimes we sat in a café, the same kind that had seemed

obnoxious but now was not. We drank Fanta with straws and watched the foreign tourists prance up and down the main street. We made fun of the way they looked—too fat, too pale and freckled, too blond, too skinny; of their socks and flip-flops, man purses, men's tank tops. We bought things: Grandpa a set of new strings for the mandolin, and ourselves new clothes—for Elif, a long silk dress that went down to her ankles, and a long-sleeved cardigan that she wore despite the heat. I told her, "You're beautiful. You don't have to hide," but she didn't seem to listen.

Every afternoon we went down to the sea. So what if the central beach in Burgas was, well, the central beach in Burgas? The sea was still the sea—calm one day and turbid on another—never the same, except in its vastness. We'd clear a spot in the sand of all the empty beer bottles, cigarette butts, and ice cream sticks and wait for the crowd to scatter with the setting sun. Then it was just us and the Gypsies, picking up large pieces of trash in their black nylon sacks, and after them the tractor, raking the sand, freeing it from any human trace. Sometimes we gathered seashells for Aysha. Sometimes we waded in the water—not even a meter from the shore—and stood against the evening wind, the sand, the earth beneath our soles giving way with each new wave. "Let's swim," I'd tell Elif, but she would only wrap herself in the cardigan more tightly.

The day before we returned to Klisura, we stumbled upon a photo booth just off the main street. "Grandpa might like a picture," Elif said, and so we took four instant photos— four tiny squares on a palm-sized sheet. That afternoon we went to the sea and waited for the sun to set at our backs. Elif's head was on my shoulder and I don't think we spoke a single word. Our shadows were a single shadow, which stretched so long it finally touched the sea and, unafraid, kept going deeper.

"Listen," Elif said at last. In the dusk, her face was blue. The distant lights of restaurants along the shoreline, of boats on the horizon, hung in the prison of her eyes. "They can take everything away from us, but not these last five days. These days are ours."

She found an empty beer bottle in the sand and tore off a photo from the sheet. She stuffed the photo in the bottle and, scooping sand in handfuls, filled the bottle up. We walked down to the sea—dark and booming and smelling fresh, of watermelon and night.

"Throw it as hard as you can," she told me, and I did. The bottle whizzed through the wind and hit the waves with a dull splash. "Whatever happens out here," Elif said, "we'll always be together, down there, at the bottom of the sea."

· EIGHT ·

I SAY TO PETAR, Petre my boy, man's heart is a lantern. And what good is a lantern unless it holds a flame? For two weeks now we've been building a school in Klisura. We've put a cross on the roof, like a church. Three crosses, like a monastery. When the Turks come back, they'll torch the school. We'll take from its flame and light our lanterns. Our bones will be timber, Petre, our blood will be oil. We'll burn with black smoke and Europe will see it.

In place of black smoke, gray dust was rolling in the skies of Klisura. We could hear the storks crying inside the dust clouds and see them, black shadows turning in wheels, like buzzards. While Elif and I had been in Burgas, the bulldozers had razed a dozen more houses. They'd cleared the rubble and leveled the ground so two excavators could dig up foundations. A crane had laid down a mesh of steel rods, a mixer had poured in the concrete. Where only a week before there had been houses and stork nests, now stood the bases of five new towers.

We found Grandpa watching the workers pour concrete for a sixth foundation. He was smoking a cigarette and by his side Saint Kosta, his wing no longer bandaged, dug in the dirt with his talons. From the dust, Grandpa's hair, the beard he still had not shaved off, and the stork's black feathers had turned so gray they both looked like one with the ruins.

When I spoke to him he didn't seem to hear me. And even after I pulled on his sleeve he watched me with eyes that said he wasn't really there. "Go with Elif," I told him. "Eat lunch. Drink some tea. I'll fix this mess."

I'd never set foot in a mosque before, but I didn't stop to admire the moment. As inside a church, the space was gloomy and for a while all I saw were green shadows and green blotches. I'd run through the village and now sweat poured down my face in rivers. Blood boomed through my temples, and at my feet the planks creaked dully beneath a thick carpet. The air smelled of sweat—my own—and the dust of the ruins, which packed my nostrils. I was just turning when my shoe caught a bump in the carpet and I tripped, stomped, and the floor shook loudly beneath me.

"For shame," someone said then. By the voice, I knew it was the imam, but all I saw was a green figure in the doorway.

"I've come to talk to you," I told him as firmly as I could.

"Show some respect," he whispered. "Come outside, we'll talk then."

Respect, I told him once we were out in the courtyard, was precisely the thing *he* was not showing. Respect for us, for the law. And then a strange thing happened. The redness of my face, the shortness of my breath, the justness of my words must have moved him, because he said, "Calm down. Have a seat. Drink some water."

He sat me down on a bench under a trellis and brought me a cold jar. He let me drink it in silence and we waited for my blood to cool down a little.

"It seems," he said at last, "there has been some big confusion. So let me dispel it. Three years ago," he said, "your grandfather came to Klisura waving about, much the way you do now, a sheet of paper. A document, which said the village school had been built in his name and so he owned it. But I knew this document was invalid and your grandfather too knew it."

"Nonsense," I cried. The ownership deed was completely valid. And Grandpa owned not just the school, but all the other houses. He'd bought them, fair and square, and later he'd transferred them, school and houses, all to my name.

"Poor boy." The imam laughed a fake laugh. "Is that what he's told you?"

And then, with a self-satisfaction I'd mistaken for kindness, he told me the rest of the story.

It was this story I was telling now, much too loudly, to Elif and Grandpa. I had run all the way back after seeing the imam to find them eating lunch on the terrace.

Here was the gist, fair and square: in the mid-sixties every single family from the Christian hamlet had been moved to the city. A state-mandated urbanization, all through Bulgaria. As compensation, in exchange for their houses, the families had been given city apartments—two entire blocks of flats in Burgas all for Klisurans. To put it plainly, in the mid-sixties the Christian hamlet had stopped being a village. The state had taken the land and transformed it into a border zone, a buffer.

Three years ago, the zone's status was reconsidered. But the land was still the property of the state and it was the state that contracted a foreign company to build on it a complex of wind turbines. The construction had just begun—see right there the unfinished tower?—when my grandfather showed up, in his hand a sheet of paper.

Every Klisuran who'd owned a house had been given in exchange an apartment. Every ownership deed had been annulled. But Grandpa's had fallen through the cracks somehow. Maybe because by that time he no longer lived in Klisura; maybe because some clerk had assumed the school must already be state-owned. After all, how could a school belong to a single person?

But it belonged to Grandpa, or so he claimed through this paper. Yet the state too had its papers, according to which no private entity could own land in the Christian hamlet.

It was a paradox. A legal casus. But until Grandpa's deed was officially annulled, until the casus was resolved, there could be no construction of wind turbines—the law did not allow for power generators to be erected within residential limits.

"So *they* took you to court, Grandpa," I said, and sat down in a chair, exhausted. "They thought, how hard could it be really, to prove your ownership deed was outdated and then annul it?"

"For three years your grandfather has jerked us around,"

the imam had told me out in the courtyard. "Forgive my language, but better words allude me."

"For three years, Grandpa," I said now in his face on the terrace, "you've dragged out this lawsuit. That's why you sold our family land, my share and my father's. Even your city apartment. You needed money to pay your lawyers."

Grandpa puffed out some air and reached for his lighter. "And you believe the imam?"

I watched him struggle to pull out a cigarette from the pack, and my heart grew heavy. To see this man the way I saw him now pained me something fierce. "I want to believe *you*," I told him. "So prove to me that we own these houses. Not once have I asked to see any papers. Now I'm asking."

Trembling, he dabbed a cigarette against his mustache a few times. When he found his lips at last he lit up and gulped the smoke in.

"We have one document," he admitted. "For this school building, which is yours now. I never owned any other houses." Then he smoked hungrily, keeping his eyes low on the table. A rotten heaviness settled in my stomach. A wave of nausea. For months now he'd lied to my face.

"Look at me, Grandpa," I told him. For there was more to the imam's story.

Each time before a court hearing, Grandpa had faked some kind of sickness. Four strokes. One heart attack. A kidney stone crisis. Six times Grandpa had entered the hospital a week before his court dates.

"Is this what happened last month? When they destroyed the first two houses?"

He began to mumble and dropped his cigarette on the table. Fumbling to retrieve it, he spilled its tip into a shower of tiny sparks, which Elif beat down. When she looked up at me, her eyes themselves were casting sparks in showers. "You're hurting him. Stop it!"

I could see he was hurting. But I couldn't stop it. And why should I? So he wouldn't fake another stroke?

"Did you fake it?" I said.

"For God's sake, my boy! You were here. You saw me."

"What about the strokes before that? The heart attack? Did you fake them?"

"For God's sake. Maybe. But understand my position. I can't let them build a wind farm right where the storks are nesting, right in the path of their migration. The turbines will kill them in thousands, it's just that simple."

"Why did you lie to me, Grandpa?" I said, so quietly that at first I wasn't sure he'd heard me. For some time he struggled to light a new cigarette from the butt of the old one. Then he took a few deep drags.

"I was afraid," he said. "I sold your land and left you nothing. I feared you'd run away if I told you the whole truth."

He had feared correctly. But it went far beyond anger. "Tell me, Grandpa, what other lies have you told me? Is Lenio a lie? Or the *nestinari*? And what about your teaching years?"

"All true, damn it," he said, and slammed his fist on the table. The plates rattled. Saint Kosta jumped in the corner and, flapping his wings, hurled at us a cloud of gray dust.

"All true?" I said, and kept my eyes fixed on Grandpa's, to see the kind of dirty flame that would ignite there.

"All true," he said, this time more softly. And there was no flame in his eye, no twitch of his eyelid. He lied to me sweetly, the way you lie to a small child too gullible to catch your deception, or too weak to handle things as they really are.

"He's lied before, your grandfather," the imam had told me out in the mosque courtyard. "Ask him why the Communist Party dispatched him to teach in Klisura. With what objective. Ask him about the kind of lessons he taught his students. About the things they did to us, he and the priest, his comrade."

My grandfather had not been exiled for his Party resignation. The Party had sent him to Klisura with his agreement. His mission—to indoctrinate the village Muslims. To make sure they grew up away from their roots; to make them believe they were truly Bulgarian.

But now on the terrace, I couldn't stand to ask him. Not when he'd lied to me with such sweet softness. I heard myself speak as if from a great distance. How stupid did he think the storks were to fly in droves into the spinning turbines? And did he understand what these wind turbines would mean for Klisura? For the whole Strandja even? Could he imagine the jobs they'd create, the new investments?

"Please, spare us," Elif said, and it was her voice, sharp and raspy from the cigarette she too was smoking, that brought me back from the distance. "You sound just like my father."

"And you?" I said, and for a long time didn't know what else to say, or how to say it. "I thought you took university classes. I thought you had exams coming. Isn't this why you studied and why every day you rode the bus to Burgas?"

Her face turned pale, then flaming. And for this shame, she had a good reason. She'd dropped out of the university a full semester back and kept it a secret. Too many failed exams; too many fights with professors. Besides, attending college had never been about the classes. It had always been about defying her father.

"Your father had sold you like a goat, you told me. For fifteen thousand deutsche marks. Is this the price tag you've assigned yourself? Why not go higher? Twenty or thirty thousand? Or are you afraid no one would pay this much for you?"

I spoke in a way no person should be speaking. I could see that each word was a slash with the dagger, which opened deep wounds. Elif was crying and Grandpa trembled and I told myself—let them.

Orhan's father hadn't bought her. She herself had promised to be Orhan's wife—because she knew his dirty name would hurt her own father and bring him dishonor. And now she'd chosen me for that same reason. "To spit in my face," the imam had told me.

"Here," I said. "I give twenty thousand in dollars. Is this enough to buy you?"

My hand shaking, I pulled the wad out of my pocket and slammed it down on the table. Again the plates rattled, again Saint Kosta jumped in his corner. For a long time Elif and Grandpa watched the money. Twenty thousand dollars. Tied with a red rubber band, a stack you'd think would be thicker. She no longer cried and he no longer trembled.

"What's this, my boy?" Grandpa asked me.

"I will make you an offer," the imam had said out in the courtyard. "Your grandpa's house is now in your name, but the deed does not hold water. It's a matter of time before the court annuls it." The next court date would be in September. "But you can't fake a stroke like your grandpa. You'll have to be present." And then, in September, once and for all, they'd take away the house and settle the casus.

This September they'd start building the turbines one way or another. But that was two months of construction squandered for nothing. Two months of financial losses. So here was the imam's offer.

"I gave them the right to build the wind farm," I told Grandpa now on the terrace. "I signed a permission form. I need the money to pay my credit card debt, my student loans. You sold my land without asking me and now I sold yours without asking. But I convinced them to let us keep the house so you can stay here. No need to thank me."

For a long time Grandpa smoked and watched me, unblinking. "You fool," he said at last. "I was so close!" And then he started laughing. His chest wheezed, a coughing fit seized him, and soon he was wiping away the tears. "In September you will be back in America. And that's another missed court date. Then they'll start sending you summonses, but how long before that mess gets settled? Two, three years? By then I'll be worm food. And with this illegal construction they've started? Who knows, the court might decide in our favor. You fool, we were so close!"

So that's why he'd transferred the house into my name—to jerk the court around a little longer? Without regard that this would put me in legal danger? I sat quietly for what seemed like an impossibly long time. I felt simultaneously outside of myself and somewhere very deep. Such weight crushed me, I could barely breathe. Nor could I think straight. There was only one thing of which I was certain—in this moment I wanted to be anywhere but here.

"Why wait until September to see me leave?" I said, and heard the words with great delay, like stones in a wall, falling. "Here," I said, and saw myself tossing him the mandolin strings I'd bought in Burgas. And at Elif I saw myself tossing the money. "To break the engagement. A gift on parting."

———————

I say to Petar, Petre my boy, man's heart is a lantern. And what good is a lantern unless it holds a flame? When the Turks come back, they'll torch the school we've been building. We'll take from its flame and light our lanterns. Our bones will be timber, Petre, our blood will be oil. We'll burn with black smoke, and Europe will see it.

And the Turks we've chased, Captain? Petar asks me. The women and the children? Who will see the black smoke when they are burning?

· NINE ·

I AM ONE THOUSAND METERS TALL. The sky is balanced firmly on my crown, but should I give a gentle nod, the sky will tumble. I've gathered the winds and clouds in my left hand, but should I squeeze only a little tighter—they'll turn to deluge. Upon my right palm rests the sun. I make a fist and down comes darkness. Elif and Grandpa, the imam and the storks, Klisura and the Strandja, they lie prostrate at my feet and at my mercy. I am one thousand meters tall here in the stork nest.

Where else was there for me to go? I climbed the trunk and all around me the black storks cried and beat their wings in horror. Why they didn't attack me, I don't know. How there were no storks in the nest at that moment, I'm not certain. But Elif's nylon baggie was there; and so was the skull in the towel. I rolled myself a joint and smoked it greedily, quickly. I'd come prepared with a lighter, but not ready for the stench of the birds, for the legions of tiny bugs—not ants, not ticks, but lice maybe?—that crawled in the straw and among the sticks.

And yet, with each new hit, my disgust gave way to curiosity, my curiosity to fascination. The more I watched these little creatures—each with the face of the others—the more they merged into a single stream of black blood, crawling, teeming, persisting up the tree, through the hay, up my legs. Ants, ticks, lice, it didn't matter what they were. They were life, life that, like a giant heart, the tree pumped, life that tickled my skin and bit me.

I could end this life with a single gesture. Down my palm went and I smeared it in circles against my calf. My skin shone black with lifeless mush, but even then the other teeming and persisting creatures went on teeming and persisting, oblivious to what had happened. I grew angry. I slapped my palm again and killed another wave and then another until my legs and palms were burning, sticky and black with stinking guts. Yet even then, the flow kept flowing. Not because the bugs were smart or stupid, cowardly or courageous, but because they *were*. Because that's what life did; it went on living.

A great, invisible heel stepped down on my chest, so hard I found it difficult to breathe. I pulled the black towel from the straw, the skull from the towel. How disappointingly light it felt in my palm now, this human skull; how quickly the teeming bugs descended from my hand and onto its yellow bone; through its nasal cavity, out its eye sockets, and like a curious thumb—my great-grandfather's—along the tooth-line, in and out of the gaps where teeth were missing.

I brought the skull to my lips as if to kiss it and whispered softly into the hollow of its eye. One evil egg after another. The storks, whom I'd sentenced to death with a single signature. Grandpa, whom I'd betrayed. Elif, whom I'd judged and ridiculed. I expelled them, one after the other. I purged myself and the skull grew heavy. But I didn't grow light. Who was I to judge Elif, when I myself had found no strength to finish grad school? Who was I to blame Grandpa for the things he'd done in his youth as a teacher, for betraying me, when I myself had betrayed him, time and again in the past? Not picking up the phone, not writing him any letters. And why? Because he reminded me of some previous, dark life I didn't want to be reminded of? If only. I'd renounced him out of laziness. It was as pitiful as that. As pitiful as spending fifteen years separated because one political regime has fallen and another has risen in its place. Because there is no money in Bulgaria for a good life. Because your father says, *We must go West!* And so you go. Money and laziness. Of all the reasons in the world.

And now here was the money. Twenty thousand dollars, held together with a red rubber band. Because isn't this why you returned? To sell your land and pay off your PlayStation, your Stratocaster, and your iBook? Or did you come for the adventure? You're in your twenties, after all, and isn't this the time to *find* yourself? Be honest. You were jealous to hear about your freshman-year roommate teaching English in Thailand. Eating noodle soup out of nylon bags, going to bed with beautiful, exotic women.

So you eat your soup out of an earthen pot now, with a wooden spoon. You drink well water out of a jar, and let's be honest, the girl you go to bed with is both beautiful and exotic. You whisper your troubles into a human skull and at your feet are bones, the bones of Thracians, Greeks, and Romans, Slavs, Bulgarians, and Turks, like stepping stones that lead you to yourself. Or that's what you've tried to turn them into anyway. Upon their bones, you are one thousand meters tall. But on your own? Be honest. No sky is really balanced on your crown. You hold no winds or clouds or suns. Bow all you want; make fists and pout. Nothing will happen. Except, in sixty years' time, at most, you'll leave a skull, like all the others.

It doesn't matter if the skull you hold was once a man's or a woman's. It doesn't matter if her eyes were blue or dark, if her nose was hooked or snubbed. To you all skulls are one skull and only the faces change like masks. Admit it, even now, you feel so proud of this revelation.

And hungry. God, what would you give, right now, for a hunk of bread and white cheese, for a fresh tomato with sunflower oil and a sprig of basil? For a jar of that cool well water? But that's life for you, isn't it, *amerikanche*? Its hunger for bread and cheese puts all the rest to sleep—shame, dignity, regrets—they all disappear when life is hungry. And so, you go on living life.

"I swear, American. You are the weirdest fucker."

It took me some time to figure out where I was. To realize Elif was standing outside the nest, not even an elbow's length away. "You've been talking to yourself for five minutes straight," she said. "How high are you exactly?"

A thousand meters high. And on my head the sky— Instead, I told her to leave me be.

"No chance," she said. "You've got my stash."

"I'll pay you back."

"You did already."

"Elif," I said. I wanted to tell her I was sorry. I wanted to tell her a hundred other things that seemed important. But would she understand me?

"Why are you here?" I said instead.

"Isn't it obvious? I've come to steal you."

· TEN ·

AND SO SHE DID. Back at the house I gobbled bread and cheese and tomatoes, sweeter than I had imagined—and then, without a word to Elif or Grandpa, retreated to my room and slept like the slaughtered.

I awoke terribly thirsty. The roosters started crowing from the Muslim hamlet, the sky grew a thinner dark, and only then did I realize Elif was in bed beside me, facing the wall, as far away as she could be lying.

Down by the well, I drank straight from the bucket. My throat iced up. My stomach swelled heavy. The chain tolled against the well walls, with a splash the bucket tumbled, and a pair of wings flapped in the blue dawn. Beyond the rows of tomatoes Saint Kosta took one, two quick steps and, wings beating, lifted a meter or two in the air. Then he was back on the ground, his left wing trembling, unable to extend like the other.

"Healed crooked," Grandpa said in a hoarse voice behind me. I hadn't seen him until now—on the bench, smoking. Most likely he'd spent the night out here. "This too is my fault," he said, and when he stood up cigarette ash poured from his lap in a gray shower.

I did not speak to him for the next three days, nor did I exchange more than a few words with Elif. Things were bad between us. We were headed in a dangerous direction and we both knew it. Each morning, I felt sicker. My head hurt and so did my muscles. By the fourth day my forehead was burning. And that fire, strangely, was what would bring us salvation.

"Is this a mole?" I asked her on the fifth day. The heat of her breath pricked my back like needles while she was checking.

"A mole?" she said. "I don't think so."

"Comrade teacher," the doctor in town told Grandpa, "we could play a game of darts on his back, it's that clear." Then he called the nurse into his office so she too could see it.

"Textbook," the nurse said, and the doctor asked if I would let him take a picture. His nephew had brought him a Polaroid from Germany and he was building an album of significant cases. He flapped the picture a few times and on it my back and the red rash came into existence. A fist-sized scarlet center, a circle of clear skin around it, and then another, larger scarlet circle. Classic presentation. No sense in wasting money on blood work.

"And the tick?" he asked.

"I burned it," Elif said from the corner.

"I would have liked to take its picture," the doctor said,

and stuck a thermometer under my armpit. "Why did you wait a whole week after you found it? You should have come sooner."

"We thought he was acting," said Grandpa.

The doctor pulled out the thermometer and read it. "Thirty-eight-point-eight. A damn good actor."

"And muscle soreness," I made sure to tell him. "And my head is splitting."

"Textbook," the doctor said, and wrote me a prescription. Ten days on doxycycline and I'd be tip-top.

"Curious luck, comrade teacher," he told Grandpa at the doorway. "To come all the way from America and get bitten." But that was the tick for you. A nondiscriminatory creature. American, Bulgarian, Turkish, or Gypsy. The tick didn't care what you were, really. All the same, it still bit you.

"We should learn from the tick," the doctor told us on parting. And once more lamented he hadn't taken its picture.

We returned to Klisura with the sun low above dark hills. Dust from the construction site rolled down the road in clouds of silver. Each time the wind gusted, the clouds' form shifted. Like mischievous spirits they whirled around for attention, slapped our cheeks, pulled our hair and ears, stole the words from our lips and let the wind take them.

One such cloud spun like a funnel by the gates of the municipal building. Two meters tall, a hundred and fifty kilos heavy, his windy flesh branded with deep scars. He didn't speak to me, he bellowed. What, I couldn't decipher. When we passed by the old church, its bells started tolling. They had been taken to the city long ago, these bells, but all the same I heard them calling. I tasted their bitter copper. From every roof, from every nest the storks were staring. Their bills sounded like metal grinding on metal and when I looked up I saw not storks but men and women cluttered in the nests, stropping long knives, the men against their sashes, the women against their headscarves. Red sparks spilled in all directions and any minute now the village would catch fire. At our house, the clouds of silver kept reshaping until a girl stood in the courtyard. Thin like a black wick, she flapped her wings, tried to fly away, but couldn't.

"We need to fix her wing," I think I told Grandpa once they'd put me in bed. "We need to let her fly away."

He jabbed a thermometer under my armpit and Elif slapped a stinking kerchief on my forehead. Vinegar trickled down my temples, cold like the fingers of the dead.

"Forty-one-point-six," I heard Grandpa say. And when they asked me how I was feeling, I told them excellent, delighted. My sickness would fix us *all*. "Where is the tick?" I said. "I want to thank him." Or maybe no one asked me. Maybe I said nothing like this.

· ELEVEN ·

THE RUMOR TRAVELED through Klisura like wind from Turkey, loud, unyielding. The teacher's boy was burning with Saint Kosta's fever. Before too long our gates were crowded with women. They'd come from the Muslim hamlet to see— what exactly? The American, wiggling across a sweat-soaked mattress, his lips spilling fire, his feet taking frantic steps in the air? And the noise of his teeth like the bills of two storks fighting? Or were they here to see the man for whom Elif had stood up to her own father?

Handsome he is, they whispered. And wealthy. He'd take her away from this mountain. Across the sea, to a new world. How they hated me and loved me in equal measure. How they envied Elif, wringing a vinegar kerchief, spreading it gently across my forehead. How they wished it was their fingers that caressed my temples, their old bodies that nestled, like serpents, beside me.

No, they were not young women. They'd lived for sixty, seventy years. They'd borne children who in turn had borne children of their own. Not once had they stood up to their husbands; not once had they done what they'd wished to. Now here was a girl who did as she wanted. How dared she expect bliss and freedom while an endless rope of women before her had received only ache and hardship? They too arose, these long-dead women, envious, outraged, indignant. At our gates they joined their living daughters. *We curse them*, they said of me and of Elif. And where they'd lain the earth gaped hollow. Their husbands groped the void and bellowed, *Where have our females gone?* In no time they too were digging; they too were sprouting like rhododendrons. A multitude of long-expired men had joined their long-expired women.

I saw them where they hung, in the yard, on my window. I heard them crying. They demanded nothing unfair. Only that the primordial order of human suffering be followed for me and for Elif as it had been for them.

Lower the curtains, I pleaded with her. Chase them away, I begged of Grandpa.

It's just Baba Mina, they told me. Bringing you thyme tea. It's just pills, not dry bones. Just turbines, not a skeleton army. Yet at the time, such corporeal matters escaped me.

Like the feverish turbine construction under way now that I'd signed my permission. Or like Elif, sneaking to see Aysha. Their father at the mosque, and their mother rushing Elif in, hoping the hag across the street wouldn't catch them. Breaking a bar of chocolate into little pieces, brewing tea, and the three of them chatting, down on the floor, forgetting their troubles, palms on their lips, laughing. Then the imam storming in, for the hag had not been outsmarted.

His boot kicking the teacups, chipping the saucers, hot tea spilling on the Persian carpet. Aysha crying, but not Elif and not her mother. For men like the imam a woman's tears were like acacia honey. Or so Elif's grandmother had once told her. *No honey,* kazam, *and the drone grows hungry. Don't feed him, then, my darling, but learn instead to make him starve.*

· TWELVE ·

JULY WAS SLIPPING INTO AUGUST. Up the slopes of the Strandja the grass was turning yellow, the leaves of the oak trees a duller green. Dry winds gusted through the streets, chased palls of dust from the construction, chapped our lips. Orphaned storks spun long, tired wheels overhead, restless it seemed to head back south. It hadn't rained in weeks and one day, far across the hills, we recognized the black snakes of smoke twisting against the cloudless blue—the brush had caught on fire.

My fever had lasted for a week. A few more days passed in weakness and I was cured. Stronger than a bull, cleverer than a fox. Thyme tea and walnut kernels had done the trick. And the antibiotics.

Grandpa and I were getting along well. It seemed like he'd forgiven me for signing the papers, and I in turn forgave him for selling my land, for feeding me nothing but lies.

There were still things that needed clarification, but I wasn't eager to unearth them just yet. As before, he spent his days out on the terrace, smoking, though now he played backgammon with Elif. He never went to the construction site and he rarely looked up at the sky. He was ashamed, I knew that much.

Elif and I too got along well. She'd forgiven me for tossing the money at her in such a lowly fashion and I'd forgiven her— Dear God. What use was it to keep composing lists, to keep on naming our transgressions and crossing them out one by one? We'd made mistakes and then had been forgiven. We ourselves forgave.

In my delirium, I'd worked out a plan, which even after I got better sounded persuasive. I wanted to marry Elif officially in August. Then take her to the States. A different culture, a new language—it wouldn't be easy. But I'd pay off my student loans, find a basic job, teach Elif English. And once we'd saved up enough money, we'd hit the road toward a brave new future.

Each time we found ourselves alone, I tried to tell her of my plan. And each time, I swallowed my tongue in fear. Was I afraid she'd say no or did I fear the plan was hogwash? Even this I was scared to consider.

It was July 28, I won't forget. We took the bus to Burgas and marched straight to the courthouse. We waited in line, made it to the clerk, witnessed the glass slide in our faces, the *lunch break* sign flip over. We waited another hour just to be informed Elif's request to change her name had not been reviewed yet.

This was, the clerk assured us, no picnic. It took time for

the court to view all cases. "Learn patience, children," she said. "It's a heavenly virtue."

I knew that Elif wanted to change her name officially before we got married. But I couldn't wait that long. So when on our way to the station she slipped into a drugstore, I waited by the door and tried to muster some courage.

A brave new world, I kept repeating. Freedom. Possibility. America.

"They were out," Elif barked, flying out of the store, and I was forced to chase her up the street to another. I asked her what she was after.

"Damn it, American," she said, not even turning. "Can't you leave me be for just a minute?"

I could see that the court's tardiness had upset her. But was I bothering her that much really? We checked three more drugstores before at last she stepped out of the fourth one clutching a paper bag.

I asked if she was hungry. "A Big Mac and fries? A large milkshake?"

"Please stop!" she said. "Please, please. Just stop."

In an instant her face had lost all color. Her eyes scurried deeper into their sockets, like frightened animals into their burrows. Even the smell her body exuded turned instantaneously sour. I was that close and I sensed it. A stream of people shuffled around us on the sidewalk. Some were watching, but I didn't care.

"What's wrong?" I said. I took her hand, fearful she might run away, glad she hadn't. For a long time, she kept her eyes on the pavement. Some cobblestones beneath our feet were loose and vibrated. Someone bumped into me, into her; the crowd tossed us about like a river.

"I'm late," she said.

At first I thought I had misheard her. I asked her to repeat and she repeated.

How late? I asked. Two weeks. No. A little over. But it had happened before—a few years back, when, to punish her father, she'd refused to eat a bite. She'd been late then, skipped two entire cycles.

We'd slipped around a corner where the sidewalk was strangely vacant. But now the sun was beating down on us, poking me in the eyes, making it really difficult to focus.

Could it be stress? I wanted to ask. Being chased out of her home, not seeing Aysha? Could it be because of my sickness?

And how? We had used protection!

Instead, I must have kept silent.

"Say something," she begged me, no longer angry sounding.

The sun was blinding, poking, irritating. I pulled her out of its reach, under the shade of a linden tree. I cupped her hand in mine and kissed the tips of her fingers.

From the drugstore Elif had bought a pregnancy test. She'd planned to use it in the toilet at the station, in secret.

"We'll do the test," I told her, and took the small bag. "But home, in Klisura."

And that, by the way she sought my embrace, seemed to please her.

We kept very quiet on the ride to the village. The driver tried a conversation, but right away Elif moved to the back of the bus and I followed. There we sat stiffly, not touching, her eyes out the window, mine straight ahead, on the plastic dice rocking from the rearview mirror, on the poster of Hristo

Stoichkov, on the picture of Samantha Fox in the nude. Not that I saw them. My mind was at once in a hundred places, all cracking with static.

I had to tell myself not to clutch the bag as hard as I clutched it. To ease up a little. What would it mean if the test turned out this way and what if the other? I tried to consider the outcomes. To sense which way I was leaning. But there was too much static, my head was too dizzy, too buzzing. I didn't know what it was that I feared. Just that I feared, wildly.

Say something, I thought. Elif needs you. Hold her hand again and kiss it. But when I tried to reach over, my muscles had turned liquid. I was paralyzed and couldn't blink even.

"Look at them," I said, beside myself, of Samantha Fox's magnificent breasts. "Enormous."

"I'd rather look at you," Elif said. "It's funnier that way."

"I'm serious," I said. "The poor woman. Think of the back pain."

"Pinned up there, nude and cold, with no one to save her."

"A martyr," I said.

"A saint even."

We burst out laughing. We snorted, choked, coughed, kept laughing with great hunger.

"What are we going to do, *amerikanche*?" Elif said, and wiped away the tears.

"We'll name her Samantha. That's what."

This too sounded awfully funny. And I simply couldn't believe it. A minute ago I'd been so scared, so uncertain. Along which path should I wish for the test to send us?

It was impossible now to envision a more senseless question.

PART
SIX

· ONE ·

I AWOKE CONVINCED that the turbines had begun spinning—
so loud was the whoosh that had roused me. It seemed like
the windows rattled. Tin cans rolled through the courtyard and a jar shattered to pieces. Then I heard crying, mad
and mournful. And Grandpa calling. I'm not sure what he
said exactly, his voice was too low and soothing.

Already Elif stood by the window.

"He's throwing a fit," she said. "The poor thing."

And really, in the yard, Saint Kosta was raising mayhem.
One moment he was atop the bench; the next he'd pushed
himself off, beating his wings grotesquely. Two, three meters,
then he'd plummet. He resembled a fish thrashing ashore,
choking. Bare-chested, a Thracian gladiator, Grandpa tried
to approach him, the shirt in his hands like a weighted net.
Once he cast the shirt, but Saint Kosta dodged it, flapped his
wings, screamed, and bounced to the well, where he perched,

breathing heavily. Grandpa watched him, his hands spread like thin wings, and the shirt he held, billowing in the wind.

It was then that I saw the reason—thick wheels overhead, hundreds of storks spinning. They'd begun to gather. They would fly south soon.

Once again Grandpa threw his shirt at Saint Kosta, and once again he missed him. The stork spooked, lost his balance, and plunged right down the well's mouth. Elif yelped. Grandpa ran to the well, cursing. He pulled on the rope and the pail and soon he was holding Saint Kosta and petting gently the base of his neck.

"Oh, no," Elif said. "Here it comes. Get ready."

She wanted her bucket. I sprinted to the hallway and brought it. It was not pretty, but it was faster this way. Each morning, her sickness seemed to get worse. As the day waned, the nausea didn't. Five in the afternoon and she'd still be retching. "That baby," she said sometimes, "she's contrary like her mother."

We believed it was a girl we were having.

"Way too early to tell, *compadre*," the doctor in town had told us. We had gone to see him at Grandpa's insistence.

Grandpa himself learned the news only moments after the test confirmed it. Elif and I walked out to the terrace. We held sweaty hands and were quite embarrassed. But on the inside we were bursting. When he saw us, Grandpa stood up.

"Old man—" I began, but he waved his cigarette *shut up*.

"Cut the crap," he said. "Is it a plus or a minus? I saw the box in the toilet. A plus or a minus?"

I stuck out the stick, to prove it. Immediately he crushed his cigarette in the ashtray. He tossed the pack over the banister. He dusted off his hands, snatched the stick, and examined it closely.

"Come here," he ordered Elif, who'd turned crimson. He gripped her cheeks and planted a kiss on her forehead. His big hand smacked me on the neck, playful-like. "Dear God," he said. "I'm now immortal. A great-grandfather."

He reached for the bottle of *rakia*—these days always on the table beside him. Then he seemed to reconsider. "We can't trust a piece of plastic. This is serious business."

The next day, we were in town at the doctor's—the same one who'd saved me from the tick, the same one who'd given Grandpa the fake medical papers to delay his trial.

"Comrade teacher, you can absolutely trust this piece of plastic. But I'll do you one better."

The ultrasound machine, he said; his nephew had brought it from Munich. So what if a horse doctor had used it there? He let Elif lie down on the couch and Grandpa and I stepped to the side, so she could expose her stomach. The doctor squirted gel from a tube, smeared it with the transducer. Elif shrieked with the cold.

"Find me one American doctor," he said, "who can do this better with what I've been given."

He called us over and we stared at the gray screen. Some people have trouble telling this from that in an ultrasound image. I am not one of those people.

"Can you see it?" I asked Elif, and she nodded, only a small nod.

"Dear God," Grandpa bellowed. "I too can see it."

A tiny thing, so small to look at you'd say it was nothing. And in that nothing already a heart beating and the emptiness taking on form and flesh, purpose and meaning.

· TWO ·

THE SMELL OF WHITE CHEESE nauseated her, and the taste of yellow cheese. The texture of ripe tomatoes. The way bread crust pressed against her palate when she chewed it. But she didn't mind couscous one bit and that's what she ate, for breakfast, for lunch and dinner. Sometimes she mixed it with yogurt, sometimes with black currant jelly. She picked it straight off the plate with her fingers. "All my life," she said, "I've hated couscous. But I guess the baby likes it."

We spoke of the baby a great deal. She'd be the prettiest, the healthiest, the strongest. We slept poorly, what with Elif's retching, and we spent our nights making things up. We'd marry right after the name change. Then we'd go to the U.S. All my fears proved groundless—I shared my plan with Elif and she said only, "You'd better start teaching me English."

So I started. We came up with a few essential phrases—

I'm hungry. I'm thirsty. How much for a packet of couscous?
Then we began to name the world around us—desk, chair,
sky, mountain. We felt like the original man and woman, giving face to the faceless.

"You realize, *amerikanche*," Elif said one night, "how
much power over me you're holding?" I could create for her
a brand-new world. A world in which the desk was an apple,
the apple a window, and she would have no way of knowing. She would have to believe me.

"Do it," she said one night. "Make me a new world."

"What do you call this?" she said, and ran her fingers
across the blanket.

"An ocean," I said, the first word I thought of.

So she pulled the ocean up to our chins, its sands and
reefs, caves, sunken ships, gold treasures, sharks, whales,
dolphins, and plankton.

"And this?" she said, and gripped one lock of her hair.

"A river."

I pressed my lips to its waters, cool and lulling. How easy
it was to change the world. All it took was to alter the way
you saw it.

Elif's hair had grown down past her shoulders. Beautiful,
glimmering black tresses. She no longer had any desire to
keep them at a boy's length. "I feel feminine," she said once.
"For the first time, a woman."

Some days we went to see the turbines. The construction
was over. The machines gone, no sign of the workers. And
the five turbines so clean with the sun setting and their metal
bodies catching the last rays. The blades stretched like arms,

perfectly still, not yet turning. Each turbine a many-armed giant. Great gods of the old days, immersed in deep meditation, at the same time creators of life and destruction.

"I hope they wait for the storks to fly off," I said. "And only then turn the blades on."

Overhead, the flocks had thickened. More and more storks arrived each day and finally, at the end of August, they set off on their journey. Grandpa poured us three shots of *rakia*—for me, for him, and for Saint Kosta. We downed ours in one gulp and the stork dipped his bill in his glass and overturned it.

"Will I live to see them next spring?" Grandpa said, and I told him—of course he'd see them.

"I hope not, my boy. I don't think I can take it."

That day Grandpa stayed on the terrace long past sunset. He didn't touch his dinner, nor did he drink any more *rakia*. Saint Kosta had perched in the corner and to me they both looked so low and defeated.

"In my mind I picture them flying," Grandpa told me when I sat down beside him. "I imagine their journey. Where they are this very moment. What the air feels like way up there." When he turned to me, his eyes were sharp, clear.

"Take me with you, my boy, will you? I want to fly on a plane. I want to see the New World."

I'm not sure if he meant this or was just talking. But why not? I'd seen older men crossing the ocean to visit their children.

You got it! I wanted to say, yet I said nothing. I knew better, and when Grandpa smiled, nodded, I saw he too knew better.

Above us the flocks were flowing, only we couldn't see

them. We heard the noise they made, like the rush of a celestial river no human eye was meant to dirty. It was close to midnight when Grandpa gave out a whistle. A loud, clean singsong that carried across the Strandja. *Take good care of them*, he was saying, though this time, nobody answered.

· THREE ·

WE RECEIVED THE COURT'S DECISION on the last day of August. A mailman delivered the certified letter right to our gates so Elif could sign that she'd gotten it. I didn't even know regular mail came to Klisura. How silly I felt, all this time paying the bus driver.

Elif ripped the envelope open in the courtyard and her eyes darted across the page. Her face was a mask of dark and bright pieces, the way the sun strained through the grapevine.

"I don't believe it," she said. She plunged down on the bench and reread the letter. "They've denied me the name change."

The court had found her reasons insubstantial.

"They change my name as a kid when I don't want it. Now I want it and they won't let me."

"Can't we appeal?" I asked.

"I don't know. Can we?"

"Sure. Maybe. Listen," I said. "Keep your old name. What's the big deal?"

The words had not yet rolled off my tongue fully and I was already regretting them. If her look could do physical damage, I'd be very badly damaged.

"You don't get it, do you?" she said, then dropped the letter and marched to the house. The door to our room slammed three times, each progressively more spiteful. Grandpa was watching me from up on the terrace. He poured himself a glass of *rakia*.

"Do you even know what happened?" I asked him.

"It seems you don't either."

He was right. I couldn't see the big deal. Or rather, I saw it—I knew Elif wanted a fresh start, to be a brand-new person—but I didn't *feel* it. How would the mere change of a name achieve all this exactly? Changing the name was so artificial. The change had to come from the inside and that's what I told her.

"Open the door," I begged from the hallway. I sat down on the floor and kept talking. I tried to make her see my point. I spoke wisely and thought I was very convincing. At last, the chair she'd propped the door with moved on the other side and her hand stuck out through the gap just a little.

I reached to hold it, but she slapped mine away.

"No, you idiot," she said. "I need the bucket!"

· FOUR ·

THE NIGHT AFTER her name request was rejected, Elif had her first in a series of nightmares. I was awake, listening to the dark and the mountain, when she started sobbing. She was crying in her sleep, which old superstition claimed was a good thing. But it wasn't a good thing. It couldn't be. She kept crying even after her eyes opened. She refused to tell me what she'd dreamed of, but the following night the dream returned and she relented. She had found herself in the nest, on the stork tree, and all around her were black storks. They watched her with gray eyes, human. Then just like that the storks began beating their wings and rose together, a black mass, terrible, awful, up, up, away from the old tree. And she couldn't stop them. She wanted to. Had to. But she couldn't.

"They took it away," she said, and the tears rolled on. "I couldn't stop them."

"It's my father," she told me the next morning. "He's laid a black spell on me. He's the imam. He's cursed me."

"Nonsense," I said. But I believed her.

When Saint Kosta came to us in the courtyard we both cowered.

"Grandpa," Elif cried. "Keep him away, Grandpa!"

"I can't stand to see you this way," Grandpa told us one evening. We had all gathered on the terrace to eat couscous for dinner. As of the last few days Elif's nausea had gone away completely, but she still retained the old paleness.

"I can't help it," she said, and started crying. This time I didn't even reach to hold her. I felt entirely helpless. I knew of nothing I could do to make her feel better.

Night after night I dreamed bad dreams and awoke each morning more fatigued, more anxious. Dry, cool winds gusted through the streets of the village. Their wailing oppressed me and I caught myself missing the noise of the storks, which had once bothered me so much. Watching the wind turbines filled me with anger. Why weren't the blades spinning? All this rushing, fighting to build them and now they stood unmovable in the wind. What were these people waiting for exactly? Turn on the switch already. Generate. Energize. Harness. The power of the ever-gusting. Of the invisible, plentiful spirits.

Saint Kosta pestered me, like a dog seeking attention, always in my way, no doubt just to annoy me. The way Grandpa smacked his lips when he drank *rakia* got on my nerves. The way he scratched his neck.

Our time was running out, I knew that much. We had to do something and do it quickly. Run away from Klisura, away from all that haunted Elif, away from ourselves. Become new people and remain together. Or remain the same people and fall apart, each in his own orbit.

"Please don't cry so much," I'd tell Elif softly. "It's not good for you or the baby."

"I know it's not good," she said. "That's why I'm crying."

That night she had another nightmare. The black storks flying. She was convinced Saint Kosta was lurking outside to take away the baby. She was convinced her father had sent him. The heat of her forehead stung me when I kissed her.

"She's burning," I told Grandpa, and we measured her fever.

"God Almighty, boy," Grandpa said in the kitchen. He soaked a kerchief in vinegar. "God Almighty."

All night Elif tossed and turned. I, on the other hand, lay frozen. Couldn't sleep, couldn't move, couldn't breathe even. A total paralysis of the body. A complete shutdown of the mind. I must have dozed off at last, with the sky growing lighter.

I was in America, back in my apartment, in my bed. The tree outside my window was heavy with black storks. The storks watched me.

"Don't let them take it from us, *amerikanche*," Elif said in English beside me. "Don't let them fly away." Then the storks began to beat their wings and the world around us to rattle. They rose up, a black veil. Nothing I could do would stop them.

"I'm sorry," I told Elif.

Her face was as hot as the fire. She rested it on my chest and we lay like this in my dream together and we watched the black storks flying.

· FIVE ·

THE ULTRASOUND let out a low hum. The gray screen—a constant whistle, which could not be denied. Flat and high-pitched, it could cross mountains, seas, whole worlds.

"I'm very sorry," the doctor told us. She was the best in town, a specialist. Grandpa's old student had sent us to her once before and we were due for a checkup soon. But here we were now, urgently. A big line snaked outside her office, but she worked us right in.

"This is the sack," the doctor said and showed us. "This is the fetus. Can you see it?"

We could see it. There was no heartbeat. And the doctor said the fetus measured eight or nine weeks old, that it had not developed past that. But it had taken Elif's body time to react, in stages. First her morning sickness had gone. Now all this.

"When did the spotting first start?" the doctor asked,

and Elif told her. She had not told me. She had kept it a secret for two whole days. She'd hoped it would go away, that
she'd feel better. Then we woke up to bright-red blood on
the white sheet.

I panicked. I cried out, "We need to see the doctor."

Elif seemed calmer. "I'll lie still," she said. "I'll get better."
But lying still was out of the question. Her back was hurting
and the blood wasn't stopping. I knew she wouldn't want
me to discuss it with Grandpa, but I discussed it. "There is
no bus until tomorrow. Can we wait that long?"

He threw away his cigarette. "We can't wait." Then he
was out the gate, down the road. I heard Elif calling. Saint
Kosta had snuck inside, perched on the chair to watch her.

"Get him out," she cried, and I did. He resisted. He beat
his wings; his talons scratched the wood floor. By the time
I'd managed to shoo him into the yard, the military jeep was
pulling over. The imam was driving.

I was afraid Elif would throw a fit when she saw her
father, but she said nothing. We spread a blanket on the
backseat and laid her down on the blanket. I rested her head
on my lap, petted her cheeks and her forehead. I dabbed the
sweat away with a kerchief. I could tell she was in pain, by
her eyes, by how hard her teeth were clenching, but she made
no sound. Up front Grandpa and the imam too kept quiet.
Only in town did they speak—Grandpa was giving directions to the doctor's office.

Now we were inside the office, cool, dark, like the mosque.
An AC unit blew overhead and the drawn blinds buzzed
when the air hit them. The ultrasound buzzed. The screen
whistled.

The doctor was talking. "This happens to many women.
You'll grieve some, then you'll feel better. And your body—

no damage to it. You're young. Healthy. You'll be pregnant again before you know it."

Then the doctor gave us an option. She could remove the fetus. Or we could wait until Elif expelled it. I thought she ought to remove it. But Elif shook her head lightly. Her face shone awash so bright with screen light—silver, perfectly calm, tender. I couldn't bear to see it. I couldn't bear to see the gray screen. I stood up. The doctor was talking. When we went home there would be more blood. Back pain. Contractions. Then Elif would start to expel blood clots, pieces of the placenta. At last she'd expel the fetus. It could be tomorrow, or in a few days. It could be next week. All in all, it could take up to six weeks.

Six weeks, I thought. Carrying the baby like this for six weeks.

· SIX ·

THERE WAS MORE BLOOD that night. There was back pain. Elif lay in bed, under a wool blanket, and her teeth chattered. She was freezing. Grandpa brought her tea, but she wouldn't look up. She kept her eyes on her hands and her hands stiff on her belly. Every now and then, when the pain got sharper, her hands made fists and her knuckles turned to snowdrops. From time to time I left my chair to open the window, to let the breeze freshen up the air. The entire mountain had sunk into silence. I'd never heard a night so quiet. No wind, no movement. Complete absence.

I must have dozed off in the chair, until Elif's sobbing woke me. I put my hand on her stomach, but she pushed me away. It wasn't for her sake I wanted to touch her.

Her voice was hoarse, distant.

"I feel so empty," she said. "No spite. No venom. No hatred." She began to sob again and only then did she allow me to sit at the edge of the bed and kiss her forehead. "I'm so clean," she said. "So new."

"Then why are you crying?"

She took my hands and pressed her cheek against them. "Don't you understand?" she said. "It's all been emptied out. Nothing's left. Nothing."

"But I still love you," I said. She leaned her face on my chest and I held her.

· SEVEN ·

WE COULDN'T LET THE EARTH SWALLOW IT, those black jaws. We couldn't let the fire. So we climbed the stork tree. We pulled the black towel out of the nest and unwrapped it.

"My *kazam*," Elif said. "My darling." She set the skull aside and laid our baby upon the towel. It was a tiny thing, but already it had eyes, nubs for arms and legs, and where the brain would be—a dark spot.

Elif had expelled it that morning, after a series of painful contractions. Four days after we'd seen the doctor.

We wrapped the towel around it. We laid it gently into the soft hay.

"What about the skull?" I said.

"What about it?"

We left the skull as it was, in the nest, and we climbed down.

"Don't look back," Elif told me.

· EIGHT ·

IT WAS SOMETIME IN OCTOBER when Elif said she was leaving. We were in bed, but turned away from each other. We rarely touched now and if we did, always by accident, we jumped, startled, as if we'd brushed against a furnace.

The winds had grown colder. The days shorter. And the rains had returned to the Strandja. It was raining now, very softly, and out the window the sky looked like a great sea. The clouds were its waves, driving madly away from us, away from Klisura, toward the edge of the world. That's where the sea emptied out. It had no shores. The nothing contained it.

"I have to leave, *amerikanche*," Elif said. "I can't stay here."

My heart understood that. But if I tried to explain it to myself I failed badly. Why couldn't we work through all that had happened and reemerge stronger together? Why couldn't we go to America, start a new life?

And what about Aysha? I wanted to ask her. *What would she do without you?* This answer too I knew already. Elif would not allow her sister to walk down the same path she herself had once taken. She would not reward the little girl's extortions. Every night for many years Elif had begged Allah to cut the rope that tied her to Aysha. Yet Allah would not cut the rope for her, as he would not for anybody. All along, Elif understood now, she'd held a knife but had feared to use it. Now at last, she was ready. Aysha would be better off without her.

"Where will you go?" I mumbled. She took some time to think it over, though I don't think she was deciding. She was afraid to tell me.

"Turkey," she said. "Where else?" She turned around to face me. "American, give me some of that money. Two or three thousand."

I brought the wad from the drawer in which we kept it. "Take it all," I insisted.

"I can't do that."

"Sure you can. I'll feel much better."

"*Amerikanche*," she said. I wiped my cheeks and tried laughing, like it was a big joke. Then something turned inside me. I almost shouted, Wait. Hear me out. Listen!

There is always suffering in life. Those before us have suffered and we too must suffer. But there is also happiness, merriment, bliss. To be alive is to hurt and to laugh, not just one or the other. To laugh after you've hurt, while you're hurting, that's a great thing. Stay with me, I wanted to tell her. Let's learn to accept the world together.

All I managed was to mumble I loved her. By now she too was crying. "What am I going to do without you?" I said, and she didn't answer.

That afternoon she made me cut her long hair.

"I can't be Lada," she said. "I can't carry you around in my hair."

I spread old newspapers on the floor of our room and when we were done I wrapped the locks in the paper. "Burn them," she said, and I promised I'd do it. She knew I was lying.

Once again, she was the way I first saw her—boyish, her cheeks sharper with the short hair. But she was not at all the same now. She bore on her face some great lightness.

We spent the night in each other's arms, crying from time to time, but saying nothing. With the dawn she kissed me. I drifted away and when I woke up it was past midday. Rain drummed on the windows. The wad of money lay untouched where I'd left it.

I heard the knocking of dice from the terrace. A silly hope seized me. I jumped out of bed, sprinted. Grandpa was rolling alone, smoking. Saint Kosta lay in his corner.

"My boy," Grandpa said when he saw me.

I pulled up a chair, sat down, quiet. But in my mind I was already running. Through the yard, toward the ruins, out of Klisura. In my mind I was crossing the fence at the border. She couldn't have gotten that far. With some luck I would catch her.

Then even in my mind I knew better. One night, when she'd first moved into our house, Elif had cuddled in bed beside me. "All my life," she'd whispered, "I thought I was a rebel. In a world of fire dancers I thought *I* was the fire. But now I see, *amerikanche*, all along it's you who's the fire. You just don't yet know it."

At last, I too knew it. Fire did not return where it had passed once. Fire did not burn backward.

PART
SEVEN

· ONE ·

LOOK. SEE: NAZAR AGA, tall, terrible, rides at the head of his fifty soldiers—the new guards of the sultan, Muhammad's Victorious Army. Tucked in his red sash—his whip, his knife, his pistol. And beside them—the grand vizier's firman. "You are to go, Nazar Aga," the firman orders, "to the Strandja Mountains, to the Hasekiya. You are to meet there with Salih Baba, its ruler. And when you do—you are to end them. Both the place and its ruler."

Nazar Aga is now an old man. Yet still, he can't ride slowly. His blood is boiling and its vapor dyes all he sees in red—the mud, the rocks and trees, the mountain. The Hasekiya, he thinks, and spits to the left of his scarlet horse. For hundreds of years the Christians there have been spared from high taxes, allowed to worship their god freely. And Salih Baba! Nazar spits to the right side. The governor who's built for his Greek wife a Christian chapel in the middle of his *konak*; who's never erected a single mosque, but with whose permission the *raya* is constructing churches! A Bektashi dervish, and once upon a time a leader of the janissaries.

No. Spittle is not enough for such a man. The knife is not enough. Nor is the pistol.

Nazar Aga pulls out his whip and lashes—the horse, his own leg, he pays no mind to what the whip is striking. The horse flies up the narrow pathway; the soldiers struggle to keep up. Scarlet clouds are thickening the sky and scarlet rain is falling.

"Wait for me, Salih Baba. I'm coming. And with me, I'm bringing you a sweet gift. The sultan's will. Allah's judgment."

It is known that Murad I, the Godlike One, established the Ottoman Empire. He brought most of the Balkans under his rule, called himself sultan for the first time, and first instituted the *devshirmeh*—the recruit, the blood tribute. Every five years the strongest Christian boys were taken away from their parents, converted into the right faith, trained harshly, and so transformed into the sultan's most faithful soldiers—the janissaries. When a janissary was ready to serve, a Bektashi dervish blessed him. It was the Bektashi order, an old and mystic brotherhood, that guided the order of the janissaries. The two entwined the way the oak and ivy do.

The centuries rolled on; the janissaries grew greedy. First they wanted more money, and when the sultan refused, they rose in arms against him. So he paid them more, and after, with each new sultan, their salary increased. As did their want—to marry, to own land, to conduct private trade. All of these privileges they were given, yet their greed remained unquenched. It turned them from servants into masters, but it also made them weak and lazy. No longer were they undefeatable in battle.

When, after a shameful military loss, Sultan Osman II vowed to disband the order, the janissaries revolted and killed him. When Salim III attempted to reform them, they had him deposed.

At last Mahmud II came to power. He tricked both the janissaries and the Bektashis; he made them think he was their ally, but secretly he plotted, surrounded himself with allies of his own. One day in June, the year 1826, he issued a fatwa—he was to form a brand-new, modern army. He knew the janissaries would revolt and when they did he torched their barracks; thousands were burned alive. Those the sultan didn't burn, he beheaded. Those he didn't behead, he exiled.

With time the janissaries disappeared, but the Bektashi roots ran deep. They had been growing, spreading for centuries on end. So here now is Salih Baba, some twenty years later. Still governing the Hasekiya.

And here now is Nazar Aga, galloping through the Strandja, and in his sash: a knife, a gun, a firman.

Nazar Aga was once a janissary. He had a different name back then, a name that Mehmed Dede, the holy Baktashi leader, had given him himself. Why Nazar chose to betray his brothers no one knows. But it is known Nazar's was the hand that brought the first torch to the barracks, and his the yataghan that slew the most men.

Another thing too is known. How Nazar first earned the sultan's trust. What he told him, what he did.

This is what Nazar told the sultan when the two first met in the throne room. This is what Nazar did to prove he could be trusted: "When I was young, Mehmed Dede himself blessed me," Nazar told the sultan. "Only, he didn't put his hand on my shoulder, as is the custom, but leaned forward and kissed my right eye. Truly a great honor. And now, to prove I can be trusted, I shall gouge out that eye."

And so he did. On his glass eye, he ordered the glazier to paint the sign of the Nazar, so it might ward off all evil.

It is an eerie feeling, people say, to stand before the aga, to face him. His left eye watches you, black, human. His right eye judges you, azure, never closing, divine.

"I have seen the Black Stone in Mecca, golden with sunrise," Salih Baba says, and takes a pull from his chibouk, "the tomb of Otman Baba, Demir Baba Tekke. And now I've seen you, Nazar Aga, the janissary who blinded himself to please the sultan. Who betrayed his own brothers and put them to the flame. And so, I've seen it all, I think. I bid you welcome."

They sit out in the courtyard of the *konak*, under the branches of a mulberry tree laden with fruit. The rain has stopped, but drops collected in the leaves still drum against the silken cloth on which the men are resting, and mulberries fall every now and then and stain the silk like blood. A band of servants lines the walls, yet no one dares to move before the master's clap has echoed.

Salih Baba smokes; his chibouk crackles. The air smells

of the summer storm just gone, and sweet, of tobacco. Nazar Aga watches, unmoving, quiet. The drops drum against the silk. Tenderly, softly. The mulberries fall.

"I planted this tree myself," Salih Baba says at last. "Thirty years ago, when my feet first touched the Strandjan mud. I brought the seed with me from Anatolia. It's best to plant a mulberry from seed. It climbs very fast at first. Then it rests. Grows deep in root and plentiful in fruit. I had it grafted. Its mulberries are now both white and black. Pleasant shade, sweet taste. This tree has always been so good to me. I hope it always shows me kindness."

Nazar Aga raises his hand. He knows what the baba is trying to say and doesn't want to hear it. Hadji Bektash Veli, the saint and father of the order, once planted from a flaming branch a mulberry whose tip, the legend claims, still burns even today. By the black fruit the baba means the dervishes, by the white the janissaries, both tied together in a sacred bond. Nazar Aga himself was never grown from seed—he was born an infidel, to infidel parents before the janissaries took him. Yet the baba knows how fast Nazar grew, thirsty for knowledge. *And now he's begging me for mercy. A coward, he speaks in tales.*

Nazar Aga pulls out a white kerchief from his jacket and dabs against his glass eye. The socket oozes sometimes, when blood is pumping through his temples much too wildly.

"I haven't come to talk of trees," he says, and puts the kerchief, stained, back in his jacket. "I've come to end all this—infidels exempt from taxes, a governor who hasn't built a single mosque. A church inside an Ottoman *konak*."

Like a gunshot, Salih Baba's clap rings out within the stone walls. At once a servant girl appears. She carries a silver tray, and buzzing on the tray—two cups of coffee, a leather pouch. Her feet are bare and shiny with grains of sand she picks up as she nears. Her hair, pitch-black and never cut, down to her heels, all but brushes the ground.

Nazar Aga watches her. It seems as though he's met this girl before. Or no, as though he's always known he'll meet her.

Just then the girl looks up and sees him. Such fright. The tresses trip her. The tray bangs loudly on the cobblestones, the cups are shattered, and gold coins roll ringing from the pouch.

"Do what you must, Aga," Salih Baba tells him later, when it's clear no amount of talk or bribery can be of use. "Just wait another day. Tomorrow the Christians hold a feast. Let me watch them one last time. Then take my head."

All night Nazar Aga tosses. All night he turns. The mountain talks to him with wind, with calling storks. He sees the girl, her bare feet, the long black hair on which she trips. She falls and he, Nazar Aga, he too is falling.

Somewhere across the hills a bird begins to sing. Another answers. It's much too soon for dawn. And suddenly the heat of fire stings him. The torch he held to burn the janissary barracks, some twenty years back. He sees himself inside this flame: a little boy. The whole village has gathered on the square. And in the coals, his father, dancing.

And now so many years later the infidels are dancing under the mulberry tree. They carry their icons across the coals, barefooted, and the coals don't burn them. From upon the terrace Nazar Aga watches and blood trickles down his face. There before him, the girl with the river for hair is whirling. There Salih Baba, the Bektashi, is kissing the eyes of Christian saints and taking them across the fire.

The drums are beating, the bagpipes shrieking. Like the surf of giant waves the blood booms through the aga. As if in a dream, he descends the staircase of the *konak*, parts the crowd of peasants in the courtyard, stands before the dancing girl. He feels the touch of wood, a holy icon, against his hand and then against his lips.

His mother is calling him from a great distance, singing that old name. His name. The saint's.

And after this—the fire.

It is said that the morning after he joined the infidels in dance, Nazar Aga himself cut down the mulberry tree. The trunk he fashioned into a stake. The stump, into a chopping log. He impaled Salih Baba. He beheaded the *nestinari*. Then he set the village on fire and watched it burn for two whole days. On the third day—or so it is said—disgraced and ruined, he laid his own head down on the stump.

This was a story Lenio once told my grandfather, of how the Hasekiya was broken up, of how the surviving *nestinari* were forced to roam the Strandja searching for a home. Nazar Aga's fire had turned all their icons to ash, except for two—one of Saint Constantine, one of his mother, Saint Elena. And so it was these saints the *nestinari* chose to follow.

This Lenio sang as many songs, strumming the mandolin out on the terrace.

It's where I'm sitting now so many years later. Perhaps the time has come for *me* to sing her story. Or rather, to bring it to an end.

· TWO ·

A WAVE OF QUIET OUTRAGE swept Klisura once people learned the news—the teacher had snuck across the border and stolen Captain Vangelis's daughter. Within a month, there was the wedding—not in the church, but in the school yard, by the well, under the trellis white with snow. That's where Father Dionysus held the service. Few villagers attended. The mayor too refused to go. "Don't ask me, my boy," he told Grandpa. "I can't." Nor could he legalize the marriage. After all, Lenio had crossed into Bulgaria in secret.

Then Lenio began to show. And for Klisurans all was clear. That's why the teacher had stolen her. That's why he'd married her outside the church. And they were right—except, the baby wasn't Grandpa's. The rest was true. He'd saved Lenio from the Greeks and when, one night in Klisura, she had cried inconsolably—that she was disgraced, that her life was over, that she would die alone—he'd taken pity and said, "Don't cry. I'll take you as my wife."

After this, Lenio stayed with Grandpa in the school. He slept in his room, she in the room that later would be mine. He taught her Bulgarian; she taught him Greek. In the evenings, she played the mandolin, sang him songs, and showed him how to whistle like a bird. So what if he was much older, if she was pregnant with someone else's child? Weren't they married before God, living under the same roof?

One February night—it was a vicious winter—Grandpa awoke with Lenio's face on his chest. "Don't cry," he said, a tired, old refrain, and kissed her. He was afraid she'd run away, but instead, she kissed him back. And after this, they slept together in the bed and often he told her stories of where he'd take her once spring arrived.

Of course he knew the Party wouldn't let him leave Klisura. Of course, in the daytime, Lenio herself refused to go elsewhere. She said the mountain held her in its fist. Saint Kosta held her. But late at night, in dreams, they traveled freely, away from parties, mountains, saints.

The baby was born when May was rolling to an end. They named him Kostadin. Then Grandpa had to leave. "You are the *vekilin* now," the mayor told him. "You have a ritual to oversee. Pack up. We're going to the Greeks."

And so they went. Captain Vangelis met them in his yard, wined them, dined them. Not once did he approach Grandpa with talk of his stolen daughter. Not once did Lenio's brothers give him a vile look. Even Michalis, whom Lenio had been supposed to wed, spoke to Grandpa with the respect his caretaking role demanded. On parting, once the dance was over, the local women kissed his hands.

Is it really this easy? Grandpa wondered. Is all forgiven? All forgotten?

Alas, it was not.

· THREE ·

I HAD DOZED OFF on the terrace, wrapped in my blanket, as I often did. Saint Kosta lay at my feet and when he stirred I woke up. A mandolin was twanging below us, deep in the bowels of the house.

Soon Grandpa emerged from the old classroom, the Cremona in his hands. Without a word, he laid it on the table, replaced the strings with the ones I'd bought him in Burgas, and set about tuning them by ear.

November. Winter in the Strandja. The days were short; the nights were dark and lonely. A new, sharp kind of gust was polishing the snow into an icy crust. It swept the roads, the hills, it beat the blades of the unmoving turbines. It no longer bothered me that no one was switching them on. Nothing bothered me these days.

Each morning we rose with the sun, and while Grandpa boiled tea I cleaned Saint Kosta's corner. He lived with us, inside the house, a skinny, sickly thing we feared wouldn't see the spring. Not only had his wing healed crooked, but somehow he'd developed a pitiful limp in his leg. We were all pitiful. If Grandpa said let's eat, we ate. If he said let's walk, we walked. We visited Baba Mina and Dyado Dacho; we stopped by the café. But if Grandpa said nothing, if he took the chair beside me, I too kept quiet in my chair. If he didn't eat, I didn't eat. If he didn't walk, I didn't walk.

This apathy seemed like a decent bargain: I didn't suffer. Nor was I merry.

"No," Grandpa said sometimes. "Laugh. Cry. But do something. That's life. Yours isn't."

"Yet here I am," I'd say, and he would tell me: "My boy, you're anywhere but here."

I guess I was. I really couldn't tell. Ever since Elif had run away, I'd lost my sense of position, both in time and in space.

"I look at you," Grandpa would say, "and see myself. I can't stand what I'm seeing. And this stork, watching me, judging me. It's too much to take!"

So one night he brought out the old mandolin. His fingers grew more assured with each new day, but I never made a comment. November passed. December came. I sat as quiet as a man can sit. And then, one evening on the terrace Grandpa spoke.

"By the end, the mayor couldn't stand me. He hated my guts. But what could he do? I was the Party. The priest was the Party. So the mayor did as we told him and let us carry out what we were sent to do."

Two years after Grandpa and Father Dionysus first set foot in Klisura, the Party started changing all Muslim names. In the end, it was not a campaign that succeeded, but they'd try again a few decades later. I knew how the priest had been baptizing people left and right. But Grandpa had kept his own involvement a secret. As a teacher, he made sure the children of Klisura learned their *a, б, в*. He taught them they were Bulgarians, not Turks. That's why the Party had sent him and the Pope there—to get things ready for what much later they'd call the Process of Rebirth.

It had all started with Grandpa, still a teacher in Pleven. He liked to tell his students stories. Of his days as a partisan fighter. Of how he'd hid in a dugout and how, dizzy with hunger, he'd raided the sheep pens, the dairy farms with his comrades. But word got around and the principal called him to his office. "The regional governor has heard of your stories. He doesn't like them."

"What's not to like?" Grandpa asked him.

"What, what! You can't be telling our children the partisans were thieving food."

"But we *were* thieving," Grandpa said, laughing. "You were thieving, the regional governor was thieving."

"Sure we were. But that's not the point. The point is the regional wants to set an example."

"All right," Grandpa said. "I'll talk to him myself."

A huge office. A secretary. Freshly lacquered paneling on the walls. A massive desk. Behind the desk—Grandpa's cousin, the regional governor.

"Listen, cousin," Grandpa told him. "What's this talk I hear, you want to punish me?"

"You're dirtying the Party's name," the regional said. "We're cousins and people are watching. I can't be giving you preferential treatment. I need to maintain a clean face."

So Grandpa told him, "You weren't worried for your

face in the dugout. And when that boy with the *kalushari* fell with a dagger in his chest, it wasn't for your face you worried."

The regional turned as pale as fresh cheese. "Leave!" he shouted. "Out of my office!"

The next day, the principal summoned Grandpa again. "Pack your bags. You're leaving for Klisura."

"And if I don't?"

"Then Belene. The work camp."

Well, devil take it. Grandpa didn't want to end up food for pigs in a work camp. With great shame he consented. He would indoctrinate the Muslims in that distant village if that's what the Party demanded.

All this I'd heard from the imam already. But it was different to hear it from my grandfather.

"They'd forced the priest too, by the way," he said. "Let's make that clear. God rest his bones, he was a decent man. God rest the mayor's too."

One morning, they found the mayor in his office. He'd shot himself in the heart with a pistol from before the Balkan War. Right by the boxes with new passports, which had just arrived from town. He'd written them a note. *I leave this pistol to the teacher. I leave my soul to the priest. He can claim it when he comes to Hell. The teacher can have the pistol now.*

"You want to see it?" Grandpa said.

I kept still, very quiet. Saint Kosta stretched at my feet and followed Grandpa with his gray eyes. Soon the old man returned from his room, a yellowish bundle in hand.

He laid the bundle gently before us and the other bundle, the black one, up in the stork nest, returned to me as if from a great distance. For the first time in many days, I felt a sting.

Here was the ancient pistol. It had belonged to Captain Kosta once. A braid of hair, thick as rope, black as tar, entwined its barrel like a serpent.

There was no need to ask whose hair this was.

· FOUR ·

AND SO, TWO YEARS AFTER Grandpa had stolen Lenio from the Greeks, the Greeks were coming back to dance across the fire. As caretaker of the *nestinari*, Grandpa was bound to meet them in Klisura. But Lenio was not.

"You and the baby," Grandpa told her the day little Kostadin turned one, "will stay in Burgas for a week. We'll rent a room in a hotel. I'll take you there and when the dancing here is over I'll come to get you."

For a long time Lenio said nothing. She rocked the baby on her knee; she kissed his forehead again and again. So Grandpa went on talking until at last he knew he'd failed. No matter how much he begged her, she wouldn't leave Klisura.

"Stay still at least!" he barked. She wouldn't. And when he touched her cheek he found out why: a whole week before the dancing she was already burning with the *nestinari* fever.

"I'm not," she cried, and kept on rocking in her chair.

They had a fight. If not of herself, Grandpa cried, she should think of the baby. To hell with ritual and dance, he'd take the baby to Burgas himself!

Now it was Lenio's turn to plead. True, her father was a wild man, but he was a man nonetheless. And so were her brothers. Hadn't they met Grandpa in their village? Hadn't they treated him with kindness and respect?

She'd disgraced herself, that too was true. She'd lost her bond to kin and blood. But her bond to the saints remained. And if she couldn't walk the fire, at least she could be close to those who did.

"Lock us up in the house," she said. "I won't go out for a week. But let me hear the bagpipes singing, the holy drum. And only when my father leaves Klisura, you let me out."

It's here that Grandpa held her and the baby. Or so I see them when I close my eyes. He smothers them with kisses and Lenio is laughing, tickled by his prickly beard. The baby giggles.

"Let go!" she cries at last in jest. But Grandpa holds them tightly. He kisses them again and then again.

At least I know I would.

· FIVE ·

I SEE THEM with merciless clarity—Captain Vangelis and his sons, coming down the mountain, like black storks. I see the bundle with the icons, roped across the captain's back, the mud on his sons' tired faces. I see the knives in their sashes, the ends of their mustaches curved up themselves like knives. With every step their musk grows thicker; the air is heating up and nearing a boil.

I know they too can see me. The jaws of time have closed. The great abyss has been erased and nothing stands between us. When they face my grandfather at the gates of the mayor's house, it's me they're facing. When Grandpa bids them welcome, it's I who really speaks.

"Welcome, welcome, Captain Vangelis," I tell him in Greek. "We've lived another year."

"May Saint Kosta give you health, *vekilin*," the captain says, and grabs my arm firmly, all the way up by the elbow.

"Come in," I tell his sons, Captain Elias and his kin, the women, some of whom I've never met before. In the yard they wash their feet. Muddy water flows into the roots of the unkempt vine. Then, dinner on the terrace.

They've heard the awful news of course, but no one asks until I speak. "The mayor died a manly death," I lie. "By his own hand. He didn't wait for old age to make a mockery of him."

"Tomorrow," Captain Vangelis tells me, "you'll take us to his grave."

"That I will do," I say, and I refill the glasses with *rakia*. "There is more stew," I tell one of the women who's already emptied her bowl. "There is *banitsa*. There is bread."

"Teacher, your Greek is very good," one of the captain's sons tells me, and for the first time I can sense spite in his voice.

"But it's a woman's Greek," another says.

This is as far as they will go. No one asks about Lenio: if she is well, if she is somewhere near. Yet I can sense that there is more to come.

That night I leave the *nestinari* in the mayor's house. Back in the school, Lenio is pacing circles, the baby in her arms. She doesn't see me right away and for a time I watch her, hidden. She carries the child the way she would an icon across the coals; her steps are just as frantic, her face illuminated and just as streaked with sweat.

"They have arrived," I say at last. She startles and when she looks at me her eyes are muddy.

"It's time," she says, "to bolt the door."

· SIX ·

FOR THREE DAYS the Greeks rested. For three days Lenio and the baby remained locked up in the house, a giant log bolting the front door on the outside. Each morning one of the Greek women called to Grandpa in secret. Each morning, she gave him some of the food she'd cooked and kissed his hands.

"Aunt Eleni," Lenio guessed with the first bite. She knew the way her auntie's dolma tasted.

And only when she ate, with an appetite Grandpa had never seen in her before, was the gloom lifted from Lenio's face. Else she sat by the window, rocked the child, and stared vacantly across the yard, the roofs, the Strandjan hills.

She was safe inside the school. And would be safe even when the *nestinari* started dancing. She'd hear their drum, the screeching of their pipes. Her heart would take a leap and she would cry just like an owl. She would be dancing, but away from them. And when they ate their meal in the *konak* she too would eat her meal. In safety.

This is the ending I would like to give: the night has passed; the sun has risen. And soon the Greeks all vanish up the hills. Only then does Grandpa roll away the log. Only then does Lenio step out of her prison, the baby cooing against her chest.

Alas. This ending isn't hers.

· SEVEN ·

JUNE 3. The feast day of Saint Constantine and Saint Elena. Early, early, Grandpa and the *nestinari* awoke Father Dionysus. Early, early, he blessed the icons in the church, and then the village boys, Vassilko in their lead, carried them to the walnut. The *konak*, the spring of Saint Constantine, the spring of Saint Elena. The ritual was followed step by step. Then the *konak* again. Back to the church, where Grandpa slaughtered a ram *kurban*.

Two carts of wood were set on fire beneath the ancient walnut tree. The crowd gathered. The sun went down. And in the dark the *nestinari* danced. At last the dance was finished. Quiet, exhausted, the *nestinari* ate their meal inside the shack. Outside, the crowd dispersed and it was time for Grandpa too to go back home.

At the threshold he bid the Greeks goodnight. He promised to meet them at the mayor's house at sunrise. They'd go to his grave once more and then—the road and the mountain.

"Till morning," Captain Vangelis said, too tired to raise himself from the floor.

"Till morning," Grandpa answered. He picked up the candelabra, the icon lamp, and hurried to return them to the church.

Father Dionysus was sitting on the church steps.

"So it's over, this godlessness of yours?"

Tired, Grandpa sat down by his side. The Pope offered him a smoke and Grandpa lit up.

"I'm tired, brother," Grandpa said. He knew he should be going home to Lenio as quickly as he could and yet his feet were brittle iron thrown into the furnace—the soles, the tendons, every little bone had caught aflame. His shoulders were on fire; his back was breaking. So just a little rest, he thought, and he'd be going home.

"I'm tired. Dear God," he said again. "What are we doing, brother? We've ruined half of Klisura. Changing these people's names."

"Dear God," the Pope agreed, and he too lit up. "Have mercy on us all."

They sat like this. The night grew very dark around them. Thick clouds had swallowed up the moon. A little rest, Grandpa kept thinking, a little rest and I'll be on my way.

And then a dog started barking far away. And after that a closer dog, and then one closer still. The priest stood up. He pushed the door open and soft light spilled out from inside the church. It was in this light that they saw Vassilko, out of breath, covered in dust, weeds and dry leaves tangled in his hair.

"Breathe, damn it," Grandpa cried, and helped him to his feet.

For a long time Vassilko couldn't say a word. Stuttering, he reached into the bosom of his shirt; stuttering, he pulled out a piece of rope and lashed it across Grandpa's hands. Of course, this wasn't rope. It was a braid of human hair.

· EIGHT ·

"MY DADDY has a hundred white sheep," she sometimes told my grandpa. "There isn't a bachelor in the village who wouldn't want me as his wife. Yet, here I am, at your threshold, a jar of yogurt in my hands."

Each day at the threshold Grandpa scooped up yogurt from the jar. He knew full well he'd have to come to a decision soon. Take the girl and the hundred white sheep, or push away the jar, before her heart had shattered.

He led her on. Day after day.

And in the end, is there a force darker than a woman with a broken heart?

· NINE ·

LENIO, BEAUTIFUL LENIO. Lend me your eyes so I may see all that you're seeing. Lend me your lips and your ears. How rosy the cheeks of the baby. How soft his skin when we kiss him. Is this his heart beating or is it yours I can hear? Or is it my heart that won't stop knocking?

A fist. Yes, a fist is slamming the front door. And a voice is calling.

Mina. The shepherd's daughter. I can smell her, stinking of wet fleece. I've seen how she watches him, how she turns crimson when he steps near. I've seen how she watches you and turns green with venom. Saint Kosta never chose her. The teacher never chose her. What does she want, the spinster?

"Lenio, beautiful Lenio, come out without fear. Your father has gone to the mayor's house and your brothers have followed. But the coals are still glowing under the old tree.

No one will see you. No one will hurt you. Dance in the fire. I'll stay here and care for the baby."

Across the yard Lenio runs, out of the house gates. Up the road, through the bushes. Her feet burning, they don't touch the ground even. When she steps in the river, the water hisses. The air is hissing as she swims through it.

There, under the walnut, some embers still glisten. But when your feet touch them, they will all wake up in fire. Wade in the coals, Lenio, fear nothing. A giant is coming to meet you. He steps out of the dark shack, there, can you see him? Tall, terrible, handsome. Hold his hand, don't let go.

The fire in the coals turns liquid, turns to blood, dark and flaming. Spilling from your chest, from my chest. Flowing out of you and into me, out of me and into you. Both ways, both directions. Hold the hand, Lenio, don't let the hand go.

Your father's hand, the saint's hand. My hand, Lenio. Hold it.

· TEN ·

THE DANCE WAS FINISHED, the crowd dispersed. The *nestinari* had retreated to their shack, but soon they too would be going. Their *vekilin*, the village teacher, had already left to take the candelabra back to the church. Even the storks had grown quiet up in their nests. Wind whistled in the branches of the walnut; thick clouds blanketed the moon, and on the riverbank, Vassilko lay in hiding. Once the Greeks had left the shack there would be no one there to see him. Alone in all the world, he'd plunge himself into the embers, invincible, barefooted. So what if whole patches of the embers were turning black; others still glistened. But he would have to enter soon. Why were the Greeks not leaving?

And as he lay, Vassilko heard twigs snapping, the rustling of grass. The splash of water. Who's that wading through the river, crossing the meadow, running toward the tree? Those braids swaying, Vassilko can't mistake them. It's

Lenio, the teacher's girl. Trampling on the coals! She'll put them out!

He gets up, dashes through the stream. If she can dance, he'll dance with her. And then he freezes. Someone has walked out of the *nestinari* shack—a terrifying giant. Captain Vangelis. There's no mistaking the way he walks—as though he hates the earth and wants to hurt it with every footfall.

And who is that behind the captain—his eldest son? And after him—his other two?

One with the dark, Vassilko watches. But what he sees he doesn't really understand. Why is Lenio prancing across the embers like this? Why is she running from one brother to another, bumping into one, falling down, then bumping into the next like a moth that shuffles inside a circle of shining lights?

Up in the branches the storks are waking. Is it the noise of their wings he hears, the rustle of running feet, or the boom of his own blood? The wind picks up some ash and slams it in Vassilko's face. He blinks, he fights to see.

Was this a cry? The girl? A stork?

He wants to yell. *Get back! I see you!* A single word and he will save the girl. But he is too afraid. He's seen their knives and so he watches, not even fifteen feet away.

The girl has fallen to the ground. She lies, unmoving. One brother shakes another by the shoulders. Captain Vangelis pulls madly on his hair. They look as if they too are just awaking from some awful dream.

"Quick, run!" the captain calls. Timid light pours out of the shack and Vassilko hears voices. Women are crying. He sees them swooping on the men. *What have you done!* In a daze, he nears the Greek girl. There she lies in the ashes, in the glimmering coals.

"Lenio," he whispers, and shakes her. Not a muscle moves.

Beside himself, he pulls out his knife, cuts clean a rope of hair. *The teacher. I must get the teacher.*

"You there!" he hears the captain yelling.

And so he runs. The braid so hot inside his shirt. *Vassilko, my sweet Vassilko,* Lenio coos in his ear. Sweetly, sweetly, the way her tresses brush against his chest.

· ELEVEN ·

"WHEN WE ARRIVED at the meadow," Grandpa said, lighting up, "the clouds had parted and we could see better."

The door of the shack was thrown open, the shack itself empty. Not a soul left, just the storks overhead crying something fierce. And the embers under the walnut tree, cold ashes, but scattered so you could tell someone had wrestled in them.

"Look!" Father Dionysus said, and in the light of the oil lamp they saw an imprint in the ash, like from a body. The body was gone, but when the Pope brought the lamp closer what glimmered was a pool of blood. Blood had turned the ash to a cold sludge, awfully sticky.

How long Grandpa knelt there, he couldn't tell me. A minute. A thousand years. But when he came to, he understood what had happened. If they wanted to stop the Greeks, there was one way for them now—up the hills, across the border.

And Grandpa had just grabbed the Pope's cassock and he was just telling him that they should go in pursuit, when a woman's cry reached them. Out of the dark came Mina, her hair messy, her lip bloodied. She'd guessed that Grandpa might be in the *nestinari* shack and that's how she'd found him.

"Teacher," she cried. "Run! They're stealing the baby!"

So Grandpa ran. Faster than the Pope. Faster than Vassilko. By then he'd lost his mind completely. All he knew was that when he arrived at the school the man was still there. Michalis, the son of Captain Elias. The boy who'd been set to marry Lenio before Grandpa stole her.

They met in the courtyard, and in his arms the baby was crying.

"I've come for my son," he told Grandpa.

"Your son?"

"My son."

"He isn't yours." And Grandpa told him: how Lenio was in love with this other boy, how that boy had gotten her pregnant.

"I got her pregnant," said Michalis. "I took her without her permission. So what? We were about to marry."

"Your son."

"My son." And the man brushed past so close Grandpa could smell the sweet smell of the baby.

If they really talked in so many words, Grandpa couldn't be certain. Nor was he sure what he did next. Only that the man was walking, up the road, out of the village, and if Grandpa let him, he'd never again see the baby.

When my grandfather flew out of the house, the Pope and Vassilko were just arriving.

"What's with the pistol?" the Pope cried, and Grandpa couldn't tell him, couldn't think straight.

He caught up with Michalis just outside the village. "Stop," he yelled, "I have a pistol." So the man stopped and when Grandpa ordered him to lay the child down in the grass he did it.

Then Grandpa shot him in the chest, from six feet away, and killed him.

For a long time Grandpa kept quiet. I could see on the table before me the pistol and Lenio's black hair. For a long time, nothing else existed. My throat had dried up, my temples were splitting, but I barely noticed. I could see where the story was heading and I couldn't bear to listen.

"Grandpa," I managed at last, that single word containing more fear than a thousand others. Please, I wanted to say, don't tell me!

But I said nothing. And so he told me.

That night, the Pope loaded Grandpa and Lenio's child into the church cart. He lashed the horse, and the cart rattled and didn't stop until they were a long way away from Klisura, until the sun was up in the sky, red like the eye of the fire. That's what Grandpa saw every time he lowered his lids—fire blazing, wild, all-consuming.

In town, they bought a bus ticket. By the next morning Grandpa and the child had crossed the Balkan Mountains. By the time the sun was once more setting, they had arrived in Pleven.

"I'm at your mercy," Grandpa said at the door of his cousin, governor of the region. "This boy's at your mercy."

Without wasting much time they snuck into the Civil Office. They forged Kostadin new papers—kept his birth date, but changed the name of his mother. And then they changed his name too.

"Grandpa," I said. I wanted him to swallow what he was about to tell me and never bring it up again. I wanted what had been a secret all my life to stay that way. But we were past that point.

"Does Father know?" I said, barely a whisper, and when he didn't answer I repeated it more loudly, my voice sharp and ugly against the night's quiet.

"No. I never told him."

"So you are not his father then? So you and I are not related?"

His hands were fire when he reached across the table. "I *am* your grandpa. You *are* my grandson."

I couldn't move. The gravity of what he'd told me pinned me down and choked me like a fist. As if for the first time I could see this man for who he really was. Fear, shame, embarrassment. I recognized them in his face. I recognized the years of deception. But there was nothing of my father in his face. In his cheekbones, nose, lips, and chin. And nothing of me.

A strange kind of chill spread through my body. My blood had come to a boil and in an instant frozen over. All the anger, all the hurt were gone and there was nothing left but empty space. At that moment, I felt no pity to see this old man demolished. And when I pushed his hand away at last, he didn't reach again to hold me.

· TWELVE ·

THAT EVENING THE SKIES OPENED UP. All night it snowed and all night I lay in bed and listened. I couldn't hear it falling. Each little flake plummeted from a terrible height, pulled down without mercy by the weight of the planet. Whatever the snow touched—the sinewy frame of the naked vine, the edge of the well, the roof of our house—it silenced it completely. Klisura, the Strandja, the entire world. All was silence. And in this silence it was my own blood I heard, speaking of Grandpa.

I hated him for his doings. Not simply for lying to me, but for deceiving Father. How would Father react to learn the whole truth? To find out that his mother, my grandma, had not died in childbirth? That the few measly pictures we kept as sacred memorabilia were those of some other woman? That the grave we visited was someone else's?

And then beneath the hatred there was hurt. This old

man and I were not related. He was not really my grandfather, and the more I considered this revelation, the more
terrible it seemed. It negated all else—the courage he had
mustered to confess; the hardship he'd accepted voluntarily,
to raise someone else's child as his own, alone, each day har-
boring an awful secret. None of this mattered to me now.

Hurting like this, I saw myself the way I once had been.
A clumsy child. In play I often fell, scraped my palms, bloodied my knees. "It's just a little scratch," Grandpa would say,
and pick me up, but even in his arms I'd keep on screaming.
It was the sight of blood that terrified me, my own blood
flowing irrevocably away. Back then, I was convinced the
human body was like a sack of milk—punch a hole and the
milk starts to gush out. Sure, you could seal the puncture,
but how would you return the milk that was wasted? What
would become of me, I'd ask Grandpa, sobbing with terror,
once all the milk had flowed out?

Nothing he said convinced me I was safe. Until one day I
was screaming like such a brat, Grandpa snatched a pocket
knife and sliced his thumb open. "Here, drink this," he said,
and shoved his finger in my mouth. I drank his blood and I
replenished mine. And after this, each time I bled, Grandpa
took the knife. Each time my blood flowed out, his flowed
in. Until my mother saw us. Until she told my dad.

So now in bed, whose blood was I hearing really? My
own or Grandpa's?

I found him still out on the terrace, snow piled in clumps
on the blanket under which he hid. Even Saint Kosta had
had the sense to go inside. The yard, the hills, Grandpa's
shoulders all blazed in the rising sun.

I brushed away the frost from his hair and only then did
he stir.

"Let's go inside," I told him. "You'll catch a cold."

His body followed me absently, but I felt as if his mind remained behind. It seemed to me he had confessed the past in an attempt to forget it. But the spark he'd rekindled had turned into a flame and that flame into a fire. The fire had raged all night and burned away the years one by one. And now my grandfather was here, but he was also in his youth again, trapped there to relive it.

· THIRTEEN ·

"HERE, *AMERIKANCHE*," Baba Mina said, "I brewed you some tea."

"Here, *amerikanche*," said Dyado Dacho, and fortified the tea with some *rakia*.

They sat me down by the stove; they threw a blanket on my back.

"Why are you here?" they asked, both smiling, both delighted to be welcoming a guest.

I told them I had come to ask for herbs. Hibiscus, chamomile, thyme, mint—whatever Baba Mina could give me. In his stupidity Grandpa had sat too long out in the snow and now I was afraid he might be coming down with the flu. And maybe it was just my imagination, but I could swear my forehead was hotter than it ought to be. My eyes were smarting and my back—

I babbled like this for quite some time. I drank my tea

and felt both warm and chilly. It was as if in talk I wanted to delay the real reason I had come. No, it wasn't for a remedy against some future cold. It was to hold this woman to account.

In her jealousy, she'd tempted Lenio and sent her to her death. She'd acted out of spite and malice. For this I was obliged to hate her.

But here she was so many years later, smiling kindly, her lips stretched to reveal a toothless mouth, serving me a tisane made with eleven different herbs—herbs she'd spent the entire autumn picking, for me and for Elif.

"Forgive me, *amerikanche*," she said, and passed me a jar of sugar. "We're out of the honey you like."

I watched her with dizzy eyes. I could hear the boom of my blood and the flow of hers. Like two rivers clashing. No, I couldn't hate her.

Almost four years ago, Grandpa had fixed up two houses in Klisura. He'd fixed the school for himself, then he'd hired a worker from the Muslim hamlet to restore another house. While the worker painted the walls, scrubbed the floors, Grandpa rebuilt the coop, bought chickens, replanted the garden. Then he traveled to Burgas, took the elevator to the eighth floor of an apartment complex, rang the bell. Baba Mina didn't recognize him until he produced a jar of yogurt from his coat.

She was retired. Dyado Dacho was retired. They hated life in town. And so, before the month was over, they moved to Klisura, into the house that Grandpa had fixed for them.

No, no, I thought, and babbled on and on about how much my muscles hurt. I hadn't come for a confrontation. I'd come to recognize my grandpa's strength and, like him, to forgive.

"Thank you, Grandma." I held her hands and kissed them and she started laughing, lightly.

"You are a funny boy," she said.

"Funny?" said Dyado Dacho, and sniffed my empty cup. "Try *drunk*."

· FOURTEEN ·

"NOTHING IS WRONG WITH ME," Grandpa was trying to convince me. "I'm healthy as a rock."

Then why, I asked him, was he sitting so close to the stove? Why did his teeth chatter and why was he sweating rivers?

"Why, why!" he said, and huddled in his coat. But when I passed him a cup of the tisane he seized it with shaking hands and drank it bottoms up.

"What do you want?" he cried. "I'm thirsty."

I pulled a chair by his side and let the fire in the stove's belly warm me up. Hot and cold waves washed down my back. A dull pain was settling deep in my muscles. Yet when I took my temperature all was as it ought to be.

"I swear I'm getting sick," I said, and shoved the thermometer in Grandpa's mouth.

Disgusted, he spat it out. For a moment he looked determined to fight, but then he shook the thermometer and stuck it under his armpit.

I went to pour myself more tea. Even Saint Kosta seemed sick under his rug in the corner. "He's shivering," I said, returning to the stove. "You let him catch a cold."

"He's fine," Grandpa assured me. He turned the thermometer this way and that to read it.

"You happy now?" he said, triumphant. "No fever."

And just like that the breath caught in his throat. His eyes grew dim.

"I couldn't stand to see you like you were," he said. "Resigned. Heartbroken. I wanted you to know you're not alone. I too suffered once and then lived on. But now I feel so bad, my boy. Much worse. Much worse."

Saint Kosta had come to his side and Grandpa was petting him with his trembling hands. And watching him like this, I felt a sudden rush of joy.

All this time I'd thought the old man had been telling me his story only so he might get relief. All this time I had been wrong. Once again Grandpa had cut himself for my sake. Once again he was letting his blood replenish mine.

I hadn't come to Klisura to sell my land and pay off my debt. I hadn't come here to fall in love and get my heart broken, to help a girl slice the rope and be free, to protect the storks, or even to assist an old man in finding peace through some confession. I hadn't come to find myself. It was my grandfather I'd come to discover; so that for the first time in our lives, we might become like one.

At least that's what I wanted to believe now as I watched him sob. And because I believed it, in that very instant, it was so.

· FIFTEEN ·

THRACIANS, Greeks, and Romans, Slavs, Bulgarians, and Turks—only those who never passed through the Strandja never brought it to ruin. How many times had Klisura burned down to the ground? How many times had its people rebuilt, as if out of sheer spite? *Let this school be a symbol of our freedom, of our resilience*, Captain Kosta had once proclaimed. *And if it burns down we shall remake it, so Klisura may be born again.* Until in the end—after all this desolation—rebuilding the school had come to signify nothing but rotten luck: erect the school again and before too long the fire will return to consume it.

Well, my grandfather had rebuilt it despite the mayor's warning. And it seemed only natural, *necessary* even, that Grandpa would be the one to bring Klisura down again.

Klisura ended with a single word: urbanization. Gone were the cooperative farms, the hundred white sheep.

Gone were Baba Mina and the *nestinari*. The Party was generous enough—as compensation for their relocation all villagers received apartments in a giant block of flats. In Burgas, *almost* overlooking the sea.

And then, devoid of people, the Christian hamlet was transformed into a border zone. Such was the end. And it was all my grandpa's doing. He'd fulfilled splendidly his job indoctrinating the Klisuran Muslims. To listen to his recommendation was the least the Politburo could do.

The years passed. Grandpa raised my father an honest, smart, hardworking man. My father met my mother, married her, and I was born. Then Communism fell and Father said, *We have no future here.* We ran away, while Grandpa stayed behind. When he retired, having heard from his student that Klisura's school was still in his name, he sold his apartment, pocketed the money, and went back to the Strandja.

He hired a lawyer. The trial began. He would be damned if he let the imam build his rotten turbines.

And now finally I understood what this stubborn fight was all about.

Grandpa wasn't saving the storks. It was Lenio he was saving.

"When one of the *nestinari* dies," Lenio had told him a long, long time ago beside the walnut tree, "a stork is hatched up in a nest. When one of the storks dies, a new fire dancer is born. Take care then, teacher, not to ogle other women once I'm gone. Because I will be watching."

I wondered if she was really watching now. If she could really see him—sitting by the stove so many years later, petting the stork, singing the songs she once had sung.

After all—I'd seen her world through her eyes. It seemed only fair that she should see my world through mine.

· SIXTEEN ·

NO AMOUNT OF TEA could chase away the fever. Our foreheads had caught fire; the marrow in our bones had come to a boil. Yet we were deathly cold. Teeth chattering, muscles contracting, and chills sloshing up and down our spines like water from an icy stream.

Why then did the mercury refuse to rise?

"Broken," I'd say, and shake the thermometer as if my spite could fix it. I'd pace across the stifling room and throw more wood into the fire.

"Dear God, my boy," Grandpa would say, and button up his coat. "Sit down. Stop acting."

But I wasn't acting. He was. Pretending he was fine. Donning shirts, wool jackets, an old, moth-eaten hat, and drinking tea by the liter.

"You keep the room so hot," he'd say. "My throat gets dry. I'm thirsty."

"Drink water, then. Eat snow."

No. We were burning up. And with each new day, denying it was proving a greater challenge. And with each new day, our heads were turning faster. We sat in the kitchen, by the stove. We even moved our beds there, too cold to go back to our rooms. We rarely spoke. Instead, we listened to the crackling of the wood and to the whistle of our breathing. Breathe in, breathe out. Breathe in and out. A delirious rhythm that spilled into my dreams.

I sometimes dreamed of Lenio. Sometimes of Grandpa as a young man. But mostly I dreamed of Elif. Each time I met her she wanted me to give her something back. The tresses I'd cut but hadn't thrown away; the little photograph I cradled under my pillow.

"They aren't yours," she'd say. "So give them back."

And soon an endless line of long-gone souls was marching through my dreams. Lenio, demanding her braid. Vassilko, claiming he should be the one to get it. Captain Kosta, asking for his pistol back, and even Nazar Aga, chasing after his severed head.

I saw refugees of war—Bulgarian, Greek, Turkish— wandering the mountains of my mind, searching for their long-lost brothers, sisters, mothers. "Give them back," they cried, "our names, our bones, our blood. Return them to us."

I tried to tell them I didn't have these things. But all the same they kept on calling.

"Why do you need your hair?" I asked Elif in one dream, Lenio in another.

"Why do you need your pistol? Your head?"

"So we may throw them in the fire," they answered like a single voice.

Until one evening, the line of souls appeared at our gates.

Grandpa was first to hear them coming. He jumped out of his chair and glued himself against the window.

"I heard it too," I said, and stood beside him. Our reflections watched us, framed by darkness.

"A whistle," Grandpa said.

"Right there over the hill."

"No, it was closer. Hear!"

He threw the window open. Wind like knuckles punched our faces and whirled around us handfuls of shaved-off ice. The flame in the lamp went out and in the corner Saint Kosta began to beat his wings. Only the glimmer of the furnace spilled out scarlet and in that light our shadows stretched thin like rope across the yard.

We listened closely, but all we heard was howling wind. It sounded like the mountain, hill after hill, was calling us with whistles. So it was only natural that Grandpa too should call it back.

That's how we saw them: swimming through the yard amid his whistles. I recognized their knives, the icons roped to the back of the one who led them. And then, as quickly as they'd come, they disappeared, returned once more into the shapes of our stretched-out shadows.

"We'd better keep the window open just a crack," Grandpa said. "We'd better let some fresh air in."

We sat down on the beds, my back to his. I could feel the room turning—the heat of the furnace leaking out, and the night flowing in, rich, intoxicating. I called for Saint Kosta, but he burrowed deeper in his blanket.

"We've got the *nestinari* fever, haven't we?" I said at last.

"Or maybe we're just pretending," Grandpa answered.

"I'd say we're doing a terrific job."

"Yes, quite convincing."

"Grandpa." I turned around to face him. "You think we ought to go along?"

"Why are you asking me?" he said, and nodded at the stork.

· SEVENTEEN ·

THE NIGHT BEFORE the big uprising, Transfiguration eve, 1903, Captain Kosta gathered his men around the fire. "Tomorrow," he told them, "we meet the Turks in battle. I've taught you how to shoot your rifles and how to wield your knives. But should you find yourself out of bullets, should your blades dull in too many Turkish skulls, don't stop your fighting. Find a burning fire and throw yourself into its flame."

Then the captain threw a handful of gunpowder in a wooden bowl and filled the bowl with wine. He mixed the two with his dagger and walked the circle, from one man to the next, so each might drink. Their hearts filled up with courage. Their blood with gunpowder.

"Grandpa," I said. I sat at the edge of his bed and shook him awake. It was still dark outside, the sun at least an hour from rising.

He didn't know right away what it was I'd laid in his

palm. He looked it over in the glimmer of the lantern. A little matchbox. Inside there was a pinch of soil, our land returned, the pinch he'd sent me in the mail so many years back. I'd brought it here with me, yet had been too ashamed to show him.

"We have no holy wine to drink," I said. I filled a jar with water, dropped in the soil. The two mixed slowly, thread by thread, as if a root were branching off in all directions.

"But this should do."

In one gulp each we drank our earth, our great-grandfathers, our dead. And we were ready for the fire.

· EIGHTEEN ·

EVERY YEAR, for thirteen hundred years, the *nestinari* dance. Come spring, come June, come the feast of Saint Constantine, the feast of Saint Elena, they build tall fires, three cartloads of wood torched and burned to embers. And then, barefooted, they take the saint's invisible and holy hand and plunge into the living coals. The drum beats wildly, the bagpipes screech. Sickness and worry, happiness and bliss—the fire consumes them all. Here in the Strandja Mountains, where the *nestinari* dance, the fire leaves nothing.

So what then if spring was still a long ways off? So what if we didn't have a drum and bagpipes? Our mandolin rang like a bell. Our backgammon board rose a mighty ruckus. And who needed icons when we had the saint himself, glorious, though limping and with a broken wing, dressed in a red wool jacket, leading our way?

Forgive us, Saint Kosta, we must tear down your shack.

Allow our ax to split these beams; allow us to pile them up under the walnut tree and torch them.

The flames loomed tall, the tips of their tongues black from the lamp oil we'd used as an igniter. A gust of wind took up the smoke and dragged it through the walnut branches. I watched it changing shapes and rising higher, free of anything to hold it back, dissolving into the bone-white sky.

When the flame from the oil began to die down, Grandpa pulled a stack of papers out of his shirt—the unsent letters he'd written me for years, the pages on which he'd copied Captain Kosta's journal, the count he'd kept of all the casualties across the Strandja in all the recent wars. The flame swallowed them and fattened up and soon the beams were burning steady.

It had begun to snow, flakes like descending storks, landing on my head, my shoulders, one by one pressing me down. Grandpa too must have felt their weight. "You want to hear something amusing?" he said. "I'm starting to suspect our stork might be female."

"Female?" I cried. "How do we know?"

"Well, that's the thing. We have no way of knowing."

I thought about this for a little while, watching the stork prance through the meadow. Saint Kosta could very well be Saint Elena then?

"You want to hear another funny thing?" Grandpa said, suddenly encouraged. He took the ax and started raking the beams. Sparks flew in our faces, but I didn't even feel their heat.

"I heard it in the Pasha Café last week," he said, "while you were sitting home, heartbroken. Well, rumor has it it's all one giant scheme."

"What is?" I said.

"The turbines. They build them and they let them sit. This way they launder the construction money."

"The hell they do. What are you saying?"

"I'm saying the turbines might never turn. According to the rumor."

I took some time to think this over too. All that fighting, kicking, screaming had been for nothing then?

"You think?" said Grandpa, and kept on raking.

"But maybe the rumor has it wrong?"

"And maybe the stork isn't really female?"

It's here I started laughing. And Grandpa too began to laugh. But in the end our laughter also vanished and quietly we faced the flame.

"Saint Kosta," Grandpa started. "I've come to tell you . . ."

He shook his great, snow-covered head. There was no need for words. Gently, he pulled out that yellowed bundle from his shirt, untied it, and took out Lenio's braid. The fire flowed like a stream between us, faster when Grandpa let it have the braid, and when I cast Elif's locks in, more turbulent still.

"Look, Grandpa!" I wanted to say, but I knew he too could see them. Rising within us and with the smoke—Captain Kosta, the endless chain of suffering Strandjans, the girls we loved—finally free from our grip, liberated through the fire.

I felt light. I felt light-headed. How I wanted to throw myself into the flame and let it free me too.

"Not yet, my boy," I heard Grandpa saying. "The embers aren't ready yet."

Or maybe it was my own voice I could hear? Or was it Lenio's? Elif's? The voice of Captain Kosta, Murad the

Godlike One's, Nazar Aga's? I couldn't really tell. Nor did it matter. The nominalia is never ending. Like a river, like wind, like flame, it always changes in its shape. But underneath that shape it's always water flowing, it's always air, always fire.

· NINETEEN ·

WHEREVER THE GODDESS LADA WANDERED, Attila followed, buried within the tresses of her hair. With each day, his weight grew greater. It drank away her beauty. It drained her strength. Her sisters begged her to forget him; her brothers ordered her to let him go. And yet, she longed to see his face once more, to hear his whisper. If only she could pry the coffin open and kiss his lips.

"You'll never bring him back this way," she heard a voice say, as rotten as the throat from which it slithered. Starost, the goddess of old age, had left her swamp and now her deathly fingers were brushing Lada's cheeks.

"Your uncle Veles loves you," Starost said. "Go to the netherworld and ask his help."

That Veles loved her was something Lada knew. More than a few times, heart filled with fright, she had thought of bowing at his feet and begging for Attila back. And yet it wasn't fright that stopped her.

"I don't know how to find the path to his world," she said, ashamed. "My eyes have never seen it."

How wickedly Starost smiled. How ugly she grew.

"Mine have."

Down the path Lada stumbled, her eyes the eyes of Old Age. All she saw were shadows, but shadows were enough to mark the way, like crumbs. Through the falls of all-purging fire the goddess plunged and then the Death Winds took her, the way a great river takes a tiny leaf. Like this she flowed through the nether, toward the One Tree.

A single tree grows at the underworld's navel, colossal, eternal, its branches alive with wind. As dirty blood must be renewed in the heart's chambers, so must the souls of men flow through the great tree. One by one the souls rush through the branches. One by one the branches catch them and strip them of their faces. There they remain, these masks, for all eternity, like fruit, while faceless the souls rejoin the rushing winds. The winds of life now.

Gently Veles plucked a face; gently he wore it as his own. And with his lips, Attila kissed Lada back.

"I've come for you," she said, and sought his hand. She was surprised to see him pull away.

"What I was once is gone," he said. "Only this mask remains. And I am not a mask."

Perhaps she understood that he was right. And yet, how could she let him go?

Wherever Lada wandered, Attila followed, rotting within the tresses of her hair. She heard him, begging her to be forgotten, his voice unshakable, incessant. Months turned to years, years into decades, but he remained. In vain, her sisters tried to console her. In vain, her brothers attempted to cut the hair and set her free. Weak of sight, tormented of hearing, she guarded Attila and his triple coffin the way the *lamya* guards a golden apple. Her gold was grief. The grief consumed her. It drove her mad.

Mad, Lada roamed fields and forests, tortured by Attila's cries. Whatever she passed, spring with the stench of rot devoured it. Crops grew tall in winter; orchards bloomed under heavy snows. But once Lada had moved along, all blossom withered. Famine swept the people up and in their anger it was Lada's father, the god Perun, they blamed. Their sacrificial fires turned to ash and soon Perun was weakened too. No longer could he force his daughter back into his mountain. No longer could he control all other gods.

Impudent Starost leapt out of her swamp, stood before Lada.

"My child," she croaked. "I'll help you drown his voice in silence. Give me your hearing and I will give you mine."

With the eyes of Old Age and with Old Age's ears, Lada was roaming the mountain. All that she heard were shadows— voices like water rushing, trapped beneath thick ice. But even in the trap of shadows, Attila's cries kept ringing loud.

Until one day Lada caught a whisper. The call of some old god, almost forgotten, a god whom Old Age had taken long before. And following the whisper, she came upon a temple in the mountains. There in the temple the maenads danced.

How beautiful their madness seemed to Lada, to worship a god so few remembered now. How furious their dance. And in the sweetness of their wine it was some distant lightness that Lada managed to recall. The more she drank, the thicker her thirst grew, the faster she forgot her father. The more fiercely she spun, the deeper Attila sank within her heart.

The wick crackles, the flame bends, and our shadows sway across the wall and ceiling. I am a boy and Grandpa is a grandpa, though Old Age is still a long ways off from him. The year is 1991. The month is maybe January. Tonight, the power won't be coming back for one more hour. It's much too soon for bed, so here we are: around the candle, in the kitchen. My father leafing through a paper in the gloom, my mother mending one of my socks. And Grandpa telling me a story.

"So dark!" my mother says. "All these stories you tell him. So unhappy."

"If you ask me, not dark *enough*," my father says, and rustles the pages of his paper. "It's good for him to hear unhappy tales."

"It's bad for *me*," my mother says, and keeps on talking. The candle flickers with her breath and our shadows stir again. Mine conquers her and Grandpa's shadows, it swallows Father's up. And then it's me and Grandpa by the candle. And no one else. No grumpy parents, no power outages, no lines for milk and bread, no mobs demanding revolutions.

Elif hasn't come to pass yet. The storks haven't come to pass, nor have the turbines. Even America is still a premonition, coiled within my father's restless gut.

I am a boy and Grandpa is a grandpa. Between us stands a candle, not the ocean.

"Tell me, Grandpa, what happened to Lada?"

"Why, see it for yourself. Look into the flame. Watch the stories that its current drags. Beautiful Lada, blind and deaf, she has long forgotten Attila. But his body remains, buried in her hair. And so his spirit knows no rest."

And sure enough, I see them, inside the flame. A face floating in a mountain creek, turning and tossing like a fish, mouth opening and closing. Lada has dipped her blistered feet to cool them and soon the face has tangled in her toes. It bites her as she peels it off and brings it to the surface. *Let go of me!* it cries. A handsome, dear face. It begs to be forgotten. Demands to be allowed to rest.

I see the goddess, stumbling down a dark path, following the trail of shadows. Tooth, nail, ax, and saber. All was in vain. No god, no mortal man could cut the tresses of her hair. So now she stands before the nether lord again and begs his help. "Release them for a day," she asks, and as before he has no strength to turn her down.

Like wild water the horde of Huns ascended. A hundred horses with their riders, a thousand. Then a hundred thousand. Hooves of gold, long dead, now crossed and then recrossed the tresses, and split them, one by one.

How heavy the ropes of hair fell at Lada's feet. How light she felt now.

"They buried Attila's coffin in the mountain," Grandpa says. "Below the stones among which danced the maenads."

"What happened to Attila's Huns?" I ask. My fingers clasp the table tighter.

Death has tricked them once before, but now it's they who have Him cheated. *Goddess*, they cry, *we've tasted sun and birdsong once again. Don't give us back to Veles!*

"She pitied them the way a mother pities," Grandpa says. "But even a loving mother holds no cure for death."

I'll let them go, said the nether lord when Lada begged him. *But in their place, you'll have to stay with me.*

"She turned Attila's Huns to birds of white plume," Grandpa says.

"Like eagles?"

"Sure. Why not. Or maybe, more like storks. And then the maenads pulled her limb from limb so she might join her uncle in the dark."

"What happened to the maenads, then?"

"Well. What do you think ought to happen?"

"She turned them into birds as well."

"Why not. She *is* a goddess after all."

"Black birds. Like storks."

"Sounds good to me. And then each spring," he says, "the netherworld is opened so Lada may ascend. And after her, the stork flocks follow."

"Wherever trees and flowers bloom."

"But in their flight," he says, "they always come back to the mountain. To that one place where Attila rests."

"And no one knows all this?" I say. "No one remembers?"

"Except maybe the storks, you know. And maybe the mountain."

"And you and I," I say.

"And you and I."

The tiny flame of the candle dances. My parents are fighting once again. We must get out of this town, my father says. Go where exactly? asks my mother. But Grandpa and I no longer hear their fight. Eyes closed, we dream. And who's to say what happens when our eyes flick open? And who's to say we're not still there, around that kitchen table, dreaming?

ACKNOWLEDGMENTS

It is important to stress that this story is a fiction and that certain locations (Klisura—not to be confused with the historical town of the same name—and Kostitsa and Byal Kamak), certain characters (most notably Captain Kosta), and certain legends (most notably those of the goddess Lada and Attila) are also fictional.

I have attempted to remain truthful in my portrayal of the rituals and mysteries of the *nestinari*. Mihail Arnaudov's *Ochertsi po balgarskiya folklor* was especially useful, as were my visits to the villages of Balgari and Kosti, the last two Bulgarian villages where the *nestinari* still dance. The volumes in Dimitar Marinov's series *Zhiva Starina* were particularly helpful in my study of the *kalushari* (*căluşari*).

I am deeply indebted to:

Emily Bell.

Nicole Aragi. Duvall Osteen.

ACKNOWLEDGMENTS

Devon Mazzone, Amber Hoover, Abby Kagan, Scott Auerbach, Brian Gittis, and everyone at FSG for their continued support.

David Holdeman, Jack Peters, Diana Holt, Kevin Yanowski. Herbert Holl and Meredith Buie. The University of North Texas Institute for the Advancement of the Arts. My friends at UNT, colleagues and students alike.

Michael Ondaatje, for his kindness, wisdom, and generosity.

Jill Morrison and the entire staff of the Rolex Mentor and Protégé Arts Initiative.

Sorche Fairbank. Carole Welch. Lisa Silverman. Kyle Minor. Raina Joines.

Boris Nikolaev. Hristo Stankushev. Ivan Chernev.

Isihia. Most of this book was written with their musical composition *Ipostas* playing in the background.

My wife, for her patience and encouragement.

My parents, for their love and support.

Thank you, kind reader, for reading.